DAWN OF DELIVERANCE

A NOVEL

James R. Peters

iUniverse, Inc.
New York Bloomington

Dawn of Deliverance

A Novel

iUniverse books may be ordered through booksellers or by contacting:

iUniverse
1663 Liberty Drive
Bloomington, IN 47403
www.iuniverse.com
1-800-Authors (1-800-288-4677)

Because of the dynamic nature of the Internet, any Web addresses or links contained in this book may have changed since publication and may no longer be valid. This is a work of fiction. All of the characters, names, incidents, organizations, and dialogue in this novel are either the products of the author's imagination or are used fictitiously.

.

ISBN: 978-1-4401-3225-4 (pbk)
ISBN: 978-1-4401-3227-8 (cloth)
ISBN: 978-1-4401-3226-1 (ebk)

Library of Congress Control Number: 2009925175

Printed in the United States of America
iUniverse rev. date: Mar/24/09

Dedications

This book is dedicated to my wife, Sallie, and to the men and women of the Ministry of Internal Affairs who tirelessly and unselfishly served their country, Rhodesia (now Zimbabwe) from 1968 – 1980.

Acknowledgments

This book could not have been completed without the loving participation of my wife, Sallie. With the help of our good friend, writer and critic extraordinaire, Beth Robles, we have tried to bring to life some historical facts relating to the terrorist war in Rhodesia that brought Robert Mugabe into power in what is now the country of Zimbabwe. We have endeavored to create a story that will enthrall the readers, enlighten them and provide a new perspective on what the people of Rhodesia faced—both white and black. I give great credit to Sallie for portraying the perspective of a spouse who has to deal with so many issues and emotional conflicts as her husband is on the front-line of the battle.

To my friend and colleague, Lewis Walter, for photos of vehicles and equipment used by the men and women of the Ministry of Internal Affairs in our struggle to win the hearts and minds of the people.

Also thanks to neighbor, Linda Painter for her last minute editing.

Bible references are taken from the *Holy Bible: New International Version (NIV)*.Copyright 1973, 1978, 1984 by the International Bible Society. All rights reserved. Also from *The Living Bible*. Copyright 1971, by Tyndale House Publishers, Wheaton, Illinois 60187. All rights reserved.

Disclaimer

Certain of the characters in this work are historical figures, and certain of the events portrayed in it happened. However, this is a work of fiction. All of the characters, names and events, as well as all places, incidents, organizations, and dialogue in this novel are either the products of the author's imagination or are used fictitiously.

Cast of Characters, Vehicles and Weapons:

Rhodesian Government, Ministry of Internal Affairs (INTAF) & Military/Guard Force/Police Officials:

Ian Smith – prime minister of Rhodesia

Jamie Ross – district commissioner

Emily Ross – Jamie's wife

Don Hardman – secretary for Internal Affairs

Dennis Cornwell – deputy secretary for Internal Affairs

Marilyn Gordon – senior district officer, Mutasa

Jack Cloete – primary development officer

Maria Cloete – Jack Cloete's wife

Angus McDonald – agricultural officer

Sixpence – Jamie's cook at Mutasa

George Barstow – provincial commissioner, Manicaland

Colonel Jock Sanders – JOC commander, Manicaland

Major John Whiting – Fourth Battalion, Rhodesian Regiment, Manicaland

Captain Mike Willis – Fourth Battalion, Rhodesian Regiment, Katiyo

Captain Gerald Boyd – Fourth Battalion, Rhodesian Regiment, Mtarazi

Major Nick Farham – officer commanding, RAR, Honde Valley

Sandy Giles – chief inspector, Special Branch, Manicaland

Sergeant Sama – head district assistant, Mutasa

Corporal/Sergeant Dande – senior district assistant, Ruda Keep

Corporal Tategulu – district assistant Ruda – replacement for Sama

Willie – cook, Ruda

Chris DeVries – district officer, Ruda Keep

Andre Pierson – construction crew boss

James Trenham – vedette officer

Garth Markham – senior vedette, Katiyo and then cadet, Ruda

Jeremy Michaels – senior vedette, Katiyo

Russell Winning – senior vedette, Simangane

Jerry Payne – assistant commandant Guard Force, Pungwe and Ruda

Corporal Brian Thompson – Guard Force, Tikwiri

Corporal Roger Brown – Guard Force, Pungwe

Corporal Jannie DuPlessis – Guard Force, Mtarazi
Corporal Alec Williams – Guard Force, Mutasa
Staff Sergeant Ryan – IANS training, Chikurubi. (Ex SAS)
Malcolm Lyle – IANS
Alan Ross – general manager, Aberfoyle Tea Estates (Jamie's brother)
Audrey Ross – Alan Ross's wife
Alex Burton – officer commanding INTAF, Chikurubi

ZANLA – ZANU Forces:

Robert Mugabe – political head of ZANU (Now president of Zimbabwe)
Rex Nhongo – overall commander ZANLA Forces
Josiah Makoni – commander, ZANLA Forces, Manicaland
Enoch Mashiri – Josiah's second in command
Morgan Tangwena – political commissar
Isaac – ZANLA guerilla
Mangwende – ZANLA guerilla

Armored Vehicles & Weapons:

MAP 45 – heavy armored truck seating twelve to fourteen people
Cougar or Rhino – built on Landrover chassis and seating four to six people
Leopard, Mark II built – built on a VW Combi chassis that could seat five to six people
Browning .303 Machine guns – relics from World War II aircraft
Garden Boys – black powder cannon for use in PVs and Ruda Keep
FN Rifles – standard NATO issue 7.62mm automatic rifles in general use by Rhodesian security forces
G-3 Rifles – secondary weapons in use by INTAF, Guard Force and militia – also 7.62mm
Uzi sub machine guns – Israeli made – 9mm
Star Pistols – 9mm
Beretta Shotguns – automatic five shot, twelve gauge shotguns.
MAG machine guns – light 7.62mm machine guns in general use by Rhodesian combat forces.
20mm cannon – heavy machine guns. Used in K car attack helicopters and DC-3 gunships

AK-47 – Russian and Chinese made automatic rifles in use by ZANLA terrorists

SKS – Chinese & North Korean made automatic rifles in use by ZANLA terrorists

RPG – rocket propelled anti-tank grenade launcher

SAM-7 – Strela 2, surface to air missiles

MP-14 – mobile multiple rocket launchers (Stalin Organs)

Terms:

Skellum – irritating or troublesome insect

Masoja – African term for soldiers

Vedette – Internal Affairs trained national servicemen deployed in psychological warfare operations

IANS – Internal Affairs national servicemen in training

INTAF – Ministry of Internal Affairs (responsible for all civil administration and psychological warfare)

DA – district assistant

Terr – terrorist

Gook – terrorist

Boys – terrorists

Magandanga – terrorists

Mambo – chief or king (a term of respect)

DC – district commissioner

Sadza – maize or corn meal thick porridge

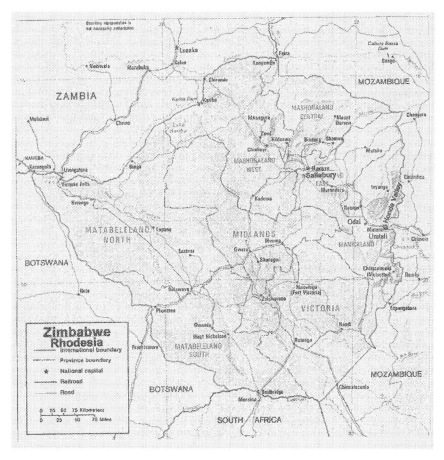

1. Map of Rhodesia/Zimbabwe

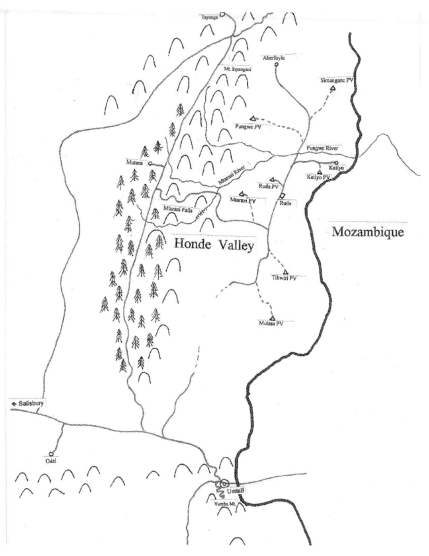

Inyanga

Aberfoyle

Mt. Inyangani

Simangane PV

Pungwe PV

Pungwe River

Mutasa

Katiyo

Mtarazi River

Katiyo PV

Ruda PV

Mtarazi PV

Mtarazi Falls

Ruda

Mozambique

Honde Valley

Tikwiri PV

Mutasa PV

← Salisbury

Odzi

Umtali

Vumba Mt.

2.   Map of the Honde Valley

Part 1 – Terrorists Control the Honde Valley

PROLOGUE

The only ingredient necessary for the triumph of evil is that good men do nothing.
> *- Edmund Burke*

Jamie eased himself into the wicker chair on the front porch. He reached for the tall glass of beer at his side. His hand shook and a knot of bile rose in his throat as he thought of the day. He took a long swig, hoping the cold liquid would wash the acrid taste away. *How was he going to tell Emily?*

A soft breeze ruffled his dark brown hair. He tried to brush the images from his mind as he looked out over the small village of Melsetter. He could see the Chimanimani Mountains in the distance—

majestic bastions of jagged rock and towering cliffs. They formed a formidable barrier between Rhodesia and Mozambique. How he loved this country. It had been his grandfather's country and Jamie knew no other land. It was his home and no one was going to take it from him.

The screen door of the porch opened and swung shut with a soft thud. He could smell her sweet perfume as she sank down on the chair next to him. Her bright floral dress complemented the colors of the evening sky—pink, blue, and purple. A strand of thick auburn hair fell across her forehead and she swept it back, pinning it behind her ear. She was so beautiful. Her gentle countenance and ready smile belied the strength and determination that lay beneath.

* * *

Josiah took a swig from his water bottle and held the tepid liquid in his mouth, hoping it would refresh him. High on the hill the ten men crouched, hidden by the thick pine forest. Josiah's body ached from the strenuous day—he was tired and hungry, but dared not light a fire. Cold maize meal cakes and water would have to suffice for the evening meal. It had been a long day, clambering up the steep incline of sharp rocks and stumbling down the treacherous slopes. The passage they had traveled over the Chimanimani Mountains from Mozambique was not well known, but it was safer. Not many people would venture such a difficult route and Josiah's hands were raw from clutching at the sharp rocks. His legs were scraped and bruised, but it had been worth it—their target was in sight.

Josiah turned to his men and spoke softly. "We have made good time. Soon we will strike another victory for freedom."

"Ah-ha." The men were tired and their responses slow.

"Last night our comrade, Morgan, and his men successfully attacked a coffee plantation. "The white pig, his whore, and their filthy offspring will no longer oppose our cause." Josiah's voice was hoarse with passion. He raised his clenched fist. "Now it is our turn. This will be our most important accomplishment yet. The white government thinks Chinyerere is an important man, but he is nothing—just a cowardly dog. He tries to block our progress in the area and has set the spirit mediums against us. We will make an example of him. We will claim a great victory for our freedom fighters. Our esteemed leader, Robert Mugabe, will be pleased."

Josiah could sense the excitement rising amongst his men as they murmured back and forth.

"Yes, we will show the white pigs," Enoch, the second in command, sniggered. "And when we have killed him we will deal with his wife as we want. His children will become our playthings."

The fervor grew amongst the men as they spewed out words of hatred. "We will drive out these white pigs from our land and take what is rightly ours. Our fallen brothers will be avenged."

"Zimbabwe, Zimbabwe," the men chanted.

* * *

Emily sighed in contentment as she settled into the chair. This was always the best time of the day. The evening light was magical, the sky a canvas of bright, changing colors. She loved how the sun reflected off the mountains, vibrant and yet peaceful.

Jamie looked at her, noted her sparkling green eyes and his heart sank. How was he going to tell her?

"Dinner will be ready in fifteen minutes. Philemon has just put the steak on." She reached for his hand. A little smile touched her lips as she heard the children squealing and giggling in the bathroom. She laughed softly as she heard Sarah, their nanny's voice, raised in mock anger.

"Look what you skellums have done. You have made Sarah's dress all wet. Now you hurry up and get out of the bathtub or your daddy will have eaten all the dinner and there won't be any of that good chocolate pudding left that your mamma made."

Emily chuckled as she heard little Deanne's high, childish voice. "Dry me off first, Sarah. Dry me off first."

"What a gem Sarah is. I don't know what we'd do without her." She turned to Jamie and her eyes clouded over as she saw the lines of tension in his face. He wasn't smiling. His face looked grey under the tan and his blue eyes were somber. "Honey, what's the matter? Something's happened, hasn't it?"

Jamie nodded, not able to look at her.

"Tell me. Has there been another attack? Is it anyone we know?"

Jamie looked at his dusty boots. His voice cracked. "Emily, it's the Viljoens."

Emily caught her breath. Her hand flew up to her throat as if to support her body. "Oh no, it can't be! Jamie, tell me they're okay. Tell me nothing bad has happened to them."

"I'm sorry, sweetheart." He squeezed his eyes shut as if to block out the images. His voice was soft but firm as he continued. "Their house was attacked last night. The whole family was killed."

Emily looked at him, her eyes wide with horror. A sob escaped her throat and her body shook. "What happened, Jamie? I need to know."

Jamie reached for her hand again but she snatched it away. She sat up straight and her eyes held his in a determined stare. "Tell me, Jamie."

"The terrorists attacked at about eight o'clock, just as they sat down for dinner."

Images of their dear friends crowded Emily's mind. The last time they had been together they had played bowls on the lawn. They often visited the beautiful little farmhouse Ken had built—with its mud stucco walls and thatched roof. He had built it to resemble an English cottage. Roses, larkspur and lilies had grown in abundance around the walls and a pebble pathway had led to the rough oak door. It nestled amid the steep hills and was surrounded by coffee bushes that Ken had planted on the slopes. One day it would be a thriving coffee plantation.

"I'm sorry, Emily. There were no survivors."

"Oh Jamie, even the children!—those precious little girls."

"I'm afraid so. It was a brutal attack. I can't describe what happened to the girls." Jamie was quiet for a moment. "Emily, promise me one thing, if we are ever in a situation like that don't let the children fall into the hands of the terrorists. Always keep four bullets."

Emily gasped. She looked at Jamie's anguished face and knew exactly what he meant. She looked at the newly installed grenade screens on the windows and a cold chill gripped her heart.

* * *

Out in the shadows Josiah and his men lay waiting. A smile spread across Josiah's lips as he saw the couple embrace and disappear into the house. He motioned to his comrades. "Soon we will attack."

* * *

Dinner was a somber affair for Jamie. He had no appetite and he noticed that Emily barely touched her food. The children sensed that something was not right and did not even bicker over who had the largest helping of pudding. Jamie tried to ask them about their day, but only little Deanne said more than just, "It was good."

He went with Emily to listen to their prayers and tuck them into bed. Rachelle and Deanne did not even demand their usual bedtime story. As he went into Barrie's room, and bent down to kiss him goodnight, he felt his son's young arms tremble and tighten around his neck. He realized that Barrie was old enough to know there was something wrong and was filled with an unknown anxiety. He daren't tell him the truth. Even though he was all grown up at eleven years old, and knew of the atrocities the terrorists had committed in the area, the Viljoens were too close, too personal. Jamie held him in his arms and whispered words of reassurance until he felt the young boy's body relax.

Jamie and Emily were silent as they sat down to listen to the eight o'clock news. Ian Smith had been meeting with John Vorster in South Africa to discuss the flow of oil; two Rhodesians had been selected to play on the Springbok rugby team; there had been more terrorist attacks in the Honde Valley and Katiyo Tea Estates were closed

Jamie immediately thought of his brother, Alan. Alan managed Aberfoyle Estates—not far from Katiyo. What would he and his wife Audrey do?

"Jamie, is there any hope for our country? We listen to the news every night and it's so depressing."

"I know sweetheart, but we must keep…"

Boom …

The loud explosion rocked the house as an RPG, rocket propelled grenade, crashed into the wall of the living room. Pieces of brick, mortar and a cloud of dust rapidly filled the room.

"Emily, hit the agric-alert!"

Emily responded without thinking. She shot out of her chair, her hand reaching for the alarm button.

Jamie shifted into instinct, pure adrenaline driving him through the next twenty seconds. "Grab the shotgun and Uzi. Round up the kids. Get them into the bathroom and tell Barrie to lock the door. Get back as soon as you can. I need you with me."

Jamie grabbed his FN and a pouch filled with loaded magazines. He flipped the main electric breaker switch. Everything went black. He ran back into the living room and dropped, crouching below the front window. He heard the distinct crackle of AK-47 rifle fire. He knew the sound of the AK. It was much sharper, not as loud as the FN. In the dark, he could now see the tracer and the muzzle flashes. Moving the change lever of the FN to semi-automatic he fired rapidly at the flashes. Every shot had to count. He had plenty of ammunition, but he knew from experience that rapid single shots would be more effective than bursts of automatic. He switched magazines and continued to fire.

Ka-boom …

The loud RPG rocket explosion shook one of the grenade screens on the window to his right. It released its fury harmlessly outside the house as shards of glass fell inside.

Jamie emptied three magazines, and felt rather than heard Emily drop to the floor beside him. She thrust the Uzi at him with her left hand while she gripped the Browning automatic shotgun with her right.

"Get to the window beside the door and fire at the muzzle flashes with the Browning. Keep firing and reload in the dark, just as we've practiced." His heart was thumping. "Are the kids okay?"

"They're in the bathroom. I told Barrie to lock the door." Emily's voice quavered.

He stopped and looked intently toward her in the dark.

"Remember to keep one spare magazine, just in case we're overrun. You know what to do."

Emily had been responding by instinct, but now panic set in. They had talked about this, but she never thought she would have to seriously consider it.

This can't be happening. God, no!

"Oh Jamie, I couldn't, I couldn't—not my own children!" She choked, finding it difficult to breathe.

He dropped the FN and grabbed Emily roughly. "You have to, Emily, there is no other choice. Remember the Viljoens. Go."

Oh God, Oh God, please don't let anything happen to my children.

She sobbed as she crawled to the window.

Picking up the Uzi, Jamie flipped the change lever to automatic and fired short bursts at muzzle flashes and tracers coming from two directions. One group fired at them from the carport about a hundred yards away and the other group fired from the grove of gum trees below and to the north of the house.

Jamie heard the loud blasts of the Browning 12 gauge shotgun. Five shots evenly spaced. A pause, Emily was reloading. Jamie dropped the Uzi and picked up his FN. It felt very comfortable in his hands, and with two magazines taped together he could get off forty rounds in less than a minute before switching. There were twenty magazines. He wouldn't run out of ammunition.

He heard his two little girls screaming. He could only trust that they were safe. He grabbed his FN and the pouch of double-taped magazines and slid over to where Emily was firing.

"I'm going out back to try and nail them from the side—by the camphor tree. They won't be expecting that and maybe I can hold them off. Keep firing to give me some cover. Here, take the Uzi and use this. Short bursts only."

Jamie doubled back through the kitchen and unlocked the back door. Crouching down behind the long flower bed he made his way to the gnarled old camphor tree. This would more than halve the distance to the nearest group of terrorists. Sliding around the side of the trunk he could see muzzle flashes not thirty yards away.

Perfect.

He raised his FN, took careful aim at the nearest flash, and fired. There was a scream and the firing stopped. Abruptly, another muzzle flash. Jamie flipped the change lever to automatic, aimed the FN, and fired three quick shots. He knew he had hit someone from the loud cry. Firing from the first group stopped and he could hear bodies crashing through the shrubs in front of him, beating a hasty retreat.

The second group of terrorists was still firing. Jamie crouched low as he ran towards the back of the woodshed. He eased around the corner, keeping his head down. The terrorists were still firing, but sporadically. Raising the FN he switched the change lever to fully automatic and, holding down the muzzle, emptied the magazine in their direction. He heard someone shout in Shona. "Run! Run!"

The firing stopped. Jamie switched magazines and continued to fire in the general direction where he thought the terrorists were headed, but there was no response. Several minutes passed. He waited. Silence ... He doubled back to the house and went in through the kitchen door.

Emily rushed up to him, threw her arms around him, and burst into tears. "Have they gone? I'm so afraid."

"Yes, they're gone." Jamie held her tightly, then picked her up and carried her to the bathroom. He called out to Barrie. "It's okay now. They've all gone. Open up. We're safe."

The door inched open. Barrie peeked through the crack then flung the door wide. Three wailing children rushed into his arms. Jamie pulled Emily and the children down onto the bathroom floor and sat with them cradled in his arms, overwhelmed by love and the instinct to protect them at all cost. His whole body pulsed to the beat of his heart as they sat there in the darkness.

* * *

Thrum, thrum, thrum.

The sound of helicopter rotors joined in the rhythm of his heartbeat. Jamie closed his eyes and took a deep breath. The response team was arriving. He gently disengaged himself from the clinging arms.

"We're okay now. The soldiers have arrived."

Chapter One

Veld Vac. Jamie tapped his pen on the desk. He stared at the open file in front of him and eased his six foot frame back into the chair. Rubbing a hand through his hair, he frowned. How could he focus on routine tasks? It was nine months since they had moved from Melsetter to Salisbury and Jamie found the endless routine of his Head Office position stifling. Planning Veld Vac was interesting, but it offered no excitement or real challenge. Watching over a bunch of school kids was not what he was trained for. He knew they had appointed him to Head Office to give him, and especially Emily, a break from the stress of running a district in a war zone. Right now, however, the mundane tasks he was assigned were providing more stress than being on the front line. He sighed. Refocusing, he tried to squelch those feelings for the sake of his family.

Rap-rap-rap.

Jamie jumped.

Dennis Cornwell, deputy secretary for the Ministry of Internal

Affairs stood in the open doorway, knocking lightly on the door jamb. "Jamie, can you spare a moment?"

"Sure," said Jamie. Anyone or anything that offered respite from the Veld Vac file was welcome. He smiled and motioned toward a chair. "Come in, sir."

Dennis took a step forward and closed the door. He was tall, lean and good looking. His hair was dark, graying at the temples and carefully groomed. Dennis was all business. He sat down, crossed one long leg over the other, and leaned back. His eyes fixed on Jamie.

Whatever it is, here it comes.

"Jamie, what I'm about to discuss with you is in the strictest confidence." His eyes were unwavering. "As you know from the daily intelligence reports, things are not going well for us along the eastern border."

Jamie's mind flashed back to the top secret reports that had passed across his desk in the preceding weeks. "Yes, our forces are facing an uphill battle. They can't seem to stop the slaughter in the Honde."

Dennis leaned forward and confirmed. "Last week they murdered twenty seven of the locals, five teachers, and two of our agricultural advisors in the Honde alone. They've had to close down the remaining tea estates, a major set-back in revenue for the area. Not only are the locals being butchered by the terrorists—they have no jobs or income."

Jamie sensed there was more to come. He clasped both hands in front of him and leaned back in his chair.

"The prime minister has asked us to send someone to the Honde who knows the people, the language, the customs, and the spirit mediums. He also wants someone who understands the psychology of the war on terror."

The pause was just long enough. The direction of the conversation sank in and Jamie began to feel his pulse rise. Veld Vac was looking more appealing.

Dennis continued. "I know you've read Mao's *Little Red Book* outlining plans for success in a guerilla war."

Jamie didn't smile. He locked eyes with Dennis and waited.

Here it comes, the crunch, and I'm not sure I want to hear it.

"You're our man, Jamie," announced Dennis. "You fit all the

characteristics. Your experience at Melsetter qualifies you like nobody else. We need you."

"But we've only just settled in Salisbury."

"Jamie, you know the area along the border, the terrain, the people and the culture. You understand how the natives think. Remember that trip you made across the border to meet with Nemanyika, senior spirit medium for the Manyika? After your visit we got a lot more intelligence from the locals."

Another lull, designed for Jamie to absorb the implications, until Dennis's voice cut through his frantic thoughts.

"You know what we're dealing with. You understand it. You've lived it. The Honde Valley is just like Ngorima in Melsetter. That's why you're unique."

Jamie felt the tension in his shoulders. Like a weight added to a swimmer struggling to stay afloat in a sea of dangerous waters, realization hit him. *If not me, who else?* Other thoughts followed, smacking at him like relentless waves. *The Honde—hottest spot for terrorist activity; top of the intelligence reports every day; main point of entry for all ZANLA terrorists entering Rhodesia; extremely dangerous and difficult for security forces to cover.*

Silence …

It was a vacuum, an abyss where Jamie frantically grappled alone with his thoughts.

Dennis waited. Jamie knew it was his turn.

Say something. Respond.

He cleared his throat. "Sir, this is a tough assignment, though I must admit I would love a new challenge."

He opened his mouth to continue, but paused. His response intercepted by thoughts of his wife and children. "I can just imagine Emily's reaction if I mentioned this to her."

"Jamie," Dennis said. "We know. We understand. Believe me we would not have come to you if we had any other options. We're not telling you to go, but the situation is critical and the country needs you. Talk to Emily. Let me know by tomorrow."

That was it. No more discussion. Let you know by tomorrow.

Jamie's mind shifted into something between panic and excitement.

Dennis stood up and put his hand on Jamie's shoulder and squeezed it. The benevolent gesture was kept in check as Dennis's eyes bored into Jamie's. "Think about it."

Jamie's brother, Alan, was in the Honde. He was the general manager of Aberfoyle Tea Estates and Jamie had been concerned for some time about him and his wife, Audrey.

Now, somewhere buried in his mixed bag of emotions, was excitement. Jamie closed the Veld Vac file and pushed it aside; it really didn't seem that important now. He needed to do something. He marched into the staff kitchen, grabbed his favorite cup and made himself some tea. Perhaps it would relax him and help him think. Back in his office, he leaned back in his chair. As he took his first sip the phone rang.

His secretary's voice bristled with importance.

"Mr. Ross, the prime minister is on the phone for you."

The prime minister! Now what?

Jamie's hand hovered over the phone. He pulled his thoughts away from the dilemma facing him. Taking a deep breath, he held the receiver to his ear.

"Jamie Ross."

"Please hold, sir, for the prime minister."

Jamie could feel his heart pounding.

"Jamie, this is Ian Smith. Do you have a minute?"

"Yes, of course, sir."

"How are Emily and the children? Your boy must be almost grown up."

Jamie laughed "Hardly, sir. He's only eleven."

"Oh yes, just a couple of years older than you were when I gave you that tanning. You know I still have that glass peashooter I took from you. I'm staring at it right now on my desk. It makes a great ruler."

Jamie's emotions eased a bit at the recollection. He laughed outright. Somehow the prime minister was easier to talk to than Dennis Cornwell. The pea shooter! The memory played back through his mind as if it were yesterday, not thirty years ago.

* * *

It was the little town of Selukwe. Jamie was nine. The Smith's lived across the street. Ian had been overseas fighting in WWII for the British and had made quite a name for himself as a Spitfire fighter pilot. During one excursion over Germany he had been shot down and suffered a wound that damaged his right eye. Through strength and determination he joined up with some partisans, and made his way back to England. After the war he had gone on to Rhodes University and had only just returned to Rhodesia and his hometown of Selukwe.

In the meantime, Jamie had made quite a name for himself—the naughtiest kid in town. The other boys loved to traipse after him because he always led them into adventures they would never have dared on their own. If there was an old mine shaft to be explored, or a bird's nest at the top of a tree, Jamie was there investigating. The other little boys followed gleefully, careful not to let their mother's know what they were up to.

That particular day Jamie had found a treasure behind the pharmacy, a glass tube about eighteen inches long. The hole in the middle was just the right size for a syringa berry to slip through. It made the perfect peashooter. Jamie climbed up into a mango tree to hone his skills with his new weapon—zap a bird or anything that caught his attention. Just then he spotted his neighbor, that young man who had just returned from university, strolling down the road. The temptation was too much. He carefully put a hard syringa berry in the peashooter and let fly. Bull's eye! Just behind the right ear. Jamie's elation was quickly doused. Ian Smith wheeled around and locked eyes with him. Jamie jumped down and high-tailed it. Who would have guessed someone that old could run so fast! Ian Smith soon overtook Jamie, relieved him of his peashooter, and cuffed him on the back of the head. And who would ever have guessed that Ian Smith would become prime minister of Rhodesia at the most controversial time in the country's history.

Jamie's admiration and awe of this great man grew daily. Here was a man who was strong and honest, determined to do what he believed was best for the country. He had stood up to the British when they dissolved the Federation of Northern Rhodesia, Southern Rhodesia, and Nyasaland—refusing to give in to their demands for immediate majority rule. The British government was determined that

Southern Rhodesia would follow its neighbors, with Britain in control, dictating the form of government. But Southern Rhodesia had never been a British colony, it had been founded by the British South Africa Company, a corporation chartered by Queen Victoria and headed by entrepreneur and financier, Cecil John Rhodes. It had been governed by the company until it gained its independence in 1923 with a freely elected parliament. Following in the footsteps of his predecessor, Winston Field, Ian Smith had refused to be bullied into giving up Rhodesia's autonomy and had declared unilateral independence for the country in November, 1965. Bucking the dictates of the rest of the world, Rhodesians struggled against blockades and sanctions. They were a proud people and refused to give up their country to the whims of a foreign government that knew nothing about the real issues, the local customs, or dreams of a prosperous future for all.

* * *

Jamie hadn't thought of that peashooter incident in a long time and he was delighted, if not a little apprehensive to hear from this man he admired so much.

"My pride is still wounded, sir, but I'm honored to hear from you."

"Jamie, I want to tell you what a great job you did in Melsetter. I know it wasn't easy. I understand you lost many friends and colleagues there."

"Yes, sir. It was tough; especially rough on Emily."

"Well, that makes it particularly difficult for me to ask you to do this. Your country needs you again, Jamie. I presume they've talked to you about the Honde."

"Yes, sir. Dennis Cornwell explained to me the situation in the Honde. He asked me to consider taking over responsibilities there. I don't know what to say."

"I understand," said Ian Smith. "I wouldn't ask you to do this if I didn't think you were the best man to handle the job. The work you did in Melsetter has uniquely qualified you for this assignment. The trouble is, we are losing ground fast in the Honde. I'm in a predicament. We have two choices. Either we push those terrorists back across the border, or we have to rewrite the borders and concede the Honde to Mugabe and his thugs." There was a pause. "I'm asking you to go to the Honde. Your country needs you, Jamie. Will you take a shot at it?"

Jamie felt the pressure build. The reality of what they were asking of him had set in. Finally, he caught his breath. "Sir, I must talk to Emily. It will affect her life too. How about tomorrow morning? Can I give you my decision then?"

"Certainly. Just think about what's at stake. I hope you will give very serious consideration to what I'm asking of you. I know the sacrifices I'm calling on you to make, but Jamie, we all have to make sacrifices. We must keep our country on the right path. You come from a long line who understood this. Your grandfather did and so did your grandmother. Think hard, Jamie. Notify Dennis Cornwell of your decision in the morning. I know I can rely on you." With that, he hung up.

Jamie's mind raced in every direction for the rest of the day.

* * *

Jamie drove faster than he should, barely noticing the other traffic. It was as if the car was on auto pilot. His mind was in turmoil. His heart raced. Each battled for the upper hand. *The Honde Valley—killing field of Southern Africa.*

On and on it went, his heart racing with excitement, his mind balking at the realities. He was almost surprised when the little Datsun pulled into the carport beside Emily's Toyota. He climbed out and looked around the yard. He had planted the flowers and tended the shrubs himself, but now they looked different. It was as if he was looking at them for the first time. They were lush and beautiful. The house looked cool and inviting with green ivy clinging to the red brick, and purple bougainvillea covering the carport. To Emily and the children it was a safe haven, away from the terrors of war.

He stepped into the kitchen and the screen door slammed behind him. He heard voices coming from the lounge, and as he made his way towards the sound his eyes lingered on the children sprawled on the carpet in front of the television. Philemon, their cook, sat with them, a full bowl of green peas on his lap, absently shelling them. Their eyes were glued to the flickering black and white picture. The Lone Ranger, his eyes hidden behind a black mask, rode high in the stirrups on his white horse as Tonto followed close behind. The children's and Philemon's eyes were enormous with suspense, even though it was obvious the bad guys never won.

"Hi, kids. Where's mommy?"

Barrie's eyes did not waver from the television. "In the bedroom—getting changed."

Jamie headed for the bedroom and stopped when he saw Emily. She was sitting on the edge of the bed.

She looked up and greeted him with a smile. The afternoon sun shone through the window, picking out the golden highlights in her hair. Her green eyes flashed and danced with life. Unassuming and unaware of her own beauty, she continuously captured his heart. "What's the matter?" she asked. "You look frazzled." He never could hide anything from her.

She continued pulling off her panty hose. How often Jamie had heard her complain, "I hate these things. I can't breathe in them. I bet some man invented them to torture women." The first thing she always did when she got home from work was to strip them off and claim her freedom. For a brief moment the picture of her sitting there took his mind off the gravity of the decision that lay ahead. What he would give to put off this discussion, to fling himself onto the bed beside her, and to pull her into his arms. He took a step toward the bed, but stopped short. The sudden alarm in her eyes snapped him back to reality.

Emily's sixth sense antenna was up; she knew him better than he knew himself.

"What's the matter, Jamie? What's wrong?"

"We need to talk." He sat down next to her. He paused, searching for a gentle way to tell her, but couldn't find the right words. There was no gentle way to broach this subject. "Emily, I've been asked to go to the Honde Valley." He swallowed.

Emily was silent. A stricken look came into her eyes.

"Ian Smith even called me himself." He reached for her, trying to soften the news, but she pulled back stiffly

"What do you mean? Just for a quick trip, right?" She knew that was not what he meant. She could feel the tension in him and knew that this was serious. She searched his eyes, hoping that was what he had said, and what she saw in his face wasn't true. Suddenly the truth of it hit her in the stomach like a clenched fist. "You're going, aren't you?" She looked away, tears welling in her eyes.

Jamie felt both fear and anger radiating from her body. Just as he couldn't hide anything from her, she couldn't hide anything from him. His heart ached for her. He knew that their experiences in Melsetter were still too fresh in her mind. She had comforted too many wives whose husbands had been killed, mothers who had lost sons; had attended too many funerals of families brutally murdered and mutilated. Her nerves were stretched taut and now, what was supposed to be a time of healing in Salisbury, was turning into another nightmare for her.

"I'm sorry, Emily." He put his arms around her.

"You can't go to the Honde, Jamie. I can't do this again. They'll have to ask someone else. They have no right to ask this of us."

"Emily, it's not that simple. You know that Alan and Audrey are in the Honde. They can't leave, even though the tea estates are closed. Everything they have is tied up in the tea estates and leaving would just signal to Mugabe's thugs that we've capitulated. The country's in deep trouble and Dennis Cornwell, and the prime minister, have asked me to go to Mutasa. They want me to coordinate a last ditch effort to get the terrorists out of the Honde. They explained to me that, because of my experience in Melsetter, I was uniquely qualified."

"Jamie, you're not being rational. This is foolish. You know it. What will happen if you hit a landmine or get shot? And what about your back? You can't go bouncing around on those roads again. Your back's a mess. The doctor warned you—any more trauma and you'll be in a wheel chair."

Jamie gently turned her toward him. He brushed aside a stray wisp of her hair. It hurt him to see the pain in her eyes. "I know, Emily. This is not an easy decision and one I wish I didn't have to make, but Ian Smith called and really put me on the spot. I said I'd give them my answer tomorrow."

Jamie glanced out the door to make sure the kids were still in the living room and not privy to their discussion. "Let's go outside, near the pool. I don't want the kids to hear us; they don't need to be involved just yet." Jamie stood up, took her hand and pulled her to him. He wrapped his arms around her and just held her until her body finally relaxed. "Come on, we'll think better outside in the fresh air."

Arm in arm they headed for the door that led to the pool.

Outside, she pulled up a chair and rubbed her arms to ward off a chill even though the evening was warm.

Jamie pulled his chair close to her and reached for her hand. For a moment he watched the reflection of the setting sun dance in the ripples of the water, and then slowly shook his head. "Emily, I hate this too. My mind tells me one thing and my heart tells me another. For the world I would not hurt you or the children, but you know how I love this country. I would do anything to save it. I also understand that we can't afford to lose the Honde Valley, because after that it'll be the whole country."

Emily's voice shook, "Oh Jamie, I'm so afraid. That's the most dangerous area in the country. What will we do if you are killed or maimed? We can't rely on a government pension."

He held her hand. It trembled in his.

"Jamie, please slow down. Think about this. We've already served our time in Melsetter. You know that you can't go back to the border. What will happen if Nkomo, or God help us, Mugabe, takes over?"

She drew her knees up tightly to her chest and wrapped her arms around them. Anger began to take the place of fear and she turned away from him, not wanting to look at his troubled face. She stared out beyond the pool and let the anger and fear wash over her as she deliberated the politics that were partially to blame for their predicament. "Jamie, don't think I don't know what's going on. The country's in a real mess and things aren't getting any better. Andrew Young and Carter are supporting Mugabe and making him promises that undermine the whole peace process." She shook her head. "The Kissinger Accord, signed off by President Ford last year, is dead isn't it? And yet we're committed." Slowly she turned to him. "Jamie, you know better than I do that the whole country's on edge. The kids and I need you.

Jamie felt torn. *Why are these decisions so hard?* "Emily, you're not making it any easier. I know this affects you and the kids even more than it does me. I'm a third generation Rhodesian and I can't let my country down. I have to think of Alan and Audrey too—they're right there in the thick of it with no support. I can do this. I've done it before." Jamie sighed.

Any hope Emily had of convincing Jamie otherwise sank along with the feeling in her stomach. She knew, well before Jamie did, that it was over. The decision had been made.

Jamie studied Emily. She looked so vulnerable and his heart ached. He waited for her response, but there was none. Philemon rang the dinner bell. They left the pool together and Jamie reached for Emily's hand. It was limp and unresponsive. Still, he gently held onto it and led her into the living room to gather the children for dinner. How would he ever tell them?

* * *

Jamie barely tasted the roast beef, mashed potatoes and green peas that Philemon had cooked. Each mouthful was a struggle, like trying to swallow cotton wool. Emily only picked at her food, pushing it around her plate, mindlessly. There was none of their usual bantering and exchanging the news of the day. The children sensed the unease and were more subdued than usual. Jamie looked at them and felt a lump rise in his throat. They were all growing up so fast. Jamie realized that he had already missed such a large part of their lives.

He looked at Barrie, tall and thin with a wild mop of blond hair. *He's already eleven years old. He could be shaving in two years. What if I'm not here to teach him those manly things that a father needs to pass on?* A vision of Barrie two years ago in Melsetter came to his mind. Barrie, just a little boy, all elbows and knees, and Jamie teaching him to fire an automatic shotgun—just in case he was ever needed to help fight off an attack. Barrie was so excited and eager to learn. He had held the gun tightly against his cheek and pulled the trigger. His slight body went flying backwards, no match for the violent kick of a 12-gauge shotgun with three-inch loads of buckshot. *What kind of world do we live in when we have to teach our children this sort of thing?*

Jamie's gaze lingered on Rachelle, a beautiful, petite, nine year old bundle of energy. The little scar above her eye, from when she fell off her bicycle, still shone pink. Of all the children, she was the one most like Jamie, determined, never willing to give up until she had accomplished what she set out to do.

Little Deanne, the baby, was already seven. Soft and rosy with golden blonde hair, Jamie could see Emily in her.

Oh God, you have given me three such precious, beautiful children. Each one is unique but made in your image and given to my care. I have already missed so much of their lives, and now I am going away again. Is this the right thing for me to do?

Jamie swallowed hard and pushed his plate away, refusing to give in to his emotions. "Kids, there is something mommy and I want to talk to you about."

Three pairs of large, solemn eyes turned to Jamie. Emily looked down at her plate, not trusting herself to look at the children.

"The prime minister has asked me to do a very special job for him. That means I will have to go away for a while."

Deanne's little face began to pucker. "My friend Anna's daddy went away and he never came back. Are you going to come back?"

"Of course he is, silly," Barrie turned to his sister, scornfully. "The prime minister is a very important man, and daddy has to do what he says." His eyes sought out Jamie's. "Don't you, dad?"

"You know, kids, sometimes in life we have to do things that we may not want to, but because it's the right thing to do, we do them anyway. I don't want to go away and leave you and mommy, but I have been asked to do this by some very important people. I'm doing it for our country, because I love our country, and because it's the right thing to do. And yes, Deanne, I will be coming back. In fact, I will try to come home every month to see you."

"Can we go with you, daddy?" Rachelle asked eagerly, thinking she had found the solution to the problem.

"No, I don't think you would have much fun there. Besides, I won't be staying in one place all the time. I'll be moving around."

"When will you be leaving, dad?" Barrie's voice betrayed a little anxiety.

"Soon. As soon I can get things organized at work."

"Will you be gone long?"

"Well, it may be as long as a year. It depends how long it takes to do the job I've been given."

Deanne brightened. "We'll pray for you every night, Daddy." She was happier now that she had found a positive thing to do.

"Thank you, Pickle. That's the very best thing you can do for me.

Jamie took Deanne's hand and they all went into the living room. He sat down on the couch with Emily and the children all crowded around them. Jamie felt a lump in his throat.

"Tell us a story, daddy." Rachelle piped up.

"Just a quick one and then you're all off to bed."

Chapter Two

Josiah grimaced. He looked behind to make sure his seven fellow comrades were matching his pace. They still had a long way to go. Earlier that day they had left the Zimbabwe African Liberation Army camp on the Pungwe River in Mozambique and made for the border with Rhodesia. It was a sixty mile journey to the border, necessitating the use of a truck for the first leg. The roads were rough bush tracks, but the comrades made good time and reached their drop off point by two o'clock. Now they were on foot, making their way down a well traveled path. They were still five miles from the border and then it was another three miles to their destination. Josiah was determined they would get there with time to spare.

Yes, this is a day to be reckoned with—it will be remembered. The Honde is now ours and the people will learn to obey.

He would complete this mission well. The people of Simangane would learn that giving information to the soldiers was unacceptable. They would understand no one was to work at the tea estates. This was their country and, he recognized that if they were ever to seize power, the whites would have to be driven back. Those that dared help the white pigs would pay a high price.

Josiah strained to look through the thick vegetation on the path ahead. The vegetation was so thick all he could see was the path. He pulled a stained bandana from his back pocket and wiped the sweat from his face. He was now the acting commander of all ZANLA forces for Manicaland, but he was not one to stay in camp—he was a man of action.

"Isaac, do you know the path? We must reach the village of Simangane before dusk."

Isaac nodded. "I know the way. This is my home. I can find even the site of my father's grave in the dark. We shall be at Simangane in good time. All the men and women will be back from their fields."

They moved quickly, traversing several streams, winding their way through dense stands of buffalo grass higher than any man. Josiah stepped carefully, avoiding the golden brown stringers of buffalo beans. Many a time he had suffered when the fine golden hairs worked their way through his clothes and into his skin. He remembered the itch for days.

They passed several villages. The locals just looked at them, but did not greet them. Josiah and his comrades dressed differently from the FRELIMO guerillas who had forced the Portuguese out of Mozambique, but they were known to be just as cruel and the people kept their distance.

Three hours later they arrived at a village that was known as the crossing-point, just inside Mozambique, and not more than half a mile from the border.

Josiah held up his hand. "We stop here. Check your guns and packs."

Their target was a local village, requiring only AK-47 rifles and bayonets. No mortars or RPG grenade launchers this trip.

"Sit down," ordered Josiah. "Morgan will instruct you."

Morgan Tangwena spoke up. The son of Chief Tangwena of Inyanga, Morgan was the political commissar, trained in China. He instructed softly, but clearly. "We will follow Isaac who knows the path to the village. He knows of a patch of forest where we can wait until dusk. As soon as the sun goes down, we will enter the village. Spread out and cover all the paths into the village. Make sure that nobody leaves. Take everyone to the clearing in front of the biggest hut. That is where Headman Simangane sleeps. Make sure that he is present, because he is the man who causes much trouble, passing information to the police."

There was a pause and the comrades all nodded their heads.

Josiah was pleased. *Good. Morgan was displaying his leadership.*

"Simangane has six wives and we want all of them present, for they, too, must be made an example of," and Morgan spat. "Look for any young men and young girls. They need to come back with us when we are finished. Don't let any escape."

There was some murmuring and snickering amongst the men.

"We will go now, but watch for anyone on the path. We do not want anyone to see us until it is time for us to enter the village. If you hear someone coming, leave the path and we will wait in the forest until they pass. Is that understood?"

Isaac quickly stood up and took the lead.

Josiah brought up the rear. He would need to alert the group if anyone tried to overtake them from behind.

The sun slowly descended over Inyangani Mountain which dominated the skyline in front of them. They moved quickly, and silently, each aware of the potential danger across the border. The Rhodesian army pigs had been spotted patrolling every day for the last month, and several groups had lost men in contacts with these soldiers, some of whom were black and of the dreaded Rhodesian African Rifles (RAR).

They came to a thick stand of forest. Tall trees towered above the path, blocking out the last rays of sunlight. Isaac motioned for them to follow as he left the path and moved into the forest. It was darker. The smell of rotting vegetation and fungus filled the air as they crept silently forward, around the boles of giant mahogany trees, and through patches of ferns and green moss.

At last, they reached the ridge at the edge of the forest. They had a clear line of sight to the village nestled two hundred yards below. There were fourteen huts nestled together. This was the headman's village, and he had huts for each of his six wives, sons and older relatives.

Josiah eased down and watched the men and women come into the village from their fields. Now he must wait. A dozen or more children played in the center of the village. One of the boys pushed a homemade cart made out of wire. Two of the girls busily pounded their long wooden pestles into a wooden mortar that held the maize for the evening meal.

Thump, thump, thump … The two girls worked rhythmically.

As Josiah watched them, remembrance of his own home crept into his mind. He pushed back the memory. Thoughts of his old life were a distraction that he had been trained to overcome. But the image returned with each pound of the pestle. He could picture his mother and sister pounding the maize. He thought of the meals his mother had made and his mouth watered—sweet maize porridge for breakfast in the morning, and thick, rich stew to dunk patties of stiff maize meal in at night. He tried once more to bury the images of his past, but the scene below was a jolting reminder. The last traces of sunlight began to fade. Josiah watched the bright orange orb descend slowly behind the mountain as the memories flooded back.

* * *

"Josiah, it's time for breakfast!"

An eighteen-year-old Josiah rushed out of his hut at his mother's voice. The golden sun edged over the horizon, its early morning rays spreading over his small childhood village in Makoni Tribal Trust Land.

It was early June, 1972. The warmth of the day would soon melt the frost that had formed on the cool grass outside Chief Makoni's kraal. Josiah thought a moment about climbing back under the warmth of his blanket, but the smell of his mother's breakfast beckoned.

What would he do today? His life was never dull with over forty brothers and sisters. He was the third son of Chief Makoni's fourth wife. A wave of excitement gripped him as he thought of his future; then a small knot of apprehension formed in this stomach. He had only six months left with his family and he would miss them. He had just passed his 'O' level examination at the nearby Makoni Secondary School and his parents were proud of him. In six months he would be enrolled at the Dombashawa Technical College where he would study agriculture. Once he graduated he would return to his home village, teach others what he had learned, and improve the farming standards of his people.

He stretched his lean, five-foot-ten-inch frame, beginning to feel the warmth of the sun. Walking back from the thatch-enclosed latrine he grabbed his old toothbrush. He took good care of his teeth, using ash from the previous night's fire to keep them gleaming white. To complete his early morning grooming he ran his fingers through his short, crinkly black hair.

He finished buttoning up a faded blue shirt and hurried to join his mother, brothers and sisters. He loved to watch his mother fix breakfast. Her welcome smile warmed him, as did the tasty, boiled maize-meal porridge she served each morning. He looked forward to it, especially served with fresh milk from one of their two nursing cows.

Josiah sat down on the freshly swept ground and reached for the plate of porridge. He began to spoon the steaming, white sadza into his mouth, when suddenly an ominous shiver ran up the back of his neck. He looked up to see six men walking towards the family gathering. The men were dressed much like every other man in the village, but carried guns with curved magazines. Josiah had never seen such weapons, but he had heard about them, and there had been talk of freedom fighters in the area. Josiah slowly put his spoon down, barely able to breathe.

His mother, his sisters and brothers froze as they stared at the men. No one moved. No one uttered a sound.

One of the men, who was taller than the others, stepped forward. His thick lips tightened in an evil grimace, revealing broken yellow teeth. He twirled a large, wooden club in one hand and Josiah's eyes followed it as it swung back and forth. He was afraid to look into the man's rabid eyes.

"Where is Mambo Makoni?" his voice was loud and rasping, and sent chills down Josiah's spine.

Silence ...

Josiah's mother still did not move. His two sisters covered their mouths with their hands to quell any sound that might escape.

Josiah gasped as the man suddenly raised the club and brought it down with lightning speed on his mothers shoulder. There was a sharp crack and Josiah knew that her shoulder was broken. She screamed as she fell to the ground.

"Where?"

Josiah's little sister whimpered, "He is over by the cattle pen."

Three of the men bounded off and within a few minutes Josiah saw them dragging his father back towards the group. Already Josiah could see blood streaming from his father's nose and split lips.

His father was flung roughly to the ground, and once again, the leader raised his club and brought it down, again, and again, striking the chief's head, his back his arms and legs. No part of Chief Makoni's body escaped the unmerciful blows.

"This is what happens to 'sellouts,'" the man shouted, flecks of foamy spittle spraying from his mouth.

Josiah could no longer bear it. He stood up and tried to grab the flaying arm of the man, but he was no match for his frenzied strength. With one blow the man clubbed Josiah and he sank to the ground next to his father who lay in a motionless, bloodied heap. Josiah could not tell if he was dead or alive.

Anger and bile rose from the back of Josiah's throat, but he lay still, knowing that any sign of opposition would mean his own death sentence. He was relieved to hear a faint moan escape from his father, and was thankful to see one of his sisters crawl to his father's aid.

"Have you learnt your lesson yet?" the man hissed, poking Chief Makoni with the barrel of his rifle.

The chief said nothing.

Josiah's lips quivered. *Say something, father, say something.*

Turning to his comrades the leader shouted, "Bring all the young people. They are coming with us."

Josiah curled his body into the fetal position. *No, this can't happen. Father, do something.*

The leader turned to the rest of his men. "Bring the boy and the girls. We are leaving now."

Josiah felt panic set in. He could hear his heart pound.

* * *

Thump, thump, thump ...

Down in the village two girls continued to prepare their evening meal with rhythmic drumming. Josiah shook the thoughts of his past from his mind. He had to focus on the mission. He felt impatient as he watched an old woman entering the village with a large clay pot on her head. *Good. She appears to be the last.*

It was twilight, and faint shadows of mist began to rise from the forest around them.

"It is time," said Josiah. He took the lead as the comrades fanned out and moved down towards the village.

As though there had been an unseen signal, they all converged and entered the village at the same time, sealing all the paths that led from it.

"Ha," said Josiah. "Where is Simangane?" He looked straight at a tall, older man wearing wire rimmed glasses. "You were expecting us?" he sneered, knowing full well that they had caught the villagers unawares. "Sit down, you eaters of dung." Josiah took three large strides up to Simangane, grabbed the front of his shirt and dragged him towards the main hut. "You think you can talk through two heads. One, telling us what we want to hear—then you tell the police where to find us." He heard Simangane's wives and children wail and cry.

Isaac and Morgan moved forward. They carried a length of barbed wire. Each took hold of one of Simangane's arms and dragged him toward a large fig tree that grew at the edge of the village. As Simangane struggled, Enoch took the butt of his AK rifle and slammed it into Simangane's face.

The sound of the blow made even Josiah wince.

Simangane went down in a heap, spitting out teeth and blood. Isaac caught hold of him by the arms and pulled him upright against the tree, with his arms pulled back behind him, one on each side of the tree. Morgan Tangwena then took the barbed wire and wrapped it tightly around Simangane's wrists, and then around his neck, so that he was pinned to the tree like a trussed pig. The women, screamed and one threw herself forward onto Isaac.

"Get off me, you whore," said Isaac. He flung the woman down. She stumbled backwards into the fire. Leaping up with another scream, she fell back among the other women who frantically brushed the hot coals off her burning dress.

Morgan stepped forward. "Now you will see what happens to dogs that sleep with those pigs of police." With that, he stepped forward and thrust his bayonet deep into Simangane's chest, just below the ribs, pulling down with all his might and disemboweling the chief in one stroke. Like a gutted fish, Simangane's entrails flopped out of the cavity that had once been his belly.

Simangane gurgled and tried to cry out, but could not. He slumped against the tree. Two of his wives screamed, throwing themselves forward to help. The comrades were ready. They thrust their bayonets in and out as they skewered the two women. They thrashed slowly on the ground until all movement stopped.

Josiah looked on, pleased with the terror on the faces of the onlookers. He nodded his head. "You have seen," he warned them, then turned to his comrades. "Bring the young men and girls. We will leave now."

There were four young boys, aged between ten and fourteen, and three young girls, a little older. The comrades immediately grabbed the seven young people, tying their hands behind their backs with bark rope

One of the wives threw herself at Morgan and shrieked.

"Don't take my only son. Please, please—he is just a boy."

The woman's screams echoed through Josiah's mind.

* * *

Josiah was wide-eyed and shaking. The screams were coming from his mother, but Josiah lay there, shaking and unable to take his eyes off his father. *Please, Father, do something.*

"Oh please, don't take my son," his mother screamed.

He looked at his father who was quickly losing consciousness. Struggling to his feet he searched frantically in all directions. He had to find a way to escape. Suddenly his head reeled as the butt of a rifle sent him sprawling to the ground. His hands were bound with bark rope that dug into his flesh. He spat out dirt and looked up to see two of his sisters being bound. Suddenly, his eldest sister, who had been hiding in the crowd, darted behind a group of people and ran behind one of the huts and into the bush. Two of the strangers ran after her but the spirits were with her that day. She quickly outran them and escaped.

The leader turned to Chief Makoni and slapped him on the face with the back of his hand. "Remember what we told you. If you speak to the police we will come back and kill you all."

Josiah stumbled as they shoved him, and his two half sisters into the middle of the group. There were armed men in front of them and behind them. Josiah felt like an animal. All of their hands were tied and there was an additional rope linking all three of them together. If one tried to escape, the others would be a hindrance.

For five days Josiah marched on, stopping only at night to sleep. He ate the dried maize cake and drank water once a day as he walked. His body was exhausted with hunger and despair. The horrible scene from his village played over and over in his mind and he was sick with anxiety, wondering what had happened to his mother and the rest of his family.

At midday on the fifth day, they came to a large river. Josiah heard the leader say it was the Pungwe. He knew they must have crossed the border and they were now in Mozambique. The trail led them through thick riverine forest of mahogany and ironwood trees and, even during the heat of the day, the mosquitoes were fierce. Their bound hands made it impossible to ward off the persistent attacks of the insects swarming around their perspiring faces. Still they marched on.

Josiah could see a large clearing in the forest. He could see many tents and people milling around. Several trucks were parked in the shade of large trees. Women were busy in an area in the center of the clearing, tending fires and stirring pots of thick maize porridge.

Josiah was separated from his sisters. He was taken to one of the huts where he was locked in. Each miserable day flowed into the next. The weeks passed by in a blur. The bark ropes binding his hands were replaced by steel handcuffs that bit into his flesh till his wrists were raw. He was chained to another young man, Enoch, even at night, so sleep was often disrupted. He felt weak with exhaustion. Escape was always on Josiah's mind, but guards with rifles were posted around the perimeter of the camp. He realized the futility of even trying.

Josiah's day started early. Before the sun was up, and while the rest of the camp slept, a guard prodded and hit him with sticks until he joined the other prisoners, standing in line with head bowed. Josiah did not dare make a sound for fear of a beating. His first job was to clean up the filth around the camp. With his bare hands he would pick up the defecation left by dogs or children, old bones or dried up maize porridge. He always felt dirty and endured the taunts and ridicule of the soldiers. There were constant beatings, sometimes for wrong-doing, sometimes for no reason at all. His food was thrown to him as if he were an animal. He was spat upon and called filthy names—no one in the camp was allowed to give him a kind word. Slowly, Josiah could feel his spirit breaking.

One morning, the routine was changed. Instead of cleaning up around the camp he was marched with the other prisoners to a covered shelter and told to sit on a rough wooden bench. Josiah looked around at the thirty or so other prisoners and knew they were thinking the same thing, wondering what would happen next.

A stranger stepped up. Tall and very thin, he wore the olive green uniform of the freedom fighters. He was not much older than Josiah, but had an air of authority. There were two other men with him. They were shorter and did not have black faces, but their skin was pale yellow. The tall man looked intently at the prisoners and began to speak in a voice of authority. "My name is Morgan Tangwena, and I have come to tell you some truths. I have brought with me some friends who can teach you many great things."

Over the next few weeks Josiah's treatment changed. He was no longer beaten and deprived of food. Each day he came to the shelter and sat on the benches and listened to Tangwena and the two men who, they were told, came from China.

Josiah tried to harden his heart. Try as he might, he could not block out the words he heard.

"We are not your enemies. You have only two enemies, the Matabele and the white pigs. Long ago, under King Mzilikazi and King Lobengula, the Matabele pillaged our lands and murdered our ancestors. These ancestors were part of the great Monomatapa Kingdom and the ruins of their great city lie at Zimbabwe where they can never be broken down." Tangwena's voice rose in anger. "The country of Zimbabwe is rightfully ours."

The guards, along with some of the soldiers who had wandered in, began to chant and clap, "Yeah, yeah! Zimbabwe, Zimbabwe!" Josiah and his fellow prisoners were prodded until they jumped up from their seats and they began to chant too, "Yeah, yeah! Zimbabwe, Zimbabwe!"

As the chanting continued, reaching a frenzy, a thin sheen of sweat broke out on Josiah's face. His heart raced faster and faster until he felt it would burst out of his chest.

Tangwena held up his hands for silence. "Now the white pigs have come and stolen our land. They have taken the best farmland for themselves and left our people with the infertile, sandy soil. For nearly a hundred years they have grown rich on the backs of your ancestors, your fathers and mothers, aunts and uncles, brothers and sisters. Will you let them make slaves of you in your own land?"

Day after day Josiah listened to Tangwena tell of how the land of Zimbabwe had been stolen from them, the rightful owners.

"Now is the time for us to rightfully reclaim the land that was ours. The struggle for freedom is yours. It is our duty to force the white pigs from our land and send them back where they came from."

Josiah listened. The change had been imperceptible but, somewhere in his heart, reason gave way to a sense of loyalty to the instructors. What he was taught began making sense. He could do more for his people now than he could by teaching farming techniques.

"We must never again be subject to the Matabele who killed your grandfathers, raped your grandmothers, and stole your aunts and uncles to force them into a life of slavery," said Tangwena. "You are brave young men, not cowardly jackals like your fathers. You will not give up this land. You will fight for it. Now you, too, are part of the resistance movement known as the Zimbabwe African Liberation Army. You are freedom fighters. We are ZANLA."

Josiah felt the pride and anger rise within him.

Morgan's voice rose to a crescendo. "Our fearless leader is Comrade General Rex Nhongo." He spat in the dirt. "He reports to Robert Mugabe who leads the political struggle under the banner of ZANU, the Zimbabwe African National Union."

Josiah's heart filled with hatred as he listened to the brutal stories of how his country had twice been stolen from his people. By the end of the second week of indoctrination the handcuffs were removed. They were no longer needed. He and the other young men sang songs of liberation. Each called his brother or sister comrade. By the third week he was instructed on weaponry—first the Chinese SKS rifle and then the AK-47 rifle. He was given limited firing practice, but taught how to fix bayonets and thrust them into sacks stuffed with straw.

After weeks of training and indoctrination, he and the others split into sections. Four new recruits were assigned to ten seasoned comrades. Josiah enjoyed the new liberty of being able to walk around the camp freely and greet people. One day he saw his half sister. She looked thin but there was a defiant fire in her eyes.

"How are you, my sister?" he asked.

"Life is very hard, Josiah. I am asked to do many things, but they tell me it is for the cause."

"We are all working for that cause. This is our land we are fighting for. You should be proud to be part of the liberation army."

"Yes, Josiah. But I do not carry a gun to fight. During the day I gather firewood and carry water. I cook. I look after the camp. They make me sleep with any Comrade who wants me. Sometimes there are many men in one night. Now I am told to carry heavy loads of ammunition and landmines for long journeys into the land they call Zimbabwe. There are many of us. It is the same for your other sister."

"You are privileged to be asked to do these things. Each thing you do is important. Your job is to help the soldiers, because it is we who are on the front lines risking our lives so that we can all enjoy our rightful land. Soon I will be amongst those who are fighting the whites and the dogs who help them."

"I am proud of you, my brother. You will be a great warrior, respected by your people and feared by the enemy. Your name will be famous. As for me, I will work hard for the cause, too. You will not be ashamed of me."

The day came. Josiah's heart swelled with pride. He was finally given his own SKS rifle, two stick grenades, an olive green uniform and a peaked cap. He was part of the Marange Section and his leader was Comrade Jeremiah. Their first assignment would be to lay landmines along the main bus routes, burn houses of any supporters of the government, and go back into his area, the Makoni Tribal Trust Land, to recruit more young men and women to join the cause.

Josiah put on his uniform for the first time and looked at the shiny new SKS rifle and bayonet that was his weapon. *Ah. Now, I, too, am a warrior. When I go back to my home my father and mother will learn and understand.*

Six months later he was sent to China for more training, before returning as a political commissar. Now, five years later, he was acting commander of all ZANLA forces in Manicaland. He understood the struggle and how to make the people support the cause and the liberators. Yes, he had learned the lessons of that great leader and teacher Mao Tse-tung.

* * *

Simangane's wife continued to cry out for her son. Josiah watched approvingly as his second in command, Morgan Tangwena, the same person who had once instructed him, took charge.

Morgan looked down at her, lifted his right foot and brought it down on her hand with all his force.

Josiah could hear the bones of her arm snap with a sharp crack. "We will still take her son," Morgan continued.

Soon it was over. The comrades had done their work. The mother lay on her back with her eyes open, blood trickling from her mouth from the wounds of a bayonet thrust into her lungs.

Now it was time to leave. There was wailing from the remaining women, two old men and the young children who remained. Josiah knew that there would be no sleep in the village that night.

Darkness descended like a black cloak as the eight comrades, with all seven captives, left the village as silently as they had come.

Chapter Three

Emily slowly pushed back the covers. She swung her legs over the side of the bed, dropping them to the floor as if they were lead. Only with prodigious effort did they respond to her will. She sat for a few moments, not yet ready to face the day. The long night had been fraught with painful images—memories she thought she had put behind her. Horrors she had faced in Melsetter returned to haunt her. So many of their friends had been murdered in the past two years.

Melsetter was bad but the Honde ... *dear God* ... the Honde was the worst. Her stomach cramped with a knot of fear. She tried to dispel it. It gnawed at her all the more. Dropping her head into her hands, her body trembled with dry sobs. She knew Jamie had not slept either. The bed had shaken throughout the night with tossing and turning; finally he had gotten up and quietly dressed. She reached over again and felt for where he had slept. The warmth was gone. She had heard his car pull out of the carport some time ago as he left for the office, skipping breakfast. Emily turned her head and looked around the room for her gown. Her feet nudged her slippers and she slipped them on. This was a new day and a new challenge. She would not let her emotions get the better of her and the children must never know her fears. Softly, she walked into their rooms, put on a smile, and woke them for school.

* * *

Jamie absently tapped his pencil against an empty tea cup. Sitting at his desk, he thoughtfully stared at the sheaf of notes spread before him. The early morning peacefulness afforded him time to jot down thoughts as he readied himself for the meeting with Dennis Cornwell.

The voice startled him.

"Well, Jamie, what's your decision?"

"Sir, you don't give a chap a chance to think." Jamie looked at his watch. *Just after eight o'clock.*

Dennis Cornwell leaned against the door and folded his arms. "Are you going to keep me in suspense?"

Jamie met his gaze. "I'll go."

Dennis stepped into the room, a broad smile spread across his face.

Jamie looked back at his notes. "I was just putting some plans down on paper so I'll have some idea what it will entail."

"That's great. I knew you were the right man for the job. Getting plans together already. I'm impressed."

"Well, let's hope the big guys are, too. It's going to be a massive undertaking and it'll need some major resources."

"You have a meeting with Don Yardman in half an hour. Finish up your ideas and we'll go together."

Jamie nodded.

By nine o'clock they were waiting outside the office of Secretary of Internal Affairs, Don Yardman. A woman of forbidding countenance, grey hair pulled severely into a bun, peered at them over tortoise shell glasses. Jamie cleared his throat.

The secretary finally offered a terse welcome as she motioned to a couple of chairs. "Have a seat. Mr. Yardman is expecting you."

After several awkward minutes they were ushered into the office, a large room with one end set up as a small conference area. As the men settled around the table, Don Yardman wasted no time.

"Well Jamie, what have you decided? Are you ready for the Honde?"

Jamie swallowed. *Ready, after only eighteen hours? No. Have I decided that I need to go? Yes.*

"Yes, sir. I'm ready."

"Good, chap! I knew we could rely on you. We'll certainly do everything we can at our end to support you."

The next thirty minutes were spent discussing details—all that needed to be done or acquired—equipment, manpower and military forces to beef up patrols and secure the border.

"Right, Jamie, when can you leave?" asked Don Yardman.

"Today is Tuesday. I could be ready to leave Monday of next week."

"February second" confirmed Dennis.

Jamie nodded, his mind turning to Emily. "I'm not taking my family with me—it would be pointless as I will be on the move the whole time. I'll come home to visit with them every four to six weeks." Jamie released a long breath.

Don Yardman stood. "It's settled. I'll call Ian Smith and you can start packing up. We're proud of you, Jamie. I know this has not been an easy decision."

Jamie stood and shook Don Yardman's extended hand.

* * *

Jamie backed his little white Datsun out of the driveway. It was a gray, damp morning. The picture in front of him etched itself on his mind. Three little children, dressed in pajamas, hair still tousled from sleep, stood in the driveway waving good-bye. Emily had her arms around them—a tight family unit. Her lips parted in a smile but Jamie saw the pain in her eyes. *Emily will be all right. She's strong. She has determination. She copes in any situation. He remembered Melsetter. She had comforted so many families that had lost loved ones. She could confidently handle an FN rifle and her aim was better than most men's. She had taught the children what each of their duties would be if the home was attacked, yet never instilling fear. Yes, Emily, you will be all right.*

He was on the road and driving fast, barely noticing lush fields of maize and tobacco. The beautiful pink and purple cosmos scattered along the side of the road seemed to whiz past in a blur of color. At one time fifty miles per hour had been the law. These days, however, prudence and safety depended on speed—limiting the time exposed to any terrorist ambush. Jamie took full advantage of the new leniency.

In just one and a half hours he was driving through the little town of Rusape. This was where his grandfather had made a name for himself during the 1896 Makoni Rebellion, not with guns or terror, but with words of persuasion. And now Jamie was on his way to a neighboring area to quell a rebellion. He hoped he could do as good a job.

The high mountains of Christmas Pass were visible in the distance. Just before reaching the pass he turned off to the left, towards Inyanga, the Eastern Highlands of Rhodesia. Cold mountain streams and heather dotted the hills. Huge pine and wattle forests were planted for timber, the area's primary industry. Orchards of apples, peaches and plums were tucked into fertile valleys.

As Jamie drove along the Inyanga road, the grasslands and msasa trees gave way to dense forests of wattle. The road wound higher and higher up to the escarpment and Jamie had to concentrate to navigate the sharp bends. He almost missed the fresh wooden sign with an arrow: District Commissioner, Mutasa – 1 mile. The ridges of corrugations in the gravel road shook and rattled the overloaded car, making it shimmy from side to side.

Suddenly Jamie rounded a bend in the road and before him was the district commissioner's station of Mutasa. It was a typical government building, long and low, with a covered verandah built around a courtyard. The station had only been built two years earlier and still looked out of place in its surroundings. The standard cream paint and brown trim added to its dreariness. Both the Rhodesian and the Internal Affairs flags fluttered feebly in front of the offices. It was not a picturesque sight, but none-the-less one which Jamie was very happy to see.

Jamie pulled up in front of the building. A small group of men walked along the verandah, laughing and talking, their black faces animated as they recounted some story. They stopped as they saw Jamie, watching curiously. From felt slouch hats trimmed with a red band, and smart khaki uniforms, Jamie knew they were his district assistants. He opened the car door and stepped onto the hard-packed red dirt. The men snapped to attention as they saw the patches of a district commissioner on the epaulettes of Jamie's khaki shirt, the equivalent of a colonel. He was now functioning in a paramilitary role. No longer would he wear a suit and tie. He was garbed in a uniform of khaki shirt and shorts, a red-and-khaki stretch canvas belt, and long khaki socks with red turnovers that came just below the knee. With his red beret carefully smoothed down over his right ear he looked more like someone from the armed forces than a district commissioner.

Suddenly, there was a shout. "Mambo Chinyerere!" A tall, handsome man broke away from the group and hurried towards Jamie. He was older than the rest and he carried himself with dignity and confidence.

Sergeant Sama!

"Sergeant. This is a welcome surprise. What are you doing here? Aren't you retired to your home in Rusape, enjoying all those wives you used to boast about?"

Jamie was delighted to see his old friend. Memories flooded back to the time, many years ago, when he had joined the Department of Internal Affairs as a cadet and was first stationed at Rusape. Sama had patiently taken every opportunity to school him in the customs and language of the people until Jamie lived and dreamed in Shona. He and Sama shook hands warmly.

Sama smiled broadly. "Mambo Chinyerere, we are so pleased to welcome you. It has been a long time, but you still remember old Sama. Now we will see some changes in the Honde."

Jamie looked around at the little settlement. Even the afternoon rains of summer weren't enough to encourage much vegetation on the hard-packed clay between the buildings. A few clumps of green grass struggled to grow and a couple of wattle trees broke the monotony of the bare, flat ground. There were a dozen houses scattered around, obviously homes for the staff. One house stood out, bigger than the rest. This must be the district commissioner's house and his new home. He could see sandbagged bunkers at the side. Another house boasted several flower beds in front and a vegetable patch to the side. Jamie smiled, musing that someone must have brought along his wife.

A small crowd of curious children gathered at a distance. Jamie waved and they broke into giggles of glee and laughter, some putting their hands to their mouths, shyly, and others waving boldly back. Jamie turned to Sama and grinned. "Sama, lead the way."

Sama motioned to the main building. "Come, I will take you to meet Senior District Officer Gordon. That is the person in charge."

Jamie followed Sama across the courtyard, up a few steps and along the verandah, where they stopped in front of a door.

Saluting smartly, Sama announced, "Mambo Gordon is inside."

Jamie entered, surprised to see a young woman seated behind the desk.

Frowning in concentration, her eyes scanned a sheet of paper she held in her hand. She looked up as Jamie entered the office. Recognizing the uniform, she leapt to her feet and offered her hand. "Welcome to Mutasa, sir. I'm Marilyn Gordon."

She was of medium build with short blonde hair. Her lack of makeup and tanned skin showed that she spent a great deal of time outside. Her grey skirt was rumpled, but the plain, white blouse she wore was crisp. If first impressions were correct, Jamie surmised she took her work seriously and that he could rely on her to keep the office running smoothly.

"Thank you, Marilyn." Pointing to the papers, "It looks like you were quite engrossed. Any problems?"

"Nothing new, sir. It's just that I'm bogged down with the preparation of estimates for additional equipment."

He nodded. "Typical of government bureaucracy. How long have you been stationed here?"

"Eight months. It's been a challenge, but a learning experience. I'm looking forward to working with you."

Jamie smiled. "Thank you. I'd like to take a quick look around and meet the staff. I'm delighted to see Sergeant Sama here. We've worked together in the past. He's a good man."

"Yes he is. He'll be a great asset to you." Marilyn rounded the desk and started towards the door. "Most of the staff is out in the field but I'll introduce you to the ones that are here."

Jamie exchanged pleasantries with the few people Marilyn introduced him to and soon they stood in front of the last door.

"This is your office, sir."

Jamie walked into the room and did a quick appraisal. *Stark, but adequate.* The room was large with only one small window. The walls, of course, were typical cream, and grey linoleum tiles covered the floor. A large wooden desk faced the door, bare except for a black telephone and a two-way radio. Two hard chairs were placed in front of the desk and a padded one behind. *Not too inviting. It could use a few things from home.* "Well, Marilyn, if you'll point me towards my house I'll dump my things off. I'll be back in a few minutes and you can begin to fill me in."

* * *

A small, black man dashed out of the kitchen door. His face was puckered with anxiety—wondering what his new boss would be like.

Jamie stepped out of the car and greeted him warmly, calming his fears. "You must be my cook and housekeeper."

The little man relaxed and a smile spread across his face. "Yes, mambo. I am Sixpence, and I am a very good cook."

"Well then, Sixpence, if you are a very good cook we will get on well together. Would you help me unload the car?" Jamie popped the trunk. "I hope my furniture from Salisbury arrived safely."

"Yes, mambo, it arrived on Saturday. I have already put it in the house." Sixpence scooped an armful of things from the car and headed for the kitchen door, Jamie following close behind.

It was a typical government house, a little bigger than most with four bedrooms and one and a half bathrooms. Jamie was pleased to note that there was running water and electricity, no bothersome generators. The kitchen had a modern stove, upgraded from the usual wood burning stoves so typical of houses in the bush. There was a big refrigerator. Nice, as the nearest grocery store was in Umtali, fifty miles away.

The few pieces of furniture Emily had scurried about to buy at the last minute were neatly placed. The sofa and two arm chairs in the living room looked inviting. He envisioned putting his feet up on the coffee table with no one around to disapprove. The dining room was adequate, a small table and four chairs—he wasn't expecting to do much entertaining. His eyes rested on the single bed in the bedroom.

A lump came to his throat. There were going to be many lonely nights here without Emily.

Jamie enjoyed the short walk back to the office. It felt good to stretch his legs and look around. The station was bigger than he had first thought, with a couple of houses partially hidden by wattle trees, and a second house with a carefully tended garden. He guessed that the agricultural officer and the primary development officer lived in the houses with gardens. They were the officers who had been living at Mutasa since it was built two years previously. Jamie heard that they had both brought their wives with them.

Jamie and Marilyn spent the rest of the afternoon going over personnel, a map of the district, a list of vehicles, equipment and weapons. Marilyn handed Jamie the keys to a brand new Leopard, delivered Friday. Together they went to inspect it. Looking like a conglomeration of items from a junk yard, there was nothing sleek about this vehicle, but Jamie had full confidence in it. He had driven one in Melsetter. This was the Mark II version, with the larger engine, and would have the extra power needed to make the steep gradients going to and fro from the Honde. Built on a VW Combi chassis it had torsion bar suspension—a much smoother ride than the jaw-breaking crunch of the Rhinos or Cougars used by the police, special branch, and the army. It was still far from comfortable, sporting a metal driver's seat with no cushioning, other than a thin piece of carpet, and bench seats on either side. Jamie knew, however, that the V-shaped body and mine-proofing could be a real life saver.

Walking back to the office Marilyn directed Jamie to the armory. "Here's a Star 9mm pistol and an Uzi. Do you want an FN as well?"

Jamie checked the weapons. "I'll need a good supply of ammunition. You can keep the FN, that way all I need to carry is 9mm ammo and a supply of spare magazines."

Marilyn handed Jamie a case of ammunition and a supply of spare magazines for the Uzi and the Star pistol. The Uzi was short, very sturdy and well proven. The Israelis had done a great job designing and building these light sub-machine pistols.

After signing for the Leopard and weapons, Jamie went back to his office to mull over all that he had seen that day. Settling down to review the reports Marilyn had placed on his desk, he heard the roar of an engine approaching. From the window, he could see the cloud of dust as another Leopard drove up. A mountain of a man eased himself out of the vehicle, his large belly indicating a passion for food and beer. He heaved his crumpled khaki shorts up and tucked the khaki shirt into the waistband as best he could. Removing his felt bush hat, he wiped his brow with a handkerchief, red with dirt.

Marilyn popped her head around the door of Jamie's office. "Jack Cloete has just arrived. He's the primary development officer. He's been dying to meet you."

A few minutes later Jamie looked up. Jack Cloete filled the door of his office.

"So you're the new DC. Man, it's good to see you. I hear you did some time in Melsetter." Jack's voice was loud and thick with a pronounced Afrikaans accent. "I have some good friends farming there. Did you know the Van der Lindens?" Jack scratched the back of his ear. "I hope you've got a good plan for this area, too. Those bastards are running wild down in the valley."

Obviously Jack did not stand much on ceremony, but as Jamie looked into that wrinkled, weather-beaten face he knew this was an honest, determined and very dependable man.

"Well, Jack, I'm going to need your help. You know the area better than any of us and I'm going to depend a lot on your expertise."

"Ja, I've been here about two years—ever since the station was built. Come over and have dinner with us tonight. I'll fill you in on what's going on. My wife's the best cook in the area." He patted his stomach and chuckled. "She's cooking mutton curry tonight and, man, that's good stuff."

Jamie suddenly realized how hungry he was. He hadn't had lunch and a curry dinner sounded wonderful.

Just before sunset Jamie walked up the path to Jack's house. Even outside Jamie could smell the sweet, spicy aroma of curry. As he had thought, this was the house with flowers in the front and a vegetable garden at the side. Before he could knock Jack opened the door and welcomed him warmly. A large woman, her ample body draped in a brightly flowered polyester dress, bustled up.

"Come in, come in. Sit down in this chair. Jack, go get Mr. Ross a beer."

Jamie looked around the room in amazement. Every spare inch was taken up with something. Ornaments and artificial flowers were placed on every table and the walls were covered with pictures. Jamie wondered how two such large people maneuvered through the room. He picked up a photograph from the table. It was a picture of one of the most beautiful girls he had ever seen. Tall and slim with black hair, a smile lit up her flawlessly featured face.

"That's our Anna. She's living in Salisbury now. This is our other daughter, Tanya, and our son Jacob. They're both married and live in South Africa." Mrs. Cloete thrust two more pictures toward Jamie. He wondered how this voluminous-busted woman with mousy hair pulled tightly back in a bun, along with a rather gruff husband, could have produced such handsome children. But Mrs. Cloete had her own beauty. As he looked again he saw softness in her face and a glow that came from a kind and loving heart.

Jamie and Jack exchanged pleasantries as Mrs. Cloete put the finishing touches on dinner. Jamie could hardly wait; the smell was so enticing he could almost taste the food. He looked appreciatively at the huge plate of steaming, yellow curry and white rice that Mrs. Cloete put in front of him. Sliced bananas and diced tomatoes were piled to one side with Mrs. Ball's chutney on the other. Before Jamie could dig in, Jack took Mrs. Cloete's hand and said solemnly, "Let us give thanks."

Jamie looked at Jack with a new respect and felt a common bond grow between them.

Jamie took his first mouthful of curry and felt the heat building in his mouth. A few more mouthfuls and a light sweat broke out on his forehead. He wiped it with his napkin. Mrs. Cloete regarded him, anxiously.

"Is it too hot for you, Mr. Ross?"

"If a curry doesn't make you sweat, it's not good curry." Jamie grinned. "This is a very, very good curry."

She relaxed only marginally until Jamie asked for seconds.

The evening passed quickly. Jack was a fountain of facts, sharing more about the Honde and Mutasa than Jamie could possibly absorb in one night. As he walked back to the house, exhausted and excited, he considered the prospects of what lay ahead.

Jamie finished unpacking his clothes and sat down on the sofa with a sigh. This was the time of night he and Emily sat together, snuggling and exchanging news of the day. Instead he picked up the book, written by General Sir Gerald Templar, on the British campaign against communist guerillas in Malaya. It was a fascinating read. He absorbed the details like a sponge. He had read the book two years previously, but now the information held more significance. It would prove to be a great reference as he decided what needed to be done in the Honde.

Constructing protected villages, building infrastructure, and protecting the people was his first priority. He would need to coordinate the training of local militia, implement curfews and create 'No Go' areas, but he realized that none of this would be successful unless they won the hearts and minds of the people. The task was daunting and Jamie had no misapprehension about the challenges he would face. He knew it would take a massive team effort. Before making decisions, he would look over the ground, meet the people who would be part of the exercise, and craft a strategic plan.

* * *

Jamie rolled out of bed. It was still dark outside when the alarm went off. A cold shower jolted him awake and the enticing smell of coffee and frying bacon drew him to the kitchen.

"Mangwanani, marara here? Good morning, did you sleep well?" which was a typical Shona salutation. Jamie sat down in front of a plate loaded with fried eggs, bacon, and toast.

"Ah, good morning, mambo. See, I have also made you some sandwiches and a thermos of hot tea to take with you," responded Sixpence.

Jamie was anxious to get his day started. He had never been a slow eater, but today it took him less than five minutes to wolf down his breakfast.

He stood up, strapped on the pistol, pulled on his red beret, grabbed his Uzi and kit bag, and headed for the Leopard.

Driving to the administrative headquarters, Jamie could see Sergeant Sama waiting for him, Beretta automatic shotgun in one hand, blanket roll in the other, and that trademark smile. He chuckled when he saw his old friend. Somehow being around Sama would soften the edge of the daunting mission ahead.

They set off down the dirt road. The morning dew was still fresh on the surface and there were no other vehicle tracks on the road. Soon they were on the tar road from Inyanga to Umtali and headed east toward the Honde. It was a quick drive to the Honde turnoff and the tea estates. The road down the escarpment was roughly paved to prevent wash-aways, but full of potholes.

The sky was just beginning to turn a dull red. Jamie smiled as he thought of that old saying—*red skies in the morning, shepherds' warning; red skies at night, shepherds' delight.* Yes, there would probably be storms that day. The Honde was known to receive over one hundred inches of rain a year and closer to two hundred inches below Mount Inyangani, where the tea estates were located. The Leopard growled as Jamie changed down into second gear to make the long descent to the Honde valley, nearly three thousand feet below. For the first time since he'd left Salisbury, Jamie began to allow himself to relax as he fought the wheel through each tight turn.

Suddenly, the whole world awoke before them. A dazzling kaleidoscope of color, a sunrise brushed with red, orange and gold tones stretched from the cloud bank on the far horizon to the earth below. It took Jamie's breath away. He could see for fifty miles, across the border and well into Mozambique.

"Sama, look, there are the Cathedral Peaks." Jamie pointed to a cluster of granite spires reaching up from a bamboo forest below, like sentinels announcing the awakening of the day. "And there beyond that is the Pungwe River. I camped there one time when I lived at Rusape. The bush is so thick and the trees like giants," said Jamie.

"Ah, but you have been here before. You know this place—that is very good. Maybe the spirits will be with you."

"It all looks so peaceful." He watched spires of smoke rise from different parts of the valley where local farmers were burning brush and weeds they had cleared from their lands. There was always smoke, even during the rainy season, because the brush was wet and green. There was no sign of the brooding troubles that were so much a part of every-day life. The road was clear with not even a bicycle to be seen.

"Sama, this is the beginning," said Jamie. "We have much to do in the next few days and I am going to rely on you to show me everything. You already know the Honde."

"You are right, mambo, I know this place and there is much work to be done."

"I want to meet Chief Mutasa, the headmen, the kraal heads, teachers, agricultural staff, and anyone who can help us understand what is happening."

Sama frowned. "This is a very troubled valley. The people are very afraid. They do not know who they can trust or who will help them."

"That is our job, Sama, to help these people, but first we need to convince them that we can help them."

"I understand." Sama nodded his head.

"I was told that Ruda is the only base camp in the Honde at this time."

"That is so. District officer Chris is stationed there, but there is nothing he can do now as the people are too frightened and will not speak to him."

"As we go, Sama, point out everything I should know about the area."

He was back in the Honde. It was hard to believe. He felt a sense of apprehension as he drove along the valley road to Ruda Keep.

Sama glanced over at him. "Mambo Chinyerere, the spirits have sent you here to bring peace. You have your grandfather's spirit and this is good."

Chapter Four

Jamie and Sama drove through the heavy chain link gate to the long, low building of Ruda Keep. A fresh-faced, well-built young man in his early twenties hurried over to greet them. He was a good six feet tall with blond hair in need of a haircut, and his smile was wide and welcoming.

"Good morning, sir. I'm Chris De Vries, district officer in charge of Ruda Keep." Chris was also dressed in khakis, wearing the red and khaki stretch belt of the Internal Affairs National Service Unit, but he was not wearing his beret.

"Chris, I look forward to working with you here at Ruda. Come and show me around. I especially want to check all security measures."

They had barely started the tour when Sama hurried over. "You are wanted on the Radio, sir."

There were two radios, one for INTAF operations and the other for general emergencies and to act as a backup. Jamie picked up the microphone, "Lighthouse one, who's calling?"

"This is lighthouse one zero, papa charlie calling. Welcome back to Manicaland, Jamie. We missed you. Over."

Jamie smiled. Papa charlie was Provincial Commissioner George Barstow, an old friend he'd first served alongside in Hartley, just before he married Emily. He had been a great support and encouragement to Jamie.

"Good to hear your voice, sir," Jamie responded. "I set up home in Mutasa yesterday and now I've just arrived at Ruda."

"Can you make it to Umtali for a briefing tomorrow at ten? We have RAR and Special Branch coming in. They want to meet you." There was a pause and Jamie thought he heard a sigh. "I don't think you know this yet. We got a call from Aberfoyle first thing this morning. They hit Headman Simangane's kraal late Sunday night. They gutted the headman and killed three of his wives. A contact group left at first light, but were unsuccessful. The terrorists were already well across the border."

Jamie tightened his grip on the microphone. They would need to get moving on things quickly.

"We've had four attacks in less than seven days," Barstow said. "We've lost fourteen of the locals, counting the three teachers and two agricultural assistants killed at Pungwe last week."

"I've heard nothing at this end," Jamie said. "Things have got to change, and quickly."

"Then I'll see you at ten tomorrow morning, Jamie. Out."

Jamie turned to Chris who had been listening in. "It seems things are pretty hot in the area. Let's finish my tour of the Keep and the security arrangements. By the way, we should always dress to show our authority." Jamie touched his head, indicating Chris's missing beret.

Chris dutifully put on his beret and followed him outside to continue touring the facilities.

The keep was surrounded by an earthen wall, about six feet high, topped with razor wire. Built as a rectangle, it was fortified with bunkers at each corner and an additional bunker in the middle of the wall facing east toward the Mozambique border. Each quadrant was one hundred plus yards and the bunkers were sighted in such a way that defenders would have a line of sight covering their left and right flanks and the arc of fire in between.

The additional bunker in the center of the eastern wall was added to provide security from any attack across the border, just five miles to the east. Walking up to the center bunker Jamie studied the construction, the placement of the sandbags, and the structure of the roof. It consisted of two layers of sandbags, supported on heavy gum poles imbedded into the earthen wall. It looked secure at a first glance, but there were no weapons.

Jamie looked around. "Where are the heavy arms? Don't we have any machine guns or mortars?"

"I'm afraid not, sir," replied Chris. "All we have are FN and G-3 rifles, and two automatic shotguns. So far, we've only been attacked once and were able to drive the terrorists off with no casualties on our side. They're lousy shots. Their 60mm mortars are mostly ineffective."

Jamie frowned as he took in the inadequacy of their weapons.

Back at the mess they walked through the living quarters. There were three small bedrooms and a larger room that could sleep four, a kitchen, and a room with two couches and six chairs that served as a living room. He noted two bathrooms and a storeroom. More than adequate, Jamie thought, and he picked out one of the smaller bedrooms for himself.

In the district assistant's quarters, there were two barracks, each with its own bathroom. Entering one, a district assistant wearing corporal stripes emerged from the bathroom, clearly not expecting visitors. Jamie stifled a smile. Awkwardly fumbling to finish fastening his belt, the man quickly stood to attention. He started to salute but stopped short when he realized he was not wearing his hat.

"Corporal Dande, sir."

The corporal was only slightly flustered, his dark brown eyes sparkling in the half light. He was tall, dark skinned and well-built.

Jamie guessed him to be about thirty years of age. "At ease, corporal. Sorry for the untimely arrival. Please, continue to dress. Take your time."

"We are very happy to have the new mambo with us. I am here alone. All the other men are out on patrol."

"How long have you been here in the Honde, corporal?" asked Jamie.

"Twelve months, sir."

"What can you tell me about the people here?"

The corporal's smile faded. "At first it was good and the people welcomed us, but in the last six months there has been much killing and the *boys* have done some very bad things. Many of the children have been taken, both boys and girls, and their mothers weep for them. Now the people do not talk to us because they are afraid."

"I see," said Jamie.

He liked Corporal Dande. There was an eagerness and lack of guile about him that was refreshing. He walked over and looked out the window, surveying the grounds.

"Come and join me as we finish our inspection."

Dande flashed a smile and grabbed his hat. "Yes, sir."

Jamie continued his assessment. The barracks were spotless. The kitchen had a large wood-burning fireplace where a black, cast iron kettle hung, bubbling with the aroma of sadza, or fresh cooked maize meal.

Jamie and Chris walked back to the main building where Chris pulled out a large topographical map of the Honde valley and laid it on the dining room table. Jamie listened intently as Chris gave a detailed overview.

"There are approximately twenty thousand local Manyika people living in the valley. Their villages are spread out between Aberfoyle Tea Estates in the north, Katiyo Tea Estates on the south side of the Pungwe River, then European-owned farms in the south. From the information we've received, another ten to twenty thousand of the people have fled across the border into Mozambique."

"I presume that we're going to have to deal with a lot of rain."

"Typically, we can expect the rains to end in April." Chris looked up, contemplating. "It will cause some difficulties, but the main roads are well-graveled and access won't be a problem."

He traced his finger along the map. "There are only two main roads through the valley. The north-western route goes to Aberfoyle and Simangane's area. The road to Katiyo turns off about a mile before you reach the Pungwe River. This is the main access to the border area."

Jamie nodded as he studied the map.

"There are seven headmen," said Chris, "including Headman Simangane. I couldn't help but overhear your radio message that he was murdered Sunday night." Chris was silent for a moment, then sighed and shook his head. "None of the villages are large; the biggest has no more than ten or fifteen huts. There are two bus companies that serve the area, but most of the people travel on foot or by bicycle. There is one secondary school and fourteen primary schools, including those run by various mission denominations."

The magnitude of the task began to engulf him. The odds of success were overwhelming. Jamie took a breath. This was not going to be a simple exercise of moving the tribes-people from one area to another. There just weren't enough roads, the villages were too spread out, and finding suitable ground to build protected villages was going to be a real challenge. The topography was difficult—hills, valleys, rivers, streams and a border that was just too close. Communications with the people would be difficult and he could see he'd be wearing out a lot of shoe leather going from village to village, checking out the lay of the land.

Chris sensed his frustration. He disappeared to rummage in the storage room, leaving Jamie for a moment to mull over the map. He returned with a sheaf of large, overlapping aerial photographs, and a 3-D viewer. Smiling, he placed them on the table.

Jamie brightened. "When were these taken?"

"Just last year. They're pretty good. They show all the current villages and paths."

Jamie positioned the 3-D glasses on their portable stand and studied the images more closely. The hills and valleys stood out in bold contrast and he could effortlessly make out the villages in their little clearings, including the paths leading to and from the villages.

"These are excellent. It's going to make our task a lot simpler and could speed up the process. I'd hate to have to wait another three months. Good work, Chris."

After a morning of studying the maps and reviewing reports Jamie stood up, stretched and yawned. "I need to get out of here and have a look around the area. Sama and I will take the Leopard and head out for a while."

"I understand, sir. But be careful. There's a lot going on out there and it's especially dicey towards evening."

"Don't worry. I have no death wish. We'll be back well before dark."

The Leopard bounced along the corrugated gravel road, jarring every bone in Jamie's body. He clamped his teeth tightly together so as not to bite his tongue. As the vehicle hit some of the potholes he could hear the breath explode from Sama's mouth. The wreckage of a small truck lay crushed beside the road, torn apart by a landmine, a grim reminder that hidden danger was ever present.

As they rounded a curve at the top of the ridge Jamie looked down at the sparkling waters of the Pungwe River. The concrete bridge straddling the gushing water looked vulnerable and out of place amongst the giant mahogany trees. Jamie slipped the Leopard into low gear and slowly labored down the steep incline. He pulled the vehicle over close to the river and stepped out onto the soft, spongy ground. He breathed deeply, savoring the sweet, musty smell of decomposing vegetation.

The beauty of the African bush had a way of drawing the tension out of him. "It's good to be back, Sama."

Cawk, cawk, cawk. The sounds of the brilliantly colored purple-crested louries calling to each other filled the air.

Jamie bent down and put his hand in the sparkling water. It was cold to his touch, a reminder that its headwaters rose high on the slopes of Mt. Inyangani. Thick vegetation filtered the water as it flowed in from a myriad of small streams that fed the river.

"When were you last in the Honde?" Jamie asked.

Sama's mind seemed elsewhere as he looked around nervously. The question sank in and he turned abruptly to face Jamie. "Last week, mambo. That's when they destroyed the school and killed all the teachers."

That, in addition to the urgency in Sama's voice, squelched any remaining feelings of nostalgia. They worked in silence as they checked for explosives under the bridge. Several locals passed them on bicycles, but none stopped or responded when Jamie greeted them. This wasn't a good sign.

After seeing all was safe at the bridge, they climbed into the Leopard and headed back to Ruda. Jamie was thinking, *Yes, he would leave for Mutasa, and then Umtali, first thing in the morning.*

Leopard MK II

* * *

Jamie breathed in deeply, savoring the familiar smells of the fresh African air blowing through the windows of the Datsun. The little car was less restrictive, unlike the Leopard—no seat belts to keep him from flying through the canvas roof, or into the bullet-proof glass windscreen if he hit a landmine. The tranquil morning scenery on the way to Umtali offered his mind a respite from deliberating the tasks that lay ahead. Climbing up Christmas Pass, Jamie looked down on the entire city of Umtali and across to Vumba Mountain to the immediate south of the city. It was here, sixteen years ago, that Jamie had asked Emily to marry him and slipped a diamond on her finger. It was a beautiful sight, a small city with the charm of the early 1900s and the modern facilities of a major center. It was the hub of Manicaland, the center from which all planning took place for the entire eastern border.

The road down Christmas Pass was much like the road descending into the Honde Valley, except this was a three-lane, tarred road and the main artery to the eastern border. Shifting down into second gear to save his brakes, Jamie began the descent. The traffic was now beginning to pick up, including an army convoy climbing up from the city, presumably headed for either Inyanga or the Honde Valley. Pulling up at the first traffic light, Jamie glanced at his watch, 1015 hours. He'd made good time. He pulled into the provincial commissioner's headquarters a few minutes later.

Sally Gordon's face lit up as Jamie walked in the door. His old friend, both receptionist and secretary to George Barstow, was elated to see Jamie.

"Hi, and welcome back. It's good to see you again, though I wish it were under different circumstances," she smiled. "I wish we had time to catch up, but the boss is waiting." She stepped around her desk and escorted him to Provincial Commissioner Barstow's office.

George Barstow was just as Jamie remembered him. Slightly built, with blond hair and a pair of bright blue eyes. He was in his late fifties, but looked ten years younger.

Jamie pulled up a chair and George leaned forward resting his arms on his desk, smiling broadly as he studied the younger man.

"You're looking well. The prospect of a little action seems to agree with you."

Jamie laughed at George's directness. "You could say that, though the task is a bit daunting."

Sally carefully nudged open the cracked door with her shoulder and came in with two cups of tea. "No sugar, Jamie—just as you like it." She sat the cups down on the desk and left the room, closing the door behind her.

"We have to be at JOC Headquarters at eleven," George added. "Go ahead and fill me in with what you have in mind. I realize you've had less than two days on the job, but we need to move on this. What was your take on the Honde yesterday?"

Jamie took a sip of tea. It would buy him a few seconds. How could he convey this quickly? The cup clanked as he sat it down.

"It's going to be tough. I was shocked to see the attitude of the people. They just looked away when they passed me on the road to the Pungwe. I can't say I blame them with what's happened there in the last six months. We've offered them virtually no protection from the terrorists, and anyone who helps us gets taken out."

George pulled out his pipe and filled it. Jamie watched in

amusement. The loose tobacco sticking out of the top looked like it needed a haircut.

"Do we know who's leading the terrorists and what resources they have?" Jamie asked.

George lit his pipe and puffed slowly, drawing the orange glow down into the tobacco.

"The best intelligence we have shows that Rex Nhongo is in overall command of all ZANLA forces. He moves around the different training camps across the border in Mozambique."

"Who's behind the most recent attacks?"

"Last week we received intelligence that it's a fellow by the name of Josiah Makoni. We believe he's responsible for the attack on Headman Simangane. Probably comes from your old stamping ground, Rusape."

Jamie immediately thought back a year. *Josiah. Is this the same guy that attacked us at Melsetter?*

George took another draw from his pipe and looked at his watch. "It's time to head out to the JOC meeting. The team is interested to hear your plans. You can expect a grilling."

* * *

As Jamie entered the conference room a giant of a man stood up and approached him, extending a massive arm. A bushy ginger mustache hid any smile that might have been on his lips and his blue eyes surveyed Jamie keenly, missing nothing. He wore camouflage and had the pips of a full colonel on his shoulders. Jamie recognized him as Colonel Jock Sanders, head of all security in Manicaland.

"Good morning. This must be Jamie Ross. Welcome back to Manicaland. I've heard a lot about you and we're glad to have you on the Team." His voice resonated around the room and the way his tongue caressed the words left no doubt as to his Scottish ancestry.

He turned, motioning to the others. "Let me introduce you to the members of the JOC. I understand you already know Major Whiting, Fourth Battalion." Jamie stepped forward and grabbed John Whiting's hand warmly, glad to see a friendly face—someone he had known since he was a boy—a friend who served as a lay preacher when not working the farm, or serving on army call-up.

"Major Whiting's here to represent the territorial forces of the Rhodesian Regiment in Manicaland," Colonel Sanders continued. "He heads up all contact groups responding to terrorist incidents. His group will be rotating with other territorial groups—six weeks in, six Weeks out." He smiled. "Beside him is Major Nick Farham of the RAR. His soldiers have the reputation of being among the best-trained regular African forces, in Southern Africa. Like you, they'll be in the Honde permanently, until the job is done."

Jamie turned to Nick Farham and the two men eyed each other intently. This was the man Jamie would be working most closely with, and it was so important that the two of them had a good rapport and understood each other. Jamie saw a man of medium height with short black hair and a steady gaze. He did not look like a man one could mess with—there was a strength and determination in the gaze. Jamie liked what he saw.

Finally Colonel Sanders turned to the last man. "And this is Inspector Sandy Giles, Special Branch—in charge of all intelligence."

Sandy Giles looked like an intelligence officer, tall, slender, with a pale face and gold rimmed glasses.

After the men had all shaken hands and exchanged a few pleasantries they sat down and all eyes turned to Jamie expectantly.

Colonel Sanders looked at Jamie, "Well, Mr. Ross, what can you tell us about your plans for the Honde?"

"I haven't had time to really familiarize myself with the valley yet, but I'll tell you what I know. There are around twenty thousand locals living in the valley, the majority of who fall under the jurisdiction of Chief Mutasa and his seven headmen. The terrain is rough and there are few access roads."

"What do you know about the people?" asked Nick Farham.

"Most of them get around on foot or bicycle. It was very obvious to me yesterday that the terrorists have the upper hand. Nobody greeted me. In fact the majority of locals avoided me."

Sanders narrowed his gaze. "What about the tea estates? Do you know what's happening?"

"I haven't had a chance to visit Aberfoyle or Katiyo, but I

understand how important the tea estates are to the economy. Recent information has it that anyone who goes to work at the tea estates will be killed, including members of their family. My brother, Alan, is general manager of Aberfoyle and I look forward to meeting with him later in the week."

Jamie looked at each of them, hoping to convey the enormity of the task he was proposing, particularly the support he would need. He spoke his next words clearly and emphatically. "This is a case where relocating the people into protected villages is the only answer. We must separate and protect the people from the terrorists. If we fail, the terrorists, through their tactics of brutality and terror, will have virtually all the support they need. As the prime minister pointed out to me, we would have to redefine the borders of the country if we don't succeed."

"Are you sure that protected villages will solve the problems?" Major Farham sounded skeptical.

"I've studied General Templar's book on protected villages in Malaya. Looking at the successes of the Mt. Darwin PV program, I'm convinced that we can win this battle if we have enough resources and work together as a team."

Colonel Sanders slammed his hand down on the table. "Then I say let's move with it. How many PVs do we need and how soon can we get started?"

"We need to proceed carefully," Jamie cautioned. "It's critical that we don't upset traditional social and tribal affiliations. There are seven headmen who owe their allegiance to Chief Mutasa, and I estimate that we'll need a minimum of seven PVs, possibly eight. The size of the PVs will vary. The smallest will have somewhere between two thousand and twenty five hundred people and the largest, close to four thousand people."

The men sitting around the table shuffled uneasily, afraid to embrace the enormity of the task.

"The terrorists have studied Mao Tse-tung," Jamie continued. "They understand his base philosophy on winning a terrorist war. You know that saying, *Where the waters are life-giving the fish will multiply and thrive—where the waters are stagnant the fish will die.* The tribal people are the waters. In simple terms, we must deny the terrorists' access to the people. We need to cut off their food supplies, eliminate their intelligence, and remove their source of carrier labor to transport their mines and munitions."

Jamie leaned back, giving them time to think. Sandy Giles quickly scribbled notes while Colonel Sanders kept his gaze locked on Jamie, nodding as he mulled over the implications.

Nick Farham sat on the edge of his chair, looking intently at Jamie.

Jamie could sense a change in attitude and excitement building in Nick's eyes.

"What do you need me to do?" Nick asked.

"First of all, step up patrols and create a 'No Go' area along the border. This is essential. We'll also need your help in relocating the locals into the PVs. They'll be reluctant to leave their villages and crops."

Colonel Sanders shot a glance at Nick. "Major Farham, what do you think? Are your guys up to providing support and policing a 'No Go' area along the border to—?"

"I agree wholeheartedly with everything DC Ross has said," Nick Farham responded before Sanders had finished his question. "My RAR guys are the very best. They've had plenty of combat experience. I'll organize our men to step up patrols as requested." Nick locked eyes with Jamie. "The Honde is the number one priority in the country right now. It's the main access route for all ZANLA forces entering this part of the country. If we begin to make inroads and recapture ground we can expect the terrorists to step up their efforts. The protected villages will become a prime target."

Jamie nodded, "I understand, but we will be prepared."

"As for the *cordon sanitaire*, we'll need to begin the process of moving people into the PVs before we finally declare any area 'No Go'. It will also mean the strategic planting of anti-personnel mines and claymores."

Jamie could see Nick's mind racing ahead, making plans.

John Whiting looked up at Jamie, his face creased with worry. "Jamie, the Honde is 'bad news'. I know because of the many contacts I've had there in the past six months. The terrain, the vegetation and now the people—everything is against you. This looks like an impossible task."

"Not impossible, but I agree it's a real challenge—a challenge we can win." Jamie's eyes flashed with excitement and his voice rang with determination.

"Okay, give us a timetable. What are we looking at?" asked Colonel Sanders.

Jamie was relieved that Colonel Sanders was willing to give the plan his go-ahead. He tapped his pen on the table and groped for an accurate prediction. "This is the beginning of February. Give me two weeks. I'll map the ground and lay out a base plan. I'd like the first construction unit to be on the ground by February twentieth. We need to have the first PV fully operational and ready for occupation by the end of March."

Jamie looked around the room as everyone nodded their heads, though he wasn't sure if it was in accord with the plan or at the enormity of the task.

"Optimistically, I think we can look at putting in one new PV a month. With two construction units, we could have all the PVs completed before the rains return in October. On second thoughts give me one construction unit to start with, but let's shoot for two construction units in April, when the rains are over."

"When can we have all the people in PVs?" asked Colonel Sanders.

"I estimate we should have them in by the end of October, depending on how soon we can have the construction units in place."

"I can have the first construction unit on the ground within two weeks," chimed in George Barstow.

Jamie was relieved to hear George's voice, so supportive and confident. "We're going to need security protection as we start to build. What can you offer?"

Jock Sanders frowned as he contemplated the situation. "The Guard Force is hard pressed at present, but I'll give you a company of Fourth Battalion farmers. Captain Mike Willis is due in with his company in two weeks. I'll have them on the ground when your construction unit arrives."

"Great."

Jamie turned to Nick Farham. "Where are you based, major, and when can we get together in the Honde?"

"I'm currently based closed to the Pungwe, but I want to be as mobile as possible. I won't be staying in any one location. No point in giving our terrorist friends a fixed target."

"Smart thinking. Lets plan to meet at Ruda on Saturday and we'll go over the plans together."

Jamie and George Barstow drove back to the PC's office, each deep in thought. Finally Jamie expressed what was most troubling on his mind.

"We're dangerously thin on the ground with weapons. We need machine guns, mortars or anything to level the playing field. The terrorists are much better armed than we are. As soon as we start work, Ruda and Mutasa will both become priority targets for our friends across the border."

Barstow looked uncomfortable. "Jamie, we're having a terrible time getting anything heavier than FNs or G-3s. Somehow the top brass seems to think we're at the bottom of the arms chain. Heavy weapons are in very short supply. I'll see what I can rake up, but no promises. We have no choice but to pull this off, so I'll be giving you all the support I can muster."

Chapter Five

Chief Mutasa stared morosely as his eyes searched the tree line that skirted the village. His ample frame overflowed the small, rickety chair placed in front of his hut. He wiped away another bead of sweat. The shade from the large mango tree was no match for the noonday heat. Amplifying the warmth, steam from the early morning rain rose from the hot earth. Sweat stung his eyes, but he did not blink. His round face, creased with age and worry, had garnered a few more lines this year. This recent unrest had accelerated the silver peppering in his short, crinkly hair and new grey streaked his scraggly beard.

She crept up, but he barely noticed her. The young woman meekly extended a plate of maize porridge and beans. With a sweep of his arm the plate went flying, the food spattering on the hard packed dirt. The woman backed away, whimpering. Chief Mutasa had no appetite. His eyes darted along the tree line. Would this be the day the *boys* would visit? It was his third day watching. The *boys* had paid visits to all the headmen. Surely his time was at hand. Desperate options flooded his mind. He let out a long, slow breath and, through clenched teeth, mumbled the name, "Chinyerere." Yes, the spirit of Chinyerere was here now, in the valley, in the form of his grandson. This would anger the *boys* and surely bring much trouble to his people. He thought of what had happened to headman Simangane and he shuddered. Simangane had given information to the soldiers, but Simangane was a fool. He, Chief Mutasa, was no fool.

* * *

The midday sun boiled the earth as humidity continued to rise. Jamie could feel the wet stickiness under his armpits. His damp shirt clung to him. One thing he enjoyed about the Leopard was the breeze blowing through the sides, but today sporadic showers just injected extra humidity and moisture to the airflow. Sergeant Sama sat on the bench seat to his left. They drove in unusual silence as they traveled to Ruda.

As Jamie parked the Leopard in front of the main building he could see Corporal Dande with two of the local men. The men looked flustered and both were shouting, their words tumbling over each other, not waiting for the other to finish before interrupting to press their point.

Corporal Dande looked up with relief as he saw Jamie and Sama drive up.

It was evident to Jamie that the corporal had a genuine concern for the people and was well respected.

"Mambo, these men are pleading for our help. The terrorists robbed their store last night and beat up the owner. He is very ill but refuses to go to the clinic. He says if he goes to the clinic the terrorists will come back and kill him."

Jamie nodded, saddened. It was always the innocent people trying to make an honest living that were caught in the middle. All the people in the valley desperately needed help. Living like this was hell for them.

"Mambo, the people are very afraid. These men risk their lives by coming to report the robbery. The *boys*, the magandanga, they are everywhere. They do as they please and show no mercy. When I first came to the Honde, it was much better. The people were glad to see us, but now they no longer bring us food. They tell us nothing because they are so afraid. These men are very brave."

"Sergeant Sama, take them to District Officer DeVries. Ask him to radio the police. They'll send out a patrol to help." Jamie sighed, there was very little that he could do at this stage to protect the people. "Corporal, come with me." Jamie's thoughts had turned to weaponry. "You're in charge of training the district assistants here at Ruda. Are you also training our cooks and helpers?"

A smile spread across the corporal's face. "Ah, yes, mambo. We have training every week. Even Willie, the cook, knows how to fire a G-3 as quick as he stirs the sadza porridge."

They walked toward the main bunker.

Corporal Dande had fallen uncharacteristically silent. Finally, he ventured. "Mambo, we have no machine gun or mortars. The magandanga have everything. They are cowards and will run when we fire at them with the FNs, but I do not know if it will always be that easy. They are getting bolder, mambo. I hear they have some big rockets that they carry on trucks. You are important. Can you get us a machine gun?"

"Well noted, corporal. I'm working on finding some heavy weapons. In the meantime, step up the training. Make sure everyone understands their duties. Do this at least twice a week. Once in the morning, and once in the evening when it gets dark."

Corporal Dande nodded solemnly. "This I will do, mambo. We will be prepared. These dogs of Mugabe's will run with their tails between their legs."

Jamie laughed. "Good, corporal." He gave him a friendly slap on the back. "Find Sergeant Sama. Tell him we're leaving in ten minutes. We'll be back before dark."

Jamie found his bedroom in the main building and tossed down his sleeping bag on the camp bed. The small room had no closet or chest of drawers, so he placed his clothes neatly on the floor. Ruda certainly didn't offer many of the comforts of home. Back in the main office he heard the rumble of an approaching vehicle. Glancing out of the window he saw another Leopard pull in next to his. Jack Cloete emerged carrying an FN in his right hand and a lunch box in his left.

"Man, but it's hot," Jack Cloete walked into the building bringing the aroma of sweat and dirt. "I heard you wanted to see me."

"Come inside, Jack. Let's grab a bite to eat. Then we'll take a ride down to Katiyo to check the lay of the land." Jamie opened a can of bully beef. "I need you to go over the aerial photos of Katiyo before we leave. I'm looking for some flat ground, preferably high, where we can site our first PV. There are just over two thousand people left in Headman Katiyo's area and we'll need an area somewhere around four hundred to six hundred yards on each side of a rectangle."

Jack shoved half a sandwich into his mouth and washed it down with a gulp of Coke. "I know just the place, man. Before you get to the tea estates there's a flat hill—cleared years ago for planting. The soil is pretty worn out and it's mostly used for grazing goats."

Jamie spooned another greasy lump of bully beef into his mouth. "Here, check these out," laying two aerial photos on the table. "Jack, take a look at this plateau. Is this the one you're talking about?"

"Ja, man, that's the place. Close to the road and about two miles from the tea estates. There must be a good three hundred acres. You have a clear view of the surrounding countryside."

"Sounds good, Jack. Let's go and take a look. You know the area, so Sama and I'll follow you."

The sun was at its brightest as they set out in the two Leopards, with Jack in the lead. Jamie felt the sweat build up on his neck and under his chin. The temperature outside was well into the nineties with the humidity about the same. They passed a business center of three stores with a bunch of chickens scratching in the dirt. There were several customers, but they did not wave or smile. Even the children ignored them. What a difference. Jamie was accustomed to having the people, especially the women and children, wave and shout when he drove past in tribal trust lands.

Turning, the vegetation on the Katiyo road changed from forest to buffalo grass and shrubs. There were planted fields of maize and sugar cane and patches of pineapples. They passed an occasional village and crossed a number of small streams. A local bus went past them, covered in mud, its roof rack burdened with chicken coops, bundles of clothing, suitcases and sheets of corrugated iron, all balanced precariously and tied down with twine, rope or string.

Half an hour later, Jack pulled off the road near a path leading through a patch of brush to their right. Parking behind Jack, Jamie climbed out, grasping the map case firmly in his left hand. He slung his Uzi over his right shoulder and checked the pouch on his belt that held the spare magazines. Sergeant Sama followed, clutching his Beretta shotgun to his chest. It was important to always be prepared.

Jack pointed to the top of a rise. "It's there but you can't see it from here. Follow me."

They set off along a well-used path, through buffalo grass, then past a dense thicket of guavas and shrubs. At last they reached the summit, a sparsely grassed plateau with small bushes. They could see for nearly half a mile along the ridge before it dropped into the forest line. This had once been fertile, arable land, but after excessive cultivation it had been reduced to grazing pasture for goats. The flat area was about five hundred to seven hundred yards wide. The factory buildings of Katiyo Tea Estates could be seen in the distance and beyond that, the Mozambique border. To the south, there were two villages, each with eight to ten huts. Green crops thrived in the fertile bottom lands, close to the streams that meandered gently towards the Pungwe River. To the west, there was thick forest and smoke rising from a patch of cleared land. Jamie could faintly make out people piling brush on a fire.

Taking the lead, Jamie walked along the ridge towards the border. The ground had obviously been cultivated at some time. A herd of goats grazed on small bushes while beyond, two donkeys and three rangy cows fed on patches of grass. Two small boys watched the animals. Jamie smiled and called out a greeting. The boys backed away slowly at first, then took off, racing down a path towards the nearest village.

Jamie frowned, turning to Jack and Sergeant Sama. "Why would they be so scared of us?"

"It is because they have seen what the terrorists do to people who support us," said Sama. "They are very frightened."

Reaching the far east of the ridge, they looked back. It resembled a shallow plateau—a perfect site. They could easily accommodate a PV of the size they needed. There would be clear fields of fire from each corner for the militia they would train.

"Perfect." Jamie turned to Jack, "How far does Headman Katiyo's territory extend?"

"From the Pungwe river in the north, to the border in the east, and then about five miles south of here. I don't know how far to the west, but it must be close to the main Aberfoyle road."

Jamie looked down at his watch. It was close to four. It's time to head back. Wiping his sweating brow with a damp, grubby handkerchief he turned and walked towards the path. Jack didn't follow. Jamie stopped and turned around to find that he was being stared at with amusement.

"What?" said Jamie, quizzically?

Jack chuckled, pointing to the red beret.

"I think I'll stay a few paces back. You make a mighty fine target. Why do you wear that hat out here?"

Jamie's crimson beret stood out like a beacon in the bright sunshine, boldly announcing their presence against a backdrop of green bushes and yellow grass.

"Well, Jack," said Jamie, "I think it makes a fine statement. It's important to show the locals that we aren't afraid. I'll be wearing it wherever I go." He smiled, adding his own friendly jab. "We've got a better spirit protecting us. Remember!"

"And I'll start soliciting his help," Jack added, laughing. "We'll need it."

"Right," said Jamie, straightening the beret for Jack's benefit. "Let's head out. Maybe we can make a quick trip to Katiyo."

Returning to the Leopards, Jamie took the lead and headed down the road to Katiyo Tea Estates, passing several villages and another business center which appeared deserted. The few locals they saw moved off the road to let them pass, turning away, not wanting to be noticed. Arriving at the main gate to Katiyo, they found the gate open with no one in sight. The gate chain was broken and the buildings deserted. Windows were broken and the grenade screens torn off several buildings. A broken chair lay outside—all signs of the constant attacks, and close proximity to the border, that had caused the evacuation some months ago.

"No sign of life here," said Jamie. "When did they all leave?"

"Must have been about two months ago," replied Jack. "The terrorists control all the ground from here to the Pungwe and beyond."

There was the sudden crackle of rifle fire and Jamie dove to the ground. The firing was coming from a grove of guava bushes to the south of the buildings. Jack and Sama had found shelter behind Jack's Leopard. Flicking the change lever of his Uzi to automatic Jamie raised the barrel and fired toward the guava grove some three hundred yards away. Jack and Sama followed suit. A brief exchange of fire lasted about two minutes and then nothing.

"That must have been a scouting party—too far out to do us any damage." Jamie looked around. "They're well on their way to the border so let's get out of here." With that, Jamie stood up and climbed into the Leopard.

* * *

Chinyerere. Chief Mutasa didn't know much about the new District Commissioner, but something didn't sit right. He promised a new peace, but at what price? He checked the tree line again. The sun was setting over Mtarazi Falls. It had been a long day of watching. He pulled at his faded khaki trousers which stuck to his skin. His sandals, made from old motor car tires, were covered in dust.

The moments ticked by. A chill erupted and traveled down the chief's spine. Four men in olive green uniforms moved down the path from the direction of the sugar cane fields. Each carried an AK-47, banana gun. The chief's heart quickened. He recognized the man in front, Morgan Tangwena. He was the son of Chief Tangwena of the Inyanga district. It was rumored he was now living in Mozambique.

The men approached and sat down in the shade of the shelter—in silence. The hush was more unbearable than the hours the chief had waited.

"Ha, Mambo Mutasa, do you not welcome us?" said Tangwena, at last.

The chief quickly called out. One of his younger wives appeared, holding out a clay pot of rich white beer made from fermented rapoka millet. The chief took it and turned to the men.

"I greet you, Morgan. Drink with me and then we'll talk."

Drinking from the pot, the chief passed the beer on to Morgan who took a deep guzzle and then passed it on to one of his comrades.

After they had all drunk, and the pot was nearly empty, Tangwena put it down in front of him, licked his lips and belched loudly.

"You heard about Headman Simangane?"

"I heard. He was a good man."

"He was a sellout and we needed to make an example of him. His people will now listen and the tea estates will stay closed."

The chief cast a questioning glance. "All I hear is that more people are being killed, our women raped and our children taken. You promised me that we would soon see our children return in triumph to claim the lands of the white farmers who live to our south. Now we have a new mudzwiti, the new district commissioner. His name is 'Chinyerere' and he is telling the people that peace will come to the Honde."

A muscle in Tangwena's jaw flinched. "It will not happen. The Honde is ours. The people must live in fear of helping the police. This mudzwiti, Chinyerere, and his men will be driven out."

"They say Chinyerere has come with the *spirit* of his ancestors to drive out the *boys*," said the chief.

Tangwena tightened his grip on the AK-47. A renewed hatred grew in him and he ached for Chinyerere's blood. "That will never happen. We have new weapons, more powerful than a herd of elephants." He leaned forward, his glower inches from the chief's face and his breath as vile as his sentiment. "Already our fearless leader, Josiah Makoni, has plans to destroy their camp at the place they call Ruda. This Chinyerere you speak of—he will soon die." Tangwena sat back, his eyes still locked on the chief, and added in a callous rasp, "Then we will see how strong his spirit is."

"What do our spirits say?" asked the chief.

"We have already consulted with Swikiro Nehandina. She tells us that the bullets of the white man will turn to water and that we will be victorious. Now, remember what happened to Simangane. Make sure that our men are received well and fed everywhere they go. Do you hear?"

"I hear you, Morgan."

It was getting dark and their time was up. Tangwena rose to his feet, followed by his three comrades, and headed toward the path. He paused. Turning slowly, he sauntered back toward the old chief, studying him. Leveling his AK he deliberately unfolded the bayonet and then thrust it into Chief Mutasa's arm, withdrawing it quickly as he watched the blood flow.

"Don't forget. We are many and we will be back. Remember whose side you are on."

The four guerillas faded into the darkness along the path from which they had come.

* * *

Jamie tried to gather his thoughts as he glanced out the window of the complex at Aberfoyle Tea Estates. Waiting for his brother, Alan, he tapped his pen on the old wooden desk. A cup of steaming tea sat untouched. *Damn. We have to pick up the pace. A burned school last night in Simangane's area, two male teachers abducted, and three women raped. No wonder the locals don't trust us. What have we got to show for our so-called protection?*

Looking out the window he scanned the thousand acres of lush tea plants with sugarcane growing in the dividing contours between the tea fields. It had rained during the night and steam was rising from the ground. The tea fields provided a beautiful emerald contrast to the darker green of the forest. Despite the fact that the tea plantation was shut down, the plants looked healthy and gave a false impression of industry in this war torn land.

He had enjoyed the drive to the tea estates that morning with Jack and Sama. It had been sixteen years since his last visit. The growth and spread of land planted under tea was impressive. In the distance he could see the tea factory, and a row of houses with grey asbestos roofs. To the right was the workers compound—neat rows of whitewashed buildings, eerily abandoned. They had once housed over two hundred permanent workers before the terrorists' heinous acts drove them away. Jarred from his thoughts, Jamie heard the door click shut.

A man wearing a safari suit walked up to Jamie, a big smile on his face.

"Well, Jamie. I can't tell you how glad I am to see you. When you called I couldn't believe it. Don't tell me the government is finally waking up to our plight and sending in the relief forces!"

Alan was older than Jamie and the past year had made the

difference even more noticeable. His hair was completely grey and his face creased with worry lines. He took a seat across from Jamie and leaned back in his chair. The two men were complete opposites. Jamie the type "A" extrovert and Alan always the thinker, but a very astute businessman.

"Well, Jamie, what can you tell me? By the way, I like the uniform. It becomes you."

Jamie laughed. "It's good to see you. I've only been in the district a few days, but I wanted to catch up with you and hear what's really going on."

"About time we had someone interested. The terrorists closed us down a couple of months ago. Killed twenty seven and threatened all the remaining workers."

"How do things stand now?" asked Jamie.

"Besides Audrey and me, we have only one other family in a holding pattern—keeping an eye on the place, so to speak. Koos Fischer is in charge of security and we have a stick of police reservists based here to give us support in case the terrorists attack."

"Have you been able to hold them off?"

"Yes, but the problem is we're outgunned. We've already had to fight off three attacks. Fortunately, no casualties on our end, but we've taken a bit of a hammering with mortars and RPG anti-tank grenades. Thank goodness our bunkers are well-fortified, and the grenade screens have deflected more than one RPG. They took out old Headman Simangane earlier in the week and now all our house servants have fled back to their villages."

Jamie nodded.

"What's your take on the situation?" asked Alan.

"First, I want you to know that the prime minister is giving the Honde top priority. We fully understand your situation and that the tea estates are shut down. The Honde is now recognized as the main infiltration point for all terrorists bound for Northern Manicaland and Mashonaland."

Alan shook his head in disbelief. "If the government knew what's been going on, then why hasn't something been done before to stop the flow of terrorists?"

"Strictly a matter of manpower and priorities," Jamie responded.

"The powers-that-be are beginning to see the light. The numbers killed each week finally got some attention."

"What's your role?" asked Alan.

"I'm coordinating a massive plan to resettle all the people into protected villages. We'll follow the basic principles that the British used so successfully in Malaya. In simple terms—isolate the terrorists from the people. We intend to deny the terrorists intelligence, food, comfort, shelter and porters to carry their munitions. A company of RAR has been moved here and we've been promised every form of support necessary to achieve our objectives."

"But how will you stop the terrorists from crossing the border?"

"With a *cordon sanitaire*. We'll create a 'No Go' area along the border, police it, put in minefields in strategic locations, and move the people into protected villages over the next six to nine months. We'll relocate the people according to their tribal affiliations. My job is to coordinate the construction of protected villages and move the people."

Jamie put down his cup and met Alan's eyes. "This war is about winning the hearts and minds of the people. From the reception I've received so far, we've a long way to go."

Alan whistled softly. "Let me get this straight. You're accomplishing this with one company of troops? There must be several hundred terrorists across the border. Then there are the others who come through on their way to Inyanga, Salisbury, or even Mt. Darwin or Bindura."

"It's going to take a massive effort," Jamie conceded. "I don't underestimate the difficulties. The one thing we have going for us is that we have a plan. Like the terrorists, we believe in a free country, but with opportunities for all of us. Unfortunately, the U.S. president doesn't see things our way." Jamie's tone rose with his exasperation. "Our latest intelligence states the U.S. is funneling cash and resources to Mugabe and his thugs. Not guns, because this would create a political uproar in America if it got out, but cash to buy guns from the Chinese. We got taken in by Kissinger when he came over to get Smith to sign the Kissinger Accord last year."

Alan leaned forward listening with interest.

"All it takes is a change in president and the American government forgets about honor and agreements. They're throwing us to the wolves. They believe they can impose their form of democracy on the country. What they don't see is that it'll take patriotic white and black Rhodesians, working together, to make this country a better place for all."

Alan sighed, his face puckered with worry. "I agree with you entirely when it comes to American policy. It's hard to believe that the major powers are so naïve."

"Yes," said Jamie. "When Ian Smith shared with us that he had been forced to sign the Kissinger Accord we thought it was a done deal. Signing Rhodesia's 'death certificate' was how Smith referred to it. Kissinger assured him he had the backing of all nations in Southern Africa and that the United States would guarantee the constitutional rights of all persons, regardless of race."

"So much for American politics," said Alan. "They change presidents and throw everything out the back door. There's no doubt Kissinger and South Africa really put the pressure on Smith."

Jamie took a breath. Despite the heat rising up the back of his neck, it felt good to talk with someone else who understood what was fueling this war, and to let his frustrations out.

"None of us liked that pressure. Smith had no alternative but to agree to a transition to full majority rule. The kicker was the guaranteed protection of our constitutional rights. No seizure of property or land and fair compensation paid to those who chose to sell and leave."

"And what about the British?"

"After the farce of the Pearce Commission we can expect no support from Britain. It seems they've washed their hands and left us to our own devices. The blockade of the Port of Beira remains and we're totally dependent upon South Africa for all oil and arms shipments."

"So, how will you proceed?"

"I'm meeting with Major Farham of the RAR tomorrow and we'll begin coordinating our strategy. Let me assure you, I'll pull out all stops to make this work and restore peace to the Honde Valley. Hang in there and give me a chance to prove it."

"You've got whatever support I can give, Jamie."

"Here's what I'd like you to do. Pass on to me any intelligence that you think might be helpful. Use your police reserve network. We'll begin construction of the first PV within weeks and we hope to move the first group in by the end of March, depending upon the rains." Jamie paused. "As it is now, we'll probably start with Katiyo because it sits right on the infiltration route. Simangane's group would be next, followed by another PV closer to the Pungwe River, and nearer to your estates. From there we'll work our way south down the valley."

Alan took a sip of his tea and looked up. "Why can't the PM work out some compromise agreement with Mugabe? Smith seems hell-bent on driving a wedge further between Rhodesia and the rest of the world."

"I wish it were as simple as that," said Jamie. "Don't forget Joshua Nkomo and the Matabele. They have the full support of Russia and Libya, and are just as determined as Mugabe that they want to be in control." Jamie shook his head in frustration. "With Mugabe getting all the support he needs from China and North Korea—and now the US, black rule is inevitable. It's just a matter of who's going to be in control and who's going to keep the country from going communist. At least Nkomo is a pragmatist, but Mugabe is an avowed Marxist."

"We're all on the same page," and Alan sighed. "Jamie, right now I need you more than you realize. I have everything invested in this company and if we can't reopen within six months, it's lost. Aberfoyle will revert back to forest and squatter lands."

"I'm with you—just give me a chance. Alan, we're going to make a difference and I want Aberfoyle to be a part of our success."

Alan tapped his pen on the table and looked up at Jamie. "I'm impressed. You've always been the patriot in the family—just like grand-father Ross."

Standing, Jamie held out his hand. "Take care, Alan. Remember, we're in this together and we're in it to win."

"Where are you headed from here?" asked Alan.

"I need to check out old Headman Simangane's area," said Jamie, standing to leave. "We need a site for a PV that's defensible and with terrain that's not too rugged. I'll drop by whenever I'm in the area and you can always contact me at Ruda or Mutasa. You have both phone numbers. Don't say anything that could compromise us. The phones are all party-line and probably monitored by the terrorists."

Alan shook Jamie's hand, the grip firm as he looked Jamie in the eye. "You know you count on me. Watch your back."

Jamie headed down the long hallway to the reception area. As he rounded the corner, he saw Sergeant Sama. "Sama, please go and find Mr. Cloete and tell him ..."

Jack emerged from the workshop before Jamie could finish his sentence, his ruddy face framing a large smile.

"I got some good information from my friend, Koos. He knows this area like the back of his hand. Says there's a flat area just below a steep ridge that we can look at and it's not far from Simangane's kraal."

Jamie grinned. "Let's go! One down, and another to follow."

* * *

A welcome breeze felt cool on Jamie's sweaty face. He shaded his eyes and carefully surveyed the ridge. It was fairly flat, about a thousand yards long by four hundred to five hundred yards wide. "It's not ideal, but I don't think there's a better site for Simangane's people." Smiling. "We can get the RAR to set some claymore mines along the top of the ridge so terrorists can't fire down on the PV. One claymore can cover over thirty yards with a single blast. That should provide adequate protection."

Jack leaned against a tree, making his own assessment. "You can build defensive bunkers on all four corners, but it will be a fairly long and narrow PV. You may need extra guards. There's nothing better so maybe it'll work."

"We do have the stream going for us," said Jamie. It'll provide plenty of water. The people won't have far to travel to their lands during the daytime, or to Aberfoyle where they can work. It's also far enough from the border that we won't have to worry too much about the *cordon sanitaire*."

* * *

Guava trees, and more guava trees. Jamie reminisced as he stepped on the accelerator. The Leopard picked up speed, hitting corrugations in the gravel road as he traveled to Chief Mutasa's kraal. He thought back to when he was a young boy biting into juicy guavas. Only when his mother grabbed a half-eaten one from him could he see the worms, or what was left of them. Here the guavas grew wild, interspersed with fields of maize, sugar cane and pineapples. Along every stream, large, dark, green leaves of elephant ear like plants produced impressive edible bulbs reminiscent of sweet potatoes.

To the west was Mtarazi Falls, the highest falls in Rhodesia. A silver strip of water and spray descending from the slopes of Mt. Inyangani fell for nearly three thousand feet. Soft, wispy clouds hovered over the top of the mountain. Jamie caught his breath. What a magnificent sight. He remembered clambering over the smooth stones and boulders as a boy, and wading through the cold, crystal-clear waters at the top before the waters plummeted, as though to the bottom of the earth.

They passed more villages. School children, kicking a soccer ball and cheering each other on, played on a bare ground that made up a sports field. For the first time Jamie noticed the children wave. This was a pleasant change. The terrorists had obviously not been as active this far south. What a contrast to the turbulence in the northern part of the valley.

"Turn right here," said Sergeant Sama. They followed a bumpy road that wound its way through scrubby forest and some msasa trees until it opened up at a grove of mango trees. Beyond were the neatly kept huts of the village.

A crowd gathered. Several small children swarmed about them, jumping onto the Leopard to examine the strange looking vehicle. Jamie smiled as a wizened old crone made her way forward. Her faded flowered top and well-worn navy skirt had endured many years. A headscarf framed snow white wisps of curly hair protruding from the front. She was missing her front teeth. All Jamie could see were her pink gums as she unabashedly smiled at him, asking in Shona if he had any cigarettes. Shaking his head, Jamie went up to her and grasped her right hand with both of his hands to show her respect. She smiled again. The wrinkles of her face resembled corrugated cardboard, surrounding her flattened nostrils.

"Where is the chief?" asked Jamie, glancing beyond her toward the huts. The old woman pointed in the direction of a large hut with new thatch and freshly daubed red mud walls.

Chief Mutasa stood in the doorway eying him warily. A faded blue shirt pulled tightly across his ample belly. Below the sleeve on his left arm was a stained bandage.

"Makadiwo, Mambo Mutasa," said Jamie. "I am the new district commissioner and I'm very glad to see you. Did you sleep well?"

"I slept well if you slept well, mambo," the chief replied, following the custom. His flat speech gave away his distrust as he examined Jamie suspiciously.

"I know that you are facing many troubles in your area. The terrorists have killed many of your people. I am here today to tell you that we are going to help you and that things will change. First, I will need your help."

Chief Mutasa said nothing but just grunted.

"All your headmen and kraal heads need to listen to me and follow all that I ask them to do. Many of your people are being killed every week and this will stop. We will build special villages where your people will be trained to protect themselves and we will be there to help them in every way."

Still Chief Mutasa said nothing and his eyes conveyed no welcome.

Two women appeared wearing headscarves and carrying young babies strapped to their backs with large flowered shawls. The younger made a couple of trips to bring out chairs. Jamie, Chief Mutasa, and Sergeant Sama took them and sat down.

Looking at the two women, Jamie could see the older was probably the chief's senior wife, and the younger woman, either a daughter or younger wife. Thanking them as they excused themselves without a word, Jamie turned his attention to chief Mutasa.

The Chief eyed him guardedly, occasionally distracted as he looked toward the trees as if someone might be watching. "You are right. We have many troubles," he began, his voice low. "Too many of our people have suffered terrible deaths. Headman Simangane was killed on Sunday night. His people are very frightened. Our children are no longer safe in school and the people are afraid to go out to work their fields. Our young people have been carried away. Some of them come back to kill their own fathers and mothers. These are very bad times, Chinyerere."

Jamie looked up as a band of curious children crowded around one of the nearby huts. Turning their inquisitiveness from the Leopard they focused on the men, but kept their distance out of respect and tradition.

For the next half hour, Jamie shared with the Chief, offering hope and explaining the importance of giving full support to the army, the police and Internal Affairs. He sensed that the chief was not listening. His body language indicated he had already made up his mind and Jamie became increasingly convinced the chief had been won over by the terrorists. He paused, silently wondering how long it would take to reach the peoples' hearts. Before he could speak again, sharp flashes of lightning erupted in the distance and delayed booms of thunder echoed across the valley. The upper reaches of the Mtarazi Falls were covered in a dark shroud as the rain began to fall.

It was breathtaking. The sun, still shining on the chief's kraal, created a stunning contrast to the dark blanket covering the north-west. He couldn't help but notice the difference between their location in the southernmost part of the valley and the dark and ominous situation that existed in the north around Aberfoyle and Katiyo.

* * *

Chief Mutasa watched warily as the Leopard pulled away. The hope Jamie spoke of was good, but he also knew it could never happen. The spirits had spoken. He walked back to his hut. As he stepped out of the sunshine into the dimness, any flicker of hope faded and his heart hardened. Tangwena's words called out from his memory. *We will destroy their camp at the place they call Ruda. This Chinyerere you speak of, he will soon die. Then we will see how strong his spirit is.*

He clutched his bandaged wound with his right hand—yes, this would be the last time he would see Chinyerere.

Chapter Six

"Watch yourself here at Ruda."

Nick Farham glanced away from the large scale map of the Honde and met Jamie's eye long enough to deliver the warning. Jamie paused from briefing Nick and Chris DeVries on the strategy for the PV program.

"You make a good target, Jamie. There are tracks crossing the border from Mozambique less than a mile from here."

Jamie reached over and gave him a playful punch on the arm. "You need to check out my Garden Boy cannons sometime. We're going back to the dark ages, but I'm told they do work. They arrived yesterday, with a Browning .303 machine gun."

Nick didn't crack a smile. He understood the gravity of the task and found it disturbing that Jamie seemed to thrive on it. The man was serious and capable, but his sanguinity ruffled Nick. Someone had to think of safety, especially if this guy was going to be walking around in the open wearing a bright red beret.

Nick looked at the map and shook his head glumly. "With these UN sanctions against us, you'd think we were the enemy. We can't get decent weapons. Mugabe gets virtually anything he wants. It makes no sense."

"You're right," said Jamie, choosing two small red flags with pins from Chris's hand. He ran his finger over several areas on the map as he studied it. "What's amazing is how successful we've been fighting this war with our limited weapons. I'm sure Mugabe is getting all the weapons he needs from China—purchased with American money."

A muscle flinched in Nick's jaw. He faced Jamie. "I heard Rex Nhongo has a couple of those mobile multiple rocket launchers they call Stalin Organs. He got them from the North Koreans. They fire about twenty rockets at one shot. Ruda would be a natural target. I have no doubt that if it wasn't for the Israelis and our South African friends, we'd have no weapons." Nick looked intently at Jamie, hoping to convey the seriousness of the dangers. "Once we start moving people into the PVs you can bet there'll be a reaction from the other side. They don't want to lose ground. The Honde is vital to their infiltration. We cut them off from the Honde and ..."

"... and they have to go north to Tete and infiltrate from the Zambezi," Jamie finished. "That's a major logistical problem for them."

He positioned the two red flags on the map, marking the sites of the first two PVs. "Chris, help me mark out the rough boundaries of each headman's area. The PVs need to be as centrally located as possible."

"Got it, sir." Chris picked up a wax marker and positioned it where Jamie indicated on the map.

"The first step is helping meet the people's needs," and Jamie waved a finger. "This is about winning their hearts and minds. They have to know we care. Access roads, water, schools, and clinics, Not forgetting the ability to get to their fields. They are all critical. We will have to allocate new fields to those who live far from the PVs."

Nick and Chris watched as Jamie pointed to the white flags.

"These are all potential PV sites. By my take, we're going to need seven PVs total, maybe eight. It'll depend on this site to the east of chief Mutasa's village. If we have enough ground, we can accommodate all four thousand of his people.

Jamie pointed to the last flag. "If the site's too small, we'll need to build the eighth PV over here."

Nick dragged a palm over his jaw. "What's the current time frame?"

"We'll start construction in ten days," Jamie moved nearer the window. "We'll be ready to move people in by the end of March, at the latest. My aim is to get all of them relocated into PVs by the end of September, certainly before the next rainy season."

Nick frowned. "How was your meeting with Chief Mutasa?"

"I met with him this morning. Sly old sod. I don't trust him. He's playing both sides. Once he sees we mean business he'll cooperate."

Nick met Jamie's eye. "I suggest you and I keep a tight lid on all our movements. We can't afford any leakage of information. You never know who to trust. The terrorists are monitoring all our radio networks."

"Agreed, I plan one day at a time and try to keep the overall plans in my head. This way there's less chance of being ambushed or taken out."

Nick nodded, approvingly. Maybe the chap would survive after all.

Chris's shoulders lifted in a questioning shrug. "What's wrong with a little action? Sitting around here at Ruda the past six months has been a hellish waste of time. While we were putting in fortifications, at least there was something to do. We've only had one attack—a couple of mortars fired from a distance. Even that was two months ago. Feeble, if you ask me."

Nick arched a brow as he eased up from his chair. He put the pen and pad back in his pocket. The lean, uncompromising lines of his face signified he wasn't amused.

Jamie fought another smile tugging at his lips. "Well, Chris," Jamie winked, "From now on I'll see to it you have long days and sleepless nights. There's more to be done than either of us could dream of."

"Since we're enjoying putting in our two-cents worth," said Nick, fixing his eyes on Chris, "I'm banking you'll have more work, and action, than you bargained for."

Jamie was barely listening. He looked out the open window, past the trees and beyond the earth embankments. The sweet smells and gentle breeze reminded him of a world left behind. He remembered walking with Emily on days like this, fingers interlaced, and the playful laughter of the kids. Then, a shadow of weariness clouded his face. He loved this country. But how much would he be willing to put on the line? He turned back and looked unwaveringly at the two men. "Once we start building the PVs we'll be pulling out all stops." His jaw set. "You can bet there'll be action."

* * *

Emily slipped quietly into a seat on the back row. She tried to push her fears aside. This new urgency for Jamie's safety had reached an unbearable pitch. She needed to get out, do something. She brushed aside her feelings of self-consciousness, but still inwardly hoped no one noticed her. She looked around. When was the last time she sat in a real church with pews and a pulpit? The air smelt of lemon furniture polish. It was cool and still and the people scattered around were quiet, no talking or whispering. No one greeted her. The woman in front of her preened a new hairdo, while many of the other ladies wore hats. She could not remember the last time she wore a hat to church.

This was so different from the church in Melsetter. As she sat in the quiet, homesickness came over her and memories of the services in Melsetter drifted through her mind. It was a social event. There was no stuffiness. How she loved those gatherings. After church, farmers and missionaries from all over the area would join them at their home, and eat lunch together on the front lawn. Denomination didn't mean a thing. They were there for fellowship. Someone always had a guitar, and after the meal they settled into lawn chairs and sang, laughing and catching up on the week's news. Despite the heartache and terror around them, there was peace and confidence in the hearts of the people as they got together and, momentarily, put aside their fears. What had happened? That peace was gone, even here in the safety of the city. Emily felt her eyes welling up. Tears began to flow down her cheeks. *God, where are you? Why have you deserted me? Do you not see the heartache I am going through, the fear that grips me every day? Do you not care any more?*

Emily was so caught up that she didn't notice the congregation had stood to sing. It wasn't until the words gently penetrated her consciousness, "Great is thy faithfulness, Lord God to me," that the tears flowed freely. The words *trust me* kept ringing in her mind. *Trust me, I am faithful.* Soft sobs escaped under her breath. How could she have slipped so far from God these past few months? How could she harbor such anger in her heart against him? Feelings of remorse and shame washed over her. An arm slipped around her shoulder and a soft white handkerchief was placed in her hand. She looked up to see a lady she judged to be a little older than herself. Short dark hair framed large brown eyes that looked sympathetically at her. Emily sniffed and wiped her face with the handkerchief.

"Thank you," she whispered under her breath. The lady smiled, giving Emily's shoulder a little squeeze, and then settled back to listen to the rest of the service.

A stream of people lined up to shake the preacher's hand as they filed out of the building, but the lady fell into step beside Emily. Once outside, she took Emily's hand in a small gesture of comfort, and pulled her aside.

"My name is Demi Rogers." She hesitated. "I can see you're troubled about something. Would you like to talk about it?"

Emily smiled gratefully. "I'm all right now, thank you."

"Are you sure?" Demi prodded gently.

Emily evaded the question, desperately searching to redirect the conversation.

Demi studied her patiently, eyes full of warmth.

Emily felt the last of her barriers melt. An opportunity to share her heart suddenly felt like coming up for air after being under water too long. The words spilled out of her. "Have you ever felt God has deserted you? I know it's terrible, but I've felt that for some time. Then, this morning, as I sat there, I began to realize something. It isn't that God has deserted me, but I've deserted God."

Demi laughed softly and gave her a hug. "Oh, I know exactly how you feel. My seventeen-year-old son was called up to do his time in the army. At first I felt just like you, but then I realized I had no one to turn to *but* God, so why would I desert him when I needed him most?"

Emily drew in a breath and slowly released it, feeling herself unwind. As they talked, Emily felt a bond grow.

They slowly walked to their cars and as Demi turned to say goodbye, she caught Emily's hand. "Why don't you come and have tea with me tomorrow afternoon when you get home from work?"

Emily gratefully nodded and they made arrangements. She no longer felt alone or deserted. Lightness came into her heart and she felt uplifted.

* * *

The young commissar didn't know much about the book he carried, but he didn't care. It spurred him on. He stopped briefly, taking a couple of steps back into the woods to read the passages again. It kept him strong—focused. Voices called from his memory, faces of those he had tortured haunted him and the words from this book helped erase them.

When the Lord your God brings you into the land you are entering to possess and drives out before you many nations … and when the Lord your God has delivered them over to you and you have defeated them, then you must destroy them totally … show them no mercy. Deuteronomy 7:1-2. They devoted the city to the Lord and destroyed with the sword every living thing in it—men and women, young and old, cattle, sheep and donkeys. Joshua 6:21.

He swatted a mosquito and wiped the sweat from the back of his neck. As the seventeen young locals, under the watchful eyes of the comrades, marched past him down the main drag to Aberfoyle, he placed the worn Bible back under his arm and fell into line.

What was that? A twig snapped. He stopped cold. Before he could turn, he felt the thud. Pain ripped through his chest as the impact propelled him backwards. Seconds fell into a surreal slowness, unfolding like a dream. Comrades and locals dispersed in all directions like mixed shapes fanning out in a myriad of colors. His vision blurred. Loose pages from the Old Testament, passages underlined, fluttered softly to the ground. Hope, also, slipped away as silently and unnoticed as his spirit. Everything went black.

* * *

Jamie dressed and got himself ready to leave. It was Monday morning. Warm rays flowed through the window and he took a moment to watch the sun break over the horizon. He thought of Emily. His fifteen minutes on the phone with her Sunday afternoon, telling her that plans were going smoothly in the Honde, had done little to calm her fears. This war was harder on her than it was on him. Her faith always seemed solid, but he could tell the growing danger surrounding him was taking a toll on her trust in God.

He caught the smell of food and suddenly he was ravenously hungry. Sixpence brought him breakfast, placing it on the table next to his chair. Jamie quickly consumed the fried eggs and bacon, topped off with two slices of bread fried in bacon grease. He looked at his watch. February sixteenth. Nice. This feature would prevent him from losing all track of days. He grabbed his kit bag full of clothes and toiletries, downed a large cup of hot tea that scalded the roof of his mouth and headed out.

Sixpence followed and helped him load the Leopard. While Jamie hoisted his bag in the back, Sixpence sat a cooler filled with food next to it and put a lunch box with tomato and cheese sandwiches up front. Jamie grabbed his Uzi and the Star pistol, fastened the ammunition pouch around his waist and climbed into the Leopard. Smoothing his beret in place he checked the radio and fuel gauge. All were in good order.

Jamie looked up at the ring of pipes newly welded onto the top of the Leopard. Quite primitive, but it did offer a sense of comfort in the event of an ambush. The twelve one-inch galvanized pipes were welded together in a circle. A lanyard was attached to release twelve strikers that would hit twelve percussion caps simultaneously—creating a blast that would shower metal ball bearings in all directions. He smiled. Well 'Betsy' you are going to be my guardian angel once we can find some black powder. Without it they were just a heap of junk pipes. He thought about the Garden Boys. Here again, these were primitive cannon made up of welded pipes mounted on a movable base. They had arrived, but with only enough powder for two charges each. Rather typical of their weapon supply system. He shook his head. This was like having an Uzi without any ammunition.

An idea struck him. Yes, he would make it himself. It had been nearly twenty years since he had taught himself how to make black powder. What fun that had been. He remembered finding some old Tower muskets while cleaning up the storeroom of the INTAF offices in Rusape and deciding to try his hand at making the powder. It was a success. He and his fellow cadets enjoyed shooting up old light bulbs down at the Rusape dam. Belching white smoke, a fifty caliber lead ball would hurl out the barrel. It worked, never mind the one-second delay from the less-than-perfect powder.

Yes, he would make his own. He could get the necessary chemicals on his next trip to Umtali.

Jamie pulled up outside the offices, stretched and drew in a breath of fresh morning air. The flags were raised and fluttering in the breeze. Sergeant Sama loaded his things into the Leopard while a group of uniformed engineers returned from checking the gravel access road for mines. A small section of engineers were posted at Mutasa for just that purpose. Surfacing the road was not an option with so many other priorities.

The corporal in charge of the engineers approached and saluted Jamie. "The road is clear, sir."

* * *

Jamie parked his Leopard alongside Jack's, then he set off with Chris and Sama up a rough track to the Katiyo PV site. He looked over the area approvingly. Jack and two assistants were busy unloading more pegs and two four-pound hammers. It had begun.

Jack looked up from his task. "Hey, what took you so long? I've been out here over an hour."

"Glad to see you so eager to get to work," Jamie laughed.

"Right. Where do you want to begin?" Jack didn't want to waste any time.

"First thing I want to do is set up a marker peg in the north-west corner and then back down towards the east. Do you have a hundred yard tape with you?"

"Ja, just show me where you want to start and we'll take it from there."

Jamie set off at a brisk pace with Jack struggling to keep up. Soon they had the four corner pegs in place—a rectangle approximately four hundred by five hundred yards. They painted the markers white. A couple of Jack's workers laid string between the pegs, marking the size and position of the proposed protected village.

On they went, marking off places for the main gate, the Internal Affairs staff barracks, the community school, the clinic and a playground for the children, painting these markers with red paint.

Jamie was pleased. He stood back and looked it over as his mind raced. After the water lines were laid, communal latrines would have to be dug. They would suffice until families could build their own. They would need to be resourceful. The clay excavated could be used to plaster between the poles of the new huts to be built. One thing for sure, there was an ample supply of trees suitable for building huts. The surrounding grass was also mature and ready to be cut to serve as thatch.

Continuing on, they marked out areas in blocks where huts would be built, leaving enough space between communities to give privacy. Jamie estimated the PV could accommodate up to twenty five hundred people without crowding.

Finally, they moved down the slope, marking out an area for the construction crews and the platoon of troops from the Fourth Battalion that would want to build camp close to the PV.

Nearby, Jamie heard the trickle of clear water bubbling up from a spring. That would come to good use. "We can easily pipe that water from the stream. That should give us a hundred foot head to provide more than enough water pressure."

It was past mid-day when the work was finally done. It had been hot, tiring work. Chris sighed, and sank down under a large mahogany tree. He let his head drop back against the trunk, enjoying several long draws of cool water from his canteen. He coughed as it went down too fast. Jamie watched in amusement.

"Had enough action yet?"

Chris managed a smile. "Not the real kind, sir. No terrorists. Dead quiet. I thought we'd at least see some curious locals ..." he lifted the canteen and sipped again, "... coming around to find out what we're doing."

Jamie grinned. "I'm sure when there are any encounters, you'll be in the thick of it." He turned and faced the other men. "Tomorrow's the big day. The first construction crews are scheduled to arrive by noon. They must be set up before dark. The Fourth Battalion troops arrive later in the afternoon." Jamie reached for the sandwiches. "Let's call it a day."

* * *

Tuesday morning, bright and early, Jamie wiped the crumbs from his mouth and took a cautious sip of Willie's steaming tea. The breakfast Willie had presented him with had left a lot to be desired, but at least the tea was strong and hot. Nick Farham had arrived at Ruda early so the two had been able to discuss preparations for the PV over breakfast.

Jamie sat the cup down with a clank and leaned forward on the metal table, "You mentioned some excitement yesterday. What happened?"

Nick swallowed the last bite of dry toast and relaxed back in his chair. "We had a tough contact yesterday at midday. We laid an ambush on the main drag to Aberfoyle. Twenty or more terrorists walked into the trap. They were heavily armed, but low on ammunition. There were seventeen locals with them—ten boys and seven girls, all teenagers or younger."

Jamie raked his fingers through his hair. "We've got to pick up the pace."

Nick repositioned himself in the chair. "As soon as we opened up, the locals fled into the bush and we had a running firefight for about twenty minutes. We killed six and I'm sure we wounded another three or four. One of my guys took a bullet in the stomach. I had a helicopter pick him up and casevacc him back to Umtali."

Jamie blinked. "Did you get the leader?"

"One of the dead terrorists was obviously their political commissar. He was carrying a bunch of papers with him, and it appears they were returning from Mrewa. He was also carrying a worn Bible with passages in the Old Testament marked up justifying the killing of everyone—men, women and children. The passages were heavily underlined."

Jamie's stomach wrenched. Not this topic. He had wrestled with its complexities on numerous occasions. Still, as Nick looked at him quizzically, he felt the obligation to share.

"It's part of their strategy. A large majority of the locals, both here and in Mrewa, have had some grounding in the Christian faith, but they've incorporated Christianity into their local animist belief system. They worship Christ with little knowledge and continue to revere their ancestral spirits. The spirit mediums and witchdoctors are still very much in control."

"So they use the Bible to justify these acts?" Nick asked, incredulous.

"The Bible can be used in many ways, Nick. The ZANLA political commissars are being trained to use passages, out of context, to justify their dastardly deeds. Nowhere do I see the Bible justifying the maiming and torture that the terrorists use for their benefit."

Nick just shook his head.

Jamie stood up and walked around the room. "The Bible is just one of many meaningless tools in the hands of terrorists. In the beginning they sweet talked the locals with promises of land, cars, new homes, the best farms and all they could dream of. Now that those promises have worn thin they're taking it to the next level. They'll use whatever persuasion works—no limits."

He walked back to the desk and slapped his palms down in frustration. "We have to change this. It won't be an easy assignment. Their objective now is horrific acts of terrorism. So traumatize the locals that they will do anything they're told. It's unmitigated fear."

"How quickly can we move?" Nick asked. "We've discussed this before. How long do you think it'll take before we can move the people into Katiyo? I can have Jock Sanders make the necessary arrangements ahead of time."

Jamie absently tapped his pen on the desk as he calculated. Clearing the access road and the fence line would take a week, he predicted. The chain link fence and razor wire would go in quickly and the bunkers within two days. Laying the water lines and piping water throughout the PV would take a week. He would need to consider the construction of internal roads and the communal latrines. Construction of the A-frame barracks, command post, school, clinic and the community center would take two weeks or more. He would be using modular materials which would speed up the process. The corrugated asbestos cement roofing would be strong and fireproof. He looked back at Nick.

"With the work beginning February twentieth, we should have the PV ready for occupation by March fifteenth to twentieth. I think we can safely project a move-in-day for March twenty first. This gives me a few days latitude in case of rain or equipment delays."

Nick didn't hide his concern. "How many villages are we talking about, Jamie? We'll need to move troops in to every village at first light."Jamie walked to the wall map. "There are fifty-eight villages in all. A stick of three or four troopies could handle up to two villages that are close together. For safety's sake, I believe you'll need two companies for this first exercise."

"I can handle it," said Nick.

* * *

The rumble of an armored police Cougar, followed by twelve trucks, broke the noon-day quiet as they pulled up on the road outside Ruda Keep. Two transporters followed carrying a D-6 Caterpillar dozer and a front end loader/back hoe combination. One truck carried fuel and nine others were loaded to capacity with fencing materials, treated gum poles, corrugated asbestos roofing, and bags of cement. The Cougar turned into the keep as the rest of the convoy stopped outside.

A young man in a police reservist uniform stepped out of the vehicle. "Johnny Mably, sir," he said, extending his hand to Jamie. "Our instructions are to escort the convoy to the construction site and then return to Umtali."

Jack Cloete and Chris walked over to the convoy, obviously delighted to see the large bulldozer and the trucks laden with supplies.

"Good to meet you Johnny. If you follow us we'll lead the way to the construction site in our Leopards. It's about a forty-five minute drive."

"I'm with you so far."

"When we get there the dozer needs to be off-loaded first so he can cut a temporary access road to the site, then the trucks can follow. There aren't any rocks or large trees to clear, so it shouldn't take more than two hours."

Johnny nodded. "I appreciate the escort. I'll have the convoy briefed and we'll be on our way in less than five minutes."

"Sergeant Sama," yelled Jamie. Sama came running from the kitchen, Beretta in hand. "Chris, you go with Jack and Sama will come with me. I'll take the lead." They climbed in the Leopards and headed for Katiyo.

As he looked in the rear view mirror, Jamie could see Jack's Leopard and the Cougar, but the rest of the convoy was obscured by a light rain. He didn't anticipate trouble but he kept his speed down to thirty miles per hour to maintain formation in the convoy. Johnny, driving the Cougar, was in radio contact with the last vehicle which had two police reservists riding shotgun.

Jamie pulled the Leopard to the side of the road, well beyond the path to Katiyo PV.

The next fifteen minutes was spent offloading the Cat D-6 from its transporter. Soon, the huge engine roared to life. The dozer swung around and rumbled up the gravel road to the path. Jack Cloete, now in charge, waved the dozer driver to follow him. The huge machine pushed its way through the shrubbery and small trees, following Jack up the ridge. It made swift progress, back and forth, pushing earth and trees aside as it created a temporary road.

Within an hour, it had reached the PV site. Then it cut a path parallel to the northern edge of the markers, over to the construction camp site. With blade down, the dozer reversed back along the road, leveling the path for the heavy trucks. The ground was soft, but not muddy, and the trucks would quickly compact the new road as they traveled up to the site.

By 1430 hours, the temporary road was complete. Jack signaled for the first of the trucks to begin the climb. The Toyota Hino five-ton trucks dropped into low gear. One after another they climbed the new road, compacting freshly turned earth as they went. In the interim, the Cat had cleared a piece of ground roughly one hundred yards by fifty yards for the construction crew camp site.

A large man, with skin burned almost black from the sun, climbed off the dozer and greeted Jamie with a rough handshake, "Andre Pierson." He had all the appearances of a seasoned construction boss.

"Welcome to the Honde, Andre. You'll have your work cut out for you here. We're on a tight schedule. Let me introduce Jack Cloete. He'll be working closely with you. He's familiar with the area and can fill you in on anything you need to know."

The two men eyed each other appreciatively. Jamie could sense already that they would work well together.

"There's a platoon of troops from the Fourth Battalion, Rhodesian Regiment on their way. They'll provide you with cover and protection throughout this exercise, and may need some help from your dozer with their defenses."

"No problem," said Andre. "We built ten PVs in Mt. Darwin and Mrewa. My crews know the drill. We'll get started right away. I'll brief my crews and we'll have our tents up before dark."

* * *

Josiah raised his binoculars and brought them into focus. Yes, there was that big machine that had cut the road, and he could see nearly fifty men milling around as they appeared to be making some sort of camp. "Hah, Enoch, the pigs have arrived. Our time is coming soon. Their blood will flow until the earth is red. Make sure you know the ground so that your comrades will be ready when the time comes."

* * *

Jamie turned and looked down the newly constructed road at the roar of approaching vehicles. Three MAP 45 armored trucks and a Rhino pulled up beside him. A stocky young man jumped out of the lead truck. The floppy camouflage hat he wore did not completely cover a mop of light brown hair. His sparkling blue eyes and infectious grin could not hide the traits of a well seasoned soldier.

"Mike Willis, sir." He saluted smartly. "Got a platoon of Fourth Battalion troopies here. Our orders are to bed down with the construction crew and provide protection."

"Jamie Ross. Glad to have you, Mike. The terrorists don't know what we're up to yet, but you can bet your life that within the next few days you'll have a visit. They don't like anyone messing in what they consider their territory."

Mike nodded towards the men behind him. "These are all good guys with me—mostly farmers and a couple of townies who can hold their own. We're ready for whatever comes our way."

"Glad to hear it. Just understand one thing. This PV site sits right along the main infiltration route into Mashonaland, and the terrorists will not give up easily."

"Don't worry about us. We can take care of ourselves. My guys have had plenty of experience. There's not a rookie among us. I only have one problem. My orders forbid me to go chase any terrorists outside a five click radius from our base. Apparently that's the RAR's job. My guys are just itching for a crack at the gooks so we can put a few notches on our guns."

Jamie smiled at the young man's enthusiasm. Despite his youth and cocky attitude, Jamie could see he led a well-trained and formidable team.

* * *

Jamie walked down the new road toward the Leopards, Sama by his side. The fresh earth of the road smelled sweet. Climbing in the Leopard he looked back. It had been a good day. The work was moving according to schedule. He buckled his seat belt harness, turned the key and with a burst of acceleration, spun the Leopard around. Yes, they would make good time without the convoy in tow.

As the trees and bushes sped by seeds of uneasiness gradually took root and began to grow. A new awareness set in. Now there would be no hiding. The machinery that hummed and sputtered over the earth behind him had put them center stage. The bright red gash in the bush stood out like a beacon where the dozer had carved its way up the ridge. He gazed into the vegetation, the emerald green deepening with the coming of dusk, and felt, even then, that there were eyes watching them.

Chapter Seven

Jamie was excited. He looked out the window as he drove his Leopard along the muddy road with Chris following behind. They were headed for an area north of the Pungwe River to check out a tract of land that might be suitable for the Pungwe PV.

He was relaxed, one hand on the wheel. He breathed in deeply, enjoying the smell of early morning. The faint smell of smoke from breakfast fires, mingling with the dank, moldy smell of vegetation, gave the Honde its own distinctive air.

Finally, they were making progress. He glanced at Sergeant Sama who sat on the passenger side. He was not very conversational, but appeared to be going over notes. Jamie shrugged. He enjoyed having time to think. The morning sun crested above the trees creating sheer bands of light that were quickly absorbed in the thick tangle of foliage. The dissipating beams left moist, warm heat hanging in the air. Jamie wiped at the sweat that stung his eyes. As they neared the turnoff to Katiyo the road became a little more difficult. He dodged some puddles, causing Sergeant Sama to occasionally glance up, seemingly concerned with the erratic maneuvers. Jamie caught his breath. Ahead was an astounding view of Mt. Inyangani. Its grandeur seemed to overshadow and engulf the area.

Jamie was watching Chris's Leopard in his rear view mirror. The heat settled like a warm, wet dishcloth that never seemed to dry. All of a sudden, this, along with the slower pace and foreboding mountain, made him feel closed in, trapped. His eyes searched the depths of the vegetation and he ignored a shudder as he tightened his grip on the wheel. *Come on Jamie. Get yourself together. You are jumpy. Get a grip on your nerves.*

In the split second he had the thought, it happened. The initial wave of the explosion slammed the underneath of the Leopard. The instantaneous pain of the land mine sheered through his body; he knew exactly what it was, but it was too late.

* * *

George Barstow drummed his fingers on the desk. His palms began to sweat. There was not much time and they were ill-prepared. Jamie had the crews up and working on Katiyo quicker than he thought possible. They needed protection. *Now.* There was no turning back. They were sitting ducks at Ruda, not to mention Katiyo. The war was heating up and they could expect an attack any time. There could be mines and ambushes anywhere along the roads. George wiped the moisture from his palms onto his pants. He picked up the phone and tapped out the numbers of Dennis Cornwell.

"Cornwell, sir. This is George Barstow."

"Yes, George."

"I spoke with Jamie yesterday. I need an update on what you're doing for Ruda. What's the weapon status? They still have no decent heavy weapons. They have two Garden Boy cannons and turret busters on the tops of the Leopards, but no black powder to operate them." Jamie tells me the Browning machine gun you sent down keeps jamming when they test fire it."

"I realize that." said Cornwell, flatly. "I've told you, we'll see what we can get our hands on."

George felt the heat rise up the back of his neck. "This should have been handled. Pull any strings you can."

"We're doing the best we can," Cornwell's voice shot back, raspy. "We're going ..."

George cut him off.

"If you're going to provide him with weapons that use only black powder, at least give him the powder. I've been trying for weeks to get heavy weapons. All I can offer him is one ancient Browning that jams and two Garden Boys—if you can call them weapons. It's a good thing the Garden Boys are made locally or he wouldn't have those."

"I assure you, George, we're doing the best we can."

George raked his fingers through his hair and shook his head, incredulously. "Do you realize Jamie's planning to load those things with any form of scrap metal he can find? I even heard talk he was going to make his own black powder."

Silence ...

George heard the rustle as Cornwell shifted uneasily. He nodded and muttered to himself, just loud enough for Cornwell's benefit. "Welcome to the dark ages. You promised him all the support he needed when you sent him to the Honde. The least you can do is follow through."

Click.

* * *

Chris saw and heard the explosion. The blast rocked the ground underneath his Leopard. He slammed on the brakes. DA Mtetwa braced himself as the Leopard came to a jarring halt. Mtetwa muttered a string of phrases in Shona, but Chris didn't hear him. In front of him the force of the blast swayed the vegetation outward like a tornado had blown through. He felt the bile rise up in his stomach as he watched a cloud of smoke slowly settle until the shape of Jamie's Leopard emerged. *Oh dear God, not the boss.*

Chris silently prayed. Sweat trickled down the back of his neck. Seconds passed like minutes. Through the swirling smoke he caught a glimpse of the wreckage ahead. The blast had blown off the whole front end of Jamie's vehicle. It had come to a grinding halt with the rear wheels and engine pointing into the air and the V-shaped cabin angled forward to the ground. One of the wheels landed on the road near Chris's Leopard. His eyes frantically raked over the scene, squinting through the settling cloud in hopes of catching any movement within the cabin. There was none. Grabbing his FN and ammunition pouch with one hand he rolled out of the Leopard, staying low and fully alert for a follow-up ambush. Mtetwa was already out on the other side and they both cocked their weapons, scanning the forest on either side of the road. There was nothing.

They crouched down and doubled forward toward the remains of the other Leopard to get a better look. It had done exactly what it was supposed to do and that gave Chris a flicker of hope. The cabin appeared to be intact with hardly a scratch. A few pieces of shrapnel took off some paint, but the body of the Leopard was basically unscathed.

Chris raised his FN, slid the safety off and fired a burst of automatic fire into the bushes on both sides of the road, just in case there were terrorists hidden in ambush—unlikely at this time of day. With no answering fire they both scrambled forward toward the disabled Leopard, in hopes of any signs of life.

Relief coursed through Chris's body as he saw first Jamie and then Sergeant Sama stagger out of the back of the vehicle. No blood. Sergeant Sama was holding his ears, his eyes wide, shock on his face. Jamie shook his head a few times, coughed and spat.

"Are you Okay?"

"I think so. I don't feel any pain and I know my heart is still beating. That sure got my adrenalin going." Jamie coughed again. "It felt like Mt. Vesuvius erupted under me."

"You are both darned lucky," Chris responded. "Without your full shoulder straps you would have gone flying through the roof. Let's check you out." He put his hand out to steady Jamie. "Can you walk? Is there anything that really hurts?"

"I'm fine—just a sore back." Jamie brushed off his pants and turned to Sergeant Sama. "You okay, sergeant?"

"Good, sir. All parts are still working."

"Well then, let's get out of here and back to Ruda. I've had enough excitement for now."

* * *

Josiah took the last four consecutive gulps of beer without a breath, sat the bottle down with a thud on the rough wooden table, and belched. Across from him in the dank bar sat a North Korean from the Fifth Brigade. He had no interest in drinking.

The foreigner sat still, trained in patience. He waited for the three men to finish their carousing. He had a scar that ran down his right cheek. His features were hard-set and emotionless. His impatience with these men would have been evident in his glare had it not been concealed by dim lighting. He too was in the business of death, but found it a repulsive waste of time to mingle it with revelry.

Josiah wiped his mouth on the back of his hand and leaned forward toward the man.

"You've got the money. Now where are the big guns?"

"They arrived in Beira last month," said the Korean, speaking in broken English in a monotone voice. "One will be here tomorrow."

"Are you sure it will do the job?"

The man narrowed his gaze.

"You have seen the pictures. These rockets will make your 60mm mortars look like toys. They sit on a special rocket launch vehicle and we provide your men a scout to help radio the position of the target."

Josiah gloated. He looked from Morgan to Enoch.

Morgan slammed his fist down on the table, a fleck of spittle reflecting on his lip as he sneered. "Let's use it on Katiyo. The bastards have set up right on our route."

"No, not Katiyo," said Josiah, slowly. The response was almost inaudible as he stared off into the shadowy room, stroking his beard. Little by little, as if something were building deep inside him, his features hardened and he snapped his attention back to the men.

Morgan looked at him, waiting for more direction.

"Not Katiyo." All signs of revelry had washed from his face and were replaced with deadly resolve. "We will wipe out Ruda as planned. Katiyo will be easy, and we will use it as a distraction. I will send both of you to take out Katiyo tomorrow. When their guard is down at Ruda I will bring in the big rockets. Then we will wipe Ruda off the map."

* * *

Jamie swallowed a mouthful of hot tea, washing down the dry peanut butter sandwich Willie had brought him. Willie couldn't even make a decent peanut butter sandwich, Jamie mused. He turned to Chris. "Well Chris, do you feel up to heading out or would you rather take a break now that you've seen a little action first hand? We still need to find a suitable site for the Pungwe PV."

"Are you kidding? Maybe I'll get a crack at those bastards on the way. Are you sure you're okay?"

"A little beat up, but ready. Grab your FN and let's head out. I'll drive, the seat is easier on my back. Sergeant Sama has a sore head and he can stay behind. We'll take Corporal Dande."

Jamie started the motor and pulled out. "We'll make a quick trip to Katiyo to check on progress and scout out the Pungwe site on the way back. It's closer to Ruda. I'd like to have Jack join us if he can get away."

As they topped the ridge at Katiyo Jamie saw the construction crews working on the chain link fence. The posts were set in concrete and the eight-foot fence was going up. At each of the four corners the dozer had pushed up earthen walls to form bunkers. A crew was busy reinforcing them with gum poles in preparation for the roofs that would be covered with sandbags. A temporary earthen wall, about five-foot high, was pushed up around the construction crew camp. In the center of the PV three A-Frame houses had been erected, two to serve as barracks for the INTAF staff and one to serve as the PV headquarters.

Climbing out of the Leopard Jamie looked around in amazement. He was impressed to see all that had been accomplished in just four days. He found Jack and Andre overseeing the laying of pipes for the water supply. "You guys have really pulled out all stops. Keep up this pace and you'll be finished in less than three weeks."

Andre greeted Jamie and Chris. "Ja, we're making good time, but there's still plenty of work to be done. Those RR troopies make it easier for us to concentrate on the job and not worry about security."

Jamie turned to Jack. "Do you think you can tear yourself away from here for a few hours? I need your help to check out the Pungwe site. You know the area and the lay of the land."

"Not a problem, I'll be glad to help."

Chris and Dande climbed into the back of the Leopard and Jack sat across from Jamie. Soon after they crossed the Pungwe River Jack pointed to a rough trail.

"Turn left here. That's the road."

"That!" Jamie was incredulous as he looked at the track branching off to the left through some tall Buffalo grass. "Well I guess the Leopard has been worse places than that."

The four men held on tightly as the vehicle bumped and bounced over the rough ground. Yes the Pungwe site would be a lot more difficult than Katiyo.

The Leopard made slow but steady progress, eventually passing one village and then another. Soon a clearing in front of an abandoned school came into view. Jamie shook his head as he noticed every window of the building was broken. *Why do they have to be so destructive? This is where their kids are educated.*

Driving behind the school Jamie saw the road had ended. He brought the truck to a stop in front of the building. Only a few miles to the west, the forest subtly blended into the dark grey cliffs of Mt. Inyangani. The mountain was ominous, dark, and brooding. Sheer cliffs descended for three thousand feet before blending into the dark green forest below.

"Okay chaps, this is where we soften our boots," said Jamie. He gingerly climbed out, slinging his Uzi over his shoulder. With Jack in the lead they set off to the west, following a path through the forest and passing several more villages clustered close together. They hiked through banana and pineapple groves and crossed several small streams. After fifteen minutes, they came to a cleared area of what had once been sugar cane and maize fields. The area would need to be cleared of undergrowth near the forest, to provide enough room for an open field of fire. The ground was rough, but Jamie was impressed by the potential. There was ample room between two feeder streams, running either side of the site.

Jamie walked down the ridge, stopping periodically to make an assessment. "It looks good to me. It may not be as big as Katiyo but we also have fewer people to cater for." He pointed down the hill. "What I like is that it slopes down on three sides, giving a clear field of fire against any terrorists wanting to attack from the north, east, or south.

It's also right in the middle of Headman Gamanya's area. Chris, are you familiar with Headman Gamanya?"

Chris nodded.

"Do you know of any objections he could raise to erecting a PV on this site? I know there will always be opposition, but I'm more concerned about spiritual objections because of the proximity to Mt. Inyangani."

Chris reflected a moment then shook his head. "None that I know of, but Gamanya is a sly dog, sir. We need to be careful. Word has it he's right in bed with the terrorists. We've heard of no atrocities involving his family and that speaks for itself."

They finished checking the area and headed back down the path, Jamie leading at a quick pace.

"The access road will prove more of a challenge," said Jack, breathing heavily as he tried to keep up with Jamie. "I think I can get that taken care of ahead of time with just the grader and a few truck loads of gravel and concrete pipes."

Jamie stopped and turned to look back up towards the proposed site. "It's defensible and large enough to accommodate all of Gamanya's people." He felt very satisfied with the outcome of their trip. Now they could head back to Ruda.

* * *

Enoch motioned to Morgan Tangwena. They squinted through the last light of dusk, studying the men at Katiyo.

Enoch whispered instructions. "That is where you will get into position," he said, motioning to the forest below the construction workers camp. "We will kill the soldiers. There must be thirty or more of them. The workers are camped separately. We will wait until it is dark and then you will take ten men with you and attack the construction camp. Take one mortar and an RPG."

They watched the soldiers for several minutes as they slowed down for the night. "They don't look like regulars," said Enoch. "They spend a lot of time talking and smoking cigarettes. When you hear the RPG explode, begin shooting. Kill them all."

Enoch watched Morgan round up his men and they faded into the depth of the forest. Enoch positioned his men in a semi-circle facing the soldiers' camp and refined his strategy. He could see the earth mounds that had been pushed up by the bulldozer. They would need to fire between each of these bolsters. Signaling his men to withdraw, he moved back into the forest about two hundred yards and briefed them.

"We will wait until it is completely dark. They light lamps so we will be able to see them, but they will not see us. They have been very careless all evening and won't expect us. They even expose themselves when they relieve themselves in the bushes. I will fire first and destroy one of their trucks with the RPG. As soon as I fire, pick your targets and begin shooting. They will panic and we will close in on them and shoot them down like pigs."

Enoch looked over the men, trying to think if he had forgotten to tell them anything. "One more thing, fix your bayonets so that you can cut their white bellies open and watch the blood spill. Any questions?"

The men stood up and came together. As adrenaline pumped, sounds of murmuring filtered through the night. A lone child sat at a distance huddled under a tree. Isaac lurched through the men, ready to kick the twelve-year-old to his feet. A small cry escaped the boy's lips. Enoch gripped Isaac's arm. The comrade stopped but continued to fix the boy with a fierce gaze. It was a look that had made, at one time or another, all the comrades quiver. Enoch released Isaac's arm, but only after he met his eyes with an unspoken warning. Enoch walked over to the boy and squatted carefully down next to him, his face inches from the boy's. He spoke softly, but there was tension around his eyes. "Come. This will be over soon," he said brightly. "You are brave and will make Josiah proud." He reached over and gave him a light-hearted nudge, then positioned the boy's SKS pointing toward the camp and mouthed, "tat-tat-tat-tat." He looked back at him and smiled, whispering, "It will be fun. You will bring down many enemies."

The boy looked at him, a hint of a smile on his quivering lips, and then pushed to his feet.

Enoch gave him a playful shove and the lithe figure scrambled toward the rest.

"What if they have a machine gun?" whispered a comrade.

"I did not see any machine guns. Even if they do have them they are not seasoned soldiers." He grinned, scoffing at the thought. "They will be food for the hyenas and jackals before the night is over. Follow me and take up your positions. Tongerayi will go to the far left with the mortar."

Silently they positioned themselves, five feet apart, lying prone so that they could watch the camp until the signal to attack.

Enoch fixed his eyes on the camp and waited. The cicadas screeched and other night sounds filtered through the warm air as the day faded from dusk to dark. There was no moon, but he could see the figures of the soldiers, intermittently, as they moved between the earthen barriers. Their vehicles were barely visible beyond, but he was sure that he had enough of a visual on one of the MAP trucks to form a target. He could not see his watch now because it was too dark. The soldiers appeared to be eating their dinner. This would be a great time to catch them unawares.

Enoch stood up slowly and stretched his legs. He could not miss. He felt his heart thump as he raised the RPG, settling it lightly on his right shoulder. Looking down the sights, he found the cab of the MAP, silhouetted by the faint light from the soldiers' camp. He flicked the switch and squeezed the trigger. A *swoosh* pierced the night as the rocket-propelled grenade soared from the launcher in the direction of the soldiers' camp. It flew harmlessly into an earthen bolster and exploded with a loud bang. Enoch cursed. He had misjudged the distance.

Immediately, the comrades opened, up firing from all directions, aiming where they thought the soldiers were, or had been. All lights switched off in the camp. They could no longer see their targets, but they kept firing.

Suddenly there was a sharp rat-a-tat, tat, tat as one of the MAG light machine guns from the camp opened up sending a hail of bullets in their direction. All Enoch saw was an occasional muzzle flash, but his men had an advantage over the soldiers, they had tracers to guide their shots.

Trees and bushes shredded around Enoch and a comrade cried out. To his right Morgan Tangwena and his group were firing furiously at the construction camp. *Boom.* Another RPG grenade exploded.

Suddenly, a second machine gun opened up from the direction of the construction camp. This was not what he anticipated.

* * *

Mike Willis jumped. They were being attacked from two fronts. *The construction camp!* His first thought was the construction workers, a hundred yards to the north. He had to get a section over there.

"Corporal McDonald," he shouted. "Take your men and MAG and move at the double to give the construction workers some support.

He spun around to Lieutenant George. "Take your section and work your way around so you can close in on the terrorists from that gulley to the south. They won't see you in the dark. Wait for a parachute flare before you open up."

Mike grabbed his FN. *These guys don't realize what they're up against.* He ran outside and dropped down behind the earthen wall as firing continued, now from both sides. His eyes probed the darkness. *They were using tracers.* He could not see the terrorists, but he knew they must be lying prone, reducing their target size. Still, they had very little protection. His men had the advantage of the trenches and solid walls of earth. After five minutes he knew at least two terrorists were down from cries that carried in the darkness.

* * *

Enoch cringed. Mortar bombs exploded in the trees around him. One shell exploded between two of the comrades, killing both instantly. This was not what he had expected. A brilliant white phosphorous parachute flare lit up the ground around him and he was temporarily blinded. Simultaneously, feet rushed at him from his left and grenades began exploding. The ground shuddered. Panicking, he leapt to his feet and scrambled. It was time to get his men out. He doubled back into the forest with the rest of the comrades following behind. Morgan Tangwena saw Enoch and his men flee into the forest as the area lit up and they followed suit.

Ten minutes later Enoch reached the rendezvous point. One by one the comrades trickled in. Of the original twenty five, twelve made it back. Enoch searched the darkness, hoping some had escaped into the bush and would find their way back to the drop-off-point across the border in Mozambique. He heard a frantic tearing through the undergrowth and turned to see Morgan. He dropped down next to him, panting and clutching his AK. "Morgan," Enoch said, his voice shaking. "These soldiers are better than we were told. We will have to find other ways to stop their work. We lost many men tonight. Did you hit anything with your RPG?"

"No, comrade, it was too dark, and their earth barriers were too high. I fired two rockets, but I don't think I hit anything. I had to leave my RPG behind as the soldiers were coming. Let us go back to our drop-off-point. We will wait till morning to see if any of our other comrades make it back. I have two who need help."

Enoch looked out into the darkness, mumbling. "This is a bad night. The spirits are against us."

* * *

Mike Willis gathered his men together inside the construction camp site. It had been quiet for fifteen minutes and soon it would be time to check on the wounded. Mike felt confident there were no casualties among his men, or the construction workers.

"Man, but that was some fight," yelled Jack Cloete still clutching his FN as he ran up to the army camp. "Seems like those terrorists bit off more than they bargained for." He turned to Mike. "Those guys of yours sure know how to fight. Took them by surprise when the flare went up and your guys ran towards them. Just like chasing a wounded leopard with dogs. They didn't even fight back, just took to the trees and ran."

Mike laughed, adrenaline still running high. "Yeah, they weren't expecting our response. We'll do a full sweep of the area in the morning. There's no sense exposing any of our soldiers to more danger. A wounded terrorist is still a threat."

* * *

Jamie slammed down the microphone and spun around in his chair. "Chris!"

Chris ran into the ops room.

"I just got the latest on the terrorist attack on Katiyo last night." Chris' face was alight with excitement, anxious to hear more details of the previous night's attack.

"Our guys put up a really good show. No casualties on our side, but seven dead and one critically injured on theirs. Mike's troopies recovered nine AK rifles, one SKS, one RPG launcher, a 60mm mortar and seven boxes of ammunition."

Chris whistled. "It looks like they came ready for a long battle."

Jamie shook his head. "One of them was only a kid, not more than ten or twelve years old."

"Well, that starts the morning with some adrenaline," said Chris. "What's planned for the rest of the day ... an attack on Ruda?"

Jamie frowned. "That's not funny, Chris. I'm meeting Angus McDonald here in a couple of hours. He's coming with me to check out a couple of sites for two more PVs."

"Angus will be glad to do something useful. This war has made his job as an agricultural officer almost impossible. What do you need me to do today?"

"Take Corporal Dande with you. Use the Hino with the sandbags since we're still short one Leopard. Go and check on our guys at Katiyo. See if they need anything."

Chris left the room at a near gallop, thrilled to be going to the place of action, even if it was twelve hours late.

Just before 0900 a Leopard pulled into the Keep. Out stepped a lanky, sandy haired man wearing a khaki shirt and shorts and a pair of heavy boots. Jamie went out to meet him as the man walked up with a broad smile.

"Good morning, sir. Angus McDonald, agricultural officer. I just got back from three weeks leave." Laughing, "It sure was nice to take a break from this place."

Jamie led Angus inside the ops room. A straightforward guy, Jamie found him easy to like. The thirty-year-old was over six feet and didn't have an ounce of fat on his body. He would be an invaluable addition to the team. His job had been to promote the planting and harvesting of sugar cane, Cavendish bananas, and small tea plantations to supply Katiyo, but since the terrorists had infiltrated the area all agricultural work had come to a halt. The locals had been warned not to have anything to do with those who came to teach them better animal husbandry and farming.

"I know things have been really difficult for you recently, but this is going to change."

"That's good to hear. The last six months have been a living hell. I've been so frustrated. Nothing can be accomplished. My Supervisor and demonstrators are scared out of their pants. They visit different villages, but keep their mouths shut so as not to be classified as 'sellouts.'"

"Welcome to the team. With our new strategic plan to relocate all the locals into PVs, I sense a new level of excitement. There's more than enough to keep you busy in the coming months—you won't get bored I promise you."

Jamie turned to look at the wall map and Angus followed his gaze.

"We need to check out two potential PV sites this morning. One is about a mile from here which we will call Ruda PV, and the other is south-west, about five miles from the border, near a village called Tikwiri."

"I know the place," said Angus. "It was a prime area for growing Cavendish bananas and sugar cane."

Jamie pointed to white flags on the map. These are potential PV sites. What do you think?"

Your Ruda site is a natural. Close to the airstrip and central to the people. You could even build the PV around the Ruda school. That will solve the problem of building a new school in the PV."

"Angus, you know the ground well. I'm going to rely on your expertise in making the final selections.

Angus nodded his head. "I probably know the area better than anyone else so will be glad to help."

"I want to hit the road and check them out. Aerial photos can only tell us so much so I always believe in a full reconnaissance on the ground."

"Let's go." Angus was already on his feet, heading for the door. "If you don't mind, I'll lead the way. I know the roads."

Jamie shoved on his beret and called for Sergeant Sama.

* * *

It was late afternoon as the Isuzu truck bumped and rattled along the corrugated dirt road that ran along beside the Pungwe River. The truck was headed west, towards the Rhodesian border. Following close behind the truck was a strange vehicle. It had an extended cab with a blunt nose. Behind the cab were two banks of cylinders, eight on the bottom layer and nine on top.

Josiah clutched the steering wheel of the Isuzu tightly. He turned to the man who sat beside him.

"Are you sure these rockets will work?"

"This is the BM-14. It is a very powerful weapon that chased the Americans back to the south in 1953."

Josiah still had a hard time understanding the sing-song accent of this fierce looking North Korean man. He shook his head in disbelief.

"When all seventeen rockets fire at once nothing will remain. You wait and see."

"How do you aim them? Don't you have to see the enemy camp?"

The Korean's jaw flinched at the naivety of the man, but there was no expression on his face. "No. We will drive to half a mile from the target and my scout will go with your attacking party to radio me the coordinates of the camp."

Josiah's face relaxed as the doubt disappeared from his mind. Looking back at the bank of enormous cylinders, he felt elated. Each cylinder was as wide as his full hand-span. Behind the cylinders, he could see a stack of rockets, neatly fitted into their carriers. A smile slowly spread across his face. *Tomorrow, there will be no more Ruda; no more Chinyerere. Thirty-four rockets. They will do a lot of damage. Each is much, much bigger than the 60mm mortars we usually carry.*

The trucks pulled up in a village two miles from the border. Josiah climbed out of the truck and stretched. "We will stay here until we see the sun setting above the big mountain. Enoch will lead the main group across the border to the track that leads to Ruda camp. We will leave the truck here until we return."

Morgan Tangwena spoke up, "Will you be coming with us or staying with the big guns?"

"I will stay with the rockets. As soon as it is dusk we will cross the border, take up our positions, and fire down on the enemy. You are not to fire at the camp until you hear the rockets explode and see them destroying the walls of the camp. Once the rockets explode, the walls will collapse. You will run in and kill them all. They will not be prepared."

Enoch turned to Josiah and sniffed. "Are you sure they have no masoja with them? The attack on Katiyo went very badly for us."

"There are no masoja," said Josiah. "The spirit medium told me yesterday that the enemy has no strength. They will fall quickly as our rockets descend. Now let us eat some food and then Comrade Enoch will lead the way."

As the men finished eating the sun began to sink behind Inyangani Mountain. Enoch stood up and thirty-one comrades fell silently behind him as he led the way down the path. They carried mortars, two RPGs, and AK-47 rifles.

Josiah looked over at the North Korean and his loader. They were conversing, so he used his time to inspect the formidable cylinders. Never before had he seen such weapons. The Rhodesian soldier pigs would get a big surprise. He was sure they had never seen anything like this.

After a few moments, the Korean, his loader, and Josiah climbed aboard the rocket launch vehicle. The driver started the engine and they drove carefully, relying on the dim evening light to follow the track. No one spoke as the strange vehicle crossed the border into the country Josiah called the 'New Zimbabwe'.

"We have only another two miles before we reach the ridge overlooking the Ruda camp." Josiah spoke softly, as if his enemy, two miles away, could hear him. "You will not see the camp because there is another ridge in front of it. Below the ridge Enoch and the comrades are positioned."

The vehicle churned slowly up the ridge, bouncing on the uneven track pitted with deep ruts. Josiah motioned for them to stop. He pointed to the ridge.

"Ruda camp is just behind those trees."

The North Korean engaged the vehicle again and positioned the BM-14 at right angles to their target. The loader jumped down and put chocks behind all six wheels. Josiah helped the loader unclip a rocket and lift the six-feet-weapon, with its shiny, pointed nose cone, into the top cylinder. Another rocket followed and

Within fifteen minutes, all seventeen tubes were loaded. With the engine still running, the North Korean engaged the hydraulics, swung the bank of cylinders around and pointed them toward Ruda. They had no map with coordinates to plot the trajectory, but the driver called in on his radio to a spotter with Enoch who gave precise aiming directions. The loader aimed, gently using the hydraulics to raise the bank of cylinders slightly. He focused the sights on a light reflected from the ground beyond the tree line where Enoch and his comrades were settled and waiting.

The North Korean faced Josiah. "We are ready. It is getting dark and the rockets are lined up."

"We wait," said Josiah, holding up a hand. "When it is fully dark, the enemy will be caught unawares. That is when we fire."

Minutes ticked by. Patiently Josiah and the North Korean waited until the last hue of grey dusk receded into blackness. Still Josiah did not move. He wanted to be sure his enemy would be tired, longing for sleep. Josiah felt the penetrating gaze of the North Korean locked on him. The man made him nervous and it broke his concentration. He tried to brush it off.

Josiah's eyes adjusted to the darkness. He could not see the Ruda camp, but he saw the reflected light from the security lights and knew that his enemy was within reach. A few more moments ticked by. The sliver of moon vanished behind a patch of black clouds and the night seemed to hold its breath.

"Now, Fire!"

There was a mighty roar. Seventeen deadly missiles left the launcher simultaneously and headed for Ruda....

Chapter Eight

GARDEN BOY GUN

Emily was delighted. It was Demi. The sound of her voice on the other end of the phone was a welcome reprieve. Since their first encounter at church, they had become close friends. Emily cherished her support and encouragement. They rarely missed a week without getting together.

"Why don't you bring the kids over this evening. John's working late," said Demi. "We can have an early supper, let the kids play, and spend time catching up with each other."

"That sounds wonderful. Would six o'clock be okay? I don't get off work until five."

"Any time would be good, Emily. Just come over as you are. I'm not going to do anything fancy. Let's just relax and enjoy each other's company."

The supper was simple, egg sandwiches and fruit salad. Afterwards Demi led the way out to the back porch. Emily could hear the children playing in the yard. She settled back in the lawn-chair across from Demi, tucked a leg under her and breathed deeply of the night air. For a moment life was peaceful. She savored the welcomed feeling of normality and let herself sink into this frame of mind—one that she had not experienced in weeks.

"What's John up to tonight?" she asked, as she covered a small yawn.

"Virtually all the men have been called up for military service so the ones left behind have to do their part to fill in gaps around town."

Emily laughed. "I know. Can you believe my seventy-year-old dad has joined the home guard of the police reserve! He patrols the neighborhood a couple of times a week armed with a baton. A very frightening sight I'm sure. At least he's making his contribution to the war effort."

Demi chuckled. "Yes, I can believe it. Let's pray he doesn't come across any thugs."

"What's John's role?"

"He goes down to police headquarters a couple of times a week to monitor the terrorist radio broadcasts from Mozambique. Your Jamie sure makes the headlines."

Emily sat up and gave her a questioning look. "What do you mean? What's he been up to now?"

"He must be doing a great job. They sure hate him. His name's right up there at the top of the list of people they intend to eliminate. Pretty nasty stuff I understand."

Emily's heart surged for several seconds. The blood drained from her face and a sick knot formed in her stomach. "You mean John hears this over the radio? The terrorists have singled out Jamie to kill?"

Demi looked at her friend's stricken face, wishing she could retract the words. "I'm so sorry Emily. I should never have said that. I just wasn't thinking what effect it would have on you. I was marveling at how successful he must be for them to keep mentioning his name."

Emily swallowed, tears flooding her eyes. "Demi, we've had so many friends killed. I couldn't bear it if ..."

Demi reached over and gently squeezed Emily's hand. "Look at me, Emily. Jamie is safe. He's very smart and obviously knows what he's doing."

They hugged for several seconds. Demi's heart ached as she realized the pain she had caused her friend. "Forgive me, Emily."

Emily caught her breath and stifled a sob as she pulled away. "It's okay. I'm glad you told me. Jamie never tells me anything about what he's facing and I know it's because he doesn't want me to worry. You're right; I need to think about what he's accomplishing, not the danger."

The remainder of the evening Emily tried to take charge of her thoughts. She smiled, shared, occasionally laughed, but her heart was miles away. Intermittently, during a lull, she softly prayed. The implication of this new knowledge slowly spread over her like burning embers. *Oh God, please be with Jamie.*

* * *

Jamie heard the whistle of the rockets just before they exploded behind the Keep. In less than a minute, following multiple explosions, Jamie was at his command post. Chris barked commands into the internal phone system that ran from bunker to bunker, and covered all four walls of the Keep. Angus McDonald was hunkered down and firing single shots with his FN, oblivious to everything happening behind him. The crackle of automatic fire drowned out all other sounds.

"They have a Stalin Organ. Fortunately all the rockets went over us," yelled Jamie.

Following the rockets there was a hail of small arms fire directed at the Keep from the east. Jamie could see the tracer and muzzle flashes clearly.

Angus returned fire as he squinted into the darkness. All he could see was an occasional muzzle flash in the dark and tracer rounds, mostly going over their heads.

Chris was hunched over the Browning .303 machine gun. It gave two quick bursts and then was silent. "Damn! It's jammed. Why don't they give us decent weapons?"

In one fluid motion, Jamie rolled over next to Chris and grabbed the ammunition belt, pulling it up. "Cock it again. See if we can loosen the belt." Chris gave the bolt another tug and it came loose. He ejected the damaged cartridge, aimed the Browning toward where he could see the muzzle flashes and tracer—*ta, ta, ta, ta, ta*, bullets spewed out of the mouth of the barrel, but then it jammed again.

"Angus," shouted Jamie. "Can you get the Garden Boys ready? Let's see if some scrap metal won't do some damage. Aim them toward that gulley at two o'clock."

Angus put his FN down and took hold of the Garden Boy, swiveling it on its mount and lowering the elevation till it was pointed toward the terrorist position. That afternoon Chris had overseen the cleaning and loading of both Garden Boys. They only had two charges of black powder for each Garden Boy and Chris had loaded a bunch of scrap metal from the Mutasa workshop. Shiny new electrical igniters had been inserted and they were connected to a 6-volt battery with a small switch.

Jamie was on the internal phone to Sergeant Sama who was handling the other Garden Boy in the south-east bunker. "Sergeant, tell me when you are ready and we will fire both guns."

"The gun is ready," called Sergeant Sama.

"Right, on my count of three fire both guns. One, two, three…"

Jamie saw flames shoot out of the muzzle of the Garden Boy and there was an immediate lull in the firing from the terrorist position, but the pause was brief. *Crump, crump.* Several mortars were fired and a barrage of shells exploded inside the Keep and near the main barracks.

Chris yelled above the noise. "We've taken one hit from the Stalin Organ so we can expect one more salvo." He was helping Angus reload the Garden Boy. "Fortunately I hear they never carry more than forty rockets."

Jamie fired several bursts from his Uzi. "Yes, we're lucky they don't have a clue how to aim them or we'd be in real trouble."

Jamie was jolted. Firing now came from a new direction as they took hits against the rear wall of the Keep. He picked up the internal phone, and called the two bunkers on the back wall of the Keep. No response.

Turning to Chris, he shouted. "Watch this front. I'm going to see what's happening behind us. There's no answering fire and they're not answering the phone."

The thought sent a chill through Chris. He stopped tamping down the cartridge in the Garden Boy. "No. There's too much fire. You'll be—"

Jamie was already gone.

He ran like a rabbit, zigging and zagging along the inside of the six-feet-high earthen wall. Spatters of dirt smacked against him as bullets collided with the wall sending a spray of earth over the top. He was near the back of the Keep and running toward the right back bunker.

Wheeeeeeeee ...

A new barrage of rockets descended towards the back of the Keep. Most were high and exploded harmlessly well beyond the Keep, but two continued their trajectory to the inside, and right toward Jamie.

* * *

Josiah felt the blast of the rockets as they left their tubes. The sound was deafening. He watched the multiple tails of fire streaming toward the target. Clasping both hands to his ears to drown the sound, he shook his head in amazement. Yes, Chinyerere would die.

* * *

Jamie heard them coming but had no time to think. He reeled as one of the rockets exploded just fifteen feet in front of him and to one side. Earth blasted with force as events unfolded in an eerie silence that he knew was really a deafening roar. He felt rather than heard the concussion of the blast. The strength of the explosion propelled him backwards and then everything was black.

* * *

Hearing the whistle and then the explosion of the rockets inside the Keep Chris felt the bile rise in his throat. *Had they got Jamie?* The terrorist fire was increasing and he realized he could not leave his post. *Got to do something or we are going to be overrun.* Back to the Browning. This, and the Garden Boys, would be their only hope. Using all his strength Chris pulled back on the bolt of the Browning and was able to free the cartridge belt. Pulling the belt out Chris picked up a fresh belt, telling himself to focus, and carefully loaded the new belt.

"Angus, is the Garden Boy loaded? I don't know what's happened to the boss, but we've got to keep up a steady rate of fire. We can't let these bastards get near us."

Swiveling the Browning Chris pulled the trigger and was relieved to hear the steady ta, ta, ta, ta, ta, as it did its job. Thinking to himself, *short bursts only. Don't want to overheat the gun.*

"Angus, tell Sergeant Sama and his men to keep firing. Use the internal phone. And, Angus, try and get through to the west bunker. Check with Corporal Dande. Maybe the boss is with him."

Another *crump* behind as a mortar bomb landed not fifteen yards away. Then there were some explosions on the main wall where two RPG rockets exploded harmlessly. The battle was continuing full force.

* * *

Corporal Dande saw Jamie running toward him and then the rockets exploded. The sound was deafening and then there was nothing. Where was Chinyerere? Running out of the bunker he saw a figure lying on his back about twenty five feet from the west wall. "Maiwe, Mambo Chinyerere is dead," he shouted. Leaning over the body there was no movement. Dande shook Jamie—no response. Picking up the limp body he ran with him into his bunker. Laying Jamie down carefully, he picked up his FN and, flicking the change lever to automatic, began firing at the terrorist position beyond the road. Dande could hear the Browning machine firing behind him—then it stopped.

He must save Mambo Chinyerere. Maybe he wasn't dead. Checking—still no signs of life. Leaving Jamie lying on his back he ran to the main bunker where Mambo Chris was shouting orders. "Mambo Chris, Chinyerere is dead. He is lying over in my bunker on the back wall."

Chris held his hand to his head in shock, but then the realization that they were still under attack forced him to react strategically. The terrorists were not known for their fancy shooting and past experience showed they did not like return fire. Turning to Corporal Dande, he said, "Get back to your post and give them everything you have. Fire on automatic and keep firing until you see the second flare. Do not leave Mambo Chinyerere."

Chris pulled out the flare gun and inserted a white phosphorous flare. It would light up the terrorist position and maybe give them a scare. "Angus, get on the line to Sama. Tell him that as soon as he sees the flare to fire his Garden Boy. This is our last shot and we must make it count. These bastards don't like being shot at. Tell everyone to give everything they've got—full automatic—five or six magazines—this'll let the bastards know that we mean business …

The flare lit up the sky and the terrorist position. The double *boom, boom* of the two Garden Boys echoed against the earthen walls. Chris could see the flames shooting out of the barrels for at least ten feet. With all the defenders firing on automatic the sound was deafening, and then silence …

As suddenly as it had started, all return fire from the terrorists ceased. Chris knew from experience that the battle was over for the night. Loading another flare he fired it over the terrorist position, but there was no response.

"Angus," Chris shouted. "Come with me. Let's go find the boss." The two men doubled to the north-west bunker just as they saw Corporal Dande emerge, holding up a very groggy Jamie.

The three men lifted Jamie and carried him to his bedroom where they laid him gently on the camp bed. Jamie's face was covered with soot and dirt and there was blood trickling out of both ears. Jamie turned and looked at Chris. "What happened? All I heard was the whistling and then nothing."

Chris sighed in relief. The boss was going to be all right.

* * *

At first light Jamie was out of bed, his whole body ached and his ears were singing. He slowly made his way to the ops room. It wasn't long before he heard the rumble of trucks and Nick appeared. He stood in the doorway looking at Jamie and shaking his head. "You're a lucky blighter. Those are a couple of colorful shiners."

Sears of pain shot through Jamie's head as he started to shake it. "You better get going to see what they left behind."

"Yeah, we're on our way now."

Outside Nick and his men formed up outside the Keep and two sections began a sweep towards the border.

Jamie walked over to the earthen barrier, climbed on top of the central bunker, watching the troopers as they began to scour the bushes and trees beyond the cleared area. Soon they were out of sight. Jamie heard nothing for three hours until Nick and his men returned.

Nick was carrying an AK-47, another of his men had a Chinese SKS rifle, a third a box of mortar rounds, and others several boxes of ammunition. "Well they didn't leave any bodies, but there was plenty of blood spoor. It appeared they must have made a litter to carry out one of their wounded."

"No actual bodies?"

"No bodies. With a ten hour start they're well across the border. Those Stalin Organs are mounted on a jeep-type vehicle. We found tracks crossing the border and ending on that small ridge about half a mile from Ruda Keep. Show me where the rockets landed."

Jamie walked over to the back wall and showed Nick the two blast craters, each about eight feet across and four feet deep. Pointing to the one crater, "This is the one that knocked me down." He bent down and picked up a silver nose cone with Chinese markings that was lying near the top of the barrier. He tossed it to Nick.

"Jamie, I don't think these guys like what you're doing. Two attacks in two days. You really need some better weapons."

"You can say that again. It's a miracle we fought them off this time."

"I'll back you up at the next JOC meeting. Maybe if we both press your case we'll see some results."

"Thanks. I need all the support I can get."

Chapter Nine

Jamie awoke to the sound of the alarm clock. He groaned as he rolled over and hit the button. He felt Emily's warm soft body next to him and pulled her close. *If only this visit could last a few more days*. But it was 2 a.m. and time to make the trip back to Mutasa. There was a job to be done and others depending on him. There was so much to do. It was already March fourteenth, and the first group of people was scheduled to be moved into the Katiyo PV the following Monday.

Jamie slipped out of bed and dressed quietly so as not to wake the kids. He kissed and hugged Emily and felt tears sting his eyes as she clung to him tightly, reluctant to let him go. He grabbed his bag and quietly closed the kitchen door behind him.

He steered the little Datsun onto the main road and put his foot down. There was virtually no traffic at two thirty in the morning so he sped through the city and onto the Umtali road. His mind was in overdrive as he thought of all that had to be done and he barely noticed the time passing. Dawn broke just as he turned off onto the dirt road and headed toward Mutasa village. The sun had not peeked above the forest and mist continued to hang in the trees like a white shroud. Occasionally, a finger of mist would reach over the road and Jamie kept his lights on low so he could see.

At five forty five Jamie pulled up to the house. Sixpence was on his hands and knees polishing the red granolithic floor. He took great pride in keeping the floors shining. The furniture could be covered in dust, but the floors always shone. He leapt up when he saw Jamie and wiped his hands on his apron.

"Ah, good morning, mambo. You are here very early."

"Yes, it is early and I'm looking forward to one of your special breakfasts."

Sixpence looked enquiringly at Jamie. "Did you bring some bacon or sausage?"

"There is some in the big box in the back of the Datsun—also some eggs and some fresh bread and butter. See what you can do."

As Sixpence busied himself with breakfast Jamie retrieved a small cardboard box from the back seat of the car. He carried it into the kitchen and examined the contents. He knew what was in it but wanted to reassure himself that everything was there. Charcoal, saltpeter and flowers of sulfur—everything he would need for his project. He would start as soon as he had finished breakfast.

Jamie took a pot from the cupboard and found a measuring cup. *I've asked head office repeatedly to get us some black powder, but it seems our request is shoved to the bottom of the pile. They just don't comprehend the seriousness of the situation.* Jamie's thoughts took on a defiant attitude. *If they can't get it for us I'll solve the problem myself, one way or another.*

Jamie looked uncertainly at the ingredients. It was a long time since he had made black powder. He tried to remember the exact proportions and the process needed to make the explosive. *I can't believe that in a war situation I have to make black powder for our weapons. It just does not make sense. Well, here goes.* He carefully measured the ingredients into the pot, added a little water and, taking a wooden spoon, began to gingerly stir the mixture into a thick, black paste. When he thought it looked about right he placed it on the stove and turned the burner onto low. Once the mixture had dried he would grind it in the pestle and mortar that he had purchased for just this purpose.

There were a few things he had to take care of at the office early, so he turned to Sixpence. "Sixpence, I want you to keep stirring this stuff, but be very careful, don't let it burn. I am going up to the office and will be back shortly."

Jack Cloete and Marilyn were waiting for him as he walked into the office. They asked how his weekend had been. Jamie wanted them to brief him on any happenings during the past few days.

"Well your brother had a bit of a fright. The terrorists attacked Aberfoyle again," Jack stated.

"What?" Jamie's face was wrought with concern. "Are they all right?"

"Ja, they're okay" Jack shifted his bulk on the small, hard chair. "It happened Friday night, but they're safe. Apparently, the terrorists went into a rage after their failed attempts on Katiyo and Ruda."

"Thankfully, no one was injured," Marilyn said.

"Nick told me that it was only a small group—ten or twelve. They had RPGs and AKs. They shot up the homes and Koos's workshop. The grenade screens protected the houses, but Koos's workshop took a hit from an RPG and blew out all his electrics. He's mad as a snake. Someone must have told them that there was only a stick of four police reservists protecting the estates." Jack stood. "The Aberfoyle people put up a good show and now there's one less terrorist for the next attack." Jack's voice rose in anger. "After they left Aberfoyle, they tied up a storekeeper and his family, locked them inside the store and then set the whole place on fire. From there, they went to a local village and killed everyone—men, women and children, leaving the bodies just lying around on the ground. Bloody animals!"

"It's all so senseless," Jamie shook his head. "What else?"

"One of the local buses hit a boosted landmine on Saturday. Seven were killed and ... "

Before Jack could finish his sentence Jamie suddenly gasped and jumped up. "Explosions! Oh no, I left something cooking on the stove." He dashed out of the door and started running towards his house.

Jamie was halfway there when he heard a muffled *whooooosh!* He saw Sixpence come flying out the kitchen door, gesturing wildly with his dish towel, hopping from one foot to the other and shouting unintelligible words. The sight almost made Jamie laugh, but when he saw a cloud of smoke wafting through the door panic overtook him and he broke into a fast run.

"Sixpence, are you all right?"

Sixpence was still shouting and panting as Jamie came to a halt.

"Mambo! The porridge has burnt the stove."

Jamie opened the kitchen door and back pedaled as a cloud of white smoke billowed out. Snatching the towel from Sixpence, he took a deep breath, holding the towel over his nose, he went inside to check for flames. The oven door was closed, but acrid smoke poured from around it. Using his free hand, Jamie quickly opened all the windows to let the smoke dissipate, then ran back outside, gulping the fresh air. "Sixpence, what happened?"

Sixpence used his apron to dab beads of sweat from his forehead. "Mambo, you told me to watch that porridge on top of the stove. It was beginning to smoke, so I put it in the oven. The next thing I knew … *bang* … and all that smoke."

Once the smoke cleared, Jamie examined what was left of the stove. It looked like the black powder mixture had ignited into a fireball, but fortunately had not exploded. It was a known fact that black powder needed to be contained to really do damage. However the entire inside of the stove was gutted and the electric wires were melted and congealed into an indiscernible mess. Jamie had to laugh at the situation—there was certainly no use stressing over it. He went outside to reassure Sixpence that a new stove would be delivered—and Jamie would no longer require him to cook explosive porridge.

Jamie walked back to the office and called George Barstow.

"Yes, you heard that right," said Jamie, grinning sheepishly. "My stove blew up.

Pause … "What's that?"

"No, it's not repairable."

Pause ….

"Yes, if you'd please get us a replacement right away, that would be great."

Pause …

"Don't ask, just do me a favor and send up a new stove. By the way, have you been able to get me any black powder?"

On the other end of phone, George Barstow smiled. *Ah ha. Now*

I know what happened. Trust Jamie. He was trying to cook up some black powder. Well, in the circumstances I can't blame him. "I've got good news, Jamie. I twisted some arms and made a little progress. You're going to get a new Browning machine gun within the next few days and six more Garden Boys." He added knowingly, "with plenty of black powder."

"Thank you, sir."

Walking into Marilyn's office, she wrinkled her nose and then went back to work. After another moment, she glanced up again, unable to stifle her curiosity. "What's that smell?"

Jamie realized he probably reeked of smoke and gun powder. After relaying the events of the earlier fiasco, they both had a good laugh.

"Just so you know, you're not allowed to try out any porridge recipes in my house. I need my stove and headquarters in Umtali may not be so forgiving next time."

"I've got some better news."

"What's that?"

"I've been promised a working Browning machine gun and six new Garden Boys." Jamie smiled. "I'll be leaving for Ruda in an hour. Could you jot down a few things?"

Marilyn took out a pen and pad, and waited.

"I won't be back at Mutasa until we've completed the Katiyo move," said Jamie. "When setting up any meetings, don't plan anything before Thursday of next week. Oh, and please check with Dennis Cornwell. He promised me four vedettes, Internal Affairs National Servicemen on call-up. We'll need them to man Katiyo until Guard Force personnel arrive, which is not for another few weeks. Even then, we may still be responsible for Katiyo as the Guard Force is stretched thin. They've committed to man just five PVs."

An hour later, Jamie called out, "Sergeant Sama, let's go."

Sergeant Sama came running, trusty Beretta in hand. The back of the Leopard looked like a junk shop. Aside from kit bags and two crates of Coke, Sama tossed in a large box of food for the DA's at Ruda while Jamie had his own box of goodies to tide him over for the next few weeks.

* * *

Jamie sat with Chris and Angus MacDonald in the Ruda dining room. He took a sip of the hot coffee Willie had brought. It tasted like burnt wood chips, but Jamie drank it anyway, hoping it would keep him alert.

"Hear about that bus attack?" asked Angus. Jamie nodded, remembering that Jack had mentioned it just before the gunpowder fiasco.

"Man, that bus took a major hit," Angus continued. "They boosted the anti-tank-mine with a case of plastic explosives. It blew the front half of the bus to smithereens." He looked down, shaking his head as he recounted the scene. "There were arms and legs lying on the road, limbs strewn among dead chickens and luggage."

Jamie grimaced. "Where did they set the mine?"

"Close to the Katiyo fork in the road. They probably hoped to take out one of the army MAP trucks. I've never seen such a mess. Nick Farham brought one of his trucks and took some of the injured to Old Umtali Mission until the ambulances could arrive from Umtali. It took the rest of the day to clear the road."

"Chris, what's the status at Katiyo?" asked Jamie. "Are the school, clinic and community center finished, and are the water stations on line?"

"Yes, yes, and yes again. There are still a few loose ends to tie up, but the security fence is complete, the bunkers on each corner fully sandbagged, the internal roads cut and latrines dug."

"That's great. What else?"

"There are three school rooms that will each accommodate about fifty kids, and three more under construction. The temporary store is ready to be occupied by local storekeepers, but they'll just have to bring their own shelving with them. Jack Cloete was very particular about drainage ditches so that the PV won't flood during heavy rain. He's a genius when it comes to understanding the lay of the land and what should go where. You'll like what you see."

Jamie nodded. "Chris, let's head for Katiyo and take a look. Angus, can you and Jack spend the rest of the week fine tuning any final construction changes. This is our first PV and we want the locals not only to feel safe, but to feel that this will be a home away from home."

Jamie paused, needing them both to understand what he was trying to accomplish. "I'm more concerned about the hearts and minds of the people. If they understand why we're doing this, and they feel safe, the impact of this move will spread throughout the valley. It will make the Simangane move much easier. From then on my hope is that the terrorist successes and influence will diminish, and the people will be more eager to move when it's their time."

* * *

"Watch out, Jamie!" Chris shouted.

Jamie looked up, but it was too late. The rocket exploded just inches from him, its blast a thunderous roar. Then darkness.

Jamie bolted upright in bed. It was early Friday morning. Thunder crashed and vivid flashes of lightning lit up the room through Jamie's bedroom window. He swung his feet over the side of the bed and sat up. Looking out the small window Jamie could see the rain coming down in sheets. He could also hear it beating down on the asbestos cement roof. There would be no more sleep tonight.

Jamie sat on the edge of the bed thinking and wondering how the people of Katiyo would react to being moved. *We have to explain to them just why they are being brought into the PV. It is so important that we communicate to them that this is about saving lives and restoring freedom to the Valley.*

Another crack of thunder made him jump. Jamie ran his fingers through his hair and his thoughts turned to security. The vedettes were arriving today and he had given instructions for them to be driven directly to Katiyo. One Browning machine gun and six Garden Boys were coming with them. The Browning and two Garden Boys would stay at Ruda Keep; the other four Garden Boys could go to Katiyo, one for each of the defensive bunkers.

The storm quieted. Jamie dressed and crept into the dining room, careful not to disturb Chris and Angus McDonald. It was only 0530 and it was still dark outside. Most of the camp was sleeping, but he could hear Willie moving around in the kitchen. He settled back into a chair and turned his thoughts to a new problem. He was reminded that the ZANLA political commissars were using the Bible to indoctrinate the people. They would read from sections of the Old Testament telling them it was God's will for them to kill all those who did not support the cause. Jamie opened his Bible and flipped through the pages. He needed to familiarize himself with the passages being used and also to find passages he could use to counter these teachings. Jamie sighed, nothing jumped out at him.

Willie shuffled in with the tea. The apron he was wearing had once been white, but now was a dirty grey, with evidence of many past meals. His trousers were dirty and ragged, but even more disturbing, was the strong smell of wood smoke and body odor that accompanied him. Jamie caught his breath; he must remember to bring some Lifebuoy carbolic soap on his next trip. He'd talk to Corporal Dande who was in charge of discipline at the Keep. Maybe he could get Willie to clean up.

"Can you spare a cup?"

Jamie turned to see Chris slump into the chair next to him. His hair was tousled and all he wore was a pair of faded rugby shorts.

"That thunder last night kept me awake. I kept jumping up thinking we were being attacked. The flashes of lightning didn't help."

Jamie smiled. "That makes two of us."

Promptly at 0800 Jamie heard the rumble of heavy trucks pull into the keep.

Nick Farham and Mike Willis joined Jamie in the ops room. The men wasted little time in pleasantries before Jamie turned the conversation to the business of the day. He looked around to make sure no one else was within ear shot, and quietly shut the door.

"The PV will be ready Saturday. We're planning to make the move Monday morning. There'll be the usual carousing and beer drinking Sunday afternoon, but the people will have sobered up by morning."

The men gathered around the large table in the middle of the room, studying the aerial photos.

"The PV can accommodate nearly three thousand people, or about four hundred families."

Nick and Mike spent some time discussing how they would divide the area up between their various troops. When everyone was satisfied with the plan Jamie turned to them.

"One important stipulation; make sure you get Headman Katiyo to the PV early. He'll be responsible for allocating spaces within the residential area. Try to keep the people together by kraal or village head, as some kraals are made up of several villages."

"I'll take care of Katiyo," responded Mike. "I've been to his kraal several times and will make him my personal assignment. You'll have him there by 0900 hours."

Jamie felt a surge of confidence as he looked at these two men. He smiled as he shook their hands. "I think we're about to see some changes in the Honde, gentlemen."

* * *

Early the next morning, Jamie was headed for Katiyo with Sergeant Sama. The gates were locked so he drove down to the construction camp where Chris had bedded down with Jack and Andre for the night. It was a hive of activity, with tents being taken down and the camp being packed up, ready for the construction crew to move to Simangane later that day.

"Good morning, sir," said Chris as he emerged from under a tarpaulin that was used to cover the dining area. "You're just in time for breakfast.

Jack sat back on the chair, replete after a very satisfying meal, holding a large mug of hot tea. He wiped his mouth with his hand and belched loudly. "Well, the PV is as ready as it's ever going to be. Andre and his crew have done a great job. We'll be heading out to Simangane later this morning. So, when's the big move taking place?"

"We'll begin preparations tomorrow. We have some National Service Vedettes arriving today and they'll be in charge of security. We're not discussing the actual move date with anyone at this time, but it'll be soon."

Jack laughed. "You don't trust anyone. I know you well." He sighed, "I expect you'll want me to stay over this weekend and keep an eye on things."

"You guessed right, Jack. I'll need you here tomorrow night and for the next few days. You can help get those vedettes settled in. Chris will be spending the next few days here as well. Because of the need for absolute security I'll announce our plans each day from now on."

Jamie turned to Angus. "Come with me. While Jack and Andre oversee the breaking of camp, we'll check out the PV. I just want to make sure we have everything in place before the construction crew leaves."

Before Jamie and Angus had a chance to start their inspection a Hino truck came lumbering into the PV and stopped near the A-frames. Four vedettes were sitting on sandbags in the back of the truck. Their khaki uniforms were creased from the heat and the long drive, but they proudly wore their Internal Affairs red berets, pulled down well over their right ears.

The first to jump off the back of the truck was someone Jamie instantly recognized. The young man was tall and slim with dark hair, bright blue eyes, and a ready smile. He landed lightly on his left leg and then steadied himself with the aluminum right leg that protruded conspicuously from his shorts. As he turned to Jamie his face beamed and he saluted smartly. "Sir, it's great to see you."

"Garth! What a surprise. It's been a long time."

"Yes, sir. Six years since that memorable trip in Tjolotjo. I've had many a free beer telling that story of how the elephants chased us."

Jamie laughed, remembering that time five years ago when Garth had come to the western border on a field trip. Garth had been sitting in the back of the open Landrover when a herd of elephants had been angered by the sight of them and charged, almost catching up to them. Garth had lost his leg in an automobile accident so it was not just a case of jumping out and running for it.

* * *

They were traversing the western border road, battling through heavy sand in four wheel drive. As they passed a herd of elephant the lead matriarch took an obvious dislike to the Landrover and charged them. She had the advantage and was gaining rapidly. Garth was sitting in the open back watching in dismay as the elephant closed the gap, her ears back and trunk curled between her front legs. Jamie could still remember looking back at Garth's panicked expression. When she was less than five yards behind them the Landrover reached firmer ground and gradually pulled away. Jamie could still remember the expression on Garth's face when he pulled to a stop half a mile down the road.

* * *

"Welcome to Katiyo and the Honde Valley," Jamie reached out and shook Garth's hand warmly. "Once a peaceful tranquil spot, but now somewhere you are guaranteed no boredom and plenty of action."

"You sure know how to give a person an exciting time so I'm prepared for anything," laughed Garth.

"Who are these other fine young men? Would you like to introduce your fellow vedettes,"

"Sir, this is Jack, Adam and Joe. We all went through IANS training together at Chikurubi. This is our third assignment."

"Now I'd like you all to meet Chris DeVries, my district officer, and Angus McDonald, agricultural officer. You'll be working closely with all three of us. Let's get you settled in. Collect your things and Chris will show you the ropes. You'll be based in that first A-frame. Later I'll come in to brief you on just what I expect of you and what we hope to accomplish here at Katiyo."

"By the way, sir, we brought six Garden Boys with us and a Browning .303 machine gun. Where do you want them?"

Jamie pointed behind him. "I hadn't forgotten those. Offload four of the Garden Boys here, plus a supply of powder and shot. The other two Garden Boys are going to Ruda with the Browning."

"Ah, sir, can't we keep the Browning?" Garth asked hopefully.

"Afraid not, Garth. You'll have to make do with the Garden Boys. Ruda is going to remain a prime target—we've already faced one major attack."

* * *

The vedettes were all seated on the floor in the ops room looking expectantly at Jamie. Chris and Angus sat to one side, it was important for them to hear the briefing too.

"This is the Honde Valley—the hottest spot in the country, where terrorists have been in virtual control of the valley for the past nine months. This is going to change and you are going to be part of making it happen." Jamie paused.

"Excuse me, sir, but will we be going out on patrol?" asked Joe.

"Sorry. No patrols at this time. Your place is here, to protect the people in the PV. Let me try to explain the principles of terrorist warfare. ZANLA is the Liberation Army of ZANU, the Zimbabwe African National Union, headed up by Robert Mugabe. Their tactics are taken straight from the *Little Red Book* written by Mao Tse-tung, the master of guerilla warfare."

The vedettes looked intently at Jamie.

"Our job is to isolate the terrorists from the people, to protect the people, to provide them a safe haven in the PVs, and to win their confidence." Jamie pointed to the map on the wall. "To do this we'll have to move the entire population of the Honde into seven PVs, build a *cordon sanitaire*, or No-Go area, along the border, and step up military activity to counter terrorist activities." Jamie paused. "It will be your responsibility to train militia to protect the PVs, and deny the terrorists access to the people. This is the first step in any hearts and minds war—safety and protection."

Jamie watched the four vedettes. Their eyes were wide with apprehension, yet they nodded their heads.

"Until recently, and even now, between ten and thirty locals have been brutally murdered, raped, and mutilated every week. This must change."

More head nodding.

"This is our first PV and it sets the standard for the rest of the program. Within the next few days, we'll be moving over four hundred families here, into Katiyo. Initially your job will be to help the people settle in, to begin to win their confidence as protectors, to make sure that the gates are closed and locked at sunset, and to ensure that the people understand the basic rules of life in a PV. They will be allowed to return to their villages and fields during the day, tend to their herds of goats, cattle, and sheep and to take care of their fields, but they must be back in the PV by sunset. Is that understood?"

More nods of affirmation.

"Now comes the hearts and minds stuff which is so critical. We have built a school and a clinic. We have also set aside space for a business center where local entrepreneurs can build their stores, put up grinding mills etc. I'm also arranging for visits by a medical orderly who will tend to the sick once a week. Your job, and this is critical, is to win over the confidence of the people, to be seen and perceived as friends and protectors—individuals they can trust with their lives. You are to be visible—that means wearing your red berets and not floppy hats. Never act as though you are more important than any of the locals, be willing to get down and dirty as you help men and women with their tasks. Be perceived as individuals in authority, but compassionate and with a concern for everyone. By that, I mean men, women, children, and especially the elderly. Learn the basics of the language which is Shona, especially greetings for both morning and evening. I will be testing each of you when I visit to see what progress you've made."

"Sir, I brought a book on Shona with me. Who would be the best person to teach us?" asked Garth.

"Find one of the local teachers, and also build a friendship with headman Katiyo. You may find him a little awkward and difficult to begin with, but as soon as he senses you respect him and want to help him and his people he will warm to you. I believe that within a month Katiyo will be a very different place to when the people first move in. Currently nobody greets us, and the children run away when they see anyone in uniform." Jamie noticed the intense look in Garth's eyes. "As you build trust and gain respect the atmosphere will change. Then you will understand what I mean by winning the hearts and minds of the people. Katiyo will become a safe haven, the children will be playing, and laughter will abound instead of cries of despair. Most of all, you'll enjoy what you were sent to do, and learn something about a people who have suffered a great deal."

"Sir, you can rely on us to do the job." After a pause Garth turned a querying look to Jamie. "What happens if we're attacked?"

"That's what you were trained for at Chikurubi. Remember to protect the PV and the people at all costs. Yes, you'll probably face an attack, so be prepared. Find the right men for a local militia and make sure you get them trained. That's a priority. Chris will help you with the final selection process." Jamie looked at the eager faces. "I'll be sending you twelve G-3 rifles and plenty of ammunition. Also make sure that you practice, and train some of the militia on the Garden Boys. I can tell you from personal experience that they are very effective. Are there any more questions?"

"Fully understood, sir" said Garth. "You can depend on us."

"Good, tomorrow will be a busy day. Get yourselves settled in, and listen to Chris. I'm heading back to Ruda."

Chapter Ten

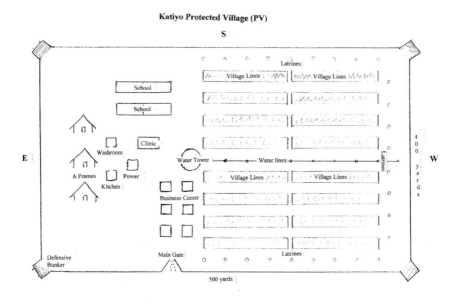

Katiyo Protected Village (PV)

Mike Willis motioned his men to move forward. He glanced at his watch. It was early Monday morning, 0430 hours. They were positioned on a ridge overlooking Headman Katiyo's village. It was still dark, but

126

Mike wanted all his men in position around the village before first light when they would actually move in. He had four men with him and the rest of the company were all positioned near other villages in the sector that he had been allocated. Everyone had been thoroughly briefed and Mike's four men moved silently into their pre-assigned positions. They had arrived on the ridge the previous evening, just before dusk, and bedded down during the night. There were sixteen huts in the village and Mike anticipated there would be fifty to sixty people, including the women, children, and the elderly. Reaching a granary hut on one side of the village, Mike lay prone with his FN cocked. Now it was just a matter of waiting for dawn to break.

At 0540 the dawn brightened the sky in the east. *Just another few minutes*, thought Mike.

* * *

Far to the south, they crossed the border at first light. There were fifteen in the group and Josiah led them at a quick pace. The Korean instructors advised finding more recruits. Over twenty of their comrades had been killed in various contacts with the Rhodesian soldiers over the past few weeks, another twenty-seven were recovering from wounds.

Josiah wiped the sweat from the back of his neck. He spat to his right and cursed. *These government pigs are getting smart. They are going to make new camps like they built in Mt. Darwin and now it will be difficult to travel through the northern part of the valley and through the mountain pass.* He thought over his conversation with Rex Nhongo several days earlier. Nhongo was enraged that their supply routes had been cut. His threatening words still rang through Josiah's mind.

Josiah, why have you let the soldiers push you back? Don't you want to be a commander? I am counting on you. The Honde is our most important supply route and the paths must be kept open. We must find carriers and food. Nearly half your comrades have been killed or wounded. Find more men, even boys, and make the people understand that we are the new power. Do whatever is necessary, but do not fail me.

He would not disappoint Rex Nhongo. He kept the group off the main paths and followed a gulley that would lead them to a banana plantation overlooking the school. He had been this way before, but in the last month had been preoccupied with the northern part of the valley. Now it was time to focus on the south, closer to chief Mutasa's village.

Josiah and the comrades climbed a ridge and lay prone. Josiah's eyes skimmed over parts of the main Honde road, villages, and a business center. There was Tikwiri School, about a half a mile to the west. This was the target.

Tikwiri was a large school. It was the only one in the area to defy the call for all schools to close.

Motioning to his comrades, they moved forward over the ridge into a belt of buffalo grass. Rising to their feet, they cautiously made their way towards the banana plantation, a few hundred yards above the school. It was still early, but in another two hours the sun would shine brightly on the school grounds.

* * *

"Now!" said Mike, leaping to his feet and running towards the largest hut. Banging on the door, he shouted, "Open up."

There were sounds of startled movement from inside. The door to the hut cracked open and a man with grizzled grey hair wedged his face in the opening and then stepped out. He was wearing an old pair of black pants, but no shirt. He appeared frightened and confused. *Why are the soldiers here?*

"Are you Headman Katiyo?" Mike asked in Shona.

"Yes, I am Katiyo." His voice shook. "What do you want?"

"Wake up your people. We are going to move to the new village today and nobody stays behind."

Headman Katiyo's eyes dropped to Mike's FN. He glanced suspiciously at the other troopers who had entered the kraal. "Why do you come here? What have we done?"

"You and your people are being moved to the wire village for your own protection. Wake up your people now and get dressed. Nobody is to leave the village. You can use the latrine, but you are to pack up your belongings and we will be leaving here in one hour."

The old man shook his head in bewilderment. *Leave now!*

"We will make two trips today so that you can carry all your personal belongings, and some food, to the new village."

One by one, the commotion caused other hut doors to open. Men first, then a few women, and several small children, came out of the darkness of their huts, many wiping the sleep from their eyes. The dawn was getting brighter and Mike could see a faint blush of pink and orange on the far horizon.

Mike shouted aloud in Shona so that they could all hear. "Listen to me. Your families and children have been murdered by those who call themselves, *boys*. These are your own children who have been given guns and told to come back and kill, even their own parents. Today you are moving to a place where you will be safe. There will be no more killings. You must listen carefully to everything I say."

There were murmurings and mumblings from some of the people and one of the women started to wail.

"Get dressed and pack up your blankets, your clothes, your pots, pans, and some food. We will be leaving in one hour and will go to the new village with the wire fence. You are to stay together and keep your children with you."

One old crone came up to Mike waving her hands at him. "I have no husband. Where will I stay?"

"Everyone in Headman Katiyo's area is being moved today and there are many soldiers in the area helping other people to move. When you get to the village Headman Katiyo will find places for you to build temporary shelters until you can rebuild your huts. The elderly people will stay behind at the new village and the rest of you will come back here with us to carry more of your belongings and food. Do you understand what I have told you?"

There was a lot more murmuring and another old woman came wagging her finger at Mike, shouting angrily at him, "Why are you making us leave our homes? We don't want to leave. This is where my children were born and where my fields are."

"Mama," said Mike. "I understand how you feel, but too many people have been killed and too many of your children are missing or dead. This is the only way we can stop the killing and protect you."

There were more angry shouts from the women. The men were

more subdued, but Mike could still see the anger in their faces and gestures.

"I understand you don't want to leave your homes and your fields, but beginning on Wednesday, you will be allowed to come back to your villages and collect more of your belongings. You will also be able to come to hoe your fields and tend to your gardens during the day, but you must be back in the wire village at night or the terrorists will find you and kill you."

There was the crackle of gunfire from the forest to their south. One of the troopers grasped his left shoulder and dived towards the eaves of one of the huts. Mike's men were quick to respond and took up defensive positions in the village. A short exchange of fire continued for about three minutes and then it was apparent the attackers had disappeared.

"That must have been a scouting party. They were probably camped just the other side of the village," yelled Mike. "Close in on me."

There was not a soul to be seen. The people had either fled back into their huts or scurried into the forest.

"Come out. You are safe now," shouted Mike. No response. "The boys are gone; you can come out."

Gradually first one, then another of the men appeared, followed by some older women.

Next to return was Headman Katiyo who was waving his fist and shouting at Mike. "We will all be killed. The boys are angry and will return with many more of our children to do bad things to us."

An older woman came out of a hut and threw some dirty water at one of the soldiers, screaming at him at the top of her voice.

For the next thirty minutes Mike was busy arguing and threatening the people. Finally, with Headman Katiyo in control, the people quieted down.

There was more murmuring and a few cries from the children. Headman Katiyo stood silently. He seemed to study his people, or perhaps mull over the words of the soldiers. Mike and the men stood, motionless with guns cocked, as only their eyes swept over the crowd, scanning for any movement out of place.

Mike was on the radio to Nick. "Had a spot of bother with a

scouting party. One minor casualty our end, but still mobile. Faced a lot of resistance from the locals, but appears to be under control. Over."

"Four seven six this is eight seven zero. Reading you loud and clear. Faced similar resistance from half the villages, especially from the women. Will complete the move as planned, but may be later than expected. Keep me abreast of any changes. See you at the RV point. Out."

* * *

Josiah crouched low. The sun shone brightly onto the school grounds. Not a cloud in the sky. Children began to arrive, mostly carrying their books in cloth bags. The teachers were already moving around the school and one of the teachers brought out a soccer ball so that the boys could play. Other children ran around and some played hopscotch, a game the white missionaries had taught the teachers.

Timing was critical. There had been reports of large numbers of soldiers in the northern part of the valley, but no activity this far south. The telephone line to the valley ran alongside the main Honde road.

Josiah leaned over and whispered to Enoch. "Take two men and go and cut the telephone lines. Do this at midday and not before. When you return we will attack. Take your time as it is still early."

"I understand, comrade Josiah. We will leave when the children are in their school rooms so that there will be less chance of anyone seeing us."

It was midday and the sun was shining brilliantly overhead. The children were all in their classrooms and it was a very peaceful scene below the banana plantation.

* * *

Headman Katiyo raised his voice. "Listen to the soldiers. We do not have any choice. They are right. We have lost many of our children. Even my two brothers are dead. Look what they did to Headman Simangane. Let us do as they say. Get dressed and get your things together."

The crowd was no longer restless. The women quieted down to listen. With the old man's few words, a new awareness seemed to cast a hush over what moments before had been a flurry of commotion and disgruntled murmurings. His message had taken root.

Quietly, the people went back into their huts to get dressed and collect their things. Some of the children came out eating cakes of dried maize meal—probably left over from their previous evening meal. Mike released a breath as he felt his own tension dissipate. He motioned for the other men to put down their guns and sit while they waited. One of the women came out of Katiyo's hut and approached them. She carried enamel cups with hot, sweet tea which she presented to Mike. She curtseyed and left. Mike thanked her and called his men over to drink the welcome tea.

The sun was now shining through the trees and dew sparkled on the leaves and thatch of the huts. Mike thought back to the attack they had fought off at Katiyo PV and what Headman Katiyo had just said. Three of the dead terrorists at Katiyo were children, probably not more than twelve or thirteen. He shook his head. The effectiveness of the indoctrination process spelled out in Mao's *Little Red Book* of guerilla warfare was baffling—these terrorists could turn even son against father and mother.

* * *

"Josiah," said Enoch. "The lines are cut."

Startled, Josiah jumped up. The three comrades had returned from behind the ridge so quietly that he had not heard their approach.

"Now is the time," said Josiah. "No teacher is to live. We have no time for sport. We must leave and cross the border as soon as possible. Use your bayonets, and only shoot if you have to. Surround the school and let us bring everyone outside to the soccer field. If anyone tries to run, catch them. Shoot them if you must."

Spreading out, they quietly moved in on the school. Their olive uniforms had dark green blotches of sweat, helping to blend with their surroundings. The comrades were armed with the latest AKs—a Chinese version with folding stocks and bayonets. Five of the comrades carried their knobkerries, clubs made from the roots of the msasa tree.

Within minutes the school was surrounded. At Josiah's signal, three comrades went up to each of the five classrooms. Simultaneously, they pushed the doors open.

Josiah was in a classroom with older children, probably between twelve and fifteen years of age.

"Sit down everyone."

The children screamed and cried, but they were too frightened to disobey.

The teacher was a well-dressed man wearing wire-framed glasses. He was seated at a table in front of a large blackboard and looked defiantly at Josiah. "What do you want? We are just here with children. This is not a government school. We belong to the mission in Umtali."

Josiah walked up to the teacher and shoved him, knocking him off his chair. The children gasped, some whimpered.

"Lie down like the dog you are." He took the butt of his AK and thrust it sharply into the teacher's neck as he tried to rise. Reversing his AK in a fluid motion, he thrust the bayonet into the man's back again and again, while the teacher cried out with his last breaths, writhing and struggling to get up. Blood flowed along the hard cement floor.

The children screamed, but remained seated. Bending down, Josiah took his bayonet and used it to flip the teacher over so that he lay looking up at him with vacant eyes, blood trickling out of his mouth. He was gone.

Josiah spun around to the children. "Go outside and do not try and run or you will be shot. My comrades will be watching you."

One by one, the children got up and obeyed. The girls cried and clung together. Some of the boys muttered to each other. Counting them Josiah could see there were forty seven children in the classroom. He herded them out to the soccer field.

"You will learn and understand," Josiah began as he walked back and forth in front of the children. "You will…"

Suddenly, a heavy woman, probably a teacher who had been visiting the latrine, came dashing from behind one of the classrooms. One of the comrades took off after her. Before she had run a hundred yards, he tripped her and she fell to the ground, screaming. The comrade reached down and grabbed the top of her dress and with one jerk ripped it from her.

"Enough," said Josiah. "No sport today. Bring her to me. The children can see what will happen to them if they try to escape."

The near naked woman, scrambling but unable to get to her feet, was dragged by her arm until she lay sputtering near the children.

"Kill her," Josiah stated, flatly.

More screams from the children.

Looking at the cowering children, "Take out the small children," He motioned with his bayonet toward the classroom he had just left. "Lock them in."

The comrades went through the children, dragging the younger ones, mostly those that looked under eight or nine years of age. They pushed them into the building. More than a hundred younger children crowded into the classroom. Josiah went inside. The children were weeping in fear.

"You will stay here until it is dark. I am leaving some of my comrades outside," he lied. "Anyone who tries to escape will be killed. Do you understand?"

There were whimpers from the children, but nobody said anything. Josiah closed the door. Taking some wire from a child's toy, he secured it shut. He had no intention of leaving any comrades behind to watch them, but they would not know that and he knew the children would be too afraid to escape through the windows.

"Separate the girls from the boys and count them," said Josiah. This took about ten minutes.

"We have fifty seven girls and forty nine boys," responded Enoch.

"Good, let us go. Keep them together, and if anyone tries to run, shoot them." He said this loud enough so that all the children could hear.

With the boys in front in one group and the girls behind in another, they set off along a path directly towards the border.

"Faster", said Josiah. "Use your bayonets to wake them up if they fall behind."

With that, the group moved at a fast pace. They had to cross the border soon, before any of the masoja arrived to track them.

* * *

"Follow me." Mike took the lead with Headman Katiyo and his people following. Mike's four men positioned themselves around the group, with one of the soldiers bringing up the rear. Stopping several times to allow two elderly women to catch up, it took just over an hour to reach their destination. At 0945 they reached the gates of the PV where two district assistants waited to direct them.

The people were apprehensive as they looked up at the chain link fence and shiny razor wire. *Was this going to be a prison?* Several hundred others from nearby villages had already gathered in the center of the PV awaiting the arrival of Headman Katiyo. He would allocate them places to build their huts in the village. People were milling around, angry, confused and shouting obscenities at the soldiers.

Garth Markham directed traffic with Corporal Dande at his side. Each family was to receive one tarpaulin and a supply of wattle poles to build their shelters.

Headman Katiyo walked slowly as he entered the PV. His eyes examined the structure warily until his gaze lit on an imposing figure striding up to him from the group of villagers. The man wore a freshly ironed khaki uniform, with red beret, and red and khaki elastic belt.

"Good morning, Headman Katiyo," Jamie Ross greeted him in Shona. "I hope you slept well and the soldiers have taken good care of you."

"I slept well if you slept well," replied Katiyo. He looked around nervously, his eyes lingering on the security fence. "Who will take care of us once the sun goes down?"

Jamie clearly understood the distrust and concern in the old headman's voice. "There are armed men who will be here to protect you. The gates are locked at sundown and the guards know how to fight. Once you and your people are settled, we will begin to train some of your own young men as guards so that they, too, can help protect your people."

Jamie handed him a sample sign, a red triangle with a black skull and crossbones, and gave him a warning.

"Do not go into areas where we have put these signs. Keep this and show it to your people. Anyone who goes beyond the signs will be in danger and could be killed."

Headman Katiyo took the sign, running his hand over it curiously as Jamie spoke.

"Now, I want you to find a place for your family first. Listen to this man," said Jamie, pointing to Garth Markham. "You and your kraal heads are to tell each family where to build their new shelters and tell them about the latrines."

"Yes, mambo. I understand," said Katiyo.

By 1700 hours, the PV was unrecognizable. A sea of brown tarpaulins, strung over wattle poles, covered the area as two thousand, two hundred and eighteen people worked to build shelters. It reminded Jamie of watching an ant colony at work through the glass walls of an ant aquarium—a highly-organized colony. Even the children worked, carrying wattle poles, setting up kitchen areas, clearing and sweeping the ground around their shelters. The first cooking fires began sending up smoke, and the breeze carried an aroma of porridge, intermixed with the occasional waft of meat roasting on open fires. By 1845 hours the sun had set, and moments later the gates were closed.

Jamie, Nick Farham, Chris, and Mike Willis sat down in the ops room just as the gates were locked. Jamie had brought a case of Coke with him.

"Well, Jamie this exercise has been challenging and we faced some resistance. Overall, however, the exercise has gone a lot more smoothly than some of us predicted," said Nick.

Jamie agreed. "I'm amazed at how little real resistance we got from the people. Yes, there was some grumbling, and a few unhappy folks at leaving their livestock behind."

"I hate to dampen your euphoria at the success of the move," replied Nick, "I just got a call that the only school open in the Honde, in the Tikwiri area, was raided this morning. They bayoneted all the teachers and rounded up over a hundred children between the ages of ten and fifteen, to take back with them for training. The younger children were left behind."

Jamie grimaced. "It seems the action is moving south."

"You're right. With the patrolling and successes we've had in the last two weeks, they're sure to shift strategies. Seventeen terrorists killed, two captured and we've virtually stopped activity along the main entry route with our *cordon sanitaire*."

Jamie leaned forward and looked at the two men. "Yes, we've a long way to go, but the fact that we're cutting off the main infiltration route will have a dramatic impact on areas to the west of us. This will have a positive impact from Inyanga to Rusape, Mrewa, Mtoko, and Mt. Darwin. None of us really know the impact we're making in this valley." Jamie paused to sip his Coke. "Six months from now we should be able to determine whether the PV program has been the success we hoped. I can't tell you how much I appreciate each of you. I'm counting on you all the way."

Mike blinked. "Look, we're in this together and today's a benchmark for the next move. Word gets around fast."

Chapter Eleven

It had been four weeks since the people had moved into Katiyo. His tour of the PV yesterday had been an emotional one and left him with a sense of wonder and pride. He had witnessed the resourcefulness and joyful hearts of a people making the best of a trying situation.

Katiyo was a community, throbbing with activity. Children ran about playing games and would stop and wave, smiling shyly. They were delighted Jamie could speak their language. He smiled as the image of Sama guarding the Leopard came to mind. This had been a sight, watching Sama shooing the curious children away with his baton and slouch hat, trying to avoid mishaps with the loaded cannons on the top of the Leopard.

Huts now lined the roads; some had been completed, their freshly thatched roofs glowing golden in the early morning sun. Women plastered while they talked and sang, taking large handfuls of thick red mud from their buckets and spreading it over wattle poles. Others smeared a paste of cow dung and water over the floors of the huts, a trick to achieve a smooth, durable surface after it had dried and hardened. The finished product would have no smell and was actually quite hygienic.

Towards the middle of the PV Jamie could see the business center. It was bustling with activity. Four stores had opened their doors, with a steady flow of women, their heads bobbing as they smiled in greeting, trying to juggle their purchases. Going inside one of the stores Jamie could see that it was stocked with bolts of colorful cotton cloth stacked up against one wall. Sugar and jam, bread, flour, and oil lined the shelves. Big sacks of maize meal and peanuts were on the floor, and bins of rice, and kapenta, the little dried fish from Lake Kariba, sat near the door. On the other side of the store, hoes, shovels, and axes were placed in piles, while bags of hard candy on the counter enticed the children.

He looked over at the school buildings. The school would be a pinnacle of hope in the community. He had no doubt that as soon as parents released their children from chores associated with the move, they would stream to the building, free from fear of terrorist abduction. Desks, chairs, and blackboards had been brought in from the old abandoned schools and sat ready for the children in the two new, large buildings. Six teachers had already volunteered to teach.

The only thing Jamie had felt was out of place on his visit was a noticeable absence of men. They returned to their old villages during the day to tend their fields and livestock. Just before sunset, they would hurry back to the PV before the gates were shut and locked— safe inside where floodlights illuminated the fence line and main gates, discouraging intruders.

The visit had given Jamie a deep sense of satisfaction. He thought of the peace and calmness amongst the people, a contrast to the fear and chaos just weeks earlier.

* * *

"You can't be serious, Alex."

A muscle in Jamie's jaw flinched and he tightened his grip on the receiver as he listened to Alex Burton's request. A vedette officer and four more vedettes were welcome, but the notion of sending a section of eight trainee IANS (Internal Affairs National Servicemen) to the Honde was senseless.

"… and you can send them out on patrol to give them a feel of the land and experience a war zone," Alex finished.

"I appreciate the officer and four vedettes," said Jamie. "But I can't accept responsibility for wet-behind-the-ears IANS. We've had no casualties thus far. I want to keep it that way. It's way too dangerous to send them out on patrol, and I really can't spare anyone to go with them."

Alex Burton sighed and shifted the phone to his other ear. "Jamie, don't worry about my guys. I'm sending an ex-RLI-instructor. He's experienced and knows the game. Just find somewhere for them to bed down, then direct them where to go."

"Alex, the area is a hot-bed of activity. Last week we fought off two attacks and one of our Leopards was ambushed. We have contacts every day. Mostly, we're fighting brainwashed kids with AKs. It's a dirty game."

Alex brushed him off. "My boys will be fine."

Jamie felt the heat rise up his neck. "Alex, I can't take responsibility for anyone not under my command. Their safety will be on your head and there's no such thing as a safe place in the Honde."

"I understand, Jamie. The responsibility rests with me. Keep them for a week and then send them back. They'll have their own transport and will arrive Thursday with the vedettes." Alex's response was laced with finality.

Jamie knew further protest was futile. The call ended, but not the gnawing anxiety in Jamie's gut. He hung up the phone and tried to shake the feeling. Everything was going well and he did not need to lose focus over a group of trainees. Closing his eyes, he leaned back in his chair and redirected his thoughts.

There was a light rap on the door. "Good morning, mambo."

Jamie sat up with a start.

Corporal Dande stood at the door greeting him with a salute and wide grin.

"Good morning, corporal. What do you need?"

The smile quickly faded as he handed Jamie the string of hand written reports that had just come in over the radio. Jamie read them.

Two European farms had been attacked in the Old Umtali Mission area and another village wiped out and burnt to the ground, just north of chief Mutasa's village. A bus hit a landmine on one of the subsidiary roads near Tikwiri with seven killed and eleven injured.

Jamie took a deep breath. He was succeeding in moving the action away from Aberfoyle, which would bode well for Alan and the people moving into Simangane, but the pressure was on for Tikwiri, Mtarazi, and Mutasa. They would have to stop the escalation of attacks in the south. He laid the report down on his desk and leaned back, looking at Dande.

"It looks like the terrorists are stepping up their attacks south of Ruda. What are the people saying?"

"Mambo, the people are very afraid. It was better for them before the soldiers moved the people into Katiyo."

"I can understand," said Jamie. "When more people are settled in protected villages the area will be safe—then we will see a change in the peoples' hearts. The terrorists are being chased from north of the Pungwe—moving south, and that is why the people are frightened. In a week we'll start a new village here at Ruda. Inform the District Assistants to keep their eyes and ears open." Jamie looked out the window. "And, corporal, let me know what the people are saying."

Corporal Dande nodded solemnly and turned to leave.

"Corporal."

"Yes, mambo?" He stopped, looking back.

"Please send Sergeant Sama. I need to talk to him."

A few minutes later Sergeant Sama walked into the room.

"Sergeant, some young recruits are arriving from Chikurubi next week to patrol the area."

"Yes, mambo. But why are they sending untrained men into the Honde? It is not safe."

"I understand. That is why I am sending you with them. I will join you later with Corporal Dande."

"Yes, mambo, but it is still not safe."

"I understand. The young recruits will arrive from Salisbury tomorrow. The next day they will be going out on patrol with their sergeant." Jamie paused. "They are coming against my recommendation, but I feel the responsibility to look out for them and that is why I am sending you with them." Jamie watched Sama's expression which told much. "Corporal Dande and I will meet with you on Friday to escort the group back to Ruda. We have much work to do before then, but with your wisdom, maybe you can keep them out of trouble."

Sama shook his head. "It is not a good plan, but yes, I will try to keep them safe."

"Sama, you are excused. I will see you in the morning," was Jamie's rather uncharacteristically terse response.

Jamie leaned over his small desk, writing down instructions for the vedettes. He occasionally looked up from his writing and tapped his pen. Next his thoughts turned to the IANS and he shook his head. *Where can I put them on patrol without getting in the way of Nick's or Mike's soldiers? Certainly not at Katiyo or Simangane. There they would be in the way, or worse, undo some of the work already complete. That leaves Ruda or Mtarazi, possibly even the western area of Ruda. Yes, the area west of Ruda and south of the Pungwe would be best.* He wrote that down. There was a lot to plan in the coming days and taking the time to plan the whereabouts and safety of eight inexperienced IANS had not been a part of it.

Picking up the microphone he called Mike Willis on the radio.

"I'd like to meet with you and Nick Farham tomorrow to go over plans for the next move. I thought it best to meet at Aberfoyle."

"It sounds like a plan," said Mike.

"They have a large, composite aerial map there and we can really see the lay of the land and pinpoint villages. I also need to check on my brother—see how they're faring. Would 1200 hours be okay for you?"

"On the dot," Mike agreed.

* * *

Alan Ross sat at his desk and peered over his glasses at Jamie. "Well, our hero of the day has arrived. I hear accolades concerning Katiyo. I hope you'll soon have some good news for me concerning our tea operations. We've been closed down for six months. Every month that we delay reopening makes it more difficult for us to get operational."

Jamie pulled up the chair Alan offered him. "Things are going a lot better than we had hoped for in the north. We've seen an escalation of violence south of the Pungwe, but nothing this side in the last two weeks."

"You're right. Both Audrey and I have been sleeping better these past few weeks. There's less tension in the air. Our maintenance workers are even laughing and joking, something I've not seen for a long while."

"Well that's good to hear," said Jamie. "My best assessment is that your tea estates should be operational by the end of June. This is not a promise, but I'll be very surprised if I'm proven wrong."

"Jamie, that's great news—far better than I thought possible. I hope you're right."

Jamie nodded, reassuringly. "I don't want you to share this information with your company directors just yet, but it would be a good idea if you developed a strategic plan for a phased build up beginning in mid-June."

Alan smiled and stood up to shake Jamie's hand.

"Remember, no promises," tempered Jamie.

The sound of a MAP truck interrupted their conversation and Jamie checked his watch. That must be Nick Farham. "Thanks for letting us use your boardroom. Your aerial photo composite is much better than what we're issued through the government. It'll make planning the relocation exercise so much easier."

"My pleasure," said Alan. "Go and meet with your military counterparts."

The division of villages for the Simangane move went quickly as both Nick and Mike knew the ropes. They decided on a Sunday morning move as the people would not be expecting them—lulled by the Saturday afternoon beer drinks.

* * *

Josiah and Enoch walked down the river from the guerilla camp with its hustle and bustle, so they could talk.

Josiah threw a rock into the darkness and cursed. "It is not going well. Our people are complaining. The masoja are everywhere north of the Pungwe. The comrades are too frightened to use our paths through the mountains and along the Pungwe River."

Enoch did not respond. He sensed that Josiah was thinking.

Josiah lay back on the damp ground and stared at the moon as he chewed on a piece of grass. "Comrade, the news is not good. These wire villages they are building are the same ones they built in Mt. Darwin. The locals are not willing to help us anymore."

Enoch snapped his head toward Josiah and burst out, "That is so. Last week five of our comrades were killed by the masoja they call RAR." He picked up a stick and began to break it into small pieces. "We destroyed the village of a sellout, we blew up one of their buses, but still work on the wire village continues. Now, even our comrades, especially the young ones, are complaining and causing trouble."

Josiah rolled over on his stomach and propped up on his elbows, looking at Enoch. He smiled and spoke with a poise that continued to get under Enoch's skin. "Yes, our attack on their base at Ruda failed. I hear that none of their people were killed and yet one of our comrades died from the iron they shot at us out of the guns that speak fire. Even now, another lies dying from wounds in his stomach." Josiah spat. "Our yellow friends told us that their rockets would destroy the base at Ruda, but today the flag still flies and they laugh at us. Tell me, comrade Enoch, what do the spirits say?"

Enoch slumped with resignation against a tree trunk, answering flatly. "We have sent word to the great swikiro, Nehandina. She tells us that we must first kill Chinyerere and destroy his spirit. Our informers have failed us. We never know which road he will travel and our comrades have lain in vain alongside the road, only to see local peasants pass by." He turned his gaze to Josiah. "Who is this 'Chinyerere' who causes us so much trouble?"

Josiah sat up and clamped his lips around a cigarette. He flicked his lighter. The brief orange glow added a speck of diversity to the blackness as Josiah took his first draw. He inhaled, drawing the smoke deeply into his lungs.

"It was my grandfather who first told me of Chinyerere. He rode his horse through the warriors of my great grandfather, Mambo Makoni. He carried no gun. Only his spirit was with him. My great grandfather's warriors were frightened; they refused to do battle with the farmers, the white pigs." Josiah paused. "My great grandfather would not give up, so Chinyerere came back with his masoja and hung him from a tree outside the cave where he was hiding. Even today, there is talk of the spirit of Chinyerere. Now it is his muzukuru, his grandson, who is causing us much trouble. Our radio has promised the people we will destroy Chinyerere. But we have not destroyed him and now his soldiers are laughing at us."

Enoch leaned closer to Josiah, straining to see his expression in the darkness. He had known from the start there was something Josiah was not telling him. He was too calm, almost smug. "Ah, but you are very clever, comrade Josiah. You must have a plan to kill this man and his spirit."

Josiah gloated. "Yes, Enoch, I have a plan. Chinyerere and his spirit will fail. I have an informer. He lives in the camp they call Mutasa."

Enoch was all ears. *How could Josiah have an informer in their own camp?*

Josiah sat in a few seconds of silence. He licked his thumb and index finger and snuffed out the remaining faint glow on the end of the cigarette stub. A faint *fizz* broke the hush. Josiah enjoyed the sound, as if it were the extinguishing of Chinyerere's spirit. He flicked the stub into the darkness.

"He works on the tractors they use to fix the roads. We have his two sons and daughter here at Pungwe camp. He has been warned, if he does not cooperate, we will send their heads back to him in a basket. We have learned this Chinyerere leaves the camp at Mutasa to go back to his family in Harare. Each time he returns it is early on a Monday morning, while the grass is still wet with dew, and before the cock crows. This will be our chance to destroy him."

A knowing smile spread across Enoch's lips. "Ah, I knew you had a plan. You are clever. An informer in their camp is a great advantage."

"Yes, he is to send word next time Chinyerere leaves for Harare."

"How can this happen?" asked Enoch.

"He will send a message through Mambo Mutasa who is his uncle. That is when we will strike. It will be too dangerous to plan an ambush that far from the border, but we have many tools and weapons we can use to destroy this man. Once Chinyerere is dead, the people will rejoice and the wire villages will fail."

Enoch returned his gaze to the dark expanse. Occasionally, he looked sideways at Josiah with a fascinated respect.

"You are the cleverest of all our leaders. The spirit of Nehandina is with you—with her we cannot fail.

* * *

Jamie sat at a table, absorbed in plans for the upcoming move. The sound of a Leopard interrupted his thoughts. He looked out the window to see the lanky figure of Agricultural Officer Angus McDonald lumbering into the office, grinning as he lugged a large box which he placed on the table.

Chris walked in just as they opened the goody box.

Jamie glanced around to make sure they were alone and lowered his voice. "The sweep will be on Sunday. The locals are expecting it on Monday, like Katiyo, but we'll catch them off guard while they're recovering from their Saturday beer drinking. We need to keep this quiet. If they're forewarned, they'll take to the hills and we'll have a heck of a job rounding them up."

"You've got it. But what about the IANS?" It was obvious Chris was still concerned about them.

"They have a staff sergeant and I'm sending Sergeant Sama with them. I plan to join them with Corporal Dande on the last leg of their patrol."

* * *

The lights were just being turned out at Elim Mission and Peter McCann closed the door to his home. He would be just in time to catch the eight o' clock news. "I'm home," he shouted.

"Just putting the children to bed, honey, responded his wife, Sandra. "I'll be with you as soon as we've finished prayers."

On his way to kiss the children goodnight Peter McCann heard a loud banging on the front door. Turning he went to open the door and was surprised to see a man outside holding a gun in his hand. The man prodded McCann aside with his gun and entered the house. Seven other men pushed in after him. One of the men was half carried and half dragged by two companions. Fresh blood oozed through a dirty bandage tied around his upper leg. The men carried the wounded man over to the couch.

Peter McCann was in shock. These must be guerillas. They all carried weapons and were wearing a motley collection of olive uniforms, heavily stained with mud and sweat. The leader wore a peaked cap with a red star roughly embroidered on the front. He was of medium build and had a scraggly beard.

"You will help our wounded comrade. Fetch your doctor."

"We have no doctor, only a nurse who tends our clinic," responded Peter McCann. "What is your name?"

"No names. Just fetch your nurse."

The commotion had woken the children and Sandra entered the room with little Joyce hiding behind her. Sandra screamed when she saw the weapons, but one of the comrades stepped up to her and put his hand over her mouth.

Peter McCann was in shock. "Don't hurt my wife and my children. Please. Just leave them alone. I will fetch our nurse."

Josiah turned. "Just get the nurse. Your children will be safe."

Peter McCann flew out the door and down the steps. It was just two hundred yards to the single women's quarters where Sister Catherine lived with two other women. Panting, he banged on the door till it was opened by a startled looking young woman. Gasping for breath, "Where is Catherine? I need her now."

Sister Catherine appeared. She was still dressed in her nurse's uniform with a starched white cap perched on the back of her head. "Peter, what do you want? It's late."

"Please come with me, but bring some bandages and surgical instruments. There are armed guerillas in our house and one of them is wounded. They are holding Sandra and the children and I need your help."

"Just give me a minute. I'll be right back."

Still panting, Peter McCann waited at the door with Sister Mary who was holding her hand to her mouth and trying to hold back her tears."

In a few minutes Sister Catherine appeared with a bag of medical supplies.

"Come with me. Please hurry."

The two left at a run for the McCann home, with Sister Catherine struggling to keep up with Peter.

The front door was still open and Peter burst inside, followed by Sister Catherine. She immediately took stock of the situation, seeing seven armed men watching her and an eighth man lying on the couch with a bloody, bandaged leg. Moving over to the couch she knelt down on the carpet and began to remove the bandages. "Peter, can you please bring me a basin of boiling water and a waste basket to put these soiled rags in."

Peter watched her. She was so professional, and appeared unperturbed by the presence of the guerillas, as she took a pair of scissors and cut away the bandages and bloodied pant leg. "Sandra, take the children to the bedroom and stay there with them. I'll boil some water and help Sister Catherine."

Josiah watched them both. He looked up as Sandra took little Joyce by the hand and led her back to the bedroom. The little girl reminded Josiah of his little Sister, Mufara. She had been only six, when he was taken, but still he remembered her pudgy face, all covered with porridge after the morning meal.

A few minutes later Peter returned with a basin of boiling water and an empty pail to put the soiled rags in.

"Peter," said Catherine, "I'm going to need your help. I have to remove a bullet and I need you to hold the leg still. Can one of these men please hold our friend down while I operate, as I don't have any anesthetic?"

"I will help," responded Josiah. "What do you want me to do?"

"Just hold his arms against his body and keep him still."

Josiah moved over to do as he had been told and Sister Catherine placed a bandage between the wounded guerilla's teeth. "Bite down on the bandage. It will help," she told the wounded man. She took a syringe and injected some morphine directly into a vein and immediately the wounded man calmed down.

With gentle skill Sister Catherine took a clean scalpel, dipped it in the boiling water and then began to cut into the bullet hole in his thigh. Holding the scalpel with her left hand she took a pair of forceps and began to probe for the bullet. The man gave a muffled scream but Josiah and Peter held him down.

Triumphantly, Sister Catherine removed the forceps holding a bloody bullet. "It's out. The worst is over." She then took a bottle of Iodine and poured it in the wound, and the man screamed again. Covering the wound with a gauze pad she gently bandaged his leg.

Josiah turned to Sister Catherine. "You did well. Now you are spared." Turning to Peter McCann, "We want a place to stay the night.

"You can't stay here. The children will be too frightened. You must leave now. Maybe soldiers are following you and we don't want them to find you at the mission."

"You are right. We will leave, but don't tell anyone we have been here. Comrades, come. Help our wounded friend. We have a long way to travel."

Two of the comrades went to assist the wounded man, who was still under the influence of the morphine, and could not walk unassisted. The eight comrades left and Peter McCann watched them fade into the darkness.

"Sister Catherine, stay here. Don't leave. It isn't safe. I'll wait an hour and then call the police. Traveling with a wounded man they won't get far tonight and will never reach the border by daylight."

An hour later Peter McCann picked up the phone to call the Umtali Police Station.

Chapter Twelve

It was Friday and the midday sun beat down fiercely. "Come on, move it. You're like a bunch of old women. You think we have all day?"

Jamie looked at the young IANS as the short, stocky man wearing the stripes of a staff sergeant dropped out of the Hino truck, slammed the door to the cab, and continued to bellow. He reminded Jamie of a bulldog growling at a litter of lanky-legged, quivering puppies. An older vedette officer jumped lightly to the ground from the back of the truck while the rest of the men awkwardly gathered their belongings.

As predicted, the convoy had pulled up at noon. A Hino truck transporting IANS and vedettes was traveling just behind the escort Rhino. There were another ten trucks behind, heavily laden with wire, poles, cement, and asbestos sheeting, ready for delivery to the next PV site—Pungwe.

Jamie greeted the new arrivals and gave instructions to the Police Reservist in charge of the convoy. He turned to see the staff sergeant marching toward him. The man stopped in front of Jamie and saluted stiffly.

"Staff Sergeant Greg Ryan, sir. Reporting with a contingent of IANS," his voice still magnified, but tempered a bit for Jamie. He motioned to a well-built, dark haired young man. "This is Vedette Officer James Trenham, with his four vedettes."

Jamie returned their salutes, smiling. "Good to have you. Your men can stretch their legs and get situated. There are refreshments inside."

It was easy to tell the four experienced vedettes from the less confident IANS. The vedettes wore khakis, sure of themselves, and unaffected by the verbal torrent as they moved into formation smartly behind James Trenham. The IANS were dressed in camo with floppy hats, and obviously unnerved as they followed suit.

Jamie felt a twinge of sympathy. *They are just kids, barely out of school. Some of them don't look old enough to shave.*

Jamie turned to Angus McDonald who watched, amused. "Angus, I'd appreciate it if you gave the IANS and Sergeant Ryan an overview of the Honde. It'll prep them for my detailed briefing when I return."

"Sure thing—after their ears stop ringing," he said, grinning. "I'll have Corporal Dande join me. He knows the area well."

Jamie turned to Vedette Officer James Trenham and shook his hand. "You must have had a grueling trip sitting on top of those sandbags. Not the most comfortable ride, but it's good to have you. Since you're an officer, you'll be stationed here at Ruda. I'll be relying on you to take charge of the office and oversee the operations and communications in the area. I understand that your term of duty is for three months so you'll get a good feel for the Honde during that time. The rest of the vedettes are only here for six weeks and they'll be stationed at Simangane. Who is your senior vedette?"

"That would be Ensign Russell Winning, sir," replied James, motioning towards a young man.

Jamie walked over to the group of vedettes and returned their salute. "Good to have you." He stood silent for a few minutes, his eyes resting on each of the young men. He smiled. "We're leaving for Simangane shortly. That's where you'll be based for the next six weeks. Vedette Officer Trenham will remain here at Ruda to direct operations and you, Ensign Winning, will take your orders from District Officer Chris DeVries and Agricultural Officer Angus McDonald."

Russell Winning interjected. "Sir, may I ask what our duties will be there?" The ensign reminded Jamie of himself at that age, impatient and eager to get started on his assignment.

"I'll brief you fully when we get there. In the meantime, take a look around. This is the center of our operations in the Honde. Not the most imposing place, but we beat off a terrorist attack a couple of weeks ago with only very minor casualties. You can see the blast craters near the back wall. Two of their rockets barely missed us. Fortunately for you, where you're going, there's no way they can bring up their mobile rocket launchers. You may be attacked with RPG anti-tank grenades, but your PV bunkers are well fortified."

They set off happily to look around, their eyes sparkling at the prospect of real action.

* * *

Thirty minutes later they were on the road. The hot sun had disbursed all evidence of a passing afternoon shower, and thick dust enveloped the trucks and everyone in them. Jamie headed toward Simangane with the truck of vedettes following close behind. He felt it would be fairly safe. The terrorists appeared to have moved south, but there was never any certainty. He prayed there weren't any terrorists in the immediate vicinity as the cloud of dust they were kicking up would be visible for miles.

Suddenly Jamie's thoughts were interrupted by a shout from Sama.

"Up ahead. Watch out!"

Jamie slammed on the brakes and the Leopard came to a shuddering halt. Ahead was the burned-out frame of an old Bedford truck. Wisps of smoke still rose from the remains. Looking around Jamie could see no signs that the terrorists were still in the area. Cocking his Uzi, he cautiously slipped out of the Leopard and silently motioned for the vedettes, watching wide-eyed, to stay in the truck. As he neared the wreckage he saw the remains of a man's body sprawled out beside the truck. Jamie grimaced and Sama stifled a gag as they looked at the badly mangled body.

"Mambo, there is nothing we can do. He has been dead for some time."

Jamie headed for the truck. "We'll call this in to Umtali as soon as we reach Simangane. We'd better not stick around here." He signaled for the vedettes to follow and got back in the Leopard. The Leopard leapt forward and the engine roared as it picked up speed, the truck with vedettes following behind.

Jamie parked the Leopard in front of an A-frame and walked back toward the vedettes, who were already throwing their gear down, climbing off the truck.

"Well, chaps. This is it—home for the next six weeks. Unload your things and meet me in the A-frame ops room in ten minutes." Jamie walked over to the construction camp where he could see Mike Willis chatting to Jack in the kitchen area.

"Mike, you and Nick have sure made an impression as most of the action is now moving south. There's still a presence in the area, however, as we passed a burned out truck one mile north of the Pungwe. Must have hit a boosted mine. One badly mangled body. I've already called it in to JOC and they're sending out a recovery team."

"Well, funny you should mention it. We had some action too last night," Jack interjected.

Jamie raised a brow. "Oh?"

The two men guffawed.

"In the middle of the night there was an almighty explosion," Jack began explaining. "Mike here has done a great job on that ridge up there. He got his engineers together and they laid a nice little surprise package of claymores, and even some of the terrorists' own anti-personnel mines. They'll shred anyone who gets within two hundred yards of the fence. We didn't think anyone could get by and attack us from that side, so got a bit of a fright when one of the mines went off early this morning. We checked it out and discovered our attacker—a large baboon."

"You've got to be kidding." Jamie laughed.

"Not much left of the poor bugger," said Jack. "They're smart animals, so I don't expect they'll mess around on that ridge anymore. We left the body there as a warning."

Jamie let the laughter subside. "I've just dropped off our new vedettes. These are young guys, but they've been deployed a couple of times previously and will be stationed here for the next six weeks. We also have eight IANS I've been instructed to send off on patrol tomorrow."

A look of consternation crossed Mike's face. "IANS! Are you talking about Internal Affairs National Servicemen in training? What you really mean is a bunch of kids who are barely out of school. I don't think it's wise to send untrained kids out on patrol anywhere in the Honde."

"I know, Mike. I'm just as worried about it as you are, but my objections were brushed aside. They're here with an experienced ex-RLI-instructor who seems pretty confidant to say the least. Notwithstanding, I feel responsible and am sending Sergeant Sama with them. I'll join them on the last leg of their patrol." Watching their numbed expressions Jamie continued, "I've got to check on the new vedettes. See you next at the Pungwe site."

* * *

Wet-behind-the-ears IANS! I can't believe it. Still I am responsible whether I like it or not. Jamie stood at the ops room door of Ruda Keep and watched Corporal Dande demonstrate how to operate the radio as James Trenham and eight IANS looked on. They stood around the corporal, giving him their full attention, while Angus McDonald sat in the living area and watched the show, his brow furrowed with lines of concern.

Dande proudly demonstrated each switch, explaining the logs and call signs, while staff Sergeant Ryan stood rigidly apart from the group.

"Hi, chaps," said Jamie, walking in. "I hope Corporal Dande has given you a good briefing."

Just then Sergeant Sama walked into the room.

Turning to Sergeant Ryan Jamie added, "Sergeant Sama will be going with you when you leave on patrol tomorrow morning. He knows the Honde better than any of us. He also knows the people and they know him."

Sergeant Sama beamed.

"Corporal Dande and I will join you on Friday—we'll meet up at a location I'll give you on Thursday."

"That's unnecessary, sir," snapped Sergeant Ryan. "I've been in this area before and I know it well," his eyes glittering with a touch of arrogance.

Jamie felt a stab of misgiving as the thought crossed his mind of the possibility of conflict. Turning to the IANS Jamie quickly diverted attention to the large map laid out on the table. "Let's take a good look at this map and examine the areas you are to patrol. I don't want you in the area of Katiyo or Simangane as it could be dangerous; and in the case of Simangane, patrolling will interfere with our operations."

He pointed to the area just south of the Pungwe River. "This is the area of Headman Mukwiri. Many of the villages are abandoned due to terrorist activity, but we've not had any incidents reported from here in the past four weeks. The people are not very cooperative. Half the children, between the ages of ten and sixteen, have been taken across the border by the terrorists. This includes both girls and boys."

"Why are they taking girls?" asked one of the young IANS.

"The girls are essential to their morale," Jamie explained. "In simple terms—they're needed as camp comforts, to cook, and to act as porters. Now, back to where you're going. It's easily accessible from the Pungwe Bridge. Your patrols will take you to the foot of Mt. Inyangani, and then south towards the Mtarazi Falls. Do you guys have any more questions?"

Silence …

Jamie continued. "On no account are you to cross the Pungwe River. Stay south of the river and travel west towards the mountain and as far south as Mtarazi Falls, but no further. The country is rugged and heavily forested. You'll find wild guava plantations, bananas and pineapples. Don't steal any fruit. If you want pineapples or bananas, buy them from the locals."

"Is there anything growing wild that we can eat?" questioned someone from the back of the room.

"You'll find a form of yam that makes good eating raw or cooked," said Jamie. "They grow along many of the streams and look like elephant ears, but the bulbs are large, white inside, and laced with purple streaks. Also, you'll find plenty of wild guavas. I suggest you only take food for three days to cut down the bulk you'll carry. Eat off the land wherever you can. Sergeant Sama knows his way around and he'll help you."

"What about the locals?" Sergeant Ryan asked halfheartedly. "I don't expect they'll cooperate."

Jamie responded, a hint of warning lacing his tone. "Whatever you do, make sure that you respect the locals. We're trying to win the hearts and minds of the people and we've made progress. Even though you're in camos, you're all part of the same unit that I am, and I want the locals to view you as friends."

The IANS nodded in agreement.

"You'll have a radio with you and should call in to Ruda every hour, on the hour, during daylight hours. Make sure we know your position when you bed down for the night. You'll be dropped off by road at the Pungwe Bridge tomorrow at 0800 hours."

The IANS studied the map intently and assimilated Jamie's instructions. Sama leaned over and looked at it with them, answering questions.

"I know this area well," said Sama. "We will be safe."

The IANS looked relieved.

Jamie felt sorry for them. It was obvious they were feeling a little out of their depth. Make sure you carry water purifying tablets with you. The streams are beautiful and the water clear, but unless you're close to the mountain, they're polluted with bilhartzia parasites."

"What about malaria?" asked one of the IANS.

"Good question. Just make sure each of you take your Camoquin tablets tonight and continue to do so for two weeks after you return to Chikurubi. You don't want to break out in malaria, especially while you're on patrol."

Staff Sergeant Ryan pulled himself up to his full five-foot-seven height and spoke with a voice of expertise. "I'm well aware of the dangers in the bush and we've come well-equipped. You don't have to worry about us."

"I'm glad to hear it, Staff Sergeant." Jamie heard a noise at the door and looked around, relieved to see Willie.

"Mambo, dinner is ready. Do you want me to bring it to this room?"

"That will be good, Willie. Just give us a few minutes to clear the table."

At the prospect of food the IANS began to relax. They laughed and talked. Jamie smiled as he caught the gist of their banter which centered on being ravenous. Unfortunately, he knew what was in store and couldn't help but wonder what their reaction would be to their next meal. Willie's cooking was nothing to rave about, but the RAT packs they would carry would be even less appetizing.

Willie walked into the room, proudly carrying a large black, iron pot. "Mambo, I have cooked a very good chicken for you. I also cooked some rice. I will get it now."

The young men each grabbed a mess tin and fork and eagerly crowded around the table, staring expectantly at the two pots. Jamie, aware of Willie's culinary skills, was less enthusiastic, and cleared his throat, masking a smile.

As Willie lifted the lid the smell was vaguely reminiscent of chicken. Soon, there were no doubts. A claw, bright yellow and curled in death, bobbed to the surface, in a gray, watery gravy. A layer of yellow fat floated in pools on the top. There were other small chunks of meat, skin, and blobs of fat, mixed with a few carrots, and onions. This was Willie's infamous chicken stew. The only consolation, Jamie thought, was that no head surfaced from the mess.

The young men regarded the dinner in silence, signs of pleasure rapidly vanishing. One of the IANS, who had been motion sick in the truck, suddenly had a reoccurrence. "You know, I'm still not feeling too good. I don't think I should eat anything tonight."

The others looked at him and then one by one began to laugh. "Come on, it probably tastes better than it looks," said a tall, fair young man as he plopped a mound of congealed rice on his plate and topped it with the watery gravy, and a few pieces of chicken. The others followed suit and soon they were eating and talking amicably.

Jamie was pleased to see that the dire repast had done more to bond the group, than would have a delicious gourmet meal at a fancy restaurant. After Willie cleared the table the young men exchanged stories, laughing and teasing each other. Jamie noted the fair-haired young man seemed to be the leader of the group—his name was Malcolm Lyle. He turned to Jamie.

"Can we expect any action, sir?"

"Well, I don't know. In the last three weeks, there've been no reported incidents in the area where you're headed, however, there are incidents to the south and east virtually every day." Watching their reaction he continued, "Last week the terrorists attacked a school, killed all the teachers and abducted over a hundred young kids. Will you be in danger? Yes. Remember, the Honde is regarded as the number one 'hot' spot in the country. Remain alert and never let your guard down. Don't for one moment imagine that you're in safe territory."

Staff Sergeant Ryan, wiped his mouth with a napkin, roused himself and addressed the IANS brusquely. "It's time you stopped pestering District Commissioner Ross and let him get on with what he has to do." He turned to Jamie, "Sir, thank you for your time. We'll be up and ready by 0800 hours."

* * *

Jamie woke early. The sky should have been grey, streaked with gold, in the early morning sun, but it was still dark, with heavy black clouds cloaking the horizon. There was so much to do and now he had to deal with a bunch of untrained IANS moving around in an area where he was still uncertain about how safe it was. He felt he was losing control.

Sergeant Ryan and the IANS were up and packing their belongings. They would each carry approximately sixty pounds, along with their FNs and ammunition. A pretty hefty load so it was a good thing they were all fit. They attacked Willie's fried eggs and bully beef with a little more relish than the previous night's chicken.

Jamie and Angus walked together outside where they would have some privacy. Making sure no one else was within hearing distance, they quietly discussed the move into Simangane scheduled for the following day. No one at Ruda, including Sergeant Sama or James Trenham, knew the date. The next few days would demand much of them. After dropping the IANS off, their next stop would be Pungwe to check on progress. Both Pungwe and Ruda PVs would need to be finished by the end of May—just five weeks away.

* * *

Jamie stood with Angus by the bank of the river. It was Saturday morning. The river flowed darkly with no sunlight reflected on the fast current. A light drizzle fell, shrouding them with a cold dampness. A stab of apprehension pierced Jamie's heart as he watched the group of ten, led by Sergeant Sama, head upstream along the banks of the Pungwe.

* * *

Early Sunday morning Jamie and Angus arrived at the gates of the Simangani PV. Jamie was surprised to see groups of people coming out of the forest below. The women, carrying pots of maize meal on their heads and babies on their backs, led the way. Behind came the men, heavily laden with bedding, tools and other precious possessions. They all seemed cheerful and greeted Jamie politely.

"This is a welcome surprise." Jamie quipped. "I guess the word has got out that the people in Katiyo are settling in and have had no trouble with the terrs."

"That, and the fact that they are all terrified after what happened to their headman," responded Angus.

Just then Jamie heard some loud shouting, screaming and yelling. Looking in the direction it came from, he saw a group of women shoving and kicking. Some had picked up hoes and shovels and swung them dangerously.

Jamie set off at a run. "What's going on, Chris." He yelled.

"They're fighting over who should have which lots."

"Get the kraal heads involved. Since there is no headman, they must take control. Stop this nonsense before it erupts into a major riot."

Chris and the vedettes pushed into the crowd. As soon as the people saw the guns and the red berets they pulled back and an uneasy peace was restored.

Once authority was established the rest of the move went relatively easily. At the end of the day Jamie looked out over the hub of activity in the new PV and was amazed that things had gone so smoothly.

Chapter Thirteen

Sergeant Sama enjoyed the feel of the fresh morning. He was fully dressed and had bathed in the nearby stream. The mist was rising as the sun began to peek through the trees and warm the wet earth. He looked over his shoulder at the handful of olive domes speckling the ground where the IANS still slept snuggly, wrapped in their groundsheets. They had spent the night in an abandoned village just below Mt. Inyangani. Maybe he would have a few more moments to enjoy the morning sights and sounds. A trumpeter hornbill called in the forest nearby and in the distance another hornbill responded. He could hear the chattering of a group of Simango monkeys and baboons barking in the distance. He was jolted by a roar that pierced the peacefulness.

"Get your asses up," yelled Staff Sergeant Ryan. "Get out of those bedrolls. Get moving!"

Sama chuckled and continued peeling an elephant ear bulb that he had pulled from the ground earlier. *If those IANS can survive that sergeant, they might survive the Honde.* He bit into the bulb. The sweet white flesh was crunchy and in a few minutes he had sleepy-eyed IANS asking where they could find their own 'Honde sweet potatoes'.

Thirty minutes later they were on the move, heading toward their rendezvous point at Mtarazi School. They made good time. They passed some women on the path, but the women kept their eyes averted and did not greet them. Three small children playing in one of the villages took off running into the forest as soon as they saw the IANS.

Sama frowned and moved up beside Sergeant Ryan. "This is not good. The people are frightened. The terrorists are in this area."

Sergeant Ryan continued up the path ignoring Sama's words of caution.

Sama fell back in line and thought about Jamie's advice. Chinyerere had taken him aside before they left and encouraged him to make the best of this difficult assignment with Sergeant Ryan.

They reached Mtarazi School just before 0800 hours. No sign of district commissioner Ross.

"Right everyone. Take up defensive positions all around the school. I don't want anyone surprising us. Sergeant Sama, you stay by me."

* * *

Jamie woke with a start. It was Friday morning and the alarm clock rang out as green digits displayed 0500 hours.

James Trenham continued snoring in his bed on the other side of the room. He rolled over and pulled the pillow over his head to block the sound.

Jamie turned off the alarm, quietly dressed, and then went to wake Angus McDonald. "Angus, it's time to get up. I want to hit the road in one hour and we still have time for breakfast. Remember, you're going to drop us off at Mtarazi School."

Jamie was wearing a light pack with his water bottle hitched to his belt. They would not be staying overnight, but it would be a good 15 mile walk to reach the pick-up point at the Pungwe Bridge. His Star pistol was holstered and the pack contained ten spare magazines, double taped, for the Uzi, and another 100 rounds of ammunition. Corporal Dande was waiting for them by Angus's Leopard. He held his FN in one hand and was struggling to fasten a pouch with loaded magazines to his belt.

The road to Mtarazi was winding and rough. Angus's messenger had a tight grip on his G-3, ready for any action. They passed a few locals who stood aside, their faces sullen and their eyes cast down. No one greeted them as they drove by. This was not a good sign. As the Leopard pulled up to the school Jamie was pleased to see some IANS hunkered down strategically around the perimeter.

"Okay Angus. I appreciate the ride. We'll see you back at Ruda this evening. Don't forget to have the truck waiting for us at the Pungwe—no later than three this afternoon. Send a couple of DAs as an escort."

* * *

Thirty minutes later they could hear the sound of a vehicle and it wasn't long before a Leopard pulled up in the shade near the school. Ryan watched as DC Ross and Corporal Dande walked up to them.

"Mambo," spoke Sergeant Sama to Jamie before Ryan could interject. "This is very bad. The terrorists know we are here. The people run when they see us. The word has been sent by the drums."

"That's a load of nonsense." Sergeant Ryan scoffed. "I haven't heard any drums."

A wave of uneasiness swept through Jamie. "I think we need to listen to Sergeant Sama. He knows the area and has a feel for what's happening. I wish I had known earlier as I would have pulled you out this morning. Now it's too late."

"Oh, let them come. We can more than take care of ourselves."

"Well, staff sergeant, you sound very confident, but we'd better get going now as we have nearly fifteen miles to cover till we reach the rendezvous point with the truck."

At mid afternoon they came to an abandoned village, not half a mile from the Pungwe River, and about one mile west of the Pungwe Bridge. Looking at his watch, Jamie noticed it was just after 1500 hours. When he looked up again, he caught sight of a movement out of the corner of his eye. Turning, he saw a goat, a sight quite out of place, tied to a stake outside one of the huts.

"Why is the goat here if the village is empty?" Jamie muttered to himself.

All the men stopped short. Sergeant Sama raised his hand in caution. "Stay here. Let me go and check." Nobody argued.

"Be careful Sama. It could be a trap," Jamie interjected.

Clutching his shotgun in his right hand Sama dodged forward carefully as he entered the village. His heart pounded.

* * *

Sergeant Ryan motioned for the IANS to take cover as he watched Sergeant Sama approach the center of the village. He begrudgingly admitted to himself that the guy had guts; he was willing to stick his neck out, even if he had no military training.

Suddenly, a fusillade of shots rang out from the forest to their north.

"Take cover and watch your backs," yelled Staff Sergeant Ryan from behind, his finger on the change lever of his FN. "Watch it. Don't move unless I say so. Return fire when you can." He looked toward the village searching for Sergeant Sama, only to catch a glimpse of him crawling as he disappeared behind a hut. Had he been shot?

The IANS sought cover among the guava trees and buffalo grass just south of the village. Jamie and Corporal Dande dodged behind an ant hill. The louder crack of the FN rifles made a very different sound from the sharp snap of the terrorist's AKs. The IANS returned fire, but were held down by overwhelming fire from two sides. From the sound of the firing, Jamie estimated there were easily a dozen or more terrorists, but he could not spot any of them. They were concealed in the forest on the other side of the village. It was pointless firing his Uzi when he had no visible target. The action went on for what seemed like an eternity, but in fact was no more than five minutes. Between firing, Jamie's eyes searched the abandoned village, trying to see where Sergeant Sama was. *Where are you, sergeant?*

* * *

As shots rang out, Sama dropped to the ground. He struggled on his hands and knees to reach cover behind one of the huts. He could feel numbness in his left shoulder. Where were the shots coming from? He sat up and pressed himself against the wall of the hut, breathing raggedly. Blood was running down, soaking his shirt. He could not see anyone. Rolling onto his belly he crawled forward. He could see the door to the hut just six feet away. If he could get inside he would have some cover. He could see someone coming. Raising the shotgun he fired two quick shots and saw the figure stumble and fall back. He was nearing the door of the hut and relative safety.

His head slammed into the ground. He spat out dirt, and blood, and his senses reeled. The foot that had just stomped roughly on his head kicked him over onto his back. Before he could regain his composure, the butt of a rifle landed twice, with force, once on his right shoulder and on the side of his head. He opened his eyes. As his vision faded in and out, he realized he lay helpless, in the open. Two terrorists stood above him, their lips curled in cruel leers.

* * *

Jamie knew they had to take the initiative away from the terrorists. The IANS were too inexperienced and no match for any well armed enemy. "Sergeant Ryan. Here. Bring Lyle with you." He could see that Malcolm Lyle was in full control and not showing any signs of panic.

Ryan and Lyle ducked low to join Jamie behind the anthill.

"Sergeant, we need a flanking movement. Can you handle it?"

Ryan nodded his head, reaching in his pocket for a container of camo grease. Without a word, they removed their jungle hats, and Jamie his beret. Each man smeared the black grease in streaks onto their faces.

"Corporal Dande. Stay here with the IANS."

Crouching down the three men doubled from their cover, heading for the long grass on the outskirts of the abandoned village. Cautiously, they stole through the grass and, a few minutes later, reached a point in the forest above the enemy. Sliding forward on their bellies, they pushed through a thick patch of scrub that merged with a section of forest overlooking the terrorists' position. Ducking low they crept through giant mahogany trees, looking for an opportune place to make their counter attack. There it was, a fallen tree covered with moss. Jamie positioned himself at one end of the old giant, and motioned for Ryan and Lyle to take their positions about twenty feet to the left, behind the trunk of the tree.

Jamie raised his head slowly to peer over the fallen trunk. He could see the backs of six men dressed in dark olive uniforms, who had each taken up positions behind large trees. The terrorists had chosen the perfect spot. They could clearly see the village, but would be nearly impossible to spot. Jamie could see clouds of dust and grass flying as the terrorist bullets pounded the IANS' position. There was little time. He motioned for Ryan and Lyle to copy him as he moved the change lever of his Uzi to automatic and checked his magazine. They quietly raised their weapons. The sergeant pointed to two terrorists on the left, assigning them to Lyle, and signaled he would take care of the two in the middle. They lined up their sights, pulled the triggers and held down the muzzles so that the bullets flew true towards their targets.

* * *

Sama pulled himself up on his knees, blinking several times, trying to focus his eyes on the two attackers. One of them had a scraggly beard. The other was tall, slim and with a scar below his right eye. The man with the beard appeared to be in command. Sama winced as he saw the boot coming, but dodged by flinging himself to the side. Grasping his shotgun with one hand he swung it around so that the heavy barrel caught the scarred assailant on the knee. The man cried out in pain. The bearded terrorist swore then raised his rifle and with a grunt thrust his bayonet through Sama's right shoulder. An involuntary cry escaped Sama's lips and in his pain his shotgun slipped from his grasp. Sama pulled back his right leg and then with all his force kicked out, catching the bearded terrorist in the groin. The man went down clutching his crotch with both hands. The scar faced man regained his footing and then, with all his strength, brought his heavy boot down on Samas's arm. There was a loud snap as the arm shattered. As Sama tried to lift himself up the sharp point of a bayonet pierced deep into his left thigh and a boot caught him squarely on the side of his chin. Waves of nausea and pain swept over him and his eyes were clouded so he could barely see, but he kept struggling, determined to fight till his last breath.

The two terrorists grabbed his feet and dragged him behind one of the larger huts in the north of the village. They released their grip, prodded and kicked him.

The bearded one jeering, "Ha, so we have one of those whores who betray us," Josiah Makoni rubbed his scraggly beard. He turned to Morgan. "You, Tangwena, teach this sell-out to talk. He has much he can tell us. I will be back."

Morgan Tangwena knelt over Sama, and a smile crept onto his thick lips as he removed his bayonet from his AK.

"Who is this man, Chinyerere, who is causing us so much trouble? Do you work for him?"

Sama blinked as he looked up at the leering face. He said nothing.

Morgan pressed the bayonet into Sama's cheek until blood dripped from the wound.

* * *

Jamie, Sergeant Ryan and Malcolm Lyle fired simultaneously. It was apparent they had caught the terrorists completely unaware. Three terrorists fell back and one doubled over clutching his belly. Sergeant Ryan and Malcolm immediately switched to other targets and another two terrorists went down. The remaining terrorist withdrew, running and firing blindly in their direction.

"Stay down. Keep firing." yelled Sergeant Ryan. "Five of the bastards are down, but there are more behind the trees at two o'clock."

Answering fire was coming in their direction, but it was sporadic, and it appeared that the terrorists were withdrawing, abandoning their fallen colleagues.

* * *

Morgan bent down to within inches of the Sama's face and hissed, "Tell me where we can find 'Chinyerere'. Where does he travel and how can we destroy his spirit?"

Sama shuddered. He worked to gather his strength and then glared at Morgan, spat and tried to pull himself up. "You … you will never catch … Chinyerere. He has a … a … powerful spirit."

Morgan Tangwena wiped the fleck of spittle from his lower lip and, with a guttural sound of rage, he stood back up, took the bayonet and thrust it down, deep into Sama's belly. Sama screamed again in agony, but still said nothing.

"Speak you whore of a hyena."

Morgan knelt with both knees on Sama's chest. He slowly thrust his left thumb into the socket of Sama's right eye as Sama thrashed and twisted in agony. "Speak you pig."

Sama's could feel himself fading but gathering the last vestiges of his strength he kicked with all his might. His left foot connected with Tangwena's chin, sending the terrorist flying backward. Sama could hear continued gunfire and knew that battle was still raging. Then slowly the explosions seemed to fade to a place far away. He struggled to hold on. He was supposed to be protecting those IANS. He couldn't let them down. He coughed and a spray of red shimmered in the sunlight. He opened his mouth again, this time to cry out a plea. There was no sound, but the message raged through his soul and into the darkness that was now his world. *Chinyerere.* He didn't know this spirit of Chinyerere, but he remembered DC Ross talking about the spirit that would protect them. There was another voice besides his own—he knew the other terrorist had returned, but then he was gone. His time was drawing short.

* * *

Josiah could see Morgan lying on his back, groaning. Suddenly a fusillade of shots rang out from the forest to their west and Josiah realized they had been outflanked by the enemy. Somehow they had managed to get behind his men. It was time to leave.

"Morgan, wake up—you must lead the men," snapped Josiah. "This pig is dead."

Morgan shook his head and slowly got to his feet.

"Run for the border as quickly as you can. The masoja will come and they will follow you. Do not stop until you have crossed the border.

Enoch and I will go straight to the river and then we will follow the mountain back to Chief Mutasa's kraal. We will see you back at camp. Go now."

Taking out a cigarette lighter he pulled down some tinder dry thatch from the hut and lit it. He looked down at Sama's body under the eaves of the hut. Soon there would be nothing left of that traitor but ashes.

* * *

There was an eerie silence. The only sound was the occasional crackling of a burning hut. Jamie, Sergeant Ryan, and Malcolm Lyle lowered their guns and waited several minutes until they were sure the firing had stopped and the terrorists had fled.

"Stay where you are. Don't move until I tell you," shouted Sergeant Ryan, loud enough to carry to the seven other IANS who had taken cover on the other side of the village. There was a movement below them and Malcolm gasped. One of the terrorists who had been hit pushed himself up and tried to grab his AK. A quick burst from Sergeant Ryan and the man was down again.

Waiting a full ten minutes to see if there was any response, Jamie looked across at Sergeant Ryan and nodded his head. The terrorists had fled. Together they ran towards the village where Jamie could see the roaring flames of the burning hut.

"Oh dear God, no," whispered Jamie. Sama's body was engulfed in flames. Holding his beret over his face with one hand, he reached out with his right hand and pulled Sama's body out from under the burning thatch. Beating out the flames with his beret, Jamie could see Sama was dead.

"Hey, all of you", shouted Sergeant Ryan. "Get over here at the double."

The rest of the IANS ran into the village with Corporal Dande in front. When they saw Sama's body most had shocked expressions on their faces—two were shaking.

Ryan shouted, "You, Brown and English, stay with the DC Ross. The rest of you take up defensive positions surrounding the village until the response team arrives. Williams, get on the radio to Ruda and report this contact and ask for immediate assistance. We need two choppers and a follow-up group. Give them our location as one mile west of the Pungwe Bridge. I'll be back in a couple of minutes to radio in a full report."

The IANS were slow to respond.

"Jump to it. This is war. Lyle, come with me."

Jamie was still in shock. Turning so that the others could not see his tears he saw another body behind one of the huts. Walking over he found a dead terrorist, still clutching his AK, with a bloody chest from numerous pellet wounds. Muttering under his breath, "Well, Sama you took one of them with you. Go well, my friend."

Corporal Dande stood next to Jamie, holding his hand over his face. The tears were pouring down and he could not control his sobs.

With Malcolm Lyle behind him, Sergeant Ryan walked back into the forest to check the injured or dead. The five terrorists lay where they had fallen. Four were dead, but they could see the chest of the fourth slowly rising and falling. He had taken a bullet in his right side and another in his lower abdomen. Blood trickled out of his mouth and it was evident one of the bullets had pierced a lung.

"Stay here and watch this guy. Give him a little water, but not too much. We want to try and keep him alive till Special Branch gets here. They'll want to interrogate him."

Doubling back to the village Sergeant Ryan was just in time to see Jamie snatch the radio from Williams and call in to the Ruda ops room. "Lighthouse one two, this is Lighthouse one. Do you read me, over?"

Lighthouse one this is Lighthouse one two, reading you loud and clear. Over."

"Contact. One casualty ours, and six on the other side. One still alive. Need immediate assistance. Map reference, 428690. Require casevacc as soon as possible. There's a burning hut that will act as a marker. Over."

"Understood. I will call in a report immediately. Stay on the air at your location. I will get back with you. Out."

Five minutes later the radio crackled and Sergeant Ryan picked up the mike as a voice came over. "Lighthouse one, we have a response team on the way. Should be at yours within twenty minutes. Stay where you are. Over."

"Roger, understood. We are not moving. Out."

One of the young IANS walked back from the bush. He had been throwing up uncontrollably after the contact and seeing Sergeant Sama's body. Sergeant Ryan called them all together. One of them was shivering, despite the heat.

"Now listen up. This is what it's all about. We're not playing war games out here. This is the real stuff. Now pull yourselves together. These things happen. You guys did great and I'm really proud of Lyle."

The IANS stared at him, their faces pale, eyes wide in shock.

"Come with me. I want you to see what the enemy looks like so that you'll know what to look for in the future."

Jamie nodded his head. "The corporal and I will stay with the body until the response group arrives."

With the seven IANS in tow, Ryan led them into the forest where Malcolm Lyle knelt on the ground giving the wounded terrorist sips of water. He had taken an old log to use as a pillow and raise his head. The terrorist was silent, but seemed grateful for the water.

"Take a look guys. These are the ZANLA gooks that ambushed us. We need to keep him alive so that Special Branch can interrogate him. Information is the key to understanding how these guys operate and where their next targets are."

Bending down, he picked up one of the AKs. "Collect the AKs and any ammunition and grenades they're carrying. Don't search the bodies. That's not our job."

He pointed to two of the IANS. "You two, Brown and English, stay here with Lyle. The rest of you come with me back to the village. We'll wait there for our response team."

Fifteen minutes later, they heard the steady *thrum, thrum, thrum* of helicopter rotors. The hut was still burning and a pillar of smoke rose like a finger into the clear air. It would be visible for several miles. Within a minute Sergeant Ryan could see two Alouette helicopters coming in from the south-east. They had spotted the smoke. Alongside the village was an old vegetable patch that had been cleared and there was plenty of room for the helicopters to land. Taking one of the IANS with him Sergeant Ryan went over to the target landing zone.

"Keep clear and leave room for the choppers to land. Don't go near them—rotor blades will cut you in half."

First one, then the other helicopter landed. Two sticks of SAS combat soldiers jumped out, with a tracker and two dogs on leashes. A slim lieutenant carrying an AK walked up to Sergeant Ryan. "Joe Markham, which way did they go?"

"They ambushed us from the forest over there," said Ryan, pointing toward the dead and wounded terrorists. "Five dead and I have two of my guys watching the wounded gook. Our last contact was thirty minutes ago and the rest of the terrorists probably took off east, toward the border."

"Good, we'll pick up their tracks. I'm in contact with Major Farham and he'll set up ambushes along the most probable paths leading to the border. We still have plenty of daylight so maybe these gooks will have a few more surprises in store for them." He walked over to the village and could see Jamie and Corporal Dande standing beside a body. "Sorry you lost one of your men. It's real tough when this happens."

"Go after the bastards. If you move fast you should catch up with them before they reach the border," Jamie responded, clenching his fist tightly.

"Come on guys, we're on our way." The eight SAS soldiers, tracker and dogs took off at a run towards the forest.

Two men, one white and the other black, dressed in civilian clothes, climbed out of the lead helicopter. They carried tote bags and a medical box.

"You must be Sergeant Ryan?" said the tall man wearing a khaki floppy hat. "Sandy Giles, Special Branch. This is Sergeant Morris Tavaziwa. Where is our subject?"

"Follow me." Sergeant Ryan led the way back into the forest where the three dead terrorists were lying. Malcolm Lyle sat beside the wounded man.

Sandy Giles bent down to check the terrorist's wounds, then looked up. "He's gut shot. We need to get him out of here, but let's see what Sergeant Tavaziwa can get out of him before we leave. In the meantime have your guys take the other bodies to the choppers. We'll run identification when we get them back to Umtali. Load your dead guy on one of our stretchers. We'll drop both you and the body off at Ruda before we head back to JOC."

Just then Jamie appeared. "Sandy, thanks for the quick response. He paused. I've just lost my right hand man—Sergeant Sama—those bastards.

Sandy Giles looked at Jamie whose face was a picture of rage and despair. "I'm so sorry. Can we drop you off back at Ruda with your men?"

"That would be great. The corporal and I will get Sama's body over to the choppers."

Leaving the two Special Branch men to do their work Sergeant Ryan organized the IANS to carry the dead terrorists to the helicopters. Three of the terrorists looked to be no more than fourteen or fifteen years old, and they were all slight of build. Even Ryan was amazed that the terrorists were just kids—much younger than the IANS he had with him.

Malcolm Lyle arrived with the weapons. "Can we keep these?"

"Not a chance," replied the pilot. "All terrorist weapons go to the Selous Scouts and SAS."

Sergeant Ryan picked up one of the body bags and called to Malcolm. "Here, Lyle. Take this over to DC Ross. The Sergeant needs special treatment. He was a real good guy and put his life on the line for all of us."

A few minutes later two of the pilots emerged from the forest with the wounded terrorist strapped firmly to a stretcher.

"Okay, time to get loaded. Put all the bodies in that chopper. The wounded and four of you can ride in this one. The rest of you will have to hoof it.

Jamie turned to the pilot. "Corporal Dande and I will ride with you. The rest of the guys can make it on their own down to the rendezvous point. With the SAS following the terrorists the area should be pretty clear from here down to the bridge." Jamie turned looking for Sergeant Ryan. "The truck should be waiting for you at the bridge. Get going and I'll see you at Ruda."

* * *

Jamie took a deep breath and turned to the IANS who had just arrived in the truck. "Okay guys, get yourselves into the base and clean up. Sergeant Ryan, meet me in the ops room. We need to talk." He longed to turn back the clock, to refuse Alex Burton's request—to again see Sergeant Sama stand before him, beaming and always so encouraging and respectful.

He lost track of how long he stood alone, but then turned with a start as he felt a hand on his shoulder. It was Corporal Dande. He had not heard him approach. Together they silently walked over to the body bag that had been left behind. Jamie unzipped it and looked down at the burnt face and body of Sama, parts of his uniform still in place. Hot tears rimmed his eyes. He turned away to say a silent prayer.

"Corporal, Sergeant Sama was our friend. Take care of him. Please make sure that the family is notified and that we do everything to take care of them. We must give the sergeant a proper burial. I will call the District Commissioner at Rusape so that he can begin making arrangements."

Chapter Fourteen

Nick Farham was patrolling the border about four miles south of the Pungwe when he got word of the attack. *Damn. The terrorists are getting brazen and that was Jamie's right hand man.* He picked up his radio. "Sergeant Major, call in all men. Rendezvous at the baobab tree."

Leading the way, Nick climbed the ridge to a lone baobab tree standing in the middle of a field, next to a small grass-roofed shelter. It was a witchdoctor's hut where locals would leave gifts to propitiate the spirits. Leaning against the trunk of the mammoth tree he waited for his men. The tree was about twelve feet in diameter at its base and the bulbous branches reached up a good hundred feet or more. It was more than likely several hundred years old. He looked up at the cream-of-tartar pods hanging from the branches. There were still some leaves remaining, but soon the tree would stand out, a leafless giant, and reminder of how puny man really was. By all standards, this was not a giant baobab, but it sure did make a statement in the middle of this field.

In the next few minutes his RAR troopies climbed the ridge to join him. Now he had two full platoons totaling sixty four men.

"Now listen up everyone," he said as they all gathered around him. "INTAF came under fire thirty minutes ago. They lost one of their men, but took out six of the other side. The terrorists are probably heading for the border right now. Not very smart of them to attack before dusk, but they probably think they can make it before anyone gets on their tail. We already have a group of SAS following their tracks. They have a tracker and dogs, but the terrorists have at least a thirty-minute start. The attack took place west of the Pungwe Bridge, and they have about nine miles to cover before they reach the border." Looking around at his men Nick continued. "We know of four main paths between here and the Pungwe and they'll probably use one of these. They have to move fast, but if we get moving now we can be in position to cover all paths within the next hour. Break up into sections. I want sixteen men covering each path. Set up your MAGs and string some trip wires and grenades along the paths. I'll take the first two sections and we'll cover the main path, closest to the Pungwe. Sergeant Major, you take the next furthest path, near that large stream. Sergeant Ndhlovu can cover the path near Chenjerayi Village. You, Sergeant Marange, cover the path that runs by that old broken store. Get going now and call up immediately if you make contact."

Experts at fading into the bush, the RAR troopies vanished into the thick green within minutes. Nick set a fast pace along a path that ran from south to north. With about five miles to cover, he wanted to make sure his sections reached their destination before any fleeing terrorists. They were at an advantage as they had been so close to the border when the call came in. He was sure that the terrorists would not try for one of the paths south of their position. They would lose too much time reaching the border.

Breaking into a run, he led his men down a slope and into a patch of forest. The going was much easier through the trees and the seventeen men moved at a slow jog. They each carried light loads as their main packs were back at camp. The MAG gunner was breaking into a sweat so Nick relieved him by taking two of his bandoliers and passing them out between other members of the troop. They crossed first one, then the second and, finally, the third of the main paths, all well known to each of them. They had just less than a mile to travel before they reached their destination, a well-traveled path that followed the Pungwe. It had once been a major infiltration route for the ZANLA terrorists before Nick's patrols forced them to move south.

They crested a ridge and Nick could see the heavy, dark green of the forest line that followed the river. They were close. Raising his right hand he motioned for the men to stop. He scanned the area.

Where would be the best place to lay an ambush?

Nick soon found what he was looking for—a low ridge in a stand of guava trees, just above a reaped field. It offered a perfect field of fire and no place for terrorists to hide. "Okay, let's head for that ridge with the guava trees. We'll have a clear field of fire for nearly five hundred yards. This will give us ample time to hold them in a killing zone before they can escape back into the forest."

They moved rapidly down the slope and up the ridge on the far side. Moving to the edge of the guavas Nick could see clearly in three directions. The path came right through the center of the field. There were a few stalks of millet still lying on the ground, but the field was virtually bare.

"This is perfect. Corporal Wilson, go and set the trip wires about seventy five yards down the path. Pull the pins from the grenades and position them behind the trip wires. That's where they'll do the most damage."

Looking to his left he could see a large quartz boulder half buried in the ground. This was where he wanted to place his MAG machine gunner. From there the gunner could cover the whole path from the forest edge.

"Moses, set up behind that rock. Take your loader with you. I don't want any jams or breaks in action so keep all your spare bandoliers ready for loading. Wait until I fire. That will be the signal for you to open up with the MAG."

Working down the ridge, Nick placed all his men so that they could see the path and still stay in cover. At least ten feet separated each trooper and between them they had an arc of fire that would cover the whole field.

Corporal Wilson and two other troopers were busy laying the trip wires and setting the grenades. "All set major. We're coming back to take up our positions."

Nick lay prone behind an old log. His men were all concealed, their floppy bush hats trimmed with grass and leaves, maximizing their cover. Looking to his left he could just make out the position of the gunner, Moses, but could not see his loader who was hidden behind a pile of guava branches that he had pulled down. It was 1730 hours. If the terrorists were taking this route they would probably be on top of them within thirty minutes. They still had another hour of daylight.

Next came the watching and waiting. Nick far preferred tracking down and initiating contacts with terrorists. Lying in ambush was not his style, but when given the opportunity it was certainly the most effective.

Suddenly a flock of guinea fowl flew up and across the field from near the forest edge. Nick quickly focused his binoculars on the path where it left the forest about five hundred yards away. His heart pounded in his chest as he saw a shadow emerge from the forest line, followed by another, then a line of small figures which seemed to blend in with the background of the forest behind them. Yes, they were coming.

* * *

Nick shifted the binoculars and the lead person came into focus. He was wearing a dark olive uniform with olive cap, and carrying an RPG anti-tank gun. Behind him the others came into view. Nick was counting them, one, two, five, seven, eleven, fourteen. He checked again. Yes there were fourteen in the group and they were moving at what appeared to be a slow jog. At the rate they were traveling, they would be in the killing zone in less than two minutes. Nick whistled softly, the call of the emerald spotted wood dove. There were answering calls. His men were ready and they had seen the target group. Nick adjusted his elbows and rested the FN on the log so that his body was protected. He checked the sights and aimed directly at a point about seventy yards down the path.

Each second seemed like an eternity and now the terrorists were less than two hundred yards away. He could see them clearly—make out the shape of their packs. They rounded a bend in the path and the lead terrorist motioned to those behind to pick up the pace. One hundred yards, and coming fast. Nick held his breath, his finger tightened slowly on the trigger.

The first terrorist reached his mark. *Crack!* The bullet went home and the terrorist spun around and fell backwards. Nick flicked the change lever to automatic just as the RAR troopers opened fire. There were three loud explosions as the grenades went off. The MAG blasted a swathe through the line and Nick watched four more terrorists go down, as others fell or tried to run through the field. One ducked down and began running from side to side as he tried to escape the fusillade of bullets. He almost made the tree line when there was a burst of fire from the edge of the forest. A group of SAS came running out, firing as they ran. The escaping terrorist threw his hands in the air, doubled over, falling flat on his face. It was over. Every terrorist was down and any who were still alive were now caught between the RAR in the east and the SAS in the west.

* * *

He felt the bullet strike his chest before he heard the shots. Falling, he was suddenly aware that they had been tricked into an ambush. He heard the blast of the grenades as they exploded behind him and the cries of his comrades as they went down. *The letter from Comrade General Rex Nhongo. I must destroy it. It lays out all our plans to regain lost ground in the Honde and lists alternate routes for our freedom fighters in the future.*

Rolling onto his side Morgan Tangwena opened his pouch struggling to pull out the letter with other papers. Taking out a cigarette lighter he lifted the papers to burn them. The lighter would not ignite so he lifted himself up onto his left elbow to get more leverage as he thumbed the igniter wheel. The pain was unbearable but he must succeed. It was like a blinding flash of light and Morgan fell back …

* * *

Nick waited two minutes and watched for any movement. There

was none. He stood up and raised his rifle to indicate they should proceed. The sixteen RAR troopers formed a line and moved in on the killing ground. The SAS troopers were running up from the opposite direction. It had been a slaughter. Not a single casualty from their side and the terrorists lay where they had fallen. Two had taken the full blast of one of the grenades and were lying in the field groaning as they held their wounds. Within minutes, the two friendly sides had met and were combing through the field.

A slim uniformed man, wearing pips on his shoulders, walked up to Nick. "Lieutenant Joe Markham, SAS. You guys did a heck of a job with that ambush. Just wish you'd given us a chance. At least you left us one bird and he'll cause no more trouble. How many have we got here?"

"Nick Farham, RAR. We're based here in the valley and this was a picnic—just what we needed after nearly three months of slugging it out with the terrorists." Nick wiped his mouth with the back of his hand. "I'm just waiting for a final count. Come with me and we'll check what the good Lord has given us in our hunting bag today."

Moving into the field, Nick and Joe Markham watched their men turn over and check every terrorist, strip them of their weapons and bring all the wounded together. There were a total of nine dead, two others who would not make it to dark, and three wounded. One with only a minor head wound that had knocked him unconscious, but now he was awake and talking like a canary to Corporal Wilson.

Nick went off to find his radio man and call in the report to his other groups, and to JOC. He got a quick response. "Sending three helicopters your way. We want all the bodies and the wounded out by nightfall. Give us your location."

"Map reference 428685. There is plenty of space to land the choppers. We'll lay out a smoke grenade when we hear your guys coming in. If you have room your SAS stick would like a ride."

"Roger, we can get them out. Good work Nick," replied Jock Sanders. "It'll make Jamie feel a bit better knowing you got the guys that took out one of his men."

"Today's kill will send a strong message to the terrorists. I'm sure that the locals, both sides of the border, saw or heard what happened. Word will get through fast."

Joe Markham was standing by and heard the response. "Glad to be a part of this contact, I just wish you'd left more rabbits for us to deal with."

"Thanks Joe. You covered the escape route and got the one terr who might have escaped. This contact today will most definitely impact our future strategies. The area we're standing on will soon become part of the southern portion of our *cordon sanitaire*."

"Glad to help. What's next?"

"As we close these northern routes it'll force the terrorists south, or north through Tete in Mozambique. Thanks for your help today, but I expect this won't be your last visit to the Honde. Our intelligence shows that ZANLA is planning a big push in the near future—we just don't know where."

As he finished his last sentence, he noticed Corporal Wilson walking toward him, concerned.

"You need to check this one." He pointed to one of the dead terrorists.

Nick and Joe Markham stopped to take a look at the body. The terrorist was carrying a Chinese-made-pistol and was clutching something in his right hand. A pack was lying open on the ground next to him with a pile of papers that had been pulled out.

"Hey, the guy was trying to burn some papers. See he has a cigarette lighter in his right hand," remarked Joe.

Bending down, Nick sorted through the papers. One consisted of a letter addressed to Morgan Tangwena and signed by General Rex Nhongo. Nick glanced at it briefly and then studied it closely. The letter contained instructions to stop the wire village settlements at all cost and giving details about future infiltration routes. There was also a tattered Bible with passages from the Old Testament heavily underlined. Yes, the same thing he had found on a dead terrorist six weeks before—passages justifying the killing of every man, woman and child.

"This guy must be the political commissar," said Nick. "I know Special Branch will be very interested in all that he's carrying. It refers to him as Morgan Tangwena, possibly related to Chief Tangwena who has been giving us so much trouble in the Inyanga area. Corporal, collect all these papers and put them carefully back in that pack. Make sure that the pack stays with the body so that our people at JOC get what they need."

"Looks like we've got some good information here," said Joe Markham, pointing to the dead terrorist. "When they pick us up, I'll make sure they give him a thorough going-over. No telling what else he's carrying."

* * *

Jamie picked up the phone and hung it up. He repeated this several times before finally dialing Alex Burton's number. His emotions were still raw and the last thing he needed was to hear Alex Burton's voice. However, the call needed to be made and unfortunately he was the only one who could make it. When he heard Alex's voice on the other end, he spoke quickly and relayed the message in one long narrative, perhaps out of frustration or perhaps to avoid dialogue with the man whose stubbornness had led to the loss of his right hand man. Now, however, he was thinking, *Alex was a good guy and had always been most supportive. We can all make bad decisions, but this one had cost someone his life.*

"Alex, what I feared most happened today. Your IANS walked into an ambush at an abandoned village. I was with them on this last leg of their patrol. I lost my best man, Sergeant Sama, who took it upon himself to act as front man for the group. He was shot, beaten and then burnt when a hut caught fire and fell on top of him."

"Jamie, I'm sorry about what happened. I know I pushed this on you, but we're in a war and these things happen. Where are my guys now?"

"Ryan and the eight IANS are all here at Ruda. I'll keep them here until your truck arrives tomorrow to pick them up."

There was silence at the other end of the phone.

"Alex." Jamie paused. "I'm short handed now. Can you help?"

"Give me a couple of days. I'll send you one of my best instructors. I have a couple in mind. Thanks again for taking care of my guys and I'm truly sorry for what happened. From all accounts, you're doing a great job in the Honde. Keep it up."

Jamie sighed and hung up the phone.

Chapter Fifteen

Jamie smiled at Garth as he walked into the ops room at Katiyo. "Well Garth, what news do you have for me?"

Garth shot to attention and saluted. "Good morning, sir. Everything's great here. I just wish we had some activity—a little excitement to liven up the place."

"Be careful what you wish for, young man. I would say no news is good news." Jamie wondered if he had another Chris on his hands.

"I haven't seen a thing or heard a single shot in the past couple of weeks—absolutely nothing since the contact between the RAR and the terrorists. We could hear the shots from here."

"Come, let's walk around the village and check the political climate."

Jamie stopped to watch some children playing soccer in a small clearing. The children were shouting and laughing, intent on their game. Women were busy with their daily chores, but were willing to stop long enough to greet Jamie. Life looked so normal.

Jamie turned to Garth. "How's your militia group coming along?"

"It's going well. We have twelve men, all between twenty and thirty years of age. We've trained them on G-3s. They have to turn in their weapons at night which we keep stocked in the armory. If we're attacked they know where to come to get them."

"You're doing a great job here, but stay alert. Terrorists are still active in the area—and Garth, I definitely will work on getting you appointed as a cadet with INTAF when you finish your deployment. I'm headed for Pungwe, but take care."

* * *

Jack was buried up to his ankles in mud. The work was nearly complete at Pungwe PV, but, true to character, he continued working full throttle, this time in a water pipeline ditch. Dropping his wrench he stepped out of the ditch as Jamie walked up. "We'll be done Monday. I'm just finishing off the water lines and the internal phone system to the bunkers."

Jamie nodded, approvingly. "Today is Friday and we may be looking at a move next week."

"Everything's in place," Jack assured. "That new generator they brought down, a Honda, it's a real beauty. Smooth as anything and starts with the first crank. A lot better than the Listers we installed at the last two PVs."

"Good, I'm headed to Ruda PV. That's going to be our big one."

Jamie and Sama headed toward Ruda. It would be their largest PV, housing about six hundred families, or close to four thousand people. The move could be daunting if the people refused to cooperate. Jamie was heavy in thought. *I need to set the groundwork by gathering the people for a meeting. Persuading them to move voluntarily will be the key to success.*

* * *

Josiah and his band of comrades crossed just below the *cordon sanitaire*. The restricted area was expanding further south every day.

The men stopped in front of one of the red signs. They knew from past experience it was not worth trying to find a way through the minefield. This meant they would have to travel south even further and this would bring them near Chief Mutasa's village. He was due another visit anyway.

An hour later, they walked into the chief's kraal and approached him.

"Ha," said Josiah, giving the chief a slight shove. "Why are your people moving into the wire villages? Each day we see more people move and now it is very difficult for us to travel up through Tangwena's country in Nyanga. The soldiers have their spies everywhere."

The old man's hands trembled. "I hear you, Josiah, but it is not easy for me. The people are afraid. Even some of the swikiros have turned against you. The spirit of Chinyerere is very strong—you must kill him first."

"Remember, we hold two of your sons and three of your daughters. Send word through your messenger when you hear anything about this man they call Chinyerere. We need to know when he leaves for Harare. Your nephew at Mutasa will send word. We must leave now. We are paying a visit to the people at Katiyo. We have to go first to the mountain and then follow the paths back to the Pungwe. It gets more dangerous for us every day."

Leaving the chief's kraal the comrades faded into the bush and made their way west toward Mt. Inyangani. They were dressed like any other villagers and carried their weapons wrapped in bundles so they were inconspicuous.

Later that afternoon they came to the Pungwe River, making their way east toward Katiyo's area. Ever alert for any soldiers, they kept to the smaller paths ...

* * *

Jamie drove down a recently graded and graveled road toward Ruda PV, but he turned off on a secondary road to the airstrip before he reached the PV. The airstrip still needed side drains, but the grass had been cut and potholes filled. A new windsock was in place and Jamie was able to drive the full length of the airstrip at a good fifty miles per hour, near the top speed of the Leopard. He could start thinking about bringing in small planes, even a DC-3. The airstrip's close proximity to Ruda Keep, less than a mile, was a convenient advantage. This had been Angus Mcdonald's project and Jamie made a mental note to thank him.

Turning back to the new road, he headed to the construction site. From the looks of it, they were indeed ahead of schedule and should be able to finish the PV by the end of May, two weeks ahead of his original schedule. Shiny new razor wire glistened in the sunlight, providing a formidable barrier for anyone hoping to climb in or out. Jamie spotted Angus McDonald's Leopard parked by the A-Frames and drove up alongside. He saw Angus chatting with two construction workers.

"Good to see you, Jamie. I'm just sorting out a spot of trouble with some workers."

They turned and walked together.

"Angus, the airstrip looks great. I also noticed you opened up the area on the east side of the PV. I'm planning a meeting of the people to try and persuade them to move in voluntarily, but I don't want them here inside the PV yet. The cleared area is perfect. I don't know how many will come, but we could have up to four thousand people. Later, it could serve as a large playground for the kids. You could put in several soccer fields and still have room to spare."

"You're right Jamie. Even with that extra clearing we're still well ahead of your schedule and should be able to wrap up here in another week. With Jack finishing off at Pungwe I've been able to spend most of my time here."

* * *

Josiah looked through his binoculars at the wire village of Katiyo. He could see the bright shiny fence, the razor wire, and the bunkers on each corner. As he watched, he could see two men dressed in uniform closing the gates. The sun was just beginning to set, but it was still light. He positioned his comrades in two sections so that they could maximize their fire against the two bunkers on each corner facing toward the border. Each section had a 60mm mortar and a light machine gun so he had plenty of fire power. Enoch was leading the section on his left and knew to begin firing when the first mortar bomb landed. Josiah looked to the comrade on his right who waited for his signal. He whispered, "It is time."

The comrade already had the mortar set up and he dropped the loaded bomb into the tube and moved back. There was a loud bang as the mortar charge exploded, followed by a delay of several seconds, and then the secondary explosion that rang out as the mortar landed short, well in front of one of the bunkers. Josiah could see the cloud of dust where it exploded. All around the comrades opened up with their AKs and two light machine guns, directing a steady hail of bullets at the two bunkers. It was not long before there was answering fire. Josiah was not worried. His men were imbedded in the forest two hundred yards from the wire village and he was sure that those being attacked could not see them. Every twenty or thirty seconds another mortar bomb discharged from its tube. Several minutes passed of continuous fire.

Suddenly, there were two loud explosions and long spouts of flame shot out from each of the two bunkers at the corners of the PV.

* * *

Garth Markham was getting ready to close the gates when the first mortar shell fell. It exploded about fifty yards short of the north east bunker. Locking the gate in one movement he grabbed his FN, his aluminum peg leg swiveling at full momentum, as he half ran, half hopped toward his command post at the north east bunker. Panting, breathless, and with adrenaline pumping, he grabbed the mike for the radio and called in for help. The twelve militia had run to the ops room and Davie was passing out G-3 rifles and boxes of ammunition.

* * *

Jamie heard the radio crackle and voices on the air as he drove back to Ruda.

"Lighthouse one, Lighthouse one, this is Lighthouse four zero. We're under attack. Just closing the gates, but we're getting hammered with mortars and machine guns from the east side. Do you read me? Over."

Jamie grabbed the mike. "Lighthouse four zero this is Lighthouse one. Reading you loud and clear. Hold tight. We'll send reinforcements ASAP. Have someone on radio standby. Out."

Jamie jammed his foot down on the throttle and roared onto the main road towards Ruda Keep. He was there in less than two minutes.

Running into the ops room he saw James Trenham at the radio.

"James, did you get that message? Katiyo is under attack. The terrs must have breached the *cordon sanitaire* and there's no way Nick Farham or Mike Willis can get there in time to help. Give me the mike."

"Lighthouse one one this is Lighthouse one. Need papa charlie immediate."

A voice came back over the radio. "Lighthouse one this is papa charlie. I have you patched in to JOC. We have two choppers ready to leave as you speak. We're also sending in a gooney bird with SAS paratroopers. They are taking off from the airfield now. They have the map reference and should be at the target location in less than fifteen minutes. Can your guys hold out?"

Jamie pressed the mike button. "I have four vedettes at the location and some partially trained militia. They have nothing other than their rifles and four Garden Boys. Our bunkers are solid and I have absolute confidence in our guys, but they are going to need help."

* * *

"Maiwe," one of Josiah's comrades to his left screamed as shrapnel caught him in the stomach. Another comrade cried out that he had been hit in the arm.

What the hell? Josiah was seething. He had not expected this. What sort of weapons were firing back at them? "Keep firing! Do not stop. We will destroy the village."

Emboldened, the comrades increased their rate of fire, but it was met by a barrage of return fire coming from the two bunkers. Again, the unknown weapons poured forth flames and shrapnel. Josiah heard leaves and bark shredding around him. The comrades took cover behind the trees. No screams. It appeared this time nobody had been hit. The battle continued, but was not going as planned. The light was fading fast.

* * *

Garth heard the sharp rattle of a light machine gun coming from the forest to the south-east. AK fire came in from the entire east side. All he could see was the tracer, faintly visible in the last rays of the setting sun. Another mortar bomb exploded. It landed close to the main fence but did no damage. As he picked up his internal phone, he caught sight of some of the people in the PV. They were running for their huts, the women shepherding the children to get them away from the perimeters of the PV.

Please, don't fire mortars into the village. Those people are helpless.

Garth barked sharply into the phone. "Get those Garden Boys loaded and fire at will. Send some militia to move the two Garden Boys from the west bunkers to our two east bunkers. Alternate your fire with the Garden Boys to maximize the effect. Davie, get the rest of the militia guys into the two east bunkers where we can direct their fire. They've had five solid weeks of training. Let's see what damage they can do."

Another mortar exploded, this time less than twenty yards from Garth's bunker. Fortunately, they appeared to be the small, ineffective, 60mm bombs, with limited impact.

Turning his head, Garth saw five militia with G-3s running toward his bunker. Pointing to the firing slits on the north side, he shouted in Shona, "Fire whenever you see flames from a gun."

It took no further encouragement. The five militia stood side by side, firing at random, deducing the location of the enemy from the muzzle flashes and tracer. The G-3s had been modified to semi-automatic so that they could only fire single shots. This would maximize every shot, saving ammunition.

Moving to the Garden Boy Garth grabbed an igniter from the safety box, swiveling the Garden Boy so that he could see down the makeshift sights to the forest edge. He was looking for the machine gunner's position. As he flicked the switch the force of the blast rocked him backwards and he stumbled to regain balance. He thought he could hear someone cry out. The militia and the vedettes were maintaining a steady rate of fire at the enemy. The second Garden Boy went off with a thunderous roar and Garth could see the flames and smoke in the slowly diminishing light. He reloaded his Garden Boy, making sure the heavy galvanized washers were well tamped down. Davie, with help from one of the militia, slipped a second Garden Boy onto the built-in mount next to the first one.

Garth shot him a glance. "As soon as you're ready, give me a signal. Both barrels should shake them up."

Thirty seconds passed. Davie raised his hand. Together they flicked the switches and a double hail of metal blazed out of the four barrels, shredding the leaves and bark of the forest where the terrorists were bedded down. Despite their archaic nature, with each discharge over five hundred heavy metal washers spewed from each weapon, cutting a ten meter swathe along the line of fire. Garth heard a desperate cry. A man wearing an olive colored uniform burst out of the forest, recklessly running and stumbling toward the fence.

* * *

Josiah cringed. Four long sheets of flame erupted from the two bunkers. The mortar man to his right cried out in agony and, holding one hand over his belly, and clutching a grenade in the other, ran with abandon toward the wire village. Before he had covered a hundred yards he lurched backward seconds before he could throw the grenade. He went down in a hail of bullets, his grenade exploding harmlessly in front of him.

* * *

Twenty minutes of the exchange passed before Garth heard the low drone of an approaching aircraft.

Reinforcements—none too soon.

The light was fading fast. Within a few minutes Garth saw a

line of olive parachutes fall away to the east and behind the terrorist position. It was hard to count them, but there must have been over thirty parachutes, and that meant the SAS had been called in. Garth closed his eyes for several seconds and silently lifted up a prayer of thanks. He had not relished the thought of fighting off the terrorists after dark with such limited forces at his disposal.

The firing from the enemy position intensified and two more mortar rounds exploded, one just inside the PV, behind the main fence where it could cause no damage. All four Garden Boys were loaded and ready and Garth gave the signal to fire. Now Garth could clearly see the long flames blasting from the muzzles of the cannon as they propelled their deadly charges into the forest. At that range they were unlikely to kill anyone, but those heavy steel washers could certainly put someone out of commission.

* * *

"Comrade Josiah," shouted one of the comrades. "Look behind. The masoja are coming."

Josiah jerked around in time to see the last of the parachutes disappear behind his line of sight.

He cursed. "Fall back, now! The pigs are fighting back and the masoja are here. Spread out and head for the river. Avoid all paths."

As he ran, burning rage escalated in him, coupled with a rush of adrenaline. His comrades fled in blind terror and he ran with them, all the while his mind racing. It was what set him apart as a leader. He would not be mocked. As head of all ZANLA forces in Manicaland he knew how to react. Someone would pay. The people would not forget who was in charge and what would happen to them if they obeyed the soldiers. Before he reached the rendezvous point, the seeds of new plans had formed. If he could not take out these men, he could handicap them, perhaps take out their equipment. Death sent a message, but better still cut off someone's face and let him live. Yes, Chinyerere would die soon, on the road to Mutasa, but he needed something sooner. Sweat ran across his forehead, behind his ears, and around his neck. The corners of his lips twitched and curled into an evil smile. Had it not required much-needed energy, he would have burst into all-out laughter. *Headman Tikwiri. Yes. He would be an easy target. His remaining days would be few.*

* * *

As Garth reloaded the Garden Boy he heard the *thrum, thrum, thrum* as helicopters approached. The heavy crack from 20mm cannon shells followed. Simultaneously, light machine gun fire came from behind the terrorist position. Garth knew the SAS was making contact. His heart hammered in his chest. Suddenly, he remembered the words he spoke to Jamie just the day before, complaining about the quiet. *Talk about being careful what you wish for. This was more than he bargained for.*

Garth mouthed a silent prayer of thanks for the reinforcements. The firing at their position stopped. He saw two helicopters outlined in the dusk as they tracked the terrorists. Suddenly, the helicopters turned and, one by one, came towards the PV, hovering, before settling slowly to the ground inside the perimeter fence. From the first helicopter John Whiting and three men leapt to the ground, as the pilot hurriedly went through shut down procedures.

Garth ran out to the lead chopper, and waited for the rotors to slow and come to a stop. He could see the insignia of a major on the first man out.

"John Whiting. You're Markham I understand. Sorry we took so long. Any casualties on your side?"

"Still checking, sir. None that I know of. There's one dead terrorist outside the fence and I don't know if we wounded any more. You don't know how good it was to hear your choppers come in. I saw about thirty parachutes drop about five hundred yards the other side of the forest line. I expect those guys are still mixing it up with the terrorists."

Garth could still hear rifle fire and an occasional grenade going off in the distance to the east of the PV.

"Good job, Markham. We got here as quickly as we could; especially when we heard that the PV was under attack—there was no way Major Farham could get to you in time. Our guys will stick around until the SAS gets here. We may need to casevacc some wounded. Heavy transport will come in early in the morning to pick up the rest.

In the meantime, can you send some of your guys to check on that gook you shot outside the fence?"

"Right, sir," replied Garth. "I'll send one of the vedettes and four of our militia. Do we bring the body here?"

"Yes," replied John. "Also any weapons with him."

Garth cupped his hands and called out, "Davie, over here. Bring four militia with you. Let's clean up before the light fades." He pointed to the dead terrorist outside the fence. "Be careful and check that he's dead before you roll him over. Bring all his weapons and dump him over there by the first helicopter. I'll turn on the lights. Once our SAS guys complete their sweep, this will help guide them in."

Garth hobbled toward the ops room and from there to the generator shed. It took some hard cranking to get the Lister engine running. He waited a minute for the engine to settle into a steady roar then threw the switch that turned on the floodlights along the perimeter fence.

The village was in turmoil, but suddenly Garth heard women ululating. Making his way to Headman Katiyo's hut he saw the women and children dancing and waving their hands in the air. *Yes*, thought Garth. *The people have seen that the PVs can protect them.*

Headman Katiyo saw Garth coming. The light had faded, but there was still enough of a glow to make out people and faces in close proximity.

"Thank you, mambo," said Headman Katiyo, grasping Garth's hand with both hands. Garth felt a slight tremble. "You have chased off the *boys* and our people are very, very happy."

Speaking in Shona Garth replied, "Thank you, Mambo Katiyo. Your own soldiers did a very good job. Thank them when they come back to the village. Now you can tell the people it is safe to prepare their meals tonight. There will be no more fighting. We have the soldiers here with us."

The last light faded and Garth walked back to the ops room to report to Ruda. Jamie was standing by for his report.

"Well, Garth, you were complaining to me only yesterday that it was too quiet. Congratulations for holding off the terrorists until the troops arrived. What's the count?"

"Sir, we know we killed one terrorist. We just brought in the body.

He's with the choppers. The amazing thing is that the locals are all celebrating. Headman Katiyo is beside himself with excitement at the success. We're now waiting on the SAS to arrive. They should have more to report, but they'll probably have to wait till morning for a thorough sweep of the area. I'll call you when they're settled in."

"Garth, the best news you gave me was the attitude of the locals. This is what it's all about. Keep it up. I'll be standing by for a full report."

"I have a major here with the response team. He wants to speak to you."

"Put him on."

"Hey there, elephant hunter."

Jamie smiled. "Is that you, preacher?"

"This is your guardian angel. It appears I'm doing more saving than preaching. Someone has to take care of your guys."

"Always good to hear from you preacher, especially tonight."

"Just wanted to say hello and let you know your guys did an outstanding job. No casualties. Everything's under control. Hate to admit it, but you were right. After today, I'm a true believer in the PV program."

"Thanks preacher. I'll see you soon. Watch your back."

John Whiting went back to find Garth. Together they walked back toward the main gates in time to see the first of the SAS paratroopers come into the PV, clearly silhouetted against the floodlights.

* * *

The sweep in the morning yielded two more bodies and one wounded terrorist. Garth called Jamie to provide him a full report.

This was exciting, and Jamie wanted George Barstow to hear the good news. "Lighthouse one one this is Lighthouse one. Need to talk to papa charlie; Over."

"Good morning, Jamie. I heard good things from JOC this morning."

"Yes, everything you heard is accurate. This was the work of our bearded friend. What I especially wanted you to know is that the program is working and the people were ecstatic after the attack ended with no casualties on our side, or in the PV. The militia really proved themselves last night and they are the heroes of the day. Celebrations are continuing as we speak."

"Great work, Jamie, and please pass on my congratulations to your chaps at Katiyo.

Jamie was thinking. *Word would get around fast that there had been two very successful contacts in the last few weeks with nearly thirty of the enemy killed or captured.*

* * *

Jamie greeted the Guard Force. The convoy had arrived at Ruda thirty minutes ahead of schedule Saturday morning. Nine men, smartly dressed, promptly saluted him. Their uniforms were khaki, but instead of red berets and the red-and-khaki stable belts of the INTAF servicemen, the Guard Force troops wore olive colored caps and black webbing. They all looked in need of a drink after the five-hour run from Chikurubi in Salisbury. A tall, well-built, sandy haired man appeared to be in charge. He stepped forward and saluted, His bushy mustache occasionally twitched as he spoke.

"Cadet Officer Jerry Payne. Reporting for duty, sir."

"Let your men grab some Cokes from our kitchen and rest before you mount up again and head to your destination. While they're refreshing, meet with me in the ops room.

Cadet Officer Payne walked into the ops room to see Jamie standing in front of a large scale map of the Honde.

"This is where you're headed," said Jamie, pointing to Pungwe PV. "James Trenham will accompany you. Effective today, you'll be in charge of all security at Pungwe PV. Your men will ultimately be responsible for five PVs. Our INTAF vedettes will stay on at Katiyo and Simangane PVs where they are doing a great job."

"Understood, sir. You can rely on us for full support. General Godwin even briefed us before we left, explaining the importance of our mission here, and the need for absolute security. No cameras, notes or anything that could compromise our mission."

"Good, security includes all plans and discussions involving the construction, movement of people or any convoys traveling to and from the various PVs. We want no breach of information. Too many lives are at stake. Any questions?" Jamie paused. "Three thousand people will be moved into the Pungwe PV Wednesday morning."

Pointing to Ruda PV, "This will be your eventual command post. It's two miles from here and I estimate there'll be close to four thousand people in Ruda PV. If everything goes according to plans, you'll move in to Ruda the beginning of June."

"Fully understood," said Officer Payne.

"Jerry, I want to make one thing very clear. We have a bigger challenge than winning this war. We're winning the peace. By that I mean you need to join with us to win the hearts and minds of the people. We've made considerable progress these past four months."

"You've got my support," said Jerry.

"Whatever you do, make sure you do nothing to alienate the locals. Let them see you as protectors and as friends."

Part 2 The Tide Turns

Chapter Sixteen

Jamie rolled out of bed and staggered to the bathroom. It was Thursday morning. He could not believe he had slept till dawn. Night after night the loss of sleep had taken its toll on his body, and now he was running on pure adrenaline. He examined his gaunt face in the mirror. The black stubble of beard, the dark circles around his eyes—he hardly recognized himself. His mind churned as he thought of all that had happened and what lay ahead.

The areas north of the Pungwe were stable and the people were secure and happy, but now the terrorists were concentrated in the southern part of the Honde. This did not bode well for the Ruda move. The people were murmuring. They were afraid, and apprehensive, and would not be easily persuaded to leave their villages to move into the PV. Jamie mulled over the problems and his plan to counter them?

This would mean a visit that he did not relish at all. He had decided to use one of the terrorists' own tools. *Nyamubvambire.*

The mudzimus or swikiros were the ones who influenced the people. These spirit mediums dealt with the dark forces and spoke of the future. The people were so entrenched in animism they blindly believed anything the mudzimu told them. Everything that happened to them, good or bad, they attributed to either good or bad spirits—particularly tribal spirits. Whether these spirits were troubled or content determined the peacefulness of their lives. Even those who professed Christianity struggled giving up these beliefs.

The terrorists had recognized the significance of these mudzimus and used them as tools. Through coercion and threats they found them a convenient means by which to increase fear, spreading their message of hate for the white man. The terrorist leaders used the mudzimus to embolden the young comrades and convince them that the bullets of the white soldiers would turn to water and not harm them. They were coerced to speak out, justifying the torture, rape and murder of men, women and children. It opened the door for bolder and more horrific acts of brutality.

As he pulled on his clothes, he thought over the day's mission: *Nyamubvambire. She's the recognized senior spirit medium in the Honde. I'm sure that the terrorists have already been in touch with her.* Anticipating the encounter had caused him some tossing and turning during the night, robbing him of precious moments of sleep. This was something he had to do.

Nyamubvambire spoke in the words of the founder of the Mutasa dynasty and her name meant, *The person who came from beyond.* She exerted great influence, controlling minds and beliefs. Timing was critical. Having her on his side, or simply ensuring she not support the terrorists, was the goal for the day, and a major step in moving Headman Mukwiri's people into Ruda PV.

Jamie's thoughts turned to Headman Mukwiri. *If I can meet with him this morning, get him to persuade his people to come to a meeting, I can talk with them, put a stop to opposition before it even raises its ugly head.* Mukwiri would know where to find Nyamubvambire. She lived in his district. If the Headman agreed, he could send his messenger with Jamie to show the way. These messengers were paid by the government to deliver messages and to assist the headmen in their duties. If he could get permission from Mukwiri to allow a messenger to lead him to the spirit medium, and win her support, the move would go smoothly.

Grabbing his Uzi, he headed for the ops room to check for messages. Corporal Tategulu stood up and saluted. Something in Jamie's heart ached. Images of Sergeant Sama's wide smile passed through his mind. He took a deep breath. Corporal Tategulu was so different, a first class leader and NCO with Chikurubi training. This separated him from the rest of the DA's. With his uniform crisply starched and ironed, he was the epitome of efficiency, but he was so different from Sergeant Sama who he had been sent to replace. An Ndebele, he was from a different part of the country. They were a proud people who had always considered the Shona subservient.

"Salibonani Inkosi," spoke Corporal Tategulu, asking how Jamie was doing in Sindebele. Jamie responded and asked him if he was well.

"No messages this morning, sir. Just one last night. Provincial Commissioner Barstow wants to meet with you on Saturday at 1000 hours, sir."

"Okay, corporal. Relax. While I am out this morning with Sergeant Dande, check the defenses of the keep. Give the rest of the DA's some training on their FNs and, maybe some Garden Boy drill."

Jamie turned to leave, grinning as he called out over his shoulder, "Oh and you may want to give them some tips about ironing their uniforms. We don't want to be outshone by the Guard Force when important people come to visit."

Corporal Tategulu stood even straighter and clicked his heels, "Yes, sir!" Not a smile crossed his face.

* * *

Jamie had promoted Corporal Dande to Acting Sergeant and Corporal Tategulu had stepped in to fill the responsibilities previously held by Dande. The early morning air was cool and crisp as Jamie and Dande bounced along in the Leopard toward Headman Mukwiri's village. Dust billowed up around them, seeping into the cab, but Jamie and Dande were so accustomed to breathing it they barely noticed.

It was remarkable how quickly these newly graded roads developed corrugations and potholes—all the heavy vehicles traveling to the PVs had taken their toll on the roads.

They turned off the main road, passing the newly constructed Ruda PV, and continued on to Mukwiri's village. By now the road was barely more than two goat tracks, not quite parallel. Using all his driving skills, Jamie avoided the ruts, careful that the Leopard did not turn over as he negotiated steep banks. Jamie gripped the wheel tightly and Dande clutched his shoulder harness as each jolt and bump slammed up and down their spines.

The sight of Headman Mukwiri's village promised a welcomed reprieve. A crowd of ragged children gathered outside the cluster of thatched huts as Jamie and Dande climbed out of the Leopard. The children were awed by the guns and backed away. Jamie smiled, greeting them in their own language, and asking whether they were happy.

This seemed to put the children at ease. They giggled, but kept their distance. Jamie estimated there were no children over the age of ten, a sad indication that these people had already suffered the consequences of a terrorist raid.

All activity in the village stopped as Jamie and Dande walked by the huts. Women stopped cleaning sadza encrusted pots and yanked toddlers to their sides. All talking ceased as they turned and looked at the two men.

In the center of the village was an open, thatched shelter. Headman Mukwiri was seated in a chair, holding court in what seemed to be a heated civil case. In front of him, sitting on the ground, were two men and a woman. The men were shouting at each other. As Jamie and Dande walked up, Mukwiri held up his hand and there was silence. He uttered a few words to the three seated in front of him, waving his hand to dismiss them. They hurried off, still arguing among themselves.

The Headman turned his attention to Jamie.

"Good morning, Mudzwiti, come sit down." He motioned to one of his wives who quickly provided two rickety chairs.

After sharing greetings Jamie got down to business. "I have come to talk to you about your people."

Headman Mukwiri just nodded.

As Jamie talked he kept a watchful eye on the Leopard. It was important that no children meddle with the turret gun.

Jamie leaned forward. "I need to talk to your people. The new wire village is nearly finished and the move will be soon. You have heard that the people in Katiyo, Simangane, and Pungwe now live in safety. They are very happy and their children are protected. Is that not so?"

The old man slowly nodded. "Yes, Mambo, it is true." He glanced away, a certain look clouding his face, deepening the furrows on his brow. "My people cry for their children taken by the *boys*. Many have been killed and our women have been violated."

"Mukwiri," said Jamie, putting his hand on the Headman's shoulder and speaking gently. "This will end and your people will soon know hope. Today is Thursday. Next Tuesday afternoon I want to meet with you and all your people in the open field next to the new wire village. You have been there?"

The chief turned his face toward Jamie. "Yes, I have been there. It is a very long fence." He paused and then shook his head. "But my people are many. It will be hard to get them to leave their villages and go inside the wire."

"If I can just speak to them, they will go."

The Headman suddenly stood, gesturing angrily with his arms. "You do not understand the people. How can you talk to them? Each day, they look for their children to come back with guns to beat them or cut them. There have been many warnings telling us not to move or this will happen. These other villages you speak of that are safe—that is because the *boys* are no longer there. But they are here, this side of the Pungwe, and they watch us."

Jamie spoke with authority. "Did you not hear? The soldiers killed many of the *boys* at Katiyo last week? None of the people were touched. Nobody got hurt."

Mukwiri exhaled and slumped back down in his chair, as if something inside him had deflated. "Yes, mudzwiti, I heard. Some of those killed were our own children. It is very bad that they would do such terrible things to my people—even to their own fathers and mothers."

"You have five days to send out word to all your kraal heads. Send out your messengers to tell the people they are to be at the wire village by mid-afternoon Tuesday. I will speak to the people when they all arrive. Nobody is to miss this meeting. Even the children must come. Tell the people to bring food with them as there will be many questions. I expect the meeting will go on till sundown."

Headman Mukwiri acquiesced but did not meet his eyes. "It will be done, just as you have said."

"Now, Mukwiri, I need you to give me one of your messengers to take us to the mudzimu. I understand she lives below the mountain."

A look of fear crept over the Chief's face. "Mudzwiti, the mudzimu has already been visited by the 'boys.' She will not receive you."

This was a blow. Jamie's heart sank, but something urged him to proceed. "Mukwiri, I understand what you say, but we must go. Call your messenger here so that he can show us the way."

Mukwiri did not look happy, but agreed.

Jamie pointed to the Leopard. "I will leave my car at your village and pay one of your men to look after it. He is to see that no one touches it. It could kill many people if the wrong part is touched."

The headman shot it a wary look. "I myself will see that no one touches your car." He left to find one of his messengers and in no time returned with a lanky young man wearing, on his left hand, the brass badge of 'messenger'.

"This is my nephew, Moses. He will show you the way."

Jamie smiled. *It was a fitting name. No doubt I'll need a miracle on this journey.*

With Moses in the lead, Jamie and Dande set off along a narrow path that meandered through fields, tall buffalo grass, a patch of bamboo, and thick evergreen forest. It was warm and the sun shone directly overhead. When they were half a mile from the foot of the mountain Jamie wiped the sweat from around his eyes and looked up. The midday sun lit up the stark cliffs. It was obvious only an experienced mountain climber could scale those granite cliffs—towering above the surrounding ground, with sheer drops of nearly three thousand feet. The path changed direction as they moved toward the base of the mountain, passing through thick evergreen forest and dense scrub.

Jamie's clothes were damp. The terrain and heat were unforgiving as they climbed over rocks and scaled steep banks, battling their way through thick underbrush. Jamie's mind whirled with trepidation at the task before him. He did not relish confrontation with anyone who dealt in the spirit world. There were too many incidents which he knew could not be attributed to mere chance—phenomena that occurred when mudzimu's acted as intermediaries with the spirit world of darkness.

As they approached the mountain, they noticed a dark cloud had descended and wrapped itself around the mountain like a shroud, hiding the upper half. Though the sun was still shining, it seemed dark. The shadowy dimness from the cloud allowed only sparse daylight to filter through the enormous canopy of leaves and branches. A strong smell of rotting vegetation pervaded the air. The path got steeper. They crossed a stream by a small waterfall. It showered them with spray as they made their way across stones slippery with moss. It was an eerie feeling and Jamie's ears and chest pounded with each heart beat as uneasiness tingled throughout his body. A brilliant flash of lightning lit up the sky and Jamie heard the thunder rumble and echo off the mountain. Turning, he watched Dande raise both hands to cover his face. Jamie could see Dande was terrified. The whites of his eyes glistened against his dark, sweaty face as he followed closely behind Jamie, constantly glancing around, and at the path at his feet.

Jamie knew what was going through Dande's mind. It was a well-known belief in African custom that the spirit mediums and witchdoctors could put a spell on a path. The spell would enter the foot of the unfortunate person, causing great pain and gradually travel from the foot, up through the leg, into the body and so destroy the hapless victim. It was also believed that witchdoctors and spirit mediums controlled the lightning and used it to kill their victims. Jamie had never seen Dande so terrified before.

They emerged into a small clearing at the foot of the mountain. Ahead there were two small huts with several goats tethered to stakes nearby.

Moses held up his hand. "It is better if I go first to speak to the mudzimu. She knows me. I will tell her that you want to visit with her."

Jamie and Dande sat down in the shadow of the forest. Jamie leant back against the bole of a giant mahogany tree and Dande sat next to him, nervously playing with a blade of grass. They watched as Moses made his way cautiously to the small village.

Suddenly the dark cloud that had been hanging over the mountain descended upon them and they were shrouded in a fine white mist. Jamie was amazed how quickly it happened. He couldn't see more than ten paces in front of him. He heard Dande catch his breath and looked over at him. Beads of perspiration trickled down Dande's face and every muscle was taut. Had Jamie not been there, he would have long fled this harrowing place.

Jamie shut his eyes and prayed for protection. A peace covered him like a warm blanket. He turned to Dande. "You know how you always say the terrorists cannot catch me because my spirit is stronger than theirs?"

Dande whispered, not wanting to offend any spirit within earshot. "Yes, mambo. That is true."

"Well, Dande, I have the spirit of Jesus. He is more powerful than any other spirit. He is here with us right now and He is protecting us from any evil spirits."

"That is good, mambo. Can your Spirit protect me too?"

"Dande, he is not just mine. He is yours too if you believe in him."

"I will do that, mambo, and then I will be protected from all the bad spirits." Jamie was pleased to see that Dande looked noticeably more peaceful.

Thirty minutes passed before Moses appeared out of the mist and gestured to them. "Come. The mudzimu will see you."

Jamie stood, fingering his pocket for the snuff and cigarettes—gifts for the mudzimu. A few minutes later, they approached the huts. One of them was open on two sides. Peering in, Jamie could see the spirit medium seated on a three-legged stool. The old crone's wizened face was cracked with a thousand lines. Wisps of stringy white hair stood out from her head. Her eyes, a dull blue, clouded from cataracts, seemed to look right through Jamie. She was wearing an old navy skirt, no top, and her withered breasts hung down to her navel. A necklace of mahogany seeds and short porcupine quills surrounded her neck. Her spindly, wrinkled legs looked as though they would hardly carry her. The only sound was the crackling of the coals from a fire burning softly in front of her.

Moses motioned for Jamie and Dande to sit down on the ground. "Great and mighty Nyamubvambire, I have brought these people to meet with you," said Moses.

The crone nodded her head and squinted her dull eyes, trying to see Jamie through a curtain of near blindness. She picked up some hot coals with her fingers and dropped them back in the fire.

"You know why we are here?" Jamie began, digging into his pockets, presenting her with the tin of snuff and a pack of fifty Gold Leaf cigarettes. She leant forward and took the gifts.

Opening the snuff, she took a pinch and sniffed it into each of her nostrils. After a few minutes she began to rock and sway. Her eyes rolled back and her body shuddered.

As Nyamubvambire came out of her trance she fixed her milky eyes on Jamie and began to speak. Her voice was low and rasping, the voice of an old man.

"I see you, Chinyerere. You have come back again. There has been much darkness in the valley and now I see that you bring peace."

Jamie was taken aback. He had never laid eyes on this old crone before and she was saying he had come back. Jamie began to speak, but Moses motioned for him to be quiet.

"There has been much suffering among our people. This is not good. The jackals are running loose and only the buffalo can trample them. You are that buffalo and the dogs of the Matabele rightly gave you that name. Even when the spear pierces the buffalo's heart he still charges the hunter, for he is invincible."

Jamie's heart was pounding and Dande was shaking his head in wonder as he knew that Jamie's Matabele name was 'Horns of the Buffalo'.

Nyamubvambire continued. "Your God is with you. Go in peace for now I must rest." She shut her eyes and once again commenced to rock back and forth.

Moses motioned to Jamie and Dande that they should leave.

They stood up and retraced their steps. Jamie was dumbfounded, amazed that the meeting had been so brief, yet successful. He knew that word she had favored them would spread quickly.

Jamie quickened his pace to catch up to Dande who was descending the mountain at a good clip, relieved to be on his way. Jamie was still puzzled by the spirit medium's greeting. "Dande, what did she mean by saying that I have come back again? I have never seen her before."

"She knows you as your grandfather and that he brought peace to Makoni. She is saying that your God is going to be with you. What she said is good."

"But how would she know my Matabele name?"

Dande answered, "The spirits know everything."

"What she said will go over well with the people,"

"Yes, the people of Mutasa and Makoni are all VaManyika. They are one people. Moses will tell Mukwiri what she said and the people will be very happy."

Moses listened and nodded in agreement with Dande.

Well, it was over. Jamie felt a sense of relief. This had not been an easy visit and yet it marked a new beginning.

What next? Word would get around about how Nyamubvambire had responded to him. But would that influence the attitudes of the people? How should he address them when they gathered next Tuesday? Would they respond? Would there be an attempt by ZANLA to disrupt or prevent the meeting? Would the terrorists attack?

Jamie was lost in his thoughts. They journeyed back to Mukwiri's village, and he hardly noticed the rugged path, the boulders, and the steep gullies.

The sun was shining brightly and he could feel the warmth penetrate his uniform, evaporating the dampness of sweat and mist. As they walked into the village, the people turned silently to observe them. True to his word, Headman Mukwiri sat under the thatched shelter, a sharp eye on the Leopard, exuding an air of pride in this responsibility. Jamie was confident no child had come anywhere near the unusual vehicle.

As Jamie, Dande and Moses approached, the headman looked up expectantly.

Moses stepped forward, clapped his hands, and greeted Mukwiri respectfully before recounting the visit to the mudzimu in detail.

A smile broke out on Mukwiri's face. "It is good," said the Headman. "Now the people will come next week. But word will get to the 'boys.' I do not know what they will do. You must tell your soldiers to be ready."

* * *

Five days later Jamie lay in bed fighting off the last vestiges of sleep. This was the day of the big meeting with Mukwiri's people. He let his mind wander over the past few days. Things seemed pretty routine and quiet. His meeting with JOC in Umtali on Saturday had gone well and he was grateful for their support and promise to keep Nick Farham and Fourth Battalion troops in the Honde until the operation was complete. The days had been a flurry of paper work in preparation for the next PV move.

Sunday morning he had said an emotional good-bye to Mike Willis and his company of farmer troops. He would miss Mike. The two of them had been through a lot together and had formed a close bond. The replacement company was due in next Saturday, just before the planned move to the new Ruda PV. They would set up base at Mtarazi, the site of the next PV. The construction crew was already setting up camp there. Nick Farham and his RAR troops had moved their base even further south, close to the proposed site of the Tikwiri PV.

Things were going well. It was time to visit Emily and the children. It felt like months since he had last seen his family, but it had only been six weeks. *Maybe I can fit in a visit after the Ruda move. All being well this would be a good time to go home.*

Jamie's thoughts jumped to today and the big meeting. He mulled over what he would say, just as he had ever since he had arranged for the meeting, but now, suddenly, that day was upon him. He needed a clear plan in place. He jumped out of bed, flung on his clothes and headed outside to climb the earthen barrier that formed the eastern wall of the base. He could always think better up here. How peaceful everything looked in the early morning light. He looked through the soft haze into Mozambique ....

The people were terrified. They did not know who or what to believe. Jamie understood their pain and confusion, but he would need to be commanding and strong. The people needed to have confidence in what he said and in the government's ability to protect them. He sat on the barrier trying to direct his thoughts. The way the terrorists were using the Bible to pervert its truths and justify their dastardly deeds kept coming to mind. Suddenly Roman's 13 took over his thoughts. *Obey the government who has authority over you ...* Jamie smiled to himself. Here was his message.

After what seemed like an hour, he climbed down and headed for the dining room. As he joined James and Chris at the table, he felt a small twinge of trepidation. He was trying to speculate what the reaction of the people would be to his speech.

As he sat down, Willie placed a large, steaming plate of fried eggs, and a thick, juicy piece of steak in front of him. Jamie's mouth gaped open.

"Willie, you are the number one cook. This breakfast looks great." Willie beamed with pride.

Slowly, Jamie chewed the succulent meat. The steak was cooked just the way he liked it, rare in the middle and slightly blackened on the outside. Normally, he would have swallowed it, barely chewing let alone tasting, but today was special and Willie's amazing breakfast certainly boded well in heralding the day's event.

Chris and James exchanged glances as they watched Jamie's reaction to the breakfast.

Jamie just smiled, nodded and chewed on, silently. When the last morsels of the steak had been devoured, he leaned back contentedly. "Well, chaps, I'm ready to take on the world now."

"That breakfast certainly got your juices flowing," Chris teased. "What's our role to be at this meeting?"

"We'll leave here at noon. I asked Jack to build a platform for me to stand on—six feet high so that the crowd can see me. I'll be speaking Shona—no interpreter. I want you chaps well to the side. There are no troops and I don't want anything that can be seen as intimidating to the people, even though they're used to seeing us with guns."

A hint of consternation laced James's voice. "Do you think it wise to be there without any military support? The terrorists must know about this meeting and they have you as number one on their death list. This will be too good of an opportunity for them to miss."

"I hear you, James. Nick Farham has his boys patrolling the

border and they'll be extra vigilant. The *cordon sanitaire* now extends four miles south of the Pungwe and that narrows the area the terrorists can use as an entry point. Trust me, I've thought this through. I'll take the risks."

* * *

It was 1230 hours and only about a hundred people had arrived. Corporal Tategulu, and Sergeant Dande, directed the people to the open space on the east side of the PV. Jamie looked up at the structure Jack had built. It was over six feet high. The frame was made of wattle poles, forming a five feet square platform.

Jamie gave Chris a worried look. "I hope it's big enough and I don't fall off the thing," he commented.

Chris chuckled. "I'm sure you'll be okay. Just think, if you do fall, the people will never forget it."

"Well, I might as well test it." Jamie climbed up the ladder to the top of the platform, tentatively stepping out onto the wattle poles. Once up, he nervously jumped up and down, satisfying himself that the structure was sound.

"It seems sturdy," Jamie yelled down to Chris. "Now I wonder if the people will be able to hear." He pointed to a pile of firewood. "Go stand over there and let me know if you can hear me. I'll be surprised if anyone more than fifty yards away can actually hear what I am saying."

Chris walked away, pacing the distance. "Ninety yards," he shouted.

Jamie talked as loudly as he could. "We are here today to talk about you. Do you want peace? Are you happy?"

Chris waved. "I can hear you, but some words were faint. We'll just have to get the people to close in."

As Jamie climbed down from the platform, he could see more people arriving. Some walked in groups, talking excitedly. Some came by themselves, quietly, wondering what it was all about. Women carried pots and food, wrapped up in cloth, on their heads. Many of them carried big bundles of firewood.

By 1400 Jamie estimated that there were more than fifteen

hundred people milling around the area. Headman Mukwiri arrived, followed by a couple of his elders. Jamie recognized Moses walking along behind them. The headman looked to be in good spirits, calling out good naturedly to the people and enjoying smiling responses. He graciously accepted the chair Dande had brought for him from Ruda and looked up as Jamie came over to greet him.

"I see some of your people have arrived but there are many that are not here."

"Ah yes. They are coming. Some come from far and they are all carrying firewood."

The people kept coming, like ants converging on a sweet bun. By 1530, Jamie estimated there were well over three thousand people present. He was anxious to start the meeting and was preparing to climb back up to the platform when Dande approached.

"Headman Mukwiri says we are to wait a little longer. The people are not ready yet."

Jamie looked out over the crowd. Women were stacking firewood in huge piles as fingers of smoke rose from other wood piles that were lit earlier. Already a smoky haze blanketed the area.

At 1630 Headman Mukwiri walked up to Jamie. His countenance had changed. He looked serious, ready to get down to business.

"Mudzwiti, the people are ready. The fires are lit and you can speak." He said nothing else, but turned and walked over to his chair.

As Jamie climbed the platform, there was excited chatter amongst the people. They turned to look at him. He stood straight and tall, his bright red beret reflecting the late afternoon sun, looking brilliant against a deep blue winter sky. The air had a slight nip to it. He knew the night would be chilly. He clutched a copy of *The Living Bible* in his hand.

Okay God. This is it. Jamie looked out over the gathering. What a sight it was. Close to thirty-five hundred people crowded together. Several dozen bonfires scattered throughout the area burned brightly. As the logs burned low, the people would be able to cook any food they had brought with them.

A sudden hush descended on the people.

Jamie began to speak.

"People of Mutasa. Sons and daughters of Headman Mukwiri, I

bring you greetings. I am Chinyerere and I come to share with you a message of peace and hope."

There was a murmuring from the crowd, but they fell silent as Jamie paused.

"For many months you have lived in fear. Where are your children? Your sons come back to kill their fathers and mothers and your daughters are bearing children to fathers they do not know."

More murmuring.

"Are you happy? Is this the peace you knew before the *boys* came? All they promised you has no meaning. They have left you with lies and hope of better times. Where are the better times? Your wives have been beaten and raped. Your men have been tied up and slaughtered in front of you. Do you sleep at night, or do you wait to hear the door being broken down and feel the sharp knives they carry at the end of their guns?"

Some of the women began to ululate, but then silence again settled on the crowd.

"Here in my hand is a book. It is the Bible. Many of you have read this book. It speaks of love and also of God's anger if you do not obey him. You have listened to the missionaries and your own teachers. Did they teach you to kill women and children? Did they teach you that it was right to violate any woman, including young girls who have not yet been married?

"Ayee, Ayee," many women cried out and others began to ululate.

Jamie held up his hand. "In Katiyo, Simangane and Pungwe the people live in peace. The people have not been harmed since they went to live in the wire villages. The soldiers of the people are trained to protect them. The people go out in the morning to tend their fields and take care of their goats and cattle. They come home at night and sleep without fear of the knock on the door, and the visit of angry *boys*."

Jamie paused. "Do you want peace, or do you want to live in fear? Is it right to listen to promises of those who cannot keep them and who turn your own children against you?"

There was more ululating and murmurs throughout the crowd.

"Jamie held up his copy of the *Living Bible*. "The boys say one thing, but God says another. Listen to His words. In Chapter thirteen of the book of Romans, listen to what God is saying to you."

There were more murmurs and then quiet. Jamie spoke in Shona directly from the Living Bible, his words carrying above the crowd: "Obey the Government, for God is the one who has put it there. There is no government anywhere that God has not placed in power. So those who refuse to obey the laws of the land are refusing to obey God, and punishment will follow. For the policeman does not frighten people who are doing right; but those doing evil will always fear him. So if you don't want to be afraid, keep the laws and you will get along well. The policeman is sent by God to help you. But if you are doing something wrong, of course you should be afraid, for he will have you punished. He is sent by God for that very purpose. Obey the laws then for two reasons: first to keep from being punished, and second just because you know you should."

There was silence from the crowd. Suddenly there was a commotion in one corner of the crowd and a fusillade of shots. Jamie saw splinters flying from the platform at his feet. He ducked, just in time to see a group of women in a melee as they descended on the unlucky perpetrator. Within seconds someone was holding an AK in the air and shouting aloud, *Ayee, ayee, ayeee.* Sergeant Dande and Chris took off at a run and soon returned with a young man whose clothes had been virtually torn off him.

Chris brandished the AK with one hand while Sergeant Dande held the terrorist's right hand up and behind his back in a wrestling hold.

The crowd was cheering and Jamie waited till order had been restored. He held up his hand for quiet, straightened his beret and paused.

"Now you have heard what God is saying to you. You understand. That is why you seized this *boy.* You are tired of the troubles the *boys* bring. Right here is your place of safety. Your leader, Headman Mukwiri, is here. Today is Tuesday. This very same day next week I want you all to move into the village behind the wire fence. There will be no soldiers here to force you, but if you want to live in peace you will come."

There was an eerie stillness in the crowd. All Jamie could hear was the beating of his own heart. Suddenly a low roar started, it built in momentum until it took his very breath away. Then above the roar the shrill, high ululations of the women pierced the air. The sound was deafening.

Spontaneously, the women began to dance, leaping into the air and crying out. They held each others' arms and danced in circles. To Jamie's astonishment some even leapt onto the fires in their bare feet, and continued dancing. Other women followed suit, and soon women throughout the area were dancing on the flames, until all that was left of the fires were the glowing coals and ashes. The dancing, shouting and joyous exultation went on for more than twenty minutes.

Jamie's emotions surged. He was caught up in the exhilaration. Never before had he experienced the likes of this. He looked over at Chris, James and Sergeant Dande, standing beside the platform. Through the fading light, he could see they stood motionless and incredulous. In one fluid motion, Jamie swung down off the platform and joined them.

Chris, his voice brimming with emotion, gushed, "Man, but that was incredible. I've never seen or even heard of such a thing happening. Look how stirred up they are."

Jamie could not see Headman Mukwiri. There was such fanfare and milling around in the crowd, he would be easy to overlook. "Where is our terrorist friend? He's lucky you were here to rescue him. Those women would have torn him apart."

"Look behind you." remarked Chris.

There, behind Headman Mukwiri, was a young man trussed like a pig, with his hands behind his back and tied to his feet so that he could not move.

"Okay, loosen his ropes a little and put him in the back of the Leopard. One peep out of him and just whack him on the head with the butt of your FN."

It had been a long and emotional evening. Jamie felt a sense of relief when at last the people started leaving, the women still dancing and laughing, some clutching babies strapped to their backs to prevent too much jostling. Despite the commotion, the babies snoozed peacefully, oblivious to the excitement around them. It was an amazing sight.

"Okay chaps, let's head back to Ruda Base," Jamie announced. "I believe a beer is in order—for all of us. Sergeant Dande, you must come and celebrate with us." Jamie looked at the bound terrorist. "Sergeant, ask Corporal Tategulu to question him before Special Branch gets here. I would really like to know why he was alone."

* * *

The next morning, Jamie showed no signs of not having slept the previous night. He was still keyed up from the evening's events, but it was time to get down to business and focus on the building of the next two PVs. The convoys were scheduled to arrive and would need escorting to both the Mtarazi and Tikwiri PV sites. Andre and Jack were already setting up camp at Tikwiri, closer to Nick Farham's forces. The replacement for Mike Willis's company of Fourth Battalion troops were also expected to arrive shortly, under the command of Captain Gerald Boyd. They would be based near Mtarazi.

The radio beeped. Jamie's call sign came over the air. Walking into the ops room he picked up the radio, "Lighthouse one this is Lighthouse one one. Do you read, over?" It was PC Barstow calling.

"Lighthouse one one, this is Lighthouse one I read you loud and clear. Good morning, sir."

"I'm sorry. I have bad news for you."

Jamie felt the euphoria drop a notch as he tightened his grip on the receiver.

"Last night the terrorists hit Headman Tikwiri."

Jamie closed his eyes.

"They bound him with barbed wire, cut out his tongue and then cut off his lips, leaving him with gaping holes in his face. Two of his wives were brutally raped and then mutilated with hoes. They did not survive. They warned his people what would happen to them if they continued to listen to the government. All the children were taken, down to those eight or nine years of age. This was apparently a group led by your old friend Josiah Makoni. He's believed to have been promoted to commander of all ZANLA forces in Manicaland."

Jamie felt sick to his stomach. "What's our response?"

"Nick Farham is at the scene right now. His men are on the trail, but the spoor is cold. The perpetrators are well across the border which is not too far from there. I'm sorry to bring you this news, but knew you would want to know."

Jamie heaved a sigh. "Thank you, sir. I was elated after a meeting yesterday with Mukwiri's people, but this shocks me back into reality."

"Okay Jamie. Sorry to be the bearer of bad news, but I know you and Nick can handle it."

"Tikwiri's area is still easily accessed by the terrorists," said Chris who had walked in and heard the conversation.

Jamie leaned on the desk as he tapped his pen, frustrated. "The southern end of the Honde still needs to be secured and that may take us another six weeks or more. I'm expecting a convoy to arrive shortly and will personally lead the group to Tikwiri. Over."

"Good," responded PC Barstow.

"What has happened to the old man?" asked Jamie.

"Nick had him casevacced to Umtali hospital where the doctors are going to graft from his buttocks to repair his lips. This is the third case of this type reported in the last two months. The psychological impact is huge. These guys are getting desperate. I hope this doesn't impact the program in the Honde. Good luck to you. I know you can handle it. Out."

Jamie finished the exchange and slowly placed the microphone back in its cradle. *No, it won't affect the move into Ruda but it will certainly have an impact on the border areas and Headman Tikwiri's people.*

Jamie slumped down in his chair, the last of the euphoria dissipating.

* * *

Just after 1000 hours a Rhino, followed by three MAP 45's, pulled into Ruda Keep. A tall, well built young man jumped out of the Rhino. He ran his fingers through his light brown hair, trying to smooth it down. On seeing Jamie he stood a little straighter. "Captain Gerald Boyd of the Fourth Battalion, sir. I'm here to take over from Mike Willis."

"Good to meet you, captain." Jamie held out his hand. "Jamie

Ross. Come into the ops room. I'll brief you as to what's happening and our respective roles in the coming months."

The captain followed him in and they sat down at the table. After a brief exchange of pleasantries, Jamie began.

"There was a nasty incident at Tikwiri last night. The headman was mutilated and his wives brutalized. I'll need to head down there as soon as we're done here."

"I'm sorry to hear this. How can we help? My men have been working their farms for the past six weeks and we're eager to get back into action."

Jamie reached for his map case. "I was hoping there wouldn't be too much action, but it seems the terrorists are getting desperate. Your chaps may get their wish." Jamie spread out his map, pointing out existing and proposed PVs.

Gerald carefully copied the information onto his own map.

"Let me familiarize you with the layout of the area. You'll be based in this area, near the Mtarazi PV site. I'll leave it to you to determine where you want to set up camp. Major Nick Farham is based near the proposed Tikwiri site. Have you met Major Farham before?"

"No, Sir, but he has quite a formidable reputation. I've heard a lot about him and his company of RAR."

Jamie chuckled softly. "All true. You'll get along just fine." Jamie folded his map and stood. "Chris DeVries is my district officer. He'll show you around and accompany you to Mtarazi. This nasty incident at Tikwiri is a setback and Nick and I need to coordinate how we can best defuse the situation. We're expecting the arrival of supplies for both the Mtarazi and the Tikwiri PV sites any minute. I need to escort one of the supply convoys to the Tikwiri site and meet up with Major Farham. Your chaps, and Chris, can escort the other convoy to Mtarazi. We'll meet here again at 1000 hours on Saturday. Nick will be here too and we can go over some strategies."

* * *

The Leopard shimmied and bumped along the road to Tikwiri. The convoy of heavy trucks lumbered along behind, carrying construction supplies for the new PV. The early winter day was beautiful, the sky a clear, light blue, with a touch of smoky haze from bush fires burning in Mozambique. The sun was directly overhead and the chill of the morning had long since been replaced by humid warmth.

"Sergeant Dande, a very bad thing happened last night. The terrorists went to Headman Tikwiri's village. They cut him very badly and killed two of his wives."

"Yes, Mambo. I have heard."

Jamie was amazed at how fast news got around. Some referred to it as the *bush telegraph.*

Dande shook his head. "That is very bad, Mambo. I thought that after yesterday we would see no more of these bad things."

"Well, Dande, so did I. Unfortunately, the ZANLA forces are determined to try and stop us. Until we have the people moved into Mtarazi, Tikwiri and Mutasa PVs we can expect more trouble on the south side of Ruda. Do you think the attack on Tikwiri will have any effect on the people of Mukwiri?"

"I do not know Mambo. The meeting yesterday was very good, but people forget the good quickly and remember the bad for a very long time. They hear the good things from Katiyo and Simangane, but they hear the bad things from Tikwiri—of what happens to people who listen to the government."

Knots of apprehension began to build in Jamie's stomach. Could the people's mood be changed so quickly? Jamie turned onto the newly cut road to the PV site. The freshly graded dirt billowed up in thick clouds of dust. Jamie was glad he was at the head of the convoy and not at the back. Those poor guys would have dust in their eyes, up their noses, and covering every part of their body.

As they arrived at the construction site Jamie called over to the driver of the lead Hino truck. "This is where I leave you. Andre Pierson is the construction boss. He'll show you where to offload and help you build any defenses. I'm going on to Tikwiri, but will be back later to escort you to the main road."

With that Jamie turned the Leopard around and drove back down the new road, veering onto a rough track leading to the southeast. They crossed a small stream before coming to another, where the bottom was corded with logs tied together with wire. Coaxing the Leopard into low gear, Jamie inched it gently into the stream, praying he would not get stuck. Lacking four-wheel-drive, the Leopard has surprisingly good traction, that is, unless it gets stuck in mud. The vehicle bucked and bounced, but soon the rear wheels bit into hard ground and churned. They were on the other side. Within moments, Tikwiri's village was visible, situated beside a grove of enormous, old mango trees. Jamie pulled underneath one and parked.

He scanned the surroundings. Not much activity and only the occasional sound of women wailing in the background. A MAP truck was parked outside a goat pen, but, except for the goats, there was little movement—no children giggling and wanting to examine the Leopard—no women pounding corn—no men sitting under a tree playing their version of checkers with little stones. Jamie clutched his Uzi and clambered out of the Leopard with Dande following behind.

Nick Farham had heard them drive up and strode toward Jamie from behind one of the larger huts. "You sure took your time getting here," said Nick, half jokingly, but clearly frustrated.

"I only got the word this morning at 0930 and had to wait on Gerald Boyd and the supply convoy."

Nick's face looked drawn and gray. "Bad stuff, Jamie. I had the headman casevacced to Umtali and they're going to transfer him to Salisbury for specialist plastic surgery. These bastards get more brutal each week. Simangane was bad, but what they did to Tikwiri made me want to puke. You should have seen what they did to his two wives." Nick's voice caught with emotion and he paused to clear his throat. "According to one of the old women, the leader claimed to be Josiah Makoni. He had a beard and was boasting about what he was going to do to you when they caught you. Apparently they took a large male goat, cut off its head and testicles and told the old woman to present them to *Chinyerere*. They are in the basket under the hut over there." Nick pointed to a basket partially visible under the eaves of one of the huts.

Jamie took off his beret and smacked it angrily against his leg. He turned away from Nick and spoke to the air. "Yesterday I was full of euphoria. I had a fantastic meeting with Mukwiri's people." He turned back and faced Nick. His voice cracked with despair. "Now, this morning, I get this news. These beasts have no soul. When's it going to stop?"

"Jamie, step back. Do you remember what it was like when we got here in February? These attacks were happening every day. It's just that the attacks are less frequent, but they're using Mao's tactics to increase the level of brutality. They're trying desperately to hold onto the southern part of the Honde."

Jamie allowed several long seconds to tick by before responding. Nick had a point, but Jamie was livid. He was repulsed and angered. "I know you're right, Nick. In my heart I know it, but I'm sick of this brutality. These beasts are the epitome of evil unleashed. They'll do anything their depraved minds can imagine to terrorize. I wish I could pour back on them all the evil they've done to these people." Gradually, calmness settled over him. He felt weak. He placed his beret back on his head and spoke, almost in a whisper, as he looked out over the village. "I need to speak to the people."

He walked over to a group of men and women seated under a large Mango tree. His gaze lingered on the anguished faces that were turned towards him. Despair hung in the air and only the sound of wailing broke the silence. Jamie greeted them gently. "My heart cries with you. This has been a very hard time and I am very sorry for what has happened to you, but peace is coming, just as it has come to other people in the Honde."

Sergeant Dande stepped up beside Jamie and spoke to the people.

"This is Mambo Chinyerere. You have heard people speak of him."

There was murmuring from the crowd.

"He has a more powerful spirit than the *boys*. They try to kill him, but they cannot, so they have turned into animals. On the other side of the Pungwe, people are safe and they are happy. You, too, will be safe and can laugh again soon. The soldiers are here to protect you now, so trust them. Tell them everything you hear about the 'boys.' These soldiers are your friends. Chinyerere will bring peace here too, and he always keeps his word."

There was silence and Jamie could feel their grief. Clapping his hands in respect, Jamie took his leave and went back to Nick.

"I presume you're going to step up patrols in this area? I still want to meet on Saturday. Gerald Boyd and the Fourth Battalion replacement company arrived this morning. He was headed for Mtarazi. We all need to discuss the move into Ruda and how we can counter these terrorist attacks in the south of the Honde."

"Jamie, believe me, I know where you're coming from. I've been here since soon after sunrise and the people have waited patiently to see if you would come. Some said you would be too afraid." Nick paused, looking around. "Now we can clean up and get out of here. They have two funerals to organize and need to get on with preparations for the proper wailing and weeping. I'll see you at Ruda on Saturday. In the meantime I'll step up our *cordon sanitaire* program, but we still have over 20 miles to cover."

Chapter Seventeen

It was Saturday morning. Jamie had some time on his hands as he waited for Nick Farham and Gerald Boyd to arrive for their meeting. He decided to check all the bunkers. Everything looked in order. The new Browning was in position and had been tested several times. It worked perfectly—amazing for a weapon pulled from a World War II fighter bomber.

Passing the door to the DA's Barracks, he caught sight of Corporal Tategulu ironing his uniform. He had never known another DA quite as fastidious about his appearance. Tategulu was not fitting in with the other DA's and it was not surprising. An Ndebele in a Shona stronghold was not an easy mix. He stopped. Maybe he could loosen him up, allay any tension before there was a problem. He turned around and walked into the barracks.

"Salibonani, Tategulu, Linjani?" Jamie greeted him in Ndebele.

"Sikona, Inkosi Impondezenyati, I see you, 'Horns of the Buffalo,'" responded Corporal Tategulu, putting down the iron and politely returning the greeting.

Jamie smiled. "Corporal, you greet me by my Ndebele name.

"Yes, Inkosi, my people still remember you by that name."

"Do you know why they call me that?" asked Jamie.

"Yes, Inkosi. It is because you always give the people two choices. Each point of the buffalo's horns is just as sharp as the other."

Jamie erupted in laughter. Even Tategulu smiled.

"Corporal, is your father, Mswigana, doing well?"

"Yes, Inkosi. He is well, but he is very old and is troubled by what is happening in our country."

"Your father is a very good man. He taught me how to speak Sindebele. That is why I can now speak to you in your own language." Jamie liked what he saw. Tategulu was a warrior. "Your home in Matabeleland looks very different from this part of Rhodesia, doesn't it?"

Tategulu nodded. A pang of homesickness coursed through him as he thought of the flat, dry Kalahari bush of Matabeleland. He was still uncomfortable with the high mountains and giant trees. The humid air of the Honde often seemed suffocating.

"Do you know that great baobab tree that lies hidden in the mopani forest?" Jamie continued. "It is the only baobab for over a hundred miles in any direction. That is where my grandfather used to camp when Lobengula allowed him to hunt elephant, many years ago."

Tategulu was incredulous. "I know that place well, Inkosi. That is where I went during my initiation rites. I also remember smoking the bees from one of the many holes in the tree and stealing their honey. Many of my people will not go there. They say that the spirit of Mzilikazi, the King, visits the tree, and that lions and hyenas are sent as spirits to protect the sacred place."

Jamie was pleased to see Tategulu laughing as he thought back on the memories of home.

Seriousness washed over Tategulu. "Inkosi, this is a great land and now we would like to see peace."

Jamie looked out the window. "Yes, this is a great land. God has blessed it with many resources. No people are hungry here as in other parts of Africa. All the children can go to school and there are many, many clinics and hospitals to take care of the sick. It is a shame to see what is happening."

Tategulu looked downcast. "Inkosi, the people have been told so many lies, they are confused. What is going to happen?"

"I wish I knew, Tategulu. I wish I knew."

Jamie caught sight of Nick Farham's MAP truck pulling in to the base. "Stay well, Tategulu. You are proud and fearless and it is an honor for me to have you serve here in the Honde."

Jamie walked to the front of the buildings as Nick climbed out of his truck. He coughed and waved his hand in front of his face.

"I could sure do with a cup of tea. That dust gets everywhere."

"Come on inside," said Jamie. "Willie will bring out the tea and some of Mrs. Cloete's oatmeal cookies. Maybe they'll keep you quiet until Gerald gets here."

Just then, a Rhino came tearing down the road and turned into Ruda Keep. Gerald Boyd jumped out wearing a jungle hat, his hair jutting in all directions from underneath it. "Hey, you guys, what's cooking?"

"Cookies," Jamie called out, smiling. "Gerald, meet Major Nick Farham." The two shook hands. "You two will be working together for the next three months. Nick has been my partner, counselor and protector these past four months. He knows more about the paths and trails in the Honde than any man in uniform. He can teach us all a thing or two. Come inside."

Willie appeared with the steaming tea and a heaped plate of Mrs. Cloete's cookies. In no time the plate was empty.

Nick wiped a crumb from his mouth with the back of his hand and sighed contentedly. "Old Jack is a lucky man. His wife sure can cook."

Gerald nodded, leaning back in his chair. "I met Jack over at the camp site, and by the size of the man, I would agree that his wife feeds him well."

Jamie's voice took on a serious note. "The move into Ruda is scheduled for Tuesday morning. After my meeting with the villagers I believe they'll be eager to move. I hope that is still true after the incident at Tikwiri. People are terrified." The two men nodded and

Jamie continued. "My big concern is that the terrorists might try and disrupt the move."

Nick leaned forward. "Jamie, I have the border covered. After Tuesday night's incident with Tikwiri, we're taking every measure to be extra vigilant."

Jamie gave an approving nod.

Nick stood up, motioning for Gerald to follow him over toward the map. "Since your guys will be covering the southern front, I'll give you some pointers on the main infiltration routes that could impact your operations"

They stood in front of the large wall map of the Honde where Nick was busy marking up what he considered 'paths of interest'.

Gerald looked it over. "I see what you mean. If they use this route then they could head north anywhere along the route between the mission and the Inyanga road. That would, however, force them into a bottleneck between Mtarazi Falls and the main Honde road." He looked at Jamie. "That's only six miles. I think I can cover that with my guys."

Nick put down the marker and eyed Gerald. "Based on what Jamie shared with us earlier, the terrorists know about the move on Tuesday. That means attacks on Monday night. They won't try anything Tuesday morning. They know they won't be able to get back across the border in daylight."

"One thing is certain," said Jamie. "This Ruda move needs to go off as smoothly as possible. It will have a definite impact on our next three moves. The area between Cathedral Peaks and Mtarazi Falls appears to be the most likely spot for them to infiltrate."

Nick and Gerald nodded as they listened. Jamie continued.

"With thick bamboo forest and buffalo grass to the north, they'll have to stick to major paths. Now, from what I know, you only have four or five paths to cover." Jamie put his finger on the map and traced an outline around the rock spires known as Cathedral Peaks. "This is all bamboo forest. I've walked through it. It will offer good cover." He glanced at Gerald to see if he was following the line of thought.

Gerald smiled. "A good spot for an ambush."

"You got it," said Jamie. "Watch what game walks into the trap. Monday afternoon would be good."

"What's your take on how the people of Tikwiri will react following the attack on their headman?" Nick asked.

"They're frightened. They're confused. What will make the difference is seeing your guys patrolling the area. A visible presence speaks wonders."

Nick dragged his hand across his jaw. "I hope you're right."

"Well, there's an old Shona saying," said Jamie. "'What you hear, you quickly forget; what you see, changes the way you think; and what you experience lives with you forever.' The people need to see your troops to change the way they think, so that they can experience safety and freedom."

Nick frowned, still skeptical. "They've just had so much happen to them. It'll be a wonder if they trust anyone again."

"True. Members of Headman Tikwiri's family will never forget what happened to them, but they will reach out to anything that offers them hope. Your troops and a strong protected village will offer that hope."

"You really think we can do this?" asked Nick.

"Yes, but it may mean a change in strategy on your part for the next month. You'll need to be far more visible. Have your guys openly greet and befriend the people. Yes, ambushes and winning the odd battle here and there does have impact, but there's something more important. It's winning the hearts and minds of the people."

"I hear you," Nick responded.

"Make the people see us as friends, not the enemy. What happened at Ruda on Tuesday afternoon was a prime example. What's happening in Katiyo, Simangane and Pungwe PVs is another. Have we lost a single life or seen a woman raped, north of the Pungwe, in the last three weeks? No. That's what it's all about."

Nick nodded. "You're right. We need to win over the people. Killing terrorists should be a secondary objective for us at this time." He looked over at Gerald. "That means we'll be driving all the fun and games your way. Will your farmer boys be ready?"

"Hey, we might have been born on farms and raised in the bush, but we've spent only half our lives farming and the rest, hunting and playing. We all grew up with a rifle in our hands. I shot my first Kudu when I was eleven and my first Leopard at thirteen. We'll take on whatever these guys bring our way."

"Sounds like hunting is second nature," said Nick. "Let's hope tracking terrorists comes as easily."

The bantering over, Nick turned to Jamie and continued on a serious note. "I'm on my way back to base. I'll stop over at Tikwiri's village and pay my respects. Based on our conversation, we'll emphasize visibility in the coming weeks. I'll split my forces. Half will act covertly and patrol the border, the other half will visit the villages, interact with the people, and make their presence known." He put his hand on Jamie's shoulder. "I hope the move goes smoothly on Tuesday. We won't be escorting the people this time, but we'll be out there patrolling the area."

* * *

Jamie sped down the road with Dande sitting in companionable silence. It had been over two weeks since they had been back at the Mutasa Base and, from what Jamie could gather from his last conversation with Marilyn, the vast amount of paper work piling up on his desk was becoming an issue. He was not looking forward to plowing through it. What he was looking forward to, however, were more civilized amenities and a good home-cooked meal.

As they pulled into Mutasa, Jamie saw Jack's Leopard parked outside the office. He speculated Jack probably needed a little break as well, getting ready for the big day on Tuesday. He was probably enjoying a good dose of Mrs. Cloete's home cooking, too. Jamie felt a touch of envy. He pushed open the door and removed his beret. Marilyn leapt to her feet. She looked decidedly frazzled standing behind a desk covered in correspondence, invoices, memos, and candy wrappers.

"Sir, am I ever glad to see you. There are a lot of things that need your attention."

Jamie sighed. How he hated this part of his job. For the next three hours he and Marilyn waded through the papers, answering correspondence, reading reports and filling out estimates for equipment needed.

* * *

Later that night, Jamie picked up the phone and dialed. In just two weeks he could go home for a weekend. His heart skipped a little faster as he anticipated hearing Emily's voice. He ached for her and the children. It had been five long months since he had arrived in the Honde and the once-a-month visits were not easy on either of them. In some ways, he thought, it was more difficult for Emily. Women were designed differently. They weren't warriors. Facing danger and challenges wasn't a woman thing. The Honde was a place where adrenaline was forever spiking. It repeated its patterns of spiking, leveling off to heart-pounding echelons, and then spiking once again. Only in the quiet of the night could he finally indulge in thoughts of her. Occasionally, a certain subconscious benevolence granted glimpses of her in his dreams, impressionist pictures of warm times together. These were all too quickly snatched away by nightmares, or unforgiving pressures, stealing away the precious images.

Emily, on the other hand, was left alone with much more than the want of memories and images. Her nightmares and fears would not go away and he knew she was hearing all sorts of stories and rumors, never exactly sure what to believe. He could picture her face and dancing eyes, now shaded with worry, as she picked up the phone.

"Oh Jamie, it's so good to hear your voice."

They whispered words of love and Jamie could tell by the catch in her throat that she was crying. He longed to take her in his arms.

"Honey, I'll be home for a couple of days in two weeks. Everything is going fine here. I've seen amazing things. We're seeing miracles every day."

He told her about the women dancing on the fires and the changed attitudes of the people. She seemed to relax.

"I still miss Sama, but Dande is proving a real gem. His wife is coming to visit with his baby daughter who he has never seen. You should see the light in his eyes."

Emily laughed.

"Now tell me about you and the kids."

"The children are fine. They miss you but are so busy with school

227

and friends. They are such a joy. Between them and work it helps occupy my mind. It distracts me from worrying about you!"

"How is work?"

Silence … "I made a disturbing discovery yesterday. I thought we just manufactured fridges, freezers and neon fluorescent lights, but I've learned something else."

Jamie frowned. "What's that?"

"I had to deliver an urgent message to my boss. I walked to the back of the building, behind the wall dividing the manufacturing side from the administrative side. We're never supposed to go back there. Now I know why. There were a group of Africans, sitting around in a circle, spooning black powder from a large bucket into grease-proof paper casings."

At the mention of black powder, Jamie had a suspicion what had happened. Emily continued.

"They were blissfully unaware of the danger. Thank goodness none of them were smoking. Jamie, one spark and the whole building could have disintegrated. I'm the personnel manager; I feel responsible for the safety of these people."

"What did you do, Emily?"

"I went to the managing director with my concerns and he just brushed me off. He said this was a time of war and they were providing the ammunition needed for something called a 'Garden Boy.' Jamie, I'm not sure what I should do."

He thought for a moment, not sure what to say. He had always known the Garden Boy was primitive, but never realized how archaic they really were. He certainly didn't want Emily's concerns to close down the operation of something they needed so desperately.

"Sweetheart, I understand your concerns. It's all right. There's really very little danger of the black powder exploding. It's not fully contained as it would be in a metal casing. The grease-proof paper cartridges just hold it together, and if it caught fire it would probably just go *whoosh*. It may cause a fire, but if I remember that building, there's little in it that could burn, just concrete and metal."

"Yes, but … "

"Honey, I really have to go. Don't worry. I'll see you in two weeks."

Jamie hated to leave her like this, but he really didn't want to get into a discussion about the Garden Boy weapons.

* * *

Jamie longed to sleep in. It was Sunday morning but, by force of habit, he was wide awake well before the sun was up. He spent so little time in Mutasa it felt uncomfortable. Tossing and turning, sleep evaded him. In resignation he flung off the covers. In a matter of minutes he had donned an old rugby jersey and a pair of shorts. Grabbing his Uzi, he headed out the door. The air was cool and crisp, just above freezing. Today there was no mist and the dry air burned his nostrils. Goosebumps covered his skin and he shivered, but it was invigorating. He walked fast, breathing deeply, to dispel the cobwebs cluttering his mind.

He followed the path for about a mile, making his way through a dense stand of wattle and reaching a granite outcrop. Climbing the rock he sat on top of it—the whole world seemed to unfold magnificently before him. He could see for at least fifty miles. Dense stands of forest gave way to slopes of msasa trees, their branches naked and brown, waiting to burst forth into vibrant colors of red in the spring. Waters of a whispery waterfall to his right glistened in the sun. Below him, he heard the call of a purple crested lourie and the *chirr, chirr, chirr* of a flock of guinea fowl. A little further out, there were gashes through the forest where roads had been cut to move out the timber. Beyond, and on the far horizon, were the low granite hills that made up this part of Rhodesia. What a beautiful sight—so peaceful, and yet he knew a churning cauldron of evil lay beneath.

Why, why couldn't Mugabe and Nkomo reach some accord? This wasn't just a struggle against the whites, it was a struggle for power between tribes and ambitious men—Russia supporting Nkomo and the Matabele in the west; China and North Korea supporting Mugabe and the Shona people in the central areas and east. Arms, ammunition, and training from these superpowers flowed freely to the insurrectionists, ensuring destruction and slaughter to anyone who stood in their way.

As he let his thoughts wander he felt some of the peace that soaked in from the beauty of his surroundings drift away. Eighteen months earlier Britain had sent the Pearce Commissioners to feel out the climate for a settlement, but nothing had come of that visit. He remembered when the two Pearce Commissioners had visited their home in Melsetter. They had been so naïve, more excited about taking home trophies and trinkets than a real peace accord. They had no clue what questions to ask, nor any understanding of the intricate political problems of the area. It amazed him that these so-called experts would visit from Britain, or the Unites States, and in three days think they had all the answers to the problems of Rhodesia. He himself was a seventh generation African, speaking both the major languages of the African people, knowing their customs, but still not fully understanding the people.

Prying himself away, but re-energized, he walked back through the forest humming to himself and enjoying the solitude.

* * *

Josiah sat on his chair by the fire. Across from him, Enoch dipped his sadza into a bowl of stewed meat and vegetables. The sun was shining and Josiah looked out at the myriad of tents and shelters that made up the ZANLA camp on the banks of the Pungwe River, sixty miles inside Mozambique. The flies were buzzing and the stench of the latrines informed all that came near that the time for the pits to be filled and re-dug had long since lapsed. Josiah did not move but turned an icy stare toward Enoch.

Enoch continued to dip his sadza, but his meal went down like bullets as he felt his leader's stare burn into him.

"Enoch, General Nhongo is not happy. Since we lost Morgan we have not been able to stop the wire villages in the Honde."

Enoch continued to look down as his mind scrambled for a reply. The lack of response was not interpreted well.

Josiah exploded forward, and with one shove, sent Enoch sprawling. "All the gains we had made are gone," Josiah spewed. "The people no longer respect us, and even the children we brought with us from the Honde are complaining. Some have even run away."

Enoch sprang to his feet, more angered than intimidated. "Does he not know what we did to Headman Tikwiri just days ago?"

Josiah approached him slowly until they were standing face to face. Enoch wiped some spilled food from his shirt and stood his ground.

Josiah glared, seething. "Yes, last week we taught the headman a lesson, but it will soon be forgotten. Our spies tell us that the people are ready to move into the wire village in Mukwiri's area."

Enoch did not blink, but a muscle in his jaw flinched at the smell of Josiah's hot breath only inches from his face.

"What is it I am to do? And what about your grand plan of attack when Chinyeyere travels back from visiting his family? Nothing has happened."

Josiah raised his fist again and then abruptly turned and paced. His next words were spoken in a more gentle tone. He needed his comrade's full cooperation.

"They tell us the people have been told to move on Tuesday next week. We have little time." He turned to Enoch. "Take thirty men with you and teach the people a lesson. You can attack the new wire village, but more important is to attack and burn villages so that the people understand that we are still in charge. Kill Headman Mukwiri and all his family. He is a 'sellout.'"

Enoch exhaled and felt limp.

"Josiah, what you say is good, but the black traitors they call RAR are patrolling the border. How do we get to Mukwiri?"

"I will have you taken to a place near the border, close to the old mission. That is where you will cross. There are no patrols on the white farms and you can travel up, into, and through the forest, then back down into the Honde. They will not be expecting you to come from there."

Enoch nodded. "When?"

"You must leave Sunday so that you cross the border and hide up in the forest until midday Monday. That will give you plenty of time to march to Mukwiri's place. It is not more than fifteen miles and you can attack early on Monday evening. That will still give you time to do what needs to be done and get back across the border that night. There is a half moon so you will be able to make good time on the return trip. We will have a truck to pick you up on Tuesday morning—the same place we drop you off."

"It is a good plan. We will do it and make those dogs eat their dung. What weapons will we take?"

"You will mostly need your AKs, but take two RPGs so that you can destroy the buildings in the wire village. Leave the mortars behind. Travel lightly so that you are ready to make the march back to the border. I will also be in the area. I will take some comrades and make sport of some of the white farmers south of the mission. They need to be reminded who controls this region. Go now and make your preparations. I will see you on Tuesday. Bring me a good report." Josiah placed his hand on Enoch's shoulder, tightening his grip as he spoke.

As he watched Enoch walk away, his thoughts turned to his plans for Chinyeyere. Yes, the time was drawing close for him to visit his family. Chief Mutasa would soon send word by Elias, the mechanic at Mutasa, and the chief's nephew. He had better not fail. Chinyeyere would visit his family, but he would never return to his wire villages.

* * *

The half moon shining through scurrying clouds provided enough pale light to illuminate the path through the forest. They crossed the border just north of Old Umtali Mission.

Enoch led, setting a fast pace as they followed the path past the mission and up into the edge of the pine forest. Climbing, they kept to the east of the main tar road as they made their way to a clearing in the forest. Reaching the clearing Enoch held up his hand. "This is where we stay the rest of the night. Rest now and we will move when the sun is overhead tomorrow."

Thirty one comrades lay down in their uniforms, using their packs as pillows. Most fell asleep.

Enoch could not shut his eyes. He was troubled and kept thinking back to the visit to Tikwiri's village. Then they had seen no soldiers and it was only a short distance back across the border to safety. This was different. There were more soldiers now south of the Pungwe, and it was a long march back to the border. Enoch jumped. An owl hooted nearby. Shivers erupted up his spine. Owls were bad medicine; they foretold death. He closed his eyes. Yes, they would need to be extra careful tomorrow, at least until they crossed the Mtarazi River. From there Enoch knew of many paths that led to Mukwiri's village and the new wire village. They would stay together until they reached the river and the place called Amagomo, where the rocks climbed out of the forest towards the sky. That would also be their rendezvous point on their return. From Amagomo, they would break up into three groups. One would go to Mukwiri's village. Another would destroy the villages below the mountain, and Enoch, himself, would lead the attack on the new wire village. Yes, it was a good plan. He closed his eyes and tried to shut out the fears that crept through his mind.

Enoch woke from a brief, disturbed sleep. He shivered with cold and his body ached from sleeping on the frosted, rocky ground. No blankets. They needed to travel lightly. No fires; that would be a signal to any of the soldiers of the enemy.

One by one, the comrades woke and began to jump and stretch to ward off the cold. An unusual sound shook the silence. They all stopped.

Enoch heard it, too. Whatever it was, it was big and it was headed their way. His skin crawled. Suddenly, there was a crashing through the forest. He whirled around to see a male baboon break through the undergrowth, barking loudly at the sight of the men. More baboons followed. The baboons had not expected to find anyone in this part of the forest. This was another bad omen. Enoch watched the baboons as they nervously paced back and forth, baring their teeth and barking to each other as they retreated into the forest. His heart raced. Were the spirits angry, trying to warn him? He waved away his concern, hoping the inward display of mock confidence would dispel his uneasiness. "Come, comrades. Let us eat. We will wait here until the sun is directly overhead, then we will move."

The comrades ate their dried maize meal cakes. One of the men passed around some boiled peanuts. They all drank from their water bottles, knowing there were plenty of streams to refill them. Two of the comrades produced packs of cards and were joined by others in whiling away the time.

As the sun climbed overhead, the soft, winter rays began to warm the men and Enoch's spirits rose. He signaled to the men. "Come, follow me. Go quietly, and if you hear anyone coming, we will move off the path and hide."

The path they were following skirted the edge of the ridge, gradually taking them down into the valley below. Mid afternoon, they reached the main road that ran down from the escarpment. They crouched low in the tall grass, straining to hear the sound of any approaching vehicle, the scuffle of footsteps, or voices of any travelers on the road, but all was silent. Satisfied, they darted across the road and onto a well-used path on the other side. They would make better time now and walked quickly, thankful for the cover of the forest trees and thick buffalo grass. The comrades made no sound, but watched for Enoch's signals. At any indication that they were approaching a village, the men would make their way around it, careful to keep out of sight. They did not want any of the locals sending warning messages to the masoja.

In the distance, Enoch could see lofty granite spires ascending out of bamboo forest. It was Amagomo, their rendezvous point. He motioned for the comrades to gather around him. "See those high rocks? That is where we are going."

The men looked up. They were tired and the rocks still seemed a long way off, but no one dared utter a sound.

"As soon as we go through those rocks, the path splits," Josiah continued. "We have already talked about our plan, so you know what you must do. Isaac will lead one group, Mandebvu the second group, and I will lead the third. Each group will move in on their targets."

The men nodded their heads in agreement and one spoke up for them all. "We are ready, comrade Enoch. We will do just as you have told us."

"Good. Nobody has seen us, but we need to be very careful. Stay together. Listen for anyone coming. Watch the person ahead of you for any signals. Now, let us go."

Forty minutes later they entered the thick bamboo forest. Ahead was an area of short grass interspersed with large boulders. The majestic spires of Amagomo rose steeply in front of them. Enoch held up his hand and the men stopped. He looked intently in all directions. He saw and heard nothing. It was just after five o'clock. The comrades clutched their weapons tightly and nodded that they were ready. Enoch was the first to cross a small clearing between the rocks. He signaled the others to follow.

The silence was broken. They stopped dead in their tracks. As if from nowhere, the sharp *rat, a-tat, a-tat, a-tat* of machine gun fire.

The sound sent electric shocks of adrenaline coursing through Enoch's now trembling body. Two of the comrades immediately behind him fell. In the split second he raised his AK, a bullet struck it squarely in the breech area. The weapon was hurled from his hands. He grimaced in pain. Hand grenades exploded all around him.

Enoch dived into the grass and called out to his men. "Get back, get back. They were waiting for us."

"*Maiwe, maiwe,*" someone called out. "I am going to die."

"Shut up you fool," Enoch hissed. Get into the grass and go back."

Enoch crawled back through the grass until he thought he was safe and then doubled back along the path as fast as he could run, holding his wrist. Bullets whizzed about him. One of the comrades ahead of him clutched his belly and fell flat. Forgetting about his wrist, and with barely a break in speed, Enoch stooped, swiped up his fallen comrade's AK, and jogged backwards, returning fire. The problem was that he could see nothing to shoot at so he just emptied the magazine in the general direction of the rocks. He turned back around and ran until he was in the bamboo thicket. His breath was ragged.

* * *

Gerald Boyd signaled his men to move forward. The ambush had been more successful than he could have hoped. The troops quickly spread out and searched the area looking for downed terrorists. They did not have to look long. Broken bodies lay in pools of blood, half hidden in the short grass, some staring in death, others moaning as they contemplated their wounds. He heard the occasional rattle of gunshots as his men fired on someone, but there was no return fire from AK rifles.

"Slowly, guys." Gerald warned his men. "We don't want to walk into an AK or a grenade. If you find a wounded terrorist, stay by him and let the others go on." The going was slow as the buffalo grass and bamboo were dense, and provided cover that could shield the enemy.

His radio man had called in the contact to JOC and a DC-3 gunship was on its way.

* * *

Enoch was frantic. "Comrades, here," he shouted. "Get back into the forest before the masoja come."

In the next few minutes, two other men appeared. The three of them ducked under branches, darting back along the path. The soldiers would follow them. They had to get into the forest and away from the paths.

Behind him, Enoch heard sporadic firing. Now, out of breath, he signaled for the two others to join him as he crouched down behind the roots of a giant ironwood tree. "Wait here. Let the soldiers go by." He spoke in ragged spurts. "They have no dogs to find us and will follow the path."

Twenty minutes passed. There were still occasional shots. Then there was a low drone overhead. It grew louder by the moment until all other sounds were drowned out by the sound of the two engines. The aircraft circled and Enoch cringed. The sharp crack of 20mm cannon pierced the air as the DC-3 gunship fired at hidden targets.

* * *

Gerald's tension slowly dispelled with the drone of the DC-3. It was a welcome sound. He fired a smoke grenade in the general direction of where he believed the remaining terrorists might try to escape. From the air the gunship had a clear view below and soon Gerald heard the cannon open up. He could not see their targets, but it was getting dark so he held back until the gunship called. He did not have to wait long.

"Found four targets. Three are down in a clearing in the forest. It's too dark to see now so we're heading home. Good hunting."

* * *

With the long-awaited cover of dark, Enoch felt emboldened to speak again, albeit a raspy whisper. "Stay here. It is nearly dark. They cannot find us."

Ten minutes later, the sound of the aircraft grew faint. There was a sudden and eerie silence in the valley.

"We must get back," Enoch ordered, now raising his voice. "They will be watching all the main paths. We will go up alongside the mountain and through the pine forests. Quick, for we have a long way to go before we reach the border. There will be others and they know where to go."

Scrambling through the undergrowth, the three comrades stumbled upon a path that traversed the base of the mountains. They followed it, eventually heading up towards the escarpment and the pine and wattle forests. They moved fast and left behind everything except their AKs, one spare magazine and water bottles. If they were to live, they would need to make it to the border before dawn.

* * *

Gerald pulled his troops back. They had located thirteen dead and four wounded. The gunship had downed another four, making a total of twenty one killed or wounded terrorists. He was fairly certain there were thirty-one. He had tried counting when he first saw them emerging from the bamboo. Ten must have either escaped, or were still down in the grass or bamboo. He would not know until morning when they could do a full sweep.

"Okay chaps, strip all the dead of weapons and anything useful. Leave the bodies until morning. I want the four wounded carried back to camp. They'll be sending in a chopper to take them back to JOC. Good job, everyone. I think we've sent the gooks a message today."

* * *

Jamie placed the radio back in its receiver. What an ambush. Gerald had just given him the report. He sat back in his chair and smiled. They had been right on target anticipating the terrorists would try to attack from the south. Gerald had positioned his men perfectly. There would not be a final count until late tomorrow morning, but even if the total killed was twenty one, that would still send a very strong message to the people in the area. The message would be carried by the drums throughout the valley.

"Amazing," Jamie mumbled to himself. "In this modern age it was still the drums that carried the message quickest and farthest."

It wasn't till well after midnight that he fell into a troubled sleep, tossing and turning until finally he could sleep no longer. The continued tension and stresses of the Honde were catching up with him and he kept imagining all the obstacles that could negatively impact the move into Ruda that morning. He needed to calm down. Nobody else was awake so he crept through the living room and out to his favorite spot on top of the east bunker. The peace around him soon lulled him into a light sleep.

"Time to wake up, sir. We need to get ready for the big move. No telling what's going to happen."

Jamie leaped up, confused for a few seconds as to where he was. "Good grief, Chris, you startled me. What time is it? We need to be out of here by 0530."

Chris laughed. "We still have a few minutes. Willie's scrambling eggs and the tea is ready."

Jamie was dressed in minutes. He barely tasted the eggs and the tea scalded his throat as it went down. He grabbed his red beret and Uzi, calling for Chris and James to join him. In ten minutes he was out the door. He could just make out Dande standing by the Leopard in the early morning light. He crunched the gears of the Leopard. With engine roaring, they tore out of the gates and down the road to Ruda PV.

The drive was a blur. As they pulled into the PV Jamie slowed to a crawl, amazed. Hundreds of peopled were camped outside the gate. There must have been at least five hundred huddled under blankets, with their possessions wrapped in bundles by their sides. Fires burning brightly in the early morning dawn could be seen scattered throughout the area.

There was a loud murmuring and excited chatter as Jamie and

Dande drove up. Many of the people got to their feet, clutching their bundles, ready to move as soon as the gates were unlocked.

"Dande, why are the people here already? We told them they would only be allowed in at sunrise this morning."

"Mambo, it was the shooting yesterday. The people are afraid and they seek safety in the PV."

A uniformed member of the Guard Force opened the gate as they drove past, saluted, and then closed it quickly, before any of the people could slip in behind the wire.

Angus McDonald and Jerry Payne were waiting as Jamie pulled up to the A frame ops room.

Jerry greeted Jamie. "It looks like we have some anxious guests. When do we open the gates?"

"Give us fifteen minutes. Barring a stampede, this should go well. Let them in just one family at a time. Angus and Chris will be in charge of the village allotments, under the direction of Headman Mukwiri. I don't want them overwhelmed. Too many people at once will create chaos."

Jerry was eager to go. "Just give me the signal and we'll get this show on the road."

Jamie looked towards the gates. People were converging in from the bush, streaming up the road. The crowd outside the gate was growing rapidly. It was only 0610 and already there were nearly a thousand people to process.

Despite the nip in the air, Jamie felt beads of sweat break out on his brow. "We need to find Headman Mukwiri as soon as possible. As soon as he arrives send him over to Chris."

Ten minutes later, Chris and Angus were in position and Jamie signaled to Jerry Payne to open the gates. The crowd stood up, surged forward, pushing and shoving. Children cried out, mothers frantically grabbed little hands, and clutched babies to their backs. Men, laden with bundles, shouted angrily at those ahead of them, forgetting the friendly camaraderie they had enjoyed just a few moments before.

Jerry and four of his Guard Force members stood shoulder to shoulder at the gate, doing their best, somewhat unsuccessfully, to hold the masses back. It was with relief that they looked back and saw

Dande striding towards them. In his khaki uniform, with his bush hat in place, and sporting a swagger stick, he was an imposing figure.

Dande looked sternly at the people, his voice rose to a roar, "What are you, a herd of wild cattle? There is room for all of you in the wire fence and fighting will not help you get a better place. If you push like school children then we will treat you like school children, and send you to the back of the line." A sudden hush and quiet stillness descended on the crowd.

Dande looked over the sea of black faces until he spotted the one he had been waiting for. Headman Mukwiri was walking down the road, followed by two of his wives and a troop of children. Dande made his way toward him as the people respectfully parted, making a path for him. Dande escorted the headman inside the fence where Jamie waited.

With Headman Mukwiri in control, Jamie could now take a back seat.

By 1100 hours over three thousand people had been processed through the gate. Others were still arriving. By noon, six hundred and forty families had been allocated their lots, and many people had already gone back to their villages for a second and third time, collecting any possessions that might prove useful in building their new homes.

Sergeant Dande approached Jamie. "Headman Mukwiri is complaining that they are running out of places to put his people. That is not true. It is because some people are trying to save places for their friends."

"Dande, you are a sergeant. Go shake up the people. No saved places. Tell Mukwiri to do his job."

Dande wasted no time and Jamie smiled as he saw him sternly lecturing Mukwiri. The headman was nodding in compliance.

Jamie turned to Chris. "It's amazing the clout these uniforms carry. Mukwiri respects Dande because he knows he also comes from a line of great chiefs."

Jamie looked out over the scene still unfolding before them. "Looks like you guys are just about done," he told Chris. "Let's head back to the barracks. We can rustle up some of those Cokes the Guard Force tried to hide in the fridge."

Chapter Eighteen

Elias' fingers trembled as he spread grease over the ball bearings on the front wheel of the Landrover. He tried to focus on his work in the machine shop at Mutasa, but he could not get his mind off his two sons and daughter. It had been six weeks, the longest weeks of his life since his children had been taken captive by Josiah. How much longer? He could not bear it. Once he passed on to Chief Mutasa the date of DC Ross' departure for Salisbury, his children would be set free. He thought of them every moment. Were they suffering? Were they alive? His wife was nearly out of her mind as she struggled to endure the horror. He looked around. No one was watching. He hurled a wrench across the shop and sank to his haunches, burying his head in clenched fists and convulsing as he sobbed. The bastard. How he hated Josiah Makoni—hated him with all his being. When would this be over? When would DC Ross leave for Salisbury? It had to be soon.

* * *

Jamie was counting down the days until he could see Emily and the kids. How strange it was. The days sped by at a break-neck pace. Still so much he needed to accomplish. There was never enough time. Yet, those very same days, between visits to his family, mercilessly dragged on. Weeks seemed like months.

It was the rumble of Gerald Boyd's vehicle. Jamie snapped out of his thoughts. Gerald parked in front of the Ruda PV and swung out of the vehicle, grinning as he spotted Jamie at the door. He was still on a high from the ambush.

He shook his head in bewilderment as he looked out over the people. It looked like the epitome of mass confusion.

"Good grief. How do you organize this lot into a workable village?"

Jamie folded his arms across his chest and laughed. "This *is* organized."

"Okay, if you say so," said Gerald, skeptically.

He eyed Gerald. "Just keep watching."

Gerald looked beyond the activity and saw it. Even Jamie had to admit it was a sight to behold. There was no mistaking that the beginnings of a village were emerging. Only a day after the move and the newly occupied village was a hive of organized activity.

"Wait until you see how fast things fall into place," said Jamie. "Within a month, you'll be convinced they've lived here forever."

Gerald took it in, mesmerized.

Women, carrying huge bundles on their heads, streamed in from the homes they had left, bringing whatever they considered their precious possessions. Men were busy stringing up tarpaulins, forming temporary shelters until their new huts could be built. Children were everywhere, running around and calling to each other in excitement, or sitting quietly in the dust, looking lost and bewildered with their new surroundings.

"By the way, great report on your terrorist encounter," said Jamie. "Congratulations."

Gerald lit up. "You were right on target locating that position for the ambush. We caught them completely unaware—about wiped them out. We did a sweep yesterday and casevacced out the wounded. Total of seventeen dead and five wounded. One of the wounded is singing like crazy. Sandy Giles says he's a mine of information. He's found out there were a total of thirty-one in the group, so nine got away. Not bad for a single contact."

"I want you to know it's had a greater affect than just the killing of a few terrorists," said Jamie. "The people see that the terrorists are not invincible. They're seeing we can really protect them and they're gaining confidence in us. I got here at the crack of dawn yesterday and there was already a crowd gathered outside the gates waiting to get in."

"You've got me sold on this 'hearts and minds' stuff. I heard that just a couple of months ago the people wouldn't come anywhere near anyone in uniform."

"That's right," said Jamie. They wouldn't even greet us. The kids all ran away if they saw us coming. Now we've got to shoo the kids off."

"What's next?" asked Gerald.

"I need some of your chaps to play a different role. Keep half your men on patrol, particularly in the area south of Mtarazi. I think that could be our next hot spot. The terrorists aren't having much success north of there. The other half needs to be seen as protectors and friends. Greet the locals, get to know them, lend a hand where necessary."

"We'll do just that," said Gerald. "Most of my guys were born and brought up on farms; they speak the lingo and are pretty familiar with the customs. They should fall into that role easily and the locals already seem to trust us. Headman Mukwiri even sent us a goat."

* * *

James Trenham lifted his head in silent greeting. He was stooped over the radio attentively listening to a message, scribbling notes on the log sheet. Jamie pulled up a chair and waited. It was Friday, June tenth and he had been so busy he barely noticed the days flying by. The radio crackled and the message ended. James jumped to his feet.

"Good morning, sir."

"Good morning. Good report today?"

"Things are pretty quiet. Only one report came in. The people from Simangane are complaining that they're not able to work and make money."

"That's one complaint I'm glad to hear," said Jamie.

James waited for the explanation.

"They must be referring to the Aberfoyle tea estates. It sounds like they want to get back to work. This is good news and good timing. I'm meeting with my bother, Alan Ross, next week to discuss starting up operations again. He'll be pleased." Jamie stood.

* * *

Alan Ross looked up. "Good to see you, Jamie. As if it weren't enough to hear all the good reports, I'm having people knock on my door wanting to know when we're going to reopen the estate. My directors are on the edge of their seats. Do you have a word for them?"

"Well, Alan, I'm the bearer of good news. We've experienced no incidents this side of the Pungwe for nearly eight weeks. The attitude of the people has shown a remarkable turn-around. I had the opportunity to take some of my senior bosses to Katiyo, Simangane and Ruda on Saturday and they were most impressed."

Alan waited with bated breath.

Jamie smiled. "What would you say if I told you to begin preparations right now to reopen the estates and the factory? How long would it take to get up and running?"

Alan pushed back is chair and leapt to his feet, his face wreathed in excitement. "This is great news. Koos has been working on the machinery. We could open the factory and drying sheds tomorrow if I had the right people. The tea is ripe for picking and we've a lot of catching up to do."

He leaned forward and looked Jamie in the eye. "You give the word today and I'll be fully operational in a week, provided I can get my labor back."

Audrey walked in with a pot of freshly brewed tea and plate of biscuits, looking perplexed when she saw the emotions on the men's faces. "This is the last of our best pickings, but it's still the best tea in all of Africa."

Jamie winked, now grinning ear to ear. "The last of it? Oh, I think you'll have plenty of fresh pickings for my next visit."

"What do you mean?"

"I've spoken to the people in both Simangane and Pungwe PVs. They're ready to start immediately. If I gave the word today you would have people lined up to work tomorrow, including many of your old workers. Just tell me when you want to start and I'll pass it on to my PV commanders."

Alan covered his face with his hands and shook his head. Audrey sat the tea tray down with a clank, her hands shaking with excitement. When they finally looked up, the fresh ray of hope that had ignited behind their eyes became a lasting memory etched on Jamie's mind—a marker of the transformation of the Honde.

* * *

Salisbury. It seemed like a dream. It felt like months since he had been home and he was excited at the thought of seeing Emily and the children. His mind reflected on the warm homecoming he was sure to receive. He wrapped up last minute items in the office at Mutasa and then headed to the kitchen for breakfast. As he finished the last bite and stood to gather his things, Sixpence abruptly entered.

"Mambo, there is a man outside who wants to see you."

Oh, no. What now?

He certainly didn't want a delay. Reluctantly, he stood up and went to the back kitchen door.

There a young man stood balancing an old, beat up bicycle.

"Mambo," he said politely. "I have brought you a gift."

Tied to the handlebars, a chicken hung upside down. Its legs were trussed together and the head hung limply down, dangerously near the spokes. Jamie wondered if it was dead, but as the young man untied the rope and handed the chicken to Jamie the bird had a sudden spurt of energy, squawked and flapped its wings in frenzied movement. Jamie finally grabbed the chicken and held it tightly, as far away from his clean uniform as possible. He had experienced traumatized chickens before. The chicken glared at him with a bright, golden eye and Jamie wondered what in the world he would do with it now, just as he was leaving for home.

"Thank you very much. This is a very good gift, I will take it to my wife and we can enjoy it together."

The young man rode off, looking very pleased that his gift had been so enthusiastically received.

Sighing, Jamie called to Sixpence, "Bring a box, Sixpence. I'm going to have to take this chicken home with me."

* * *

Elias stood in the shadows beside the workshop. He carefully rolled a plug of tobacco in a piece of newspaper, lit it and drew in a mouthful of acrid smoke. He sighed contentedly. Finally, the day had come. He felt stimulated; having forced aside his worry for his children in order to function at the machine shop, keep his job, and just survive for this day—so his children could survive. He dared not dwell on the thought. With Josiah, one never knew. Still, a flicker of hope existed; he buried it deep inside. He peeked around the corner of the building. He could just make out DC Ross's house from where he stood. He looked with interest as he saw the gift being accepted and then watched as Mambo Ross put a suitcase in his car and drove out of the station. His heart surged. This was what he had been waiting for.

He looked around. No one was paying any attention to him. He knew he would not be missed right away. The work he was supposed to be doing on the Landrover could wait; after all, he had already postponed it for two days. He took a last draw on his cigarette then reluctantly crushed it with his foot, imagining it was Josiah's neck. He started off, walking briskly, towards Chief Mutasa's kraal. His uncle's home was about twenty miles away. It would take him most of the night to get there, and then it would take the messenger another half day to find Josiah. Mambo Ross usually returned early Monday morning—that would give Josiah enough time to arrange whatever he was planning to do.

* * *

"Daddy's home! Daddy's home!"

As Jamie opened the car door Deanne flung herself into his arms. He tossed her into the air and caught her as she squealed in delight.

Rachelle was jumping up and down, waiting for her turn, but she had grown, so Jamie could only pick her up and hold her tightly.

Barrie was beaming, not yet too old for a hug and a kiss.

"You kids can help me take my luggage in."

Barrie grabbed the suitcase from the back seat as Jamie opened the trunk.

Rachelle reached for the cardboard box. As she lifted it a loud squawk startled her. She jumped back in surprise. Slowly, she bent her head and peered through the narrow opening in the top of the box. Her eyes widened in surprise, "It's a chicken," she whispered. Then more loudly, "It's a chicken! Daddy brought us a chicken!" She ran, with the box clutched in her arms, towards the house. "Mom! Mom! Daddy brought us a real, live chicken."

Emily dried her hands on a dish towel and tossed it aside. She hurried out of the kitchen door, eager to embrace Jamie, to feel his arms around her. She stopped as Rachelle ran up to her. She glanced at the box and then turned a questioning look to Jamie. "A chicken, Jamie?"

Jamie could read her mind. *What in the world were they going to do with a real, live chicken in the middle of Salisbury?* Jamie looked apologetic, "It was a gift, just before I left Mutasa."

The children were no longer interested in Jamie or Emily. They were crowded around the chicken box, carefully lifting the lid.

"I think my hopes of chicken stew are dashed. At least as far as this chicken is concerned," Jamie whispered into Emily's ear. The two of them laughed out loud as they clung to each other and looked at their delighted children.

At last the children had the chicken out of the box and Barrie undid the bindings on its legs. It shook and ruffled its feathers, glad to be free at last. Jamie thought he had never seen such a scrawny bird. Its legs were long and sinewy. Not much of a drumstick there, he thought. Its comb flopped over its left eye at a rakish angle and its golden eyes had a fierce gleam.

Rachelle clapped her hands in delight. "Oh, isn't he beautiful, daddy? His feathers look so pretty in the sunlight. All black, red and orange. And look at his tail. It looks just like he has a pony tail." Rachelle picked the bird up and hugged it to her chest, whispering sweet words of endearment. Jamie could only hope it didn't have lice.

* * *

The weekend went by far too fast. Jamie lay awake, tense, waiting for the alarm to pierce the silence, telling him it was 1:30 in the morning. This was his last night at home and he wanted to prolong it, savor each moment. He felt Emily's warm, soft body beside him and he turned his head to breathe in the sweet fragrance of her hair. He would take these memories with him; hold onto them till he was home again. He longed for life to get back to normal—coming home every night for dinner, playing with the kids, spending evenings loving and talking with Emily. Except for church, and a doctor's visit that produced a disheartening report on his blood pressure, he had allowed nothing else to pry himself away from them this weekend.

He looked at the clock. It was time. He reached over and turned off the alarm, seconds before the raucous beep could startle Emily. Climbing out of bed, he padded begrudgingly to the bathroom and looked at himself in the mirror. There was no time to shave. He would wait until he got back to Mutasa. He kind of liked the look of the one day stubble. It seemed manly. In fact, if it didn't itch so much he might even consider a beard. But then he knew Emily wouldn't go for it.

He put on his uniform, slipped into the bedroom and kissed Emily gently on the cheek. She mumbled in her sleep then snuggled further into the blankets. He looked in at the children. It was amazing what weird contortions children could sleep comfortably in. He picked up his bag, checked his Uzi, and headed out to the little Datsun.

* * *

A sliver of a moon was etched on the night sky. Not much else but the street lamps. Driving through Salisbury at two in the morning there was hardly a movement—virtually no cars. Something felt different this morning. Strangely, despite the solitude and eerily desolate surrounds, he felt unusual warmth, an assurance he was being watched over.

By the time he reached the main Umtali road, he felt invincible and had the urge for an adrenalin rush. He pushed his foot flat down on the accelerator. Soon the needle was flickering between ninety and a hundred and ten miles per hour. He held that speed for the next fifteen minutes. It was exhilarating. Hopefully, no animals were on the road.

Passing through the little town of Marandellas, he settled down and maintained a steady, but safe speed until he reached the Inyanga turnoff around 0445. From there it was an hour's run to the Mutasa road. He would be at his second home in time for breakfast.

As he drove, his mind skipped from one thought to another. He took pleasure in going over the high points of the weekend. The children were growing up so fast, and Emily seemed so much more self assured and capable. She had become used to making decisions on her own, dealing with problems he would normally have dealt with. At church on Sunday morning everyone had been so friendly and glad to see him.

Driving home, there was always the excitement of seeing Emily and the kids. Driving back to Mutasa, however, those memories faded, and all he could think about were the challenges that lay ahead.

Jamie drove through the pine and wattle forests. He could just make out the road through the brightening dawn as the first rays of light progressively illuminated the scenery. His headlights lit up the Mutasa signpost. Slowing down, he looked at his watch, 0540 hours. He would be at the village in just minutes. The gravel road was covered with dew. In the faint light of dawn, he could see no other tracks. The road was narrow, just wide enough for two cars to pass. Either side of the road was a grass verge with freshly cut drains every fifty yards or so. His thoughts turned to the week ahead and all that needed to be done. There was so much to do.

What? Something yanked the steering wheel from his hands. He was out of control. Wide awake, there was no doubt the steering wheel was still being pulled to the left. The left-side wheels of the Datsun bounced over the grassy verge with a sharp bump as the car flew over one of the side drains. Jamie wrenched the wheel to the right and was back on the road. His heart hammered. What was that all about? The little Datsun had purred along fine for the entire trip. What sort of malfunction was this?

He drove on cautiously. His adrenaline rush was tempered by the incident and he slowed down until, with relief, he saw the lights of the village of Mutasa. He would get one of the mechanics to take a look at the Datsun. There must be something wrong with the steering mechanism, or maybe just an odd bump in the road. He shrugged it off.

Sixpence was waiting to help unload the boxes of groceries as Jamie drove up to the house. First order of business was always to call Emily and let her know he was safely home. He could hear the phone ringing at the other end and then a sleepy voice. "Is that you, Jamie?"

"Hi Emily, I just got back to Mutasa. I wanted you to know all is well. Give the kids a hug from dad. I'll call you tomorrow evening. Love you."

Jamie sorted through his clothes. He would need to leave some at Mutasa and re-pack others for the Honde. He zipped up his bag and tossed it next to the door.

It had only been fifteen minutes, when the phone rang. It was Marilyn Gordon. Her voice was terse. "Jamie, come down to the office right away. The engineers are still on their road patrol, but have asked that you meet with them. They're about half a mile from the village. Pick me up on your way."

"I'm sorry, what?

"Just get here as soon as you can."

Click.

Something was not right. He drew a breath. Shoes on and laces tied, he picked up his Uzi and headed for the Leopard. No breakfast today.

Here we go. Crunching the gears he backed up and drove straight to the office. Marilyn was standing on the front verandah with Sergeant Dande, and a young engineer whose name he did not know.

"Mambo, there's big trouble on the road. Muvundhla asks that we go with him. The rest of the engineers are waiting for us," said Dande in an excited voice.

Jamie's pulse quickened. This job was certainly doing a number on his blood pressure.

"What gives, Marilyn? Why the sudden panic?"

Her eyes were wide. "I don't know, but I don't like the sound of their voices. Muvundhla found Sergeant Dande and they came rushing in to tell me to call you."

"Okay, jump in. Let's go."

They had only driven a short distance when they caught sight of the remaining three engineers standing by the side of the road. The only tracks on the road were the tracks of his Datsun from earlier that morning. Jamie frowned. He slowed to a stop. They had placed red triangles in the middle of the road to stop any traffic. He climbed out and was immediately approached by Corporal Makuviri who stopped in front of him. The corporal was obviously perplexed. He paused as if searching for words. The man could speak perfect English; why the fumbling?

"Sir," the corporal began, his brow wrinkled. "Why did you drive off the road? Did you see something?"

At first Jamie did not know what he was talking about, but then, looking at the tracks, his blood ran cold. Abruptly, he remembered. *The incident with the steering wheel.* He could see clearly where the Datsun's tracks had veered off onto the verge and then back on again.

"I don't really know. Is there something wrong?"

"Yes, sir, we think there is a landmine in the road. If you look closely the dirt in the middle of the road is a slightly different color to the rest of the dirt. We wanted to speak to you before we checked further."

Jamie was stunned. Memories of that morning came crashing back. He had not been alone.

"Muvundhla," said Corporal Makuviri, "Get your probe and check the road."

The engineer picked up the long aluminum probe. He lay flat on his stomach and gently used it to move the soil. Suddenly, he stopped and withdrew the probe. "There is a mine here."

"Keep checking," said Makuviri.

Gradually, as the earth was moved away, Jamie could see the metal top of a landmine.

Makuviri whistled in amazement. "There's more. There are hand grenades all around the mine. This will take time."

Jamie stood back with Marilyn and Sergeant Dande, watching while the engineers continued their probing for the next hour. With long metal forceps, one by one, four Chinese-made stick grenades were removed and brought over to show Jamie, after they had been disarmed. Finally, Makuviri inserted a larger probe lifting one side of the landmine and enabling them to insert a harness to drag it towards them. It was a standard Russian-made, anti-tank mine about eighteen inches in diameter and four inches deep.

"Wait, shouted Muvundhla. There's more." He slid forward and with a shorter probe unearthed a wooden box. With careful maneuvering, they soon had it removed. The box, with Chinese lettering, represented twenty four pounds of plastic explosive. Jamie sucked in a sharp breath.

I should be dead. The thought immobilized him.

Marilyn turned to Jamie, her tears came without warning.

"That little package would have blown you all the way across the border. Someone was determined to take you out and we'd have had nothing to ship home, especially in that little Datsun of yours."

The color had drained from Sergeant Dande. "This is very bad, mambo. Somebody must have told the *boys* you would be driving back this morning. No other cars or trucks are expected." Dande walked briskly over to the engineers where a spirited conversation took place, out of earshot of Jamie and Marilyn. After a few minutes he walked back to Jamie.

"They all want to know what spirit warned you about the landmine. You could not have seen it with your eyes while driving, even in the daylight."

"Well Marilyn, it's good to know I'm still top of the hit list and they haven't forgotten me." He put a hand on her shoulder. "Come, we could both do with breakfast. I know a great local chef in need of diners and he's cooked up a hearty meal."

Jamie looked up. *Thank you, Lord.*

* * *

"What do you mean, he is not dead. You are telling me lies." Josiah's voice was low, raspy and menacing.

"It is true, my esteemed leader. He is not dead." The young boy cowered in front of Josiah. His lips quivered as he delivered his message. "I hid in the bushes all night and he passed by in the morning. I saw with my own eyes that his car was not hurt."

"How is it that he is not hurt. Were the explosives not placed in the road?"

"Yes, Mambo. They were there but the car left the road and did not go over them."

"Isaac!" Josiah bellowed.

Isaac scurried into the room and stood before Josiah. His heart was pounding. He had never heard Josiah so angry.

"I am here, Mambo."

"You fool." Spittle formed at the corners of Josiah's mouth, his eyes flashed. "You did not hide the mines well enough. Chinyerere spotted them."

"No, Mambo. I hid them very well. No man could have seen them."

"Then how do you account for the fact he drove his car around them.?"

"Mambo, the people say that Chinyerere has a very strong spirit. I think maybe his spirit protected him."

"Chinyerere has one spirit. How can his one spirit be more powerful than the many spirits of our ancestors?" Josiah spat contemptuously. "You will see. I will show you that this spirit he has is like a newborn jackal. Go! I must think."

Despite the bravado that Josiah showed, a small seed of fear crept into his mind. *Was this spirit of Chinyerere more powerful?*

Chapter Nineteen

Josiah stood in the hallway outside the old farmhouse dining room. He smoothed his olive green uniform over his stomach. He had refused the chair offered to him by the young comrade on duty; he did not want to crease his uniform by sitting down. Three days ago he had received word that Rex Nhongo, and the great leader of the revolution, Robert Mugabe, wanted to see him. Josiah had taken special care to see that his uniform was freshly washed and ironed—even his boots were polished to a bright sheen. He stood tall and stiff, proud to be commander of the Manyika division of ZANLA. He wondered if there was to be a new honor bestowed on him, or perhaps a new command. He waited patiently.

The door opened and a young comrade motioned him into the room. He stood at attention and saluted smartly. Rex Nhongo he knew. Comrade General Nhongo had been his leader for the past five years, but Josiah's eyes were riveted on the man sitting beside him. Robert Mugabe was smaller than he had imagined. Not the large imposing build of a great warrior. His face was as black as Josiah had ever seen and his eyes glistened from behind the thick round lenses of a heavy pair of tortoise shell glasses. Around him the air seemed to crackle with tension and his presence dominated the room. Josiah felt a slight shiver travel down his spine.

Rex Nhongo motioned to a chair. "Sit." He turned to Mugabe, "This is Josiah Makoni, sir, the one who has been leading our forces in the Honde."

Josiah swallowed hard as he pulled up a chair. "It is a great honor for me to be in the presence of so great a man; the comrade who is leading our struggle for freedom."

"Ah, yes, Makoni." Mugabe's voice was smooth as silk. Josiah felt the glistening eyes bore right through him. "So you are the commander General Rex Nhongo has been telling me about." His eyes never blinked and never left Josiah's face. "Comrade General Nhongo is the hero of the people. He has led us to great victories in the Honde Valley and the forests of Chimanimanis."

"That is true, my esteemed leader." Josiah tried to control the quiver in his voice. "I have been greatly honored to work under him."

The thin slit of Mugabe's mouth suddenly turned down at the corners and his face contorted in anger. "But now what is happening in the Honde? You understand that with the Honde closed, we have to move all our comrades north through Tete. This is causing us many problems. What do you have to say?" His words cut malevolently through the air.

Josiah's heart dropped down to the hollow pit of his stomach. Were they blaming the problems in the Honde on him?

Mugabe half rose in his seat and leaned forward. Josiah gasped at the fetid smell of his breath. "Comrade Makoni, you know how important it is for all the people to understand our struggle for freedom—the sacrifices we must make. We have seen much of our good work in the Honde undone in the last few months. We cannot lose ground in other parts of the border, especially at our crossing points. You have not answered me." His voice was shrill and menacing.

Josiah squirmed in his seat. He could not find the words to answer.

Rex Nhongo looked disdainfully at Josiah. "We still have our paths open through the Vumba, and at Chimanimani. We cannot lose more ground. As commander of the Manyika Division I am relying on you to keep these paths open. Most important of all, is for our people to understand the struggle. Only absolute loyalty to our cause can bring about the freedom we fight for. Local tribal leaders are wavering in their support, and passing information to the police, and the enemy. This cannot be tolerated."

Josiah's heart pounded. "Comrade Mugabe and Comrade General Nhongo, I hear you. My heart is heavy with the losses we have suffered in the Honde. The spirits turned against us and our enemy, Chinyerere, has avoided all the traps we set for him."

Mugabe sat back in his chair and pressed his fingers together. His eyes narrowed behind the glasses as he peered at Josiah. "Maybe there is one thing you can do that will make up for your failures."

Josiah nodded eagerly. "Yes, Comrade Mugabe. Anything."

Mugabe's tone was conciliatory and the corners of his lips turned up as he explained his plan.

Josiah's eyes widened as he listened. Yes, this would be a deed that would teach a vicious lesson and catch the attention of the whole world. "I can do it Comrade Mambo Mugabe. I know the place you speak of. I have been there."

Nhongo lit a cigarette and looked out the window, slowly exhaling and sending a puff of smoke floating upwards. "You understand there is no place for failures in our struggle." He paused and looked at Josiah, his lips tightening in a grimace. "You have heard the words from our esteemed leader, Comrade Mambo Mugabe. Do not disappoint us. Failure to support our cause will not be tolerated. You are dismissed."

Josiah walked out of the room. His face burned with the reprimand, but his determination soared. Now he would show the people just what he could do. No one would be able to deny he was a great commander. He would not disappoint the great Comrade Mugabe.

* * *

Josiah quietly thanked the spirits. The dark clouds vanished as quickly as they had arrived. The sun came out briefly, rays of light brightening the misty valley below. As they topped the ridge, Josiah stopped. He looked across the valley to the plains in the distance, illuminated by the last rays of sunshine. There were fourteen in his group. Early that morning, they had set out from their camp in Mozambique, prepared to travel most of the day.

They crossed the Rhodesian border at midday and kept to hidden paths. Reaching Vumba Mountain was no easy journey. The trails were narrow and crossed three mountain ranges. Crystal clear mountain streams were plentiful and offered reprieve for the thirsty comrades. Maize meal cakes provided scanty fare, but hunger was of much less concern than the Rhodesian security forces that patrolled the border in their helicopters. The rhythm of the rotors matched the quickening hearts of the men on the ground as they heard one. *Thrum, thrum, thrum.* The whirling blades broke the silence, skimming over the forest, as gunners watched intently for intruders, like hawks circling for prey. The men below moved quickly, practiced in deftness and experts at concealment. They remained attuned to every footstep and breath, continually gauging speed against energy reserves.

They were getting closer. Josiah turned toward Enoch. "Make sure the rockets for the SAM missile launcher are ready. We could be spotted."

"I am ready," said Enoch, adding under his breath, "I would love the chance to shoot down one of the vultures."

Josiah heard him and realized the absurdity. Chances were slim to none that any missile could arm itself before a twenty millimeter cannon turned and sought them out, spraying an angry volley of bullets that would shred all in its path.

Josiah's heart raced. Now they were crossing the ridge of Vumba Mountain. Just below was an old convalescent school. His lips quivered. He felt fear and anticipation. A few minutes later he could see a narrow tar road, clawing its way up the mountain, with sharp turns and steep gradients. Looking below Josiah could see their target, Elim Mission Secondary School. Yes, they had treated his wounded comrade, but then turned them away. From the information they had given him back at the ZANLA camp he learned that the missionaries came from England and that there were over two hundred students and fifteen African teachers. *Yes, this was the opportunity to redeem himself. Comrade Mugabe and Comrade General Nhongo would shower him with praise at the audacity and success of this mission. The world would know that the power of ZANU was not be trifled with.*

Stopping near a clump of rocks Josiah held up his hand. The comrades gathered around. Looking down Josiah watched the lights come on at the mission. There was a distant sound of children singing. Turning, he pointed down towards the mission. "You see the cricket field and pavilion. That is where I want you to take everyone. Sit down now. We will wait here until it is dark." He glanced at his watch—just after six. Night settled around them like a black wreath. The comrades took out the last of their maize cakes, probably their last meal before they crossed the border back into Mozambique. Talking in low tones, they ate and waited for the signal to proceed.

Josiah settled against a boulder. He was not hungry. Squinting, he focused his eyes on the missionaries' houses above the school. He saw occasional movement through the windows. His mind drifted.

Someone coughed softly in the deepening dusk.

Josiah sat up with a start. He jumped to his feet. It was time. He gathered the comrades around him. "We will enter the school as one. Mangwende will lead his men and go immediately to the teachers' houses, just outside the main perimeter. The teachers will understand and will be quick to follow orders. Is that understood?"

Murmurs of agreement followed and heads turned as he pointed to the large field below.

"All teachers and their families must be taken to the pavilion near the cricket field, and wait there for the students. Mangwende, you are responsible for the teachers. Make sure they understand their duties—to watch over the students when they arrive. Is that clear?"

"Yes, Comrade Makoni. I understand," responded Mangwende.

"Good. Take two men with you."

He pulled Enoch aside. "Take three men. Wake all the students. Go into both the girls' and boys' dormitories and take them to the cricket field. Have them sit in a large circle. They must see everything that happens."

The men nodded in agreement.

"I will take six comrades with me. We will bring the missionary families to the cricket field. Understand this—tonight, there will be no easy death. Nobody is to fire a rifle unless it is absolutely necessary. More murmurs of agreement.

"When I give the call of a nightjar, move in."

They all settled back as they watched and waited. Finally, the first lights went out. At eight, the lights in the main courtyard of the school were switched off. That was the signal. Josiah motioned to the men. The comrades jumped to their feet, checking AK rifles, spare magazines, the SAM missile launcher, and the rockets.

The comrades followed Josiah as he led the way down the crest of the ridge. They padded along barefoot with their boots slung over their necks, to avoid making noise. The path meandered from left to right, around large rocks, and ever downward towards the mission school. Moving like a pack of wild dogs, they closed in on their prey.

The few remaining lights burned brightly. The comrades moved in and crouched down just two hundred yards from the school. The night was quiet, except for the clicks of bolts being drawn back as weapons were cocked.

"Fix your bayonets," whispered Josiah in a raspy order. "Make sure they are tight. Use your knobkerries first."

Mangwende, and two other guerillas with knobkerries, held them up, shaking the clubs.

Enoch tightened his grip on the SAM missile launcher in his left hand and a demo, small axe, in his right hand.

Josiah and Enoch separated the comrades into three groups. Enoch and Mangwende, with their men, moved towards the teachers' housing and dormitories. Josiah led his six men toward the three missionaries' houses just above the school. Upon his signal, they would kick open the doors to the three houses at the same time. He called quietly for two of them to follow him, pointing to the remaining four to break up and head for the other two houses. Moving silently, he neared the largest of the three buildings, the headmaster's home. He had been here before. Each group moved in and waited for Josiah's signal.

Josiah's heart pounded. Mugabe's words rang through his mind. *There is a high price for disloyalty and lessons to be learned.*

The men were in position. It was time. Josiah whistled the shrill call of the nightjar—a plaintive wail in the still night air.

Josiah kicked open the headmaster's door. A dull light shone from the bathroom. Josiah headed there and pushed the door open. What a sight. The headmaster and his wife were undressed and in their nightclothes.

Josiah stared with revulsion.

Yes. These are white pigs.

He grabbed the woman, tearing her blue nightdress, and simultaneously pointed to the man in his under shorts. "Come with me. Don't shout or I will kill."

He yanked the woman's hand, dragging her behind him as he used his bayonet to drive the man forward and down the hall. In the living room two young children stood, dressed in bright yellow pajamas. The girl squealed in fright.

The frantic woman's fear now turned to hysteria. "Please, please don't hurt them. They are only small children."

Josiah slapped her. "Shut up."

The man instinctively wheeled around to protect his wife. Josiah prodded him sharply with the bayonet. Blood trickled down the man's belly, leaving a crimson trail on the beige living room carpet as Josiah continued to shove him along. Both children backed away from the blood and screamed. The boy cried out for his father. Isaac drew back his knobkerrie and smacked it down on the small shoulder. The slight frame slammed to the floor, and stayed down, afraid to move. A warm, dark red blotch soaked through his yellow pajamas. The little girl, desperate to run to someone, anyone, whimpered uncontrollably. Isaac kicked the boy with his foot and commanded him to stand up.

Using bayonets, the three comrades herded the wailing family out in the cold and down to the cricket field. Other screams joined theirs as cries filled the dark night. Students were gathering on the cricket field.

A man, woman, and a young girl wearing a bright red dressing gown, struggled to hold onto one another as they were forced forward. The cry of a baby rose above the noise. A half-dressed woman, clutching an infant to her chest, was herded alongside her husband and made to stand in front of the students. Three other women joined them. One was much older than the rest and Josiah recognized her as the nurse who had treated his wounded comrade some weeks before.

Josiah called out to the teachers and students, his voice carrying above the screams. "Sit down now and watch what happens to traitors."

Children cried out as teachers protectively pushed to the ground any students still standing. A sudden aura of silence settled over the field.

Enoch looked over the crowd and chose a teacher. Within seconds, he was standing before the quivering man. Wrenching him from the group, he pulled him to the pavilion.

"Turn on the lights," he bellowed.

The ground in front of the pavilion flooded with the brilliance of four large flood lamps. The sudden brightness was temporarily blinding.

Josiah turned to the cowering missionaries. They were huddled together, clutching each other, and praying aloud to their God.

"Shut up!" He stamped his foot on the ground. "Be quiet you cowardly dogs."

He spun back around to the teachers and students and shouted, "You are now going to see for yourselves what happens to those who are not loyal. Tonight you will understand ZANU justice." Quickly scanning the group, he settled on the man in the under shorts. Blood still trickled from his belly. He pointed. "Enoch. That one. Let him be first."

Enoch grabbed the man and pulled him out of the group.

Daddy, daddy!

The man's wife silenced her children as she dropped to her knees in horror, pulling them with her and burying their heads into her chest to shield their eyes. Her mouth fell open but she could not scream.

One of the comrades stepped forward with his knobkerrie. He struck the man a hard blow to the side of his head. The man crumpled to the ground. Another comrade shoved him over with his foot and thrust a bayonet into the man's belly, slowly pulling it down, spilling guts and innards. There were several screams. He repeatedly stabbed the writhing man with the bayonet until, finally, there was no sign of life.

A quivering female's voice repeatedly screamed, "Oh God, no, please, please stop."

It caught Josiah's attention and a malevolent smile crossed his lips. He pointed to the woman. "Comrades, have some fun. See which woman will be the first to cry for mercy."

Twelve of the comrades grabbed the six adult women and the young girls. One of the comrades laughed as he tore the nightdress off one of the women, leaving her standing naked in the bright light from the flood lamps. Two other comrades ripped off the clothes of another woman who was still fully dressed. She clutched both arms around her private parts, falling to her knees, as her panties were torn off.

"Oh please don't hurt me," she sobbed.

The comrades dragged the women to different corners of the cricket field, remaining in full view of the teachers and students. Josiah watched as Isaac grabbed the young woman with the baby.

In another corner, Mangwende tore off the blouse and bra of the older woman. He jeered when he saw her sagging breasts.

"This one is too wrinkled. She looks like a dried up lizard." All the comrades laughed,

He shoved the older woman backwards. "Let's see how fast you can run. Here, I'll give you a little help."

He thrust his bayonet into her shoulder and again into her side. From where he stood, Josiah could hear flesh tear as the bayonet was pulled out with a ripping sound. She hit the ground. Again, unsteadily, she stood. Mangwende spat on her.

"You bastard."

He booted her back into the dirt. Yet again, she gathered strength and pushed herself up.

Josiah shook his head. *The old hag is strong. He had watched her before when she treated his wounded comrade.* The woman looked up and, for a few seconds, her burning eyes locked with his. Josiah frowned. He had seen this same look several times tonight, but not quite so intense. Yes, there was a fear and unmistaken panic in her eyes, but there was something stronger. It stirred a feeling deep in Josiah. He remembered his mother. It was in the eyes. When he had done something wrong, there was anguish in her eyes, yet behind them, unbelievable strength. He quickly looked away from the woman. Whatever peculiar feeling this was, it would succumb to anger. It was the only way. He was a leader. He would not be weakened. Maybe it was the baby's cry getting to him. He turned toward it in a rage. As soon as Isaac was finished with the woman, he would have him kill it.

The woman holding the baby screamed and kicked frantically. Isaac held her down with one knee on her chest while Enoch unbuckled his trousers. Forcing the woman's legs apart, he moved on top of her shouting, "Now you can feel a real man." The young woman never let go of her baby. Clutching her tightly to her chest, she pleaded, "No, no, Jesus help me. My baby."

* * *

Sister Catherine coughed as the blood trickled from her mouth.

Oh, God, save us.

She frantically searched for a way to hide her nakedness as she stood under the bright floodlights of the cricket field.

Dear God, we came to this Mission for you. Please don't let this happen.

Her blouse and bra were ripped off. The man laughed and said something, she was not sure what. Others laughed. She could not focus.

Suddenly, an intense pain burned through her as a bayonet drove deep into her shoulder. Flesh ripped as the bayonet was withdrawn. More pain, and nausea. Next, she felt the bayonet thrust into her side. When she hit the ground, she did not feel the impact.

God, why … ?

Dizzy, she pushed to her elbows and slowly lifted to her knees. The man spat on her. She didn't see his kick coming and went reeling again into the dirt. Laughter, mixed with sounds of thuds as clubs broke flesh. Gasps and screams of panic and death surrounded her from all directions. She offered another plea to the one who mattered most, her God. A new surge of adrenalin flowed through her. Pulling herself up, she regained focus. She caught the eye of the leader, the one giving the orders. It was him. She recognized him—the terrorist who had brought the wounded guerilla to the mission.

"Get up, you white pig."

The sneer came inches from her. She drifted.

No. I can't lose consciousness.

She spat blood and dirt from her mouth and looked up. The images were terrifying. There were at least a dozen terrorists. Her heart stopped cold.

"Oh, Jesus, save my baby."

It was Joyce. She was on the ground clutching her baby as a man held her down and another moved toward her, unbuckling his belt. Joyce's cries rented the air.

She heard little Becky scream and scream again and again. She looked, but could not see what was happening to her. She had watched as the terrorists had dragged the child onto the cricket field, lights shining on her bright red dressing gown. That precious little girl. She was only four years old.

"Where *are* you God?"

She could see the students and teachers sitting untouched in a circle, forced to watch. Then it came to her—what was really happening. This group was being used. They would live, but suffer far more than those who were dying. They would experience a torment designed to traumatize them beyond anything they could imagine; the ramifications of which would reach undeniably deeper than any thrust a bayonet, or any act of hatred could inflict.

A new panic set in.

I am going to die.

Her eyes darted beyond, to the forest. She weighed her chances.

Keep thinking. Clear my thoughts ...

She gagged, not sure if the nausea was from searing pain of her gashes, the hot, sticky blood running down her side, or from the pungent, sweaty stench of Mangwende, who was still shouting, just inches from her. She had to get away. Her eyes again darted toward the edge of the forest. It was just one hundred yards away.

"She's too old," said Mangwende derisively. "I don't want her." He loosened his grip. "Let's see how fast she can run."

Her limbs were weak, but she dove forward, out of the rough hands, and ran, stumbling, tripping through the crowd of whimpering students and teachers, on toward the forest. She heard footsteps running behind her and the voice of the leader.

"Let her go. She is finished and won't live long."

It was the last thing she heard as she ran out of the circle of light, into the thick bush, and darkness beyond the field.

* * *

Josiah approved as he watched the old woman run. "Yes, she is finished. She can die in the forest."

"Spare the children," shouted one of the teachers.

Josiah ignored him.

"It is time to finish it," he shouted to his men.

The comrades grabbed each of the remaining whites. They beat them, sometimes with their knobkerries, sometimes with the butts of their AK rifles. Screams and cries rent the air. Josiah continued to oversee. He watched as the missionaries tried to fend off the blows while the comrades fought over them like dogs fighting over a bone—stabbing, kicking, hitting with their knobkerries until the last of the missionaries fell and lay in pools of their own blood.

There it was again. The cry of the baby. Josiah looked at Isaac and pointed toward the sound. As a final gesture, Isaac took his bayonet and thrust it right into the back and heart of the tiny infant who was still clutched in his dead mother's arms. The baby gave a shudder and fell to one side, still grasping her mother's finger as she convulsed twice before lying still.

Josiah turned to the teachers.

"Now it is finished. Tonight, you have seen justice. Do not call the police. Do not leave until morning or we will be back to give you the same message. Take the students back to their dormitories and then go back to your houses and stay there."

Josiah shouted to Enoch. "Get the group together. We have a long way to travel before dawn."

They set off, moving quickly. They would need a good head start to reach the border of Mozambique, before the Rhodesian helicopters and Special Forces were sent to cut them off. It would be a long night.

* * *

The sergeant did not bother to knock. He skidded to a stop in front of Colonel Sanders.

"Terrorists just hit the Elim Mission," he gasped, out of breath. "We got a call a few minutes ago that all the missionaries have been killed. Only one possible survivor—an older woman. Old Mac from Eagles Nest called in on the agric-alert."

Colonel Jock Sanders, Nick Farham, John Whiting and Jamie Ross were sitting in the ops room drinking coffee. Jamie and Nick had spent the night in Umtali, ready for an early morning briefing. Hearing the news they all sprang to their feet.

"Damned animals!" cursed Sanders, slamming his fist on the desk. "Send out an immediate red alert."

Within minutes, all members of the JOC had gathered in the ops room. The Colonel had finished gathering the initial information and stood to address them, waving the report angrily.

"We've had another beastly attack. The bastards hit the Elim Mission last night and wiped out the missionaries and their families. Initial reports say there is one woman survivor. The farmer who took her in doesn't think she'll make it."

Colonel Sanders turned to John Whiting.

"Major, get two choppers ready for immediate take off and have two sticks ready to board ASAP. See if you can get some SAS guys dropped on the border, just South of Vumba Mountain. A full platoon if we have one."

Jamie's eyes were fierce as the heat washed over his face. "Those bastards will head straight for the border. You'll have to catch them before they get there. They've had a good eight to nine hour start."

Jock turned to Jamie, Nick Farham, and Sandy Giles from Special Branch.

"I want the three of you at the mission, pronto. Sandy, you'll need to fully brief the press. All the teachers and students will have to be dealt with. Close down the school. That's your job, Jamie. Nick and Sandy, I'm relying on you to put together a full picture, including photos for debriefing this evening. John, you head up the response group. Catch the bastards. Don't let them cross the border."

* * *

The scene was ghastly. Jamie drew in a sharp breath. He had to turn away as he felt bile rise up in his stomach.

Just yesterday, he had marveled at how he had been protected from the mine, and now this. Jamie wanted to turn and walk away, as much from the gruesome scene as from the questions that plagued him. But he could not.

Jamie fought back emotions as the rims of his eyes reddened. "Those animals," He yelled to no one in particular. "I can't believe what I'm seeing. Why the missionaries, and babies too?" Tears finally spilled over as he saw a baby's tiny fist clenched around her mother's index finger.

Sandy's face was drained of color. "What a bloody mess. They massacred them all."

Jamie went from body to body while Nick accompanied him in silence. He had seen many bodies brutalized by terrorists, but nothing compared to this. He walked back to the Leopard and picked up the radio receiver. "Lighthouse one calling, Lighthouse one zero. Do you read me? Over." There was silence and then the radio crackled to life.

"Lighthouse one zero here. Who is calling?"

"Lighthouse one zero, this is Lighthouse one. I need immediate assistance. I need to speak to papa charlie."

As he waited, the logistical nightmare ahead of him began to set in. Hundreds of students and teachers needed a way back to their homes in the Mutare Tribal Trust Land, or rides to the train station in Umtali where they would begin their journey home.

"Lighthouse one this is papa charlie. I heard about the mission. I'm so sorry. What can I do?"

"I'm at Elim Mission. You've heard the reports. We need to close down the school. Send up eight trucks with escorts. We have over two hundred and fifty people to move. I'll need these people on their way by midday."

"Roger. Understood. I'll be back in touch in thirty minutes. Hold tight and wait. Out."

Jamie slumped back in the seat of the Leopard. George Barstow, would move heaven and earth to find the necessary trucks to transport the people. All he could do now was sit and wait while images haunted him, and questions whispered through his mind. The door creaked open and Sergeant Dande slipped inside the Leopard. His face looked grey through his black skin.

"Mambo, why do these people kill missionaries? What good did it do to kill small children, even babies? I am so ashamed."

Jamie turned to his friend. "What we see today has nothing to do with freedom. These people think that by killing innocent missionaries in this manner they will win the support of the people."

"This is not freedom," Dande spat out.

"I think we both know that. It is only the beginning of the end of freedom."

"Who could do this?" asked Dande.

"This is the work of Nhongo," said Jamie. "Maybe even Josiah Makoni. I wonder why he has left the Honde Valley to come this far south."

Dande dropped his head into his hands.

Jamie raked both hands through his hair. "I know Mugabe is behind all this bloodshed. We can never understand what's in his mind. I fear the day if he ever gains power in this land. He is such a smooth talker. The Americans and British think that all he wants is a peaceful transition to power. He and his thugs got their training in North Korea and China."

"Mao Tse-tung?" asked Dande, sitting back again.

Jamie nodded. "They follow the *Little Red Book*. Look what Mao did in China. Did he allow opposition? Millions were slaughtered after he gained power. Mugabe will do whatever it takes to make sure the Matabele never gain power again."

Dande frowned. "What is happening to our government?"

Jamie sat silently for a moment and then continued. "Rhodesia is in for a long struggle. You can be sure that any peace and order in a new black government will give over to corruption and eventual starvation. Hunger for power replaces reformation."

The radio crackled to life again. "Lighthouse one this is papa charlie. Eight trucks and two police reserve sections are on their way for the evacuation. They'll be there by ten. Thank you Jamie. I am glad you are there to help. Out."

* * *

Click. Click. Camera shutters snapped. Police photographers milled around the scene of the massacre, hovering over bodies and taking images of corpses just as they lay. Two medics arrived and began unloading a stack of black plastic body bags. Jamie finished answering questions posed by two reporters from the Rhodesian Information Services, and a visiting reporter from South Africa. He had no doubt this would make international news.

As the reporters walked back to the scene, Sandy approached Jamie with his account. "Eleven dead, including one baby, aged six weeks. I've just received word about the one survivor."

Jamie swallowed hard.

"The older woman died on her way to Salisbury hospital."

Sandy stared out at the scene and shook his head. "Maybe now the international press will understand what we're dealing with. That bastard Mugabe, and his thugs. He oozes oil when he speaks, but underneath he's a power hungry animal willing to stop at nothing to seize power."

"God help the people if he ever gains control of the country," said Jamie.

Sandy glanced over at the teachers. Dande was directing them to gather under the pavilion. "I hope you have a smooth evacuation."

"It will take some logistics to get these people home," said Jamie. "A bigger concern is dealing with the psychological trauma they've experienced. We don't have counselors."

Sandy nodded. "I'm sure this will affect them the rest of their lives."

Jamie looked toward the pavilion. All the teachers were now sitting down on the bleachers, waiting in silence. "It's time," he said.

"You have a difficult task ahead," said Sandy, turning back to the scene to finish writing up his report.

Jamie walked toward the dining room where the teachers were gathered. He wanted to be anywhere but here. He searched for the right words, but was aware nothing he could say would erase their anguish.

* * *

Great plates of hot maize porridge sat before the children, along with jugs of milk and jars of sugar to sweeten the food, as though this would alleviate the pain. It was ten o' clock and the students and teachers were sitting down in the dining room to eat. They ate in hushed tones. There was no laughter and very little talking.

Jamie opened the door to the dining room and walked in. This was the first time he had seen all the students and teachers in one place. The students looked up at him, many with vacant eyes, having retreated into their own worlds. Some sat, lips quivering, and arms wrapped around themselves. Others just looked startled, not knowing whom to trust or what would happen next.

Jamie spoke words of consolation and comfort that, although poured from the depths of his soul, seemed empty and inadequate compared to the trauma the children had endured. He explained procedures for evacuation. Some would be transported by trucks to their homes in Mutare Tribal Trust Land. Others, who had come from afar, would be taken to the train station and given tickets to the station nearest their home.

* * *

Alouette Helicopters

John Whiting held the binoculars close to his eyes. He searched the ground in front of the helicopter. It was rugged, with forest, deep valleys, and dense buffalo grass—virtually impossible to see paths or recognize the border. John thought back to the call from JOC that came in just as he took off. "No gooney birds available," they had announced. That was the slang for the old DC-3 aircraft used by the SAS. The information meant no paratroopers to seal the border.

Turning to the pilot, Alan, he asked, "How much fuel have we got left? We've been in the air just over an hour."

"About thirty minutes, then we'll need to turn back."

Looking to his right John watched the second helicopter. The gunner was hunched over the optical sights of the 20mm Browning cannon.

"I can't see a damn thing. It's just so darn thick down there," announced the voice over the radio from the second helicopter.

"What we need is a good fire to burn the bastards out," barked the pilot into the radio.

The first rays of early morning sunshine lit the sides of the mountains, leaving the valleys in deep shadow. Breathtaking greens and browns painted a contrasting picture to their cheerless mission.

The radio crackled. The pilot acknowledged the message and turned to John. "Jack thinks he's spotted movement over in the valley just north of Himalaya Mountain. If this is our target group, they made it much further south than we would have guessed. Let's go take a look."

The two helicopters made a sharp turn to the right and down towards the valley floor.

Alan's pulse quickened and he tightened his grip on the controls as a streak of white smoke arced its way toward the lead helicopter. "The bastards, they think they can get us with a SAM," said Alan as the SAM streaked by them and headed up into the atmosphere above. "We're too low, so the missile won't arm. We have them now and they're still five hundred yards from the border."

John looked down. No sign of movement through his binoculars. "Fire a quick burst into that long grass," he shouted. "Maybe we can flush them out and catch them moving."

Rat, at at, at at, barked the Browning. Suddenly, they saw them. The group of figures sprinted through the long grass, heading for the border.

"There's nowhere to land," shouted John. Follow them. See if we can nail the bastards before they get into that next forest line."

Both helicopters turned abruptly and the sharp crackle of cannon fire drowned out all other sounds. One of the figures on the ground threw up his hands and fell on his back. Another fell, trying to rise up, but unable to stand. By now, the remaining terrorists were on the edge of the forest line, one hundred yards from the border.

"Give them another burst," shouted John over the din of the rotors. "We have to stop them. This is our last chance."

Once again, both cannons roared. The grass shredded below them, and just before the figures reached the forest, one of them spun around and staggered backwards, falling flat on his face. It was over. Three terrorists were down. What appeared to be eleven others had escaped across the border.

"Set down in that clearing, five hundred yards to our right. We can make it back and see what we've bagged."

The helicopters hovered as they got in position and settled side-by-side in a clear patch that used to be an old maize field.

As the rotors wound down John Whiting was the first to hit the ground. "Follow me," he yelled. With his men fanning out he ran in the direction of the contact. Holding their FNs tightly across their chests, they pushed their way through the long buffalo grass, jumped through a stream, and were at the scene within minutes.

"Over here," shouted one of the troopies. "I have one of the bastards. He's still alive. He's taken a cannon shot through his hip and isn't going anywhere."

"Roger, I'll be with you," shouted John. He rounded a small bush and there was one of the terrorists lying on his back in a pool of blood. He was moaning, his whole left hip a bloody mess, and the crimson pool below him was spreading fast. It was unlikely he would survive more than a few minutes.

"Find the others," shouted John. He bent over the wounded terrorist, taking a field dressing from his first aid kit to try and stem the flow of blood. The terrorist looked at him, eyes desperate and pleading in his moments before death.

"Who sent you?" asked John gently in Shona. There was no response. Again he asked, "Who was your leader? Was it Makoni?" The wounded terrorist nodded and with that he turned his eyes and tried to roll over. That was his last response. John checked the man's heart and it had stopped beating.

"He's gone," said John. "We know it's that bastard Makoni. Check the other two when you find them. See if we got Makoni. He has a beard."

One troopie called out, "I have the first one. Dead. No beard."

A few minutes later another call. "I have the last of the bastards. Took a shot right through the middle of his lower back. No beard."

"So," said John, "Makoni has got away again."

John examined the other two dead terrorists who were lying prone where they had fallen. "Okay, we have them all," said John. "Drag them back to the choppers and let's head home."

They lugged the bodies through the brush and grass, zipped them up in black body bags then hoisted them aboard waiting helicopters. The helicopter rotors began to wind up with a high pitched scream, then the choppers took off heading back to JOC headquarters.

John Whiting picked up the radio and reported. "We got three of the bastards, but another eleven escaped across the border. This was Makoni's work. Unfortunately he got away."

John turned to Sergeant Major Johnson. "As soon as we get back, let's get a full report on what happened at Elim Mission. I hate that we missed that bastard, Makoni."

"Even more," said Johnson, "I hate to hear what he's left behind."

John shook his head. "It's all I can do not to head over the border and track him right now. That damn Kissinger Accord Smithy signed last year. The Americans and Brits have really tied our hands in forbidding 'hot pursuit.'"

John closed his eyes. He thought about the horrors and buried his head in his hands. *Why God, Why?*

Chapter Twenty

Jamie woke with a start. His sheets were damp. Cold sweat trickled down his face and chest. Most of the night sleep evaded him as images of horror haunted his mind. When troubled sleep came the nightmares were so realistic and brutal that he woke, exhausted and sick to the stomach. So it had been each night since the massacre. He could clearly see them. The missionaries' ravaged and brutalized bodies—distorted as they lay in their own blood. God, how could you let this happen? Jamie tossed and turned. He gave up on rest and swung his legs over the edge of his bed, held his head in his hands. There was still so much to be done.

* * *

Josiah squeezed his eyes shut. Maybe this night sleep would come. It had been two weeks since the attack at the mission and two weeks since he had slept. How long could he endure this? The fight was not over, there was still much to do. That white pig, Chinyerere. He was gaining the respect of more and more of the people. The attack on the mission had not had the desired effect. In their terror the people were turning more and more to the security offered by the government. Now the people from Tikwiri were in a wire village. It had happened last week. According to informers, two more of the villages were nearly complete. The attack at Mutasa had failed. How could he stop the moves? The people needed to know he was still the one to be feared. *But what?*

He was so tired, he could not think. He rolled over as his thoughts drifted. A soft veil of sleep slipped over him. It was brief. Screams filled his ears. He clasped his hands over his ears, but the blood-curdling sounds radiated through his body. Images of bloodied bodies filled his dream. He saw the young girl, her red blood mingled with the red of her gown; the baby clutching her mother's finger in death; the man cut down before he had a chance to protect his wife. He heard the voices crying out, *Jesus, Jesus.* The piercing look in the older woman's eyes burned through his mind, clawing at his heart. And then he saw the hyenas circling around, their glowering red eyes staring—not at the lifeless victims, but at him. In the background was the lion, pacing, flashing brilliant golden eyes that never left Josiah. They seemed to search the depths of his soul.

Josiah bolted up and hugged his blanket tightly around him. Cold sweat encased his body. He shivered. Once again, a night would pass with no sleep. He dared not shut his eyes. The images would return. They always did.

* * *

Jamie poured himself the second cup of tea. It would take more effort to focus this morning. He channeled his thoughts. His brother, Alan, was expecting him at Aberfoyle. He had promised to brief Alan's directors from Salisbury. They wanted information on the current status of the tea estates and the present condition of the Honde. Before the meeting, he would check the progress at Mtarazi. The move was scheduled for the following week and he needed assurance that Jack and Andre would be ready.

The end was in sight. Soon he would be returning to Salisbury,

Emily and the children. After the move into Mtarazi, there would be only one more PV to finish—Mutasa. He could only hope it would go as smoothly as it had for Tikwiri. After a quick breakfast, Jamie met Dande and they set off in the Leopard towards Mtarazi PV.

Outside the gates of the PV, a large crowd had gathered. They turned and looked at the Leopard, talking loudly and gesturing.

"What's going on, Dande?"

The sergeant frowned. "I do not know, Mambo, but I will find out."

He climbed out of the vehicle and held up his hands for quiet. An uneasy hush settled over the crowd and one man, obviously a leader in the group, spoke up, his voice rising in anger.

Dande turned to Jamie. "Some of the *boys* have been seen in the area. The people fear for their children at night. They do not understand why they have not been allowed to move into the PV when the people at Tikwiri have already moved in."

Jamie smiled. "Well, this is a new complaint, not being able to move in soon enough."

Dande looked concerned. "Mambo, there were three of the *boys* here last week. They asked many questions but did not do anything. The people are very frightened and want to move into the protected village. They see that the people in the other PVs are safe and happy."

"Sounds like a scouting party," said Jamie. "I guess they are staying low, trying not to attract too much attention."

Jamie stepped down, shut the door of the Leopard, greeting the people in Shona. "I know you are all eager to move into the wire village, but we must finish our work. This will take another week. As soon as the village is finished, you may move in. Now, go home and wait until we call you."

There was murmuring, but slowly the group disbursed.

* * *

Jamie settled into a chair, gratefully accepting Audrey Ross's cup of tea. Alan and his two directors from Salisbury looked at him, expectantly.

One of the directors leaned forward. "Can you give us an update on the protected village program?"

Jamie took a slow sip, using the few seconds to organize his thoughts. He understood what they really wanted to know—the stability of the valley and what they could expect in the future. As clearly and concisely as possible, he explained the PV program and how the attitude of the people had changed.

"I've just come from an area where the people are clamoring to be let into a PV. They are upset about having to wait. The program has been an outstanding success. Now the people who used to work in both Aberfoyle and Katiyo want to return to work. Unfortunately the Katiyo estate has been utterly destroyed, but the local farmers have formed a cooperative. I have suggested to Alan that Aberfoyle consider buying the tea from them. This would significantly increase your output and could be very profitable for both sides."

Several directors nodded in agreement.

"Sounds like a beneficial proposition. When do you expect the first tea to be ready for shipment?" asked one of the visitors.

Alan was delighted to offer an answer. "In another week to ten days we'll have enough tea for our first shipment. The wholesalers have been calling me virtually every day. I have no doubt our tea will command good prices. Consumers generally recognize our tea to be the best in Africa; better than Malawi or Kenya tea."

The directors looked pleased.

Alan rose. "Let me show you around and you'll see for yourselves the enthusiasm of the people."

Outside, the men slowly made their way through the drying and packing sheds, stopping to talk to workers. Climbing into Alan's open Landrover, they drove to the lush, green slopes where rows of tea bushes grew. The sweet smell of the fields filled the air. Jamie joined a line of pickers, walking along with them and asking questions. The women laughed and chatted as they plucked green leaves, throwing them into baskets slung over their shoulders. This was a social occasion for them. The competition was friendly and the atmosphere jocular.

As they drove back to Alan's office it was evident that all the men were encouraged.

Turning to Jamie one of the directors commented, "Well, Mr.

Ross, we all owe you a debt of gratitude. It certainly looks like peace, even prosperity, has returned to the valley. We'll report to our directors and to the Prime Minister that tea is back in production. It will be a valuable export for the country. Even sanctions and that blockade along the Mozambique coast won't hold it back. The world wants our tea."

* * *

Tension was in the air and the people were impatient. They bumped into each other, pushing and shoving to get closer to the entrance, craning their necks to see if the gates were open. There would be no trouble getting the people into the Mtarazi PV; the dilemma would be keeping peace as people jostled for position.

"Dande!" Jamie yelled. "Get Headman Mushaya up here to talk to the people. We need to keep order." He questioned the strength of the gates.

The crowd parted as Dande led Headman Mushaya to the front, pulling over a chair for him to stand on so he could speak to the crowd.

As the morning wore on, Jamie watched and marveled as he thought how each move had been unique in its challenges as well as successes, yet the outcome for all had been the same—cooperation and security. Soon, the people were all inside and following instructions. Several more hours passed and, wearily, Jamie and Dande drove back to Ruda. Six down, and one to go.

* * *

Corporal Tategulu sat proudly next to Jamie. He was the benefactor of Dande's sour stomach. It had been a rough Saturday morning for Dande, and Jamie felt a twinge of guilt at having to leave him at Ruda with the stomach flu and a bottle of Kaopectate. However, Tategulu had been more than eager to fill his shoes. After a brief stop at Mtarazi PV to check on progress, they headed out for Chief Mutasa's kraal. Jamie stifled a smile. Tategulu sat next to him, firmly grasping his FN. No doubt it was impetus from the warrior blood on his grandfather's side, though it was doubtful they would see any action. It was just as well to be prepared.

"Inkosi Impondozenyati, your wire villages find great success," said Tategulu, impressed by Mtzarazi.

They turned onto the main road and drove towards Chief Mutasa's kraal. The eroded track to the chief's village showed fresh signs of a heavy vehicle, probably the tracks of a MAP truck. Jamie parked the Leopard under a mango tree. The chief was sitting on his chair in the shade of a thatched shelter and stood up as Jamie approached.

"I am so happy to see you, Mambo Chinyerere. You have brought peace to my people and we can sleep again."

The chief's words were smooth and conciliatory, but Jamie had learned to be wary. He looked at the old man, weighing whether his words were genuine.

"Makadiwo, Mambo Mutasa." They shook hands in the traditional way. "Are your people ready to move into the wire village?"

"We are ready, Mambo. But now, you must sit and we will drink tea and talk." He beckoned to a young woman who disappeared into the hut.

Conversation encompassed the weather and the fact that many of the winter crops had failed, as the people were too frightened to go and plough, or cultivate their fields. The girl, either a wife or a daughter, brought out a tray with three enamel mugs of hot, sweet tea made with goat's milk.

Jamie dutifully took the strong, smoky brew, and forced a sip. "The new village will be finished in about ten days. When will your people be ready to move?"

"The people are ready to move right now."

Jamie hid his surprise at the apparent cooperation. This was unusual, but with the chief's next words, he understood why.

"We still have some of the *boys* in the area. Two of them came to my village three nights ago and told me we must not move into the new wire village. My wives are very frightened. They remember what happened to Headman Simangane's wives."

Jamie frowned. "What did you do after the visit?"

"I sent my messenger to the masoja. They came here yesterday to look for the 'boys.' They have not found them. I think they are hiding very well. We have not heard any guns."

Later, Jamie and Tategulu traveled the rough track back towards Ruda. Had he truly won over Chief Mutasa? If so, this may well be the final hurdle.

* * *

Josiah lay on his back in the thick grass. Soothing sounds of rippling water from the Pungwe River beckoned a few paces away, yet its peace belonged to another world—a world he could not find—a world he longed for. The sun was directly overhead and its warmth burned into his chest. Enoch sat silently next to him, contemplating the smoke that rose from his cigarette. Finally he coughed and broke the silence.

"What troubles you, Josiah?"

Josiah stirred and turned onto his side. "Enoch, you are my comrade and friend. I trust you with my life. We have been through much together."

"That is true. We have been together many years now, since you were a young boy and joined the cause."

"It is the dreams. I cannot sleep at night. Over and over, I hear the cries of the women and children at Elim. I see that small baby holding its mother's finger. I see the way that older woman looked at me. I see blood and hear the screams." Josiah quivered. "And then there are the hyenas. They circle around, cackling and sneering, but their evil eyes are on me, not the screaming people. There is a lion on the hill. He sits there, his golden eyes never shut as he stares at me. In my dreams, I turn and run, and keep running and running, but I cannot escape."

Josiah paused, taking in gulps of breath. "This happens every night. I think it is the spirit of those people, tormenting me."

Enoch regarded the desperation in his friend. He was uneasy and his forehead wrinkled as he thought.

"Josiah, you are a fearless leader. This is a bad omen, something you cannot fight on your own. It would be better for you to see the nganga. The witchdoctor will know. He will throw the bones and tell you who has cast this evil spell. Then he will give you medicine for protection." Enoch's face cleared and his voice was decisive. "Come, we will visit the nganga tomorrow. Then you will sleep again."

* * *

Wednesday was dreary. Smog from Mozambique fires hung over the valley in a thick mantle. Jamie sleepily drew the back of his hand across his eyes and took a swallow of tea to ease a scratchy throat. This was the last protected village. Today, Mutasa's people would move in. He looked out the window. The thick smog offered a convenient cloak that might lend itself to a surprise from Josiah's men. Despite Mutasa's smooth words, Jamie did not trust the old chief and had warned his men to be prepared for anything. His unfinished cup of tea clanked as he sat it on the metal table. He decided to pass on breakfast. It was time to go.

Not more than an hour later, with Dande and Tategulu along with him, he pulled the Leopard up to the new PV. Dande and Tategulu were silent, eyes glued to the armored glass windows. Even Jamie was astounded. There appeared to be well over two thousand people crowded together, restless and jostling for position outside the gates. The Guard Force members were being heckled as the crush of people pushed against the gates.

Occasional shouts rose above a continual clamor of voices. "Why do you keep us waiting out here? Do you want the *boys* to come and see us here? They will kill us all if they come. Open the gate!"

The Guard Force men stood stoically behind the gates, keeping their emotions in check. Periodically they ordered, "Keep back!" but their voices were barely audible in the tumult.

Jamie pulled the Leopard up sharply at the edge of the crowd.

"Go and look for Chief Mutasa," he ordered Dande and Tategulu. "Tell him to talk to his people. Until the crowd is calm, the gates will not be opened. No one will be let into the village. Any trouble makers will sleep outside the wire tonight and won't receive their plot until tomorrow."

Feared and respected by his people, Chief Mutasa walked through the noisy throng, threatening any rabble rousers. Soon the crowd quieted and the move proceeded without incident.

* * *

The hut was large, and an old tree stump with a myriad of dry branches was buried in the ground near the front door. Josiah and Enoch approached cautiously. Seated on a wooden stool was an old man. His grizzled white head was covered with a crown of mahogany seeds. Bones, feathers and a wildebeest's tail hung from a cord around his neck. On his chest dangled a necklace of white shells and beads that surrounded the shell of a tortoise which had been sealed at one end and was open at the other. He wore the skin of a hyena as an apron and had anklets of python skin with beads of snakes' teeth on each foot. No shirt covered the wrinkled skin over his belly.

The nganga looked up and motioned for them to be seated. His weathered face crinkled as his sunken lips stretched into a toothless grin.

His voice was raspy. "I have been waiting for you, Comrade Josiah. Sit down."

Josiah and Enoch's eyes were wide with apprehension. This was truly a great nganga, considered to be the most powerful in the whole of Manicaland. He knew they were coming. They eased down and sat cross legged in front of Nyagudza.

"We see you, oh mighty one."

Nyagudza bent down over a woven basket positioned on a reed mat in front of him. His fingers were clumsy as he struggled to open it. He removed two castor oil seeds and inserted one in each nostril. His body began to weave from side to side and he wheezed as he rocked. Next, he pulled out a carved image of himself from the basket and placed it in front of him. His voice quavered as he addressed it.

"Did Josiah try to cross the Pungwe and fail?"

He then clapped his hands at the carved image. The image appeared to respond in a low hiss, but Josiah and Enoch could not make out its words.

Josiah's insides wrenched. He wanted to flee from the place but found he could not move. He sat mesmerized.

Nyagudza sprinkled some herbs on the fire at his side. Acrid smoke rose from the burning leaves and Josiah began to choke and cough. Then the witchdoctor leant over the fire absorbing some of the smoke through his open mouth. He wheezed. Without looking up, he spoke again.

"You are very troubled, Josiah; the spirits are angry. I see that you are tormented and cannot sleep."

Turning toward the weathered old stump, he removed a large horn and a woven pouch. Placing the horn to one side and the bag to the other, he left a space in the middle of the mat. From the pouch, he pulled out 'hakata', three small, flat pieces of ivory, each the size of large pocket knife, but with different markings.

Cupping the ivory pieces in both hands Nyagudza rocked from side to side and chanted. The words were inaudible as his voice droned on. His eyes rolled back in his head. Leaning over the center of the mat he opened his hands and let the ivory pieces fall. They lay in different positions with their markings visible only to Nyagudza. Bending down, the witchdoctor studied the ivory bones. There was silence. Finally, Nyagudza looked up and fastened his coal black eyes upon Josiah.

"It is the spirit of one who watches over Chinyerere. It will take much to drive off that spirit." He paused. "What have you brought me?"

Josiah put a shaky hand in his pocket and pulled out a bundle of Mozambique escudos.

"This will buy you ten cows. Is it enough?"

He passed the bundle of banknotes over to Nyagudza who took them, held them tightly, and then placed them in the basket.

Nyagudza delved into the woven pouch and pulled out a gona, the hollow horn of a duiker, suspended from a cord that had been woven from the hairs of a wildebeest's tail.

"This gona contains the gallbladder of the crocodile, the tooth of a hyena, and part of the claw of a lion. It is the only medicine that can protect you from the lion that is following you. Keep it with you at all times."

Josiah shuddered when he thought of the lion in his dream. He took the horn of medicine with shaking hands, placed the cord around his neck, clapped his hands and then they left. They walked briskly in silence for several minutes, trying to steady their nerves.

Enoch finally stopped to rest against a tree and catch his breath, more from nerves than exertion. He glanced back from where they had come and then turned to his friend.

"It is good, Josiah. Now you can sleep again."

Josiah was pale, visibly shaken. "No, Enoch. It is just as I feared. This is the spirit of the one who watches over Chinyerere. Has he ever failed him?"

* * *

Jamie sank into bed and rolled over, exhausted. Satisfaction, along with fatigue, washed over him. It was finished. Everyone in the Honde valley was safe in the protected villages. Nick and his men were shipping out within a couple of weeks; Andre would remain another month, but only to put final touches on the airstrips he was building at each PV. Jack would spend more time enjoying Mrs. Cloete's home cooking and, best of all, Jamie would be going home to Emily and the children. With a deep breath, his heavy lids closed and, for a welcome change, he fell into a dreamless sleep.

Chapter Twenty One

Jamie bolted upright. The thunderous rapping at the door jarred him awake. The loud, insistent voice that followed told him something was amiss.

"Mambo," announced Corporal Tategulu, several decibels higher than necessary. "It is the telephone. The Deputy Secretary, Mambo Cornwell, wants to speak to you."

Jamie looked at his watch.

Good grief! It's eight o'clock.

Leaping out of bed, wearing only a pair of rugby shorts, he made a dash for the telephone in the ops room. Picking up the phone he heard Dennis Cornwell's voice booming over the line.

"Good morning Jamie. I'm hearing some good things about the Honde. The Prime Minister himself mentioned it at our last security briefing. Congratulations."

"Thank you, sir," said Jamie, catching his breath. "We've made good progress. In fact, the last move took place yesterday. Chief Mutasa's people moved without a hitch. Everyone seems happy."

"That old fox. I trust he cooperated."

"Well, yes. He finally decided which horse to back. He did a good job convincing the people to move."

"Jamie, we made a deal before you left for the Honde. Your job is nearly done and it will soon be time to bring you home."

Jamie caught his breath. He had known it would be coming soon, but to actually hear the words filled him with excitement. It had been a long, hard seven months and now he could hardly wait to be home with Emily and the children. Being away from them for so long had left a gap in his life. He had missed so much of the children growing up, and even when he was home for the occasional weekend, it had been difficult fitting back into the family. They had become so used to getting along without him and it had not been easy for him to bend to their ways. Now it was time to bridge gaps, to once again become a family unit.

"Sir, that's wonderful news," he said. "I'll miss the challenge and involvement that I've experienced here, but I'm looking forward to being home again."

"I think you'll like what we've worked out," continued Dennis Cornwell. "You're to take over as district commissioner and officer commanding the Chikurubi Training Center. You'll be responsible for the training and deployment of our IANS, our Vedettes, and new District Assistant recruits. Alex Burton will take your place as DC Mutasa."

"Thank you, sir. I will enjoy the new assignment. When do I make the move?"

"Well you've done such a good job with your team, but there's one more thing I want you to cover."

Jamie felt his heart miss a beat. What next?

"The media have been hounding us for weeks to see for themselves just how successful the PV program is in the Honde. Word has leaked to them and now we have both national and international media crews clamoring for interviews.

"But, Sir, the media don't know what's going on. They have a history of misreporting everything."

"I know, Jamie, but you are a great spokesperson, and the Honde is one of our very few success stories. I need you to make the best of it. We have television crews lined up from South Africa, Britain, Australia and the United States. It will be just four weeks and I'm relying on you to be our spokesperson. This should be easy after all you have gone through in the past seven months."

Jamie sighed. "Okay, sir. I'll do my best, but all I hope and pray for is that these reporters tell the right story. We've made such great progress, I would hate for the media to put a negative spin on what has been accomplished by the people. We don't need them to upset the applecart."

"Understood, Jamie. I trust you and you have our full support. Remember you will be home in about four weeks."

* * *

Jamie woke early and dressed carefully in freshly ironed khaki trousers and shirt. It was Monday the 26th of August. His blue eyes had dark circles around them and a few extra creases at the corners. The Honde had taken its toll on his youthful looks. A few gray hairs had sprung up at his temples, a more mature look, he consoled himself. In today's situation, that would be an advantage. Three weeks had passed with ten media crews, but today was different. He was expecting the big shot reporter from America and had been warned to make the best of it.

Soon it was time to leave.

"Sergeant Dande, are you ready? The plane will be here any minute."

Jamie glanced up briefly when Dande walked in, uniform immaculate, with sharp creases in his trousers.

Ten minutes later they pulled onto the Ruda airstrip with Chris following close behind in his Leopard.

Chris scanned the horizon. "Stop worrying, Jamie. No one can deny the Honde operation is a great success. We've spit and polished everything in sight." He smiled, glancing sideways at Jamie. "Maybe we'll all be on international TV. After that, who knows? Hollywood?"

Jamie rolled his eyes. "I'm sure we'd be cast as villains."

They could hear it before it was visible. The speck grew in size and Jamie identified it as a Beechcraft Baron, big enough to seat at least seven people. The plane lost altitude quickly and came in low over the airstrip, allowing the pilot to read the windsock. The wind was coming from the southeast so the pilot banked and made his approach from the north, touching down and rolling to a stop at the far end of the airstrip. He turned and taxied toward the Leopards. Both engines shut down, the door opened, and a tall figure stepped onto the ladder. He paused, taking in the sights and sounds, then his gaze settled on Jamie, Chris, and Sama.

Jamie had to admit the man was very handsome. He was at least six feet tall. His body was trim and the slacks and soft silk shirt he wore accentuated his elegant build. His dark hair shone in the sunlight and his face was smooth and lightly tanned.

The man seemed to glide down the ladder. As he approached Jamie his lips parted in a practiced smile, revealing gleaming white teeth. Jamie stepped up and grasped the man's outstretched hand in a firm handshake.

"Jamie Ross, district commissioner. Welcome to the Honde."

"Don Raster, CBA News." His voice was low and resonant. "It's very good of you to meet us and offer to show us around." He turned to the other two men. "Let me introduce my two companions. Joe Lester, my cameraman and Dave Withers, my assistant director."

Both men paled in the shadow of Don Raster. Except for the two cameras draped around his neck, Joe Lester was average in every way and had no distinguishing features. He greeted Jamie with a nod. The other, Dave Withers, showed every sign of having been up all night. As he finished jotting a quick note on his legal pad, he placed the pen behind his ear which quickly disappeared in an unruly tangle of brown curls. He reached out to shake Jamie's hand. His eyes were tired and bloodshot, a tell-tale sign of a demanding boss, Jamie surmised.

"This is Chris DeVries, district officer at Ruda," Turning to his right. "And this is Sergeant Dande, my confidante, protector, and right hand man."

Again, the flash of white teeth as hands were gripped firmly. "Good to meet you. I look forward to talking with you and learning all I can about the Honde."

Don Raster had made an impression. Dande's face beamed with pleasure, delighted with Jamie's introduction.

"I've worked up a schedule for your visit covering the next three days," Jamie said. "I need to go over it with you to see if it meets with your approval. We've also set aside space in our Keep for you to spend the next two nights. We have two spare beds; I'm afraid the others will have to rough it on the floor."

Don Raster held up his hand. "We don't want to put you out, so don't worry about accommodations. We have suites reserved at the Cecil Hotel in Umtali. We'll fly back there each evening."

Jamie got the impression Mr. Raster was more concerned about his personal comfort than any inconvenience he was causing.

By this time the two pilots had emerged and were in the process of securing the Beechcraft.

Jamie continued. "I think it best if we made Ruda Keep our first stop. You can freshen up and the pilots can stop over there while we make our visits. I'll brief you in our operations room so you'll have an overall understanding of the Honde Valley, the importance of the tea industry, and where the seven different protected villages are located."

"Very good. We're at your mercy, so lead the way."

Jamie had his doubts Don Raster was ever at anybody's mercy. "I would like you and your team to ride with me and the two pilots can ride with Chris. Our Leopards can each carry six people in a pinch, but don't expect too much comfort."

Don Raster climbed into the vehicle and sat down across from Jamie while Dande and the other two men squeezed in behind.

"Please, strap yourselves in with the shoulder harness. It provides extra protection in the event we hit a landmine."

Don Raster looked startled. "I thought terrorist activity was no longer a threat. You still have land mines?"

"Land mines are always a possibility," said Jamie. "We never take our safety for granted, though in recent months the threat has been mostly eliminated. Hang on; the ride is short." Within minutes Jamie pulled up in front of the Ruda Keep buildings. He led the way into the ops room where a pot of tea was waiting for them.

As the men sipped their tea Jamie turned to the map on the

wall. He pointed out the Mozambique border and the position of the protected villages.

"How big is the Honde Valley?" asked Raster.

"About eighteen hundred square miles. The Valley is roughly sixty miles long by an average of thirty miles wide, narrower in the north and wider in the south." He pointed to the white flag markers. "These indicate the protected villages—seven in all. Here is Aberfoyle Tea Estates which we'll visit later today. Nearer the border is Katiyo Tea Estates, abandoned last October."

"Explain to me some of the dynamics leading up to the situation here." Don Raster stood and walked over to the map to examine it more closely.

"This is not a new struggle. It's something that's been going on for generations. There has always been animosity between the Shona and the Matabele, but now there's a new ingredient thrown into the mix. The Chinese and North Koreans have weighed in on the side of the Shona in the east, and Russia and Libya have given their support to the Matabele in the west." Jamie swallowed some tea. "The Shona, led by Robert Mugabe, represent the Zimbabwe African National Union (ZANU) and their military wing, the Zimbabwe African Liberation Army (ZANLA). Joshua Nkomo, the first real leader of liberation factions, heads up the Zimbabwe African Peoples Union (ZAPU). I believe you've already been briefed on these issues. Just six months ago the Honde was the center of some of the worst terrorist atrocities in the country. Now you will see for yourselves how this valley has been transformed to a peaceful haven."

"Why does this area have the reputation of having been the center of terrorist activity?" Raster probed.

"For all of last year, and through about April of this year, the Honde Valley was the central route for ZANLA terrorist groups infiltrating the country," explained Jamie. "In order to ensure the absolute cooperation of the local people, they were brutally murdering between ten and thirty people per week and abducting thousands of young boys and girls to serve as trainee guerillas, porters, cooks and sex slaves."

"What were these acts of terror that you mention?"

"The atrocities they committed were unbelievable, principally focusing on tribal leaders and their families, school teachers, and other leaders of the community. For example, Headman Simangane was beaten, tied to a tree with barb wire around his neck, and then gutted like a fish so his entrails hung out of his body. He was left to die a slow, agonizing death. His wives were beaten, raped, and bayoneted. Another, Headman Katiyo, had his lips and tongue cut out. His wives were also beaten, raped, and killed. School teachers were raped if they were women, or mutilated if they were men, all in front of the children they were teaching. In another case over a hundred young children, aged between ten and fifteen, were forcibly abducted to training camps in Mozambique after their teachers were all bayoneted."

"It's hard to believe that freedom fighters would do such things to their own people," said Don Raster, slightly derisive.

Jamie felt his blood pressure climb but ignored the comment and pressed on.

"When I came to the Honde Valley, at the beginning of February, the locals wouldn't greet me or talk to me. Children ran away when they saw anyone in uniform. This was the Valley of Terror. Now the people are settled and safe in protected villages. We have not had a single death due to terror in the past two months."

Don Raster shook his head, incredulous. "No acts of terror! How unbelievable—quite a turnaround."

"Correct. The people are laughing, not crying. The children are back in school. They live in the midst of their business centers and clinics and they can now work their fields which had been all but abandoned. The tea estates are back in operation, even though Katiyo is not functioning as an actual entity. Their tea is tended and picked by local farmers, and trucks from Aberfoyle arrive daily to buy the pickings. In the evening the people come back to a safe haven where they can sleep at night. Their own trained militias are their guardians."

Don Raster leaned forward, clasping his hands behind his back as he continued to examine the map.

"So, how many people have moved into these protected villages?"

"Our current count is just over twenty two thousand people, including women and children. The numbers grow each day as people return from Mozambique where they fled. The smallest PV has just over twenty seven hundred people and we now have thirty nine hundred people at Mutasa PV, the largest and the most recently settled."

Raster frowned. "Has the whole population of the area been moved into protected villages?"

"All those that remained in the valley. We estimate twenty thousand or so fled into Mozambique when the terrorist acts began. Many of these are returning as they hear that peace has been restored."

Don Raster turned to Jamie. "I look forward to seeing these, what do you call them, protected villages?"

Jamie seized the moment. "If you're ready, we'll head out." Our first stop will be Ruda PV, just west of Ruda airstrip. You would have seen it as you landed."

As they drove through the gates of the PV, Don Raster looked with interest at the Guard Force men who snapped to attention at their arrival. A group of militia formed up to greet them. They were smartly turned out in brown uniforms and maroon floppy hats.

"I see your guards are well-armed," Don Raster commented, implying what Jamie was not sure, but he detected the negativity.

"Yes, the Guard Force has FNs and the local militia has G-3 rifles. They're necessary to protect the people in the event the village is attacked."

"Mmmm." There was no other comment.

As the men started to walk through the village, crowds of people gathered. News had spread throughout the valley of the important TV man from America. The people were curious to know why these visitors were different from the hoards of other newsmen they had seen. As in every case, when the camera was pointed, people vied to be in the forefront.

Their first visit was to the school. The headmaster, forewarned, waited at the door to greet them. Tall and impressive, his curly black hair was flecked with white. A large pair of tortoiseshell glasses, perched on his nose, gave him a distinguished look. Jamie was doubtful he could see as well with them as he could without them.

"Welcome to our school," he said, smiling. "We are so pleased to meet an official from America." The headmaster spoke fluent English so Jamie did not need to translate. "Our children are all well-behaved and studious." He motioned inside, welcoming them in. "They have prepared a song for you."

Don Raster was affable. "I am flattered. I would be delighted to hear it."

With that the headmaster signaled for the children to stand. They proudly stood, donned in their finest clothes with shiny, scrubbed faces. Sweet voices rang out in harmony as they sang the Rhodesian National Anthem to the tune of *Ode to Joy*. Joe panned his camera over the group, careful not to exclude any child.

As they finished Don Raster looked over the giggling group. "These are all very young children. Where is the class for the older children?"

The headmaster looked pained. "Sir, there are no older children. The *boys* took them all."

"You mean all the older children left to join the Freedom Fighters?" Don Raster responded.

The headmaster looked perplexed. "No, Sir. They did not go to join the Freedom Fighters. They were kidnapped and forced to go over the border to terrorist camps. Sometimes they return with the terrorists, but then they are not our children anymore. Their minds have been turned and they do not even acknowledge their own parents."

Jamie was proud of the Headmaster. It was good that the TV crew was hearing the truth from someone else intimately involved with the problem.

Jamie escorted the group to the business center. The cameraman busied himself taking pictures of the stores and other enterprises.

"Why are the people lined up there?" Don asked, pointing to a group of women standing in line holding bulging burlap bags.

"They are waiting to grind their maize," replied Jamie. "This is a new luxury for many. The majority of families had to grind their maize by hand in large wooden mortars before they moved here."

There was no comment.

They walked on through the village lines until they came to Headman Mukwiri's huts. The headman had roofed his main hut with old sheets of corrugated iron salvaged from a burned out business center. The freshly thatched huts were far more appealing to the eye, but the headman was proud of his 'modern', metal roof. He sat in the shade of the open shelter surrounded by his senior wives, a beautiful picture in their brightly colored cotton dresses and bandanas. Determined not to be outshone, the headman sported a shiny, navy blue suit. His rectangular brass Headman's badge was suspended prominently around his neck and a gray fedora hat was pulled down over his forehead with the brim turned up. He gripped a long, black umbrella like a walking stick, with a black briefcase by his side. There was no sign of rain, but he had obviously seen a picture of an Englishman in similar attire and felt he was in the height of fashion. The headman stood up as they approached. He reached out to shake hands with each of them.

"Please, sit. I am honored to meet you," a rehearsed greeting that, surprisingly, was quite intelligible. His English was not good but it was apparent he had practiced a few phrases.

Don Raster began firing questions, barely giving Dande a chance to translate the answers.

"Why did you move into the protected village?"

"Were you forced to move in by the government?"

"Why weren't you allowed to bring your cattle and goats with you?"

"Are the people free to leave any time?"

"Isn't it true that there is no work for you now?"

"Isn't Mugabe a friend of the people?"

"Are there any people left outside the protected villages?"

"Now that the government is keeping you here, in this wire enclosure, will you ever see your children again?"

"Don't you want to go back to your villages?"

The old man looked confused at the barrage of questions. He stammered, unable to keep up as he tried to answer. Sergeant Dande stiffened as he began to understand the direction the questions were taking. He looked from Mukwiri, to Don Raster, to Jamie, but battled on, translating each question and answer as accurately as he could.

Jamie could not contain himself. "Is life better for you now than before you moved here?" he chimed in.

If he had ever doubted the notion that this news anchor was not the least bit interested in any information that might shed a different light on his own preconceived ideas, it was gone. Anger crept up the back of his neck, but he remained calm and responded candidly to questions Don Raster asked him.

Finally Don Raster shook hands with Headman Mukwiri and they took their leave to return to the Leopards. Both Don Raster and Jamie were quiet. Jamie did not trust himself to converse. He was seething at the exchange he had witnessed.

After a brief visit to Aberfoyle Tea Estates they arrived back at Ruda Base where they picked up the two pilots and returned to the airstrip.

"We'll return tomorrow around ten," said Don Raster. "From what you've told me we'll be flying in to four of the protected villages. Is that correct?"

"Yes, Mr. Raster. Each of the protected villages now has an airstrip. We'll begin in the north by visiting Simangane and Pungwe PVs and then come south to Katiyo and Tikwiri PVs. We'll wrap up by late afternoon, depending upon how much time you'll need at each. We'll visit the last two PVs, Mtarazi and Mutasa, Wednesday morning."

* * *

Tuesday came and went with a similar line of questions. Wednesday, they visited Mtarazi PV and were flying east to their last stop, Mutasa PV. Jamie was the only additional passenger with the cameras and equipment taking up the remaining space.

The Beechcraft, flaps down, leveled off and made a perfect landing, rolling to a smooth stop near the two Guard Force Rhinos.

Corporal Alec Williams was there to meet them. The men climbed aboard the two Rhinos and drove into Mutasa PV. It was nearly lunch time.

Jamie suggested they first have lunch in the main ops room where Corporal Williams would answer any questions from a Guard Force perspective. This proved wise. Alec was not shy and took every chance to explain how well the people had settled in; the many gifts of chickens and eggs they were receiving; and how quickly and eagerly the militia had taken to their new roles as guardians of the people.

After lunch they made brief visits to the school and business center, before walking through the village lines and watching the militia drill.

Raster stopped every now and then to talk to locals, surprised at their friendliness, and how eager they were to have their pictures taken.

Finally, they arrived at Chief Mutasa's huts. Jamie was glad to see that the roof was now finished on the main hut and that the chief's open courthouse had also been thatched. The chief was seated at his table, his large belly bulging over the tight belt of the black pants he wore. The bright blue shirt was obviously new, neither the cuffs nor collar showed any signs of wear. His dark green jacket, however, hinted of having been a former purchase made during his younger and slimmer days. He proudly wore his crescent shaped chief's badge, polished until the luster that reflected from it matched the polished brass of the emblem on his white pith helmet.

Chief Mutasa rose as they approached and came forward to shake hands with everyone, welcoming them to his tribal area. His senior wife, with the traditional teapot handy, poured hot, sweet tea with milk for everyone. Don Raster began to put up his hand to refuse when Jamie touched him gently on the arm.

"The tea is delicious," he lied. "This is a sign of hospitality to honor you. He would be most offended if you refused."

Except for slightly watery eyes that only Jamie amusingly picked up on, the anchor concealed his aversion well as he braved a swig of the strong, smoky, sweet brew.

Raster quickly sat down the cup, clearing his throat. "It is a real pleasure to meet you Chief Mutasa." He looked around. "It must be very hard for you to live in a place like this after you were used to so much freedom. All this wire and the guards at the gate must make you feel like you are living in a prison compound. Are you happy that the government has made you move into this area that is surrounded by wire?"

Chief Mutasa raised a brow. He was a wily old fellow himself and knew well the art of using devious comments and questions. This man from America was trying to put words in his mouth.

"I am Chief Mutasa. The government has not made me do things I do not want to do. My people are very happy living here and were not forced to come. I had to work hard to prevent them coming here before the wire was finished. They are tired of their children being taken and their wives beaten and raped. When the day came for us to move, there were so many people lined up, they were like an endless herd of buffalo ready to stampede to water."

There followed a few awkward seconds of silence.

Don Raster cleared his throat again. "I am sorry, chief; I did not mean to upset you. What I really want to know is, are you happier now than before the troubles came to your land?"

"That is a different question. Before the *boys* came we were all very happy and lived in a peaceful valley where food was plentiful, and there was always work for the men in the neighboring farms and forest estates. Then the *boys* came and they promised us motor cars and big farms. They said we could have anything we wanted. Once the people learned that this was just talk and the promises had no meaning, they no longer wanted to listen to the *boys*. That is when our troubles started. First they took our young men and their sisters. Later our young men came back to beat up and kill their own fathers and mothers. Then the *boys* came back and they did terrible things to us. We could no longer sleep at night and lived in fear every day."

"How long have you been living in fear?"

"Our troubles began with the rains more than a year ago. We have seen strangers from other parts and other tribes. They treat us like dogs to be whipped and used as they want. One of my headmen had his lips and tongue cut off. Another was cut open so that the dogs could feed on his insides. It would have been better if we had all died than to live such a life of misery."

"If the troubles end, will you go back to your villages?"

"If this happens, some will go back and some will stay. My people like to be near to the schools and clinics, and to have stores, a grinding mill and water near their homes. This is a good life and we are safe at night. The only trouble is carrying the grain back from our fields, but we have plenty of donkeys to help."

"What do you think about these villages, which are like small towns?"

"I am very happy. I thank Mudzwiti Chinyerere. He has seen much suffering of my people and he and his people have worked hard to make us safe. Chinyerere has a very powerful spirit that protects him and the people respect him."

"I thank you, Chief Mutasa for talking with us. I would like to have my picture taken with you so that the people in America can see what a real chief looks like."

He moved beside Mutasa and draped his arm around the chief's shoulder. Chief Mutasa stood tall and rigid, no smile crossed his face, but Jamie knew that underneath, the chief was pleased at the thought of having his picture broadcast to the world.

Jamie and the TV crew made their way through the crowd of curious onlookers and headed back to the Leopard.

On the drive to the airstrip, Don Raster remarked offhandedly, "Your Chief certainly knows which side his bread is buttered. He was obviously trying to impress you. He knows I'm just visiting but you will be in control for a long time. He was careful to say just what you wanted to hear."

Jamie seethed. "You know Mr. Raster, I don't understand you. Everywhere you've been you've seen happy, smiling faces and heard the same things. Why is it that you are so prejudiced about the protected villages and the peace that has returned to the Honde?"

"Jamie, don't get me wrong." Don Raster's voice was conciliatory. "My job is to dig deep and to ferret out the real facts and feelings. I'm not here to judge, just report what is happening. Yes, I believe this is a more peaceful place than it was, and that the people are now safer than they were six months ago. What I don't agree is that this is the best option for them. They've been forced to leave their homes and villages because your government is unwilling to work out a political solution."

"Mr. Raster, how much do you know about the 'Kissinger Accord?'"

"Not very much."

Obviously, thought Jamie.

"I know President Carter sent Andrew Young to meet with the heads of state of all of Southern Africa and then decided it was not in our best interests to ratify the agreement."

"Well, Sir, I'm not a politician," said Jamie, "but we all thought that when our prime minister, Ian Smith, signed off on the accord worked out by Secretary of State Kissinger, and agreed to by President Ford, that the United States would honor that agreement. What we did not expect was to see the United States reverse its position, turn its back on us, and begin supporting the likes of Robert Mugabe and his thugs. We also understand that Ambassador Young advised President Carter of the consequences of failing to ratify the Kissinger Accord and that there was a danger of the country falling into communist hands."

"I see that you're very much a patriot."

"I'm a third generation Rhodesian and I love this country as much as any of the people you've met. I've seen the tragedies of this brutal terrorist war and agree that a political solution is our best course. President Carter chose to ignore the advice of his own Ambassador, and now we see an escalation of the war as the US covertly channels funds into Mugabe's organization. All war is hell, but a terrorist war is the worst kind." Jamie paused briefly for emphasis. "I hope that when you return to the United States you will present a fair picture. Fairness in your reporting, Mr. Raster, will help us work toward a political solution that will protect the interests of all people—black, white, and even the minority Indians who have settled here."

The flight back to Ruda went quickly. Jamie said good-bye to the team with mixed relief, his stomach in knots.

The Beechcraft taxied to the end of the airstrip, turned, and picked up speed to take off.

Jamie looked over his shoulder as Chris walked over to join him. "Chris, I don't know about you, but I'm just about ready to puke. Reporters. They come from other countries with their minds made up. In three days they think they have all the answers and proceed to undermine what we've done to make life better for everyone, black and white. We're pre-judged and condemned because they don't understand the people, the culture, and what it takes to make democracy work in Africa."

Chris muttered a mild expletive. "He sure didn't gain a fan in you. Come on. It's over. Let's head back to Ruda." Then he smiled and added, "You can give me the full scoop."

Jamie nodded. "This is one afternoon I could use a beer."

Chapter Twenty Two

Sweat glistened on Josiah's face. He leapt up from the crude bed and checked his watch in the moonlight. It was just after midnight.

Why? Why were the dreams still there?

Fingering the amulet around his neck, he shivered, confused, and then angry. The nganga had promised him that the dreams would go away. Helpless and desperate, he sank back down and looked up at the full moon that peeped through the canopy of giant mahogany trees.

Another hour of tossing and turning gave way to more troubled sleep.

He heard her cry. The young woman with the baby. She called out to Jesus and cried again. The bayonet sank deep while blood spouted like a fountain, drenching everything and covering Josiah.

Panic. He had to escape. He spun around, but more terror. The hyenas and the lion stared at him and slowly moved in. He ran, but the lion was closing fast as it chased him. Escape, escape ... running, faster, and faster. Still the lion came on. Down the mountain Josiah scrambled, but the lion gained. Panting, Josiah slipped and grasped at a tree limb. He felt himself falling—down, down, into blackness.

Screaming, he bolted upright. Sweat poured down his face. "Why, why?"

* * *

The news of Jamie's transfer spread rapidly to even the furthermost parts of the area. Jamie wanted to leave everything in ship shape order, but every time he tried to settle down to complete the paperwork, there was a knock at the door. There was a never ending stream of people stopping in to say good-bye.

The final visits to the PVs had been especially difficult. Throngs of locals gathered at each PV, pleading for him to stay. With alarm in their eyes and panicked voices, they shared their fears of the terrorists returning once he left. Jamie spent time talking with them, reassuring them that nothing would change. The new district commissioner would carry on the work, that the Guard Force would remain to protect them, and that District Officer De Vries and the vedettes would take care of any problems arising in the PVs. He also reminded them of the great job their own militia were doing.

The most emotional visit had been to Chief Mutasa. The old chief had the reputation of being difficult, not quite trustworthy. He had held back his support of the protected villages until he was assured that it would be a success, but once convinced, he was a stalwart ally.

* * *

Jamie, Dande, Chris, Garth and Corporal Tategulu drove together to Mutasa PV. Jamie wanted to say a special *good-bye* to the Chief and had brought one of his chairs from Mutasa to give him as a parting gift.

Soon after they left Ruda Keep Jamie noticed an unusual number of travelers on the road. As they neared the turnoff to Mutasa PV, there was a stream of men, women, and children, all walking towards the PV. Pick-up trucks crammed with people roared along, bouncing from pothole to pothole. People were hanging on for dear life, but brave enough to release their hold and to wave cheerfully as they shouted greetings. Bicycles, each carrying at least one additional passenger, more often two, perched on any part of the bike that was exposed.

"What on earth is going on? Is Chief Mutasa getting married again? Looks like these guys are ready for a party."

Chris shook his head, dubiously." A new wife! He has enough trouble with the twelve he has already. It sure looks like there's going to be a big party. No doubt there'll be some hangovers tomorrow."

Jamie parked the Leopard in front of the A Frame ops room. Old cars, a bus, trucks, and hundreds of bicycles were parked haphazardly outside the main gates. Corporal Williams of the Guard Force walked over to greet them. Jamie eyed him, suspiciously.

"Look's like something's going on here."

The Corporal grinned. "Darn right, there is. Come on." He threw his arm over Jamie's shoulder. "Chief Mutasa is waiting for you at the school."

Jamie walked with him towards the school building, followed by Chris, Garth, and Dande. People were lined up along the way. The shrill cries of women ululating and shouts and laughter reverberated in the air.

It slowly, dawned on Jamie. The celebration was for him. He looked incredulously at the mass of people; there must have been several thousand crowded outside the school building. As he approached they all turned and looked at him, their faces beaming.

Chief Mutasa, dressed in all his chiefly finery, sat under a thatched canopy on the school playground. It had obviously been constructed for the occasion. His white pith helmet stood out brightly in the sunlight and the crescent-shaped brass chief's badge reflected the morning sunlight. Several wooden chairs, and a small table with a beautifully crocheted white tablecloth, were placed under the shelter. The chief rose and stepped out to greet Jamie.

"Welcome, Chinyerere. As you see, my people have come from all the villages to honor you. You have brought peace to the valley."

Jamie gripped the old man's hand and looked into his eyes. A bond had grown between them in the last month, affection between adversaries that had developed into respect for each other.

"Our children wish to thank you. They no longer live in fear of the *boys* taking them away. They sleep at night. They are safe in school each day." He motioned toward a chair. "Please, sit down."

Several hundred giggling, excited children filed out of the school buildings and shuffled into formation before Jamie. The headmaster eyed them sternly and with a quick word quieted them down. They began to sing as their clear voices blended in natural harmony, a musical gift that seemed inherent to Africans. The well-known Zulu song, Inkosi Sikelele Africa, drifted through crowd. The people could no longer contain themselves and broke out in song, clapping and dancing where they stood. They continued long after the song had finished.

The crowd parted, making way for a group of men and women dressed in traditional regalia. Short, pleated, navy skirts swirled around the women's legs as they swayed and gyrated to the rhythm of drums, clapping and singing as they danced. Their upper bodies were covered with brightly colored cloths, thanks to the influence of the missionaries. Men wearing khaki shorts danced into the center of the clearing, chanting and singing. Anklets of mahogany beads and seed pods rattled in rhythm as they stamped their bare feet. Puffs of dust rose and covered their legs as the chanting and singing escalated. The women formed up in front of the men and, swaying to the rhythm of the chant, began to dance their way forward toward Jamie and the group. Back and forth they went until they were only a few yards away, the dust rising in clouds as feet stamped in unison.

Suddenly a young girl threw herself forward and grasped Jamie's feet, lying prone on the ground in front of him. Jamie was taken aback, unsure what to do. After much urging from the crowd he stood up, grasped the girl by her hands and lifted her to her feet. He began to dance with her. Forgetting his self consciousness, he stamped and clapped, blending in with the dancers. The crowd went wild. Shouts and ululations echoed throughout the PV. Even Chief Mutasa beamed.

After a few minutes, Jamie was wet with perspiration. He slipped back to his chair and laughed. Out of the corner of his eye, he could see Chris' amused expression and readied himself for the comment he was sure was brewing. He did not care. Making a fool of himself was worth cementing the love and respect the people had for him.

Chris wasted no time. He leaned over and whispered. "Gosh, sir, I hope that wasn't a marriage proposal. It could have been a fertility dance. Maybe there will be a wedding at Chief Mutasa's village after all. You only have one wife you know."

Jamie pointed. "Watch out, Chris. Here comes a girl to ask you to dance and she knows you're single."

The dancing continued for several minutes until, finally, the chief held up his hand for silence. The dancers slipped back into the crowd and gradually the excitement calmed down. At a gesture from Chief Mutasa, Headman Mukwiri came forward.

Mukwiri held a soapstone carving of a buffalo in his hand and carefully laid it on the table in front of Jamie.

"Mambo, you have been our strong protector. As our mudzimu spoke, you have been the buffalo that trampled the *boys* and drove them away."

Jamie picked up the beautiful carving and admired the way the sunlight brought the iridescent green stone to life. He felt a lump rise in his throat as he grasped the headman's hand.

One by one, headmen and kraal heads came and laid their gifts before him. Soon the table was piled high with clay pots, crochet and embroidered table cloths, soapstone and wood carvings. Baskets of eggs, pineapples, and bananas encircled his feet. Some brought chickens and even a young goat. Jamie envisioned arriving home with a flock of birds and a goat. He smiled as he remembered the look on Emily's face when he brought home the last live chicken. It still reigned, King of the yard, as Rachelle's beloved pet.

Just when Jamie thought he had received the last gift, Chief Mutasa stood up and presented him with a long, slim parcel, wrapped in brightly colored cloth. He unfolded the cloth and caught his breath as he saw what it was. He held it up for all to see. The crowd cheered and clapped as they saw how delighted Jamie was with the gift. Chief Mutasa held up his hand for silence. He turned to Jamie.

"You, Chinyerere, are the one who talks softly and carries a big stick. This is what your name means. We have found it to be true. You talked softly to us, yet your big stick chased out the *boys* who would murder us, steal our children, and do many bad things to us. I asked my wife's father's uncle to carve this stick for you. He is a very old man now, but there is no better wood carver in the whole of Africa. This wood is Ironwood, which is strong, like you."

Jamie ran his hand over the smooth, black wood.

"You will see at the bottom of the stick is a snake," Chief Mutasa explained. "This represents the *boys*, cunning and evil like a snake."

Jamie stood, looking at the intricately carved snake winding its way halfway up the stick. Its body was covered in scales and its eye indeed looked evil. The top half of the stick was carved with the faces of people, some Jamie even thought he recognized.

The chief continued in a voice for all to hear. "These represent my people; they are the ones you have saved from the *boys*. At the top of the stick is the mighty lion. That is you. You have crushed the snake and freed the people. Although we now live behind a wire fence, it has been a long time since we have enjoyed such freedom. You may be leaving us, Chinyerere, but your spirit will live on here forever."

Jamie took the magnificent cane and once again held it up for the people to see. He felt tears pricking the back of his eyes, but he was determined not to let them flow. The people must remember him as strong and undefeatable; tears would be a sign of weakness to them. He stepped forward to thank the chief.

A fusillade of shots rang out and Jamie fell back onto the ground, still holding the walking stick. It appeared that shots had come from two directions in the crowd.

Chris, Dande and Corporal Tategulu picked up their weapons and aimed at the crowd.

"Don't shoot," yelled Jamie. "They're in the crowd."

A mighty roar arose from the crowd—it was not a roar of panic, but the roar of a mother lion protecting her cubs. Several minutes passed before the crowd parted in two places and groups of men dragged six bedraggled *boys* towards Jamie and Chief Mutasa. The terrorists' clothes were torn—they looked beaten physically and in spirit. Two of them could not walk. Suddenly, one of the men, sporting a beard, broke away from his captors, brandishing a pistol. He turned on his captors, fired at one of the men and ran. Then he was running back toward the edge of the crowd, firing his pistol randomly.

Corporal Tategulu took off after him, but by the time he reached the edge of the crowd the bearded man had disappeared....

The five terrorists were dragged up to Chief Mutasa who got up, walked up to them, paused, and spat on each.

Chris was checking Jamie who was now sitting back in his chair holding his left arm. Pulling out his knife Chris cut away Jamie's shirt until the arm was exposed—a flesh wound right at the top of the arm—it was bleeding profusely.

One of the women brought over a beautiful crocheted cloth and proceeded to wrap it tightly around the arm to control the bleeding.

Meanwhile Sergeant Dande and Corporal Tategulu were tying up the remaining five terrorists, some of whom looked as though they needed medical attention. Within minutes the Mutasa militia arrived with their G-3 rifles and maroon floppy hats. There would be no escaping for these terrorists.

Jamie clenched his teeth to stifle the pain, but stood up. He could barely trust himself to speak, but he knew the people expected some words from him. He cleared his throat and tried to bury his emotions as he looked out over that throng of expectant faces.

"I am very honored by your presence and by these wonderful gifts. Today you have truly shown that you are free and that the dogs who call themselves 'comrades' will not be allowed to trouble you. I will remember you always. We have been through hard times together, but now I see you are happy and determined to be free. You say that I am the strong one, but I say that you are the strong ones. It is you who have defeated the terrorists. You worked together and built new homes—made new lives for your families." Jamie paused, looking around the crowd. "You have done what it takes to chase out the terrorists. Look at these dogs now." Jamie pointed to the trussed terrorists. "Now you have strong militia forces from your own people who will help protect you. Each one of you should be very proud of what you have accomplished. The Lion that has watched over me is the spirit of my God, Jesus. He will remain to watch over you. Read the Bible and you will understand the truth of his promises."

There was a moment of silence. Then the crowd broke out into loud cheers and ululating. Chief Mutasa again clasped Jamie's hand.

"We will miss you, Chinyerere. May the Spirit of your God protect you and give you a long, happy life."

* * *

Josiah, his pistol waving in front of him, ran through the edge of the crowd. *Ha, why had the people turned on them. These were his people, and yet they were protecting Chinyerere.*

He was through the crowd and dodged behind some huts toward a latrine. The filth of a covered latrine was disgusting, but he must live—yes to enjoy the victory of the new Zimbabwe.

Josiah lowered himself through the hole of the latrine and stood to one side—out of sight and out of the filth. The stench was overwhelming. He took an old handkerchief out of his pocket and bound it over his nose and mouth. There he waited—leaning against the earth walls of the pit until it was dark. Two fingers on his left hand were broken and he was bleeding from the cuts where the women had scratched him. He took several deep breaths through the handkerchief and gagged. As he stood there his thoughts constantly went to the events of the day. *How could he have missed, but just as he fired Chinyerere had stepped forward. Yes, Chinyerere was not dead—he was invincible. Getting into the wire village had been easy—they blended with the crowd—their AKs, with folding stocks, hidden in the bundles they carried.*

Long after it was dark Josiah clutched the edge of the hole and pulled himself up. He knew he must smell worse than a pig, but he was free. Clutching his pistol in one hand he stealthily made his way past the school buildings to an area of shadow behind one of the stores. He watched and waited. His heart was pounding. All the guards were in the eastern bunkers and there was no movement in the south-west corner. Dodging between buildings he made his way to the shadows near the west bunker. Lying flat he pulled out a pair of wire cutters and cut a hole in the fence. Patient—he waited. Yes it was safe and he crawled through the hole and darted through the floodlit area, running for the safety of the trees ...

* * *

In that last week, Jamie finally found the moments to tie up loose ends. He had not anticipated that saying good-bye to Ruda and the Honde would have been quite so difficult. Chris and Garth he knew he would see again. In fact, Chris had implied that he would like to join him at Chikurubi as an instructor.

Jamie could have stood there for hours, reliving the past few months. He took one final look and stepped into the Leopard to join Dande.

Who would ever have thought I'd be sad to leave this place?

As they drove out of the gate, heading for Mutasa, he looked back to see Chris, Angus and Garth standing with a small gathering of people, waving good-bye.

After ten minutes of silence, Dande spoke. "Mambo, you came to bring peace and now you leave. It has been my honor to serve in the place of Sergeant Sama, who was like a father to me."

"Dande, you are a man among men. Keep up the good work and always remember we are here to serve the people—not the people to serve us."

Later at Mutasa, Mrs. Cloete dabbed a tear with an already dampened tissue as she handed Jamie a fresh-baked, large batch of koeksisters, warning him to spare some for the children. Jamie held out his hand to say good-bye to Jack. The big Afrikaner ignored the hand and Jamie found himself enveloped in a robust bear hug.

"Jamie, my brother, we'll miss you. I know that God had you here for a purpose. Now I know he has another purpose for you, so I must not be sad to see you go. You go on and do whatever God has for you, but always remember it is through his power that everything is possible."

The day passed in a blur. With the little Datsun packed to the hilt, Jamie was on his way home.

* * *

Jamie had been at Chikurubi nearly two years. It was a far cry from the Honde, but he was enjoying the change of pace. He was particularly enjoying being home with the family. He still got a thrill when he drove up to the house in the evening and the children would come hurtling out and fling themselves at him, all talking at once. "Daddy, daddy, you're home. Guess what happened at school today." They could never wait to tell him about their day. He hoped this would never change, that the novelty of having him home every day would not wear off.

As he stepped into the house Emily would be waiting for him. There was no need for words. Her sparkling eyes and soft lips said all that was necessary. As they embraced, events of his hectic day melted away. There was definitely no place like home.

He leaned back over his desk and picked up his pen.

The intercom buzzed.

"Mr. Cornwell is on the line, sir," his secretary's voice crackled.

Jamie's hand hovered over the phone. In the past Dennis' phone calls had not brought good news.

"Hey, Jamie," the familiar voice boomed. "How are things going at Chikurubi?"

"Everything is well, sir. It's very different from what I'm used to, but I'm enjoying it, especially helping these kids and vedettes understand the importance of winning the hearts and minds of the people."

"Good, good." There was a slight pause. "I just got a message from the PM. He wants to see us tomorrow in his office about ten. Come to my office around nine thirty and we'll walk over together. There will be several others with us, but the PM specifically asked that you join us."

Jamie's heart sank. His mind went into high gear. What could the PM want? Surely they weren't going to ship him out again—just when he was making his mark at Chikurubi. For the rest of the day, and all that evening, his emotions churned. He did not mention it to Emily. There was no need to upset her until he knew what the PM wanted.

It was a long night of tossing and turning. The next morning, Jamie was filled with trepidation as he and seven other officials entered the prime minister's office. Ian Smith rose from behind his desk and greeted them all by name. He looked tired. His once sandy hair was grey and his face was pale and gaunt. His right eyelid seemed to droop more than ever. The fifteen years he had been in office had taken its toll, especially the stress of defying the world and leading a country through eleven years of terrorist war on two fronts. It had aged him beyond his years and yet he still exuded toughness and determination.

He clasped Jamie's hand in a firm shake. "Jamie, you did a great job in the Honde. The country owes you a debt of gratitude."

"Thank you, sir." Jamie's voice was low. He felt very humbled. His trials seemed minor in comparison to the ones Ian Smith faced.

"There is something I want you all to hear." Ian Smith was never one to engage in small talk and considered it a waste of time. He liked to get right down to business. "Please sit down. I've brought you here because each of you has gone above and beyond in serving your country. Now the end is in sight." He paused and Jamie saw the shocked look on Dennis's face. "Vorster called me yesterday. He can no longer meet our needs for oil and weapons. In simple terms we are being forced to capitulate. Vorster wants to meet with me in Pretoria tomorrow."

"But we can't just give up, sir," responded Dennis.

"I don't intend to give up—not without a fight. Unfortunately Vorster is under tremendous pressure from America—and we are his sacrificial lamb. I wanted to tell you all personally and thank you."

Jamie was still in shock as each of his fellow officers stood, shook hands with the PM and then they took their leave.

* * *

Back at Chikurubi Jamie bent forward and placed both hands around his head as he prayed. "Lord, you protected me throughout my time in the Honde. I saw miracles such as I would never have believed. You never forsook me. I can see that you were preparing me for something bigger and now I must answer that call."

He picked up the phone to call John Whiting ...

Chapter Twenty Three
(Two Years Later)

Josiah left the witchdoctors cave. It was no use. He ran, scrambling down the mountain, tripping, grabbing onto roots, and slapping branches out of the way. This was the end. It was time. He headed recklessly for the city and the building where it would happen. He knew where he was going. In death, he would find peace. The sky darkened with an impending storm. Now he was in the city, running toward his destination. The silhouette of the edifice lay ahead. It loomed larger as he ran toward it. Like a sepulcher, the double doors looked like an ever-widening mouth waiting to devour him. He halted; something inside him balked. Was there another way? His heart pounded, counting out the seconds. Desperation again welled up. No, it had to be done. *Blood, voices.* They plagued relentlessly.

Boom! A loud crack of thunder jolted through him. He lurched forward, fell again, gathered himself, and then stumbled toward the building. He stopped in front of it. His hand shook as he laid it on the door. A new wave of despair raked through his heart, shredding it seemed, what remained of his soul until he could no longer see or feel. It was as if someone else, not him, slowly pushed at the door. It creaked to a stop. He stepped inside. Yes, though it was hard to see, he could tell it was the church. His eyes were slow to adjust and the inside seemed dim and ominous. He did not care. It matched his black-stained heart. He wanted to fade away into it, right along with the voices and the blood. His legs were weak from having traveled through the heat of the day, up and over Vumba mountain. He let them give way. He dropped to the wooden-hewn floor, his hands torn from scrambling down the mountainside. Blood he could not see, but knew was there. He was barely aware of the numerous thorns that were sewing into his flesh. If there were any real sounds in the building, they were inaudible through the thunder, his ragged breathing ... and the voices. The voices of those he had slaughtered reached a fever pitch. Now his own blood streaked his face as he clasped raw, splintered hands over his ears.

Trembling and weak, he grabbed onto a wooden pew and pulled himself up, slumping against the hard back of the bench as he tried to control new waves of sobs.

Focus. This was it. It was the proper way, the only way to bring it to an end.

He heard footsteps. Yes, it was time.

* * *

Jamie wiped the sweat off his brow. It was late evening following a hot, dry day. He placed his pen on the desk, taking a break from writing his sermon. Leaning back in his chair as he sat outside on the back verandah of his house, he hoped for a breeze. Today was Saturday, October 31, 1981, but the scorching heat remained. October was the hottest month of the year and often referred to as the 'suicide month.' Air conditioning was unheard of. It was just a matter of how well one could adjust to temperature changes. He scanned the horizon. The rains should come any time, maybe even tonight. There had been promise of it at sunrise, that red and orange sheen to the clouds, a trusty harbinger of rain. How similar it was to the new political climate, the dawn of a new era yet clouded with hints of something foreboding on the horizon. What was in store?

Zimbabwe. What a different world. Rhodesia was only a memory. His mind drifted back. A year ago, preparations were being made for the elections in Rhodesia. In one reckless act, the British and American governments had foolishly pulled back all government troops, allowing Mugabe and his thugs to intimidate the people into voting for ZANU as the new government. Now Zimbabwe was a communist nation. Surprisingly, Mugabe had encouraged all the white farmers to stay. No doubt he recognized their crucial role to both the economic future and the food supply of a rapidly growing country. Considered the bread basket of Southern Africa, Rhodesia had been proven capable of producing three times the food needed to feed the population. Tobacco generated nearly forty percent of the gross national product and vital foreign exchange. Mugabe surprised everyone with his pragmatic outlook—at least on the exterior. He was quick to display a willingness to reach out to everyone. Jamie fingered the condensation that formed on his glass of ice water. Mugabe was making an appealing impression. That was on the surface. What simmered below left him feeling uneasy. What stirred beneath the new government would in due time emerge. Despite Mugabe's smooth promises, Jamie had strong reservations. There had been rumors of major reprisals against the opposition in Matabeleland—involving the North Korean Fifth Brigade. A leopard cannot change its spots.

Jamie pushed aside misgivings and refocused on his sermon. He enjoyed this. What a far cry from relocating people into protected villages, or overseeing the training and deployment of vedettes and district assistants. The transition had been a smooth one. He knew God was working through him. He felt it. He was the acting pastor of the Mutare Christian Evangelical Church and his congregation of both black and white was steadily growing. There had never been apartheid in Rhodesia, but in past years the two cultures had remained somewhat separate. That was changing. More than half the congregation were black families representing the new order of Zimbabwe.

Sounds of giggles came from inside the house as the children chased each other. Jamie smiled. Emily loved the garden—the flowers and vegetable garden behind the house. The aroma of roast beef, roast potatoes, and fresh green peas from the garden was a reminder it would soon be time for dinner. He picked up his pen to jot down a few more thoughts before they escaped him. A faint breeze lifted the edges of his papers. *In another month he would finish his dissertation for his theological degree.*

This was his third day preparing for the sermon, yet the topic had pulled at his heart, at first quite gently, but then with relentless fervor for well over a month. What was it about that New Testament story— the conversion of Saul on the road to Damascus? How could he best convey the drama of the journey of a man who had been persecuting the Christians and was struck down, lost his sight, and then became the most powerful advocate of Jesus of all time? He closed his eyes to pray, remembering that Jesus would sometimes spend the whole night praying.

Crack! The sudden explosion of thunder shook him from his reverie. His mind flashed back to memories of mortar bombs and rockets as the western sky behind him lit up with jagged flashes of lightning. More thunder boomed and echoed through the valley, bouncing off the mountains to the north and the south. The first sporadic drops of rain fell. Large drops rang out as they ricocheted off the corrugated iron roof of the verandah above him. Sensing a downpour Jamie grabbed his raincoat and ran from the manse to the side entrance of the church. He still needed to prepare the altar for communion in the morning. There was much to be done and perhaps he could get some of it done before dinner. He made it to the building before the sky opened up. The door was never locked so he pushed it open, dashed inside, and hung up his raincoat. Switching on the lights at the front of the church, he began to make his preparations. He set the altar and then prepared to pour the communion wine.

He stopped short. *What was that?* He heard it again, a noise in the back. The lights were still off in the back of the church and he could not see anyone. He listened more intently over the drumming of the rain. Soon, there was no doubt. Someone was seated in the darkness on one of the back pews sobbing uncontrollably. Putting down the wine, Jamie quietly walked to the back of the church, leaving the lights off. In the dimness he could make out a man wearing dark clothes, sitting on a pew with his head buried between his hands. He had never seen anyone more stricken with grief. Jamie sat down next to him and put his right arm around the man's shoulder and held him. Several minutes passed and the man finally raised his head and looked at Jamie.

"Chinyerere?"

"Yes, I am Chinyerere, the priest of this parish. Do you know me?"

The man bent down again and continued to sob for several minutes. Finally, he looked up at Jamie. "I have not slept for four years—not since Elim. Because of that night I have no peace." Josiah held his head. "We were enemies, but your spirit prevailed."

Jamie fought the instinct to recoil, but took a deep breath. "Are you Josiah Makoni?"

The man grabbed a hold of Jamie's shirt with a look in his eyes analogous of a desperate, trapped animal. "Yes, I am Makoni. Now I have come. You still have a gun? Take me outside and shoot me so that I am no longer tormented by the spirits of those we killed."

The words pelted Jamie in rhythm with the rain spattering on the roof, edging him on. Emotions assailed him from his memory. He could not block out that day when he saw the unbelievable horrors inflicted by Josiah and the terrorists on the missionaries at Elim.

Animals. That's what he had called them.

He felt a wave of nausea. The familiar instinct of the hunter rose within him. Kill.

Oh God, help me. He is my enemy—there are no consequences.

Warmth washed over him. A familiar, gentle voice somewhere within him whispered, *Trust me.*

Then it came. All the thoughts the Holy Spirit had given him as he prepared for his sermon on Saul's conversion poured through his mind. Saul had personally been responsible for the persecution and death of many Christians, including Stephen. The voice of the Holy Spirit coursed through his mind.

What did I do to Saul? I struck him down and then built him up.

Yes, Jesus forgave even Saul. How many times had Jamie reflected on John 3:16 in the New Testament and missed the depth of the meaning? Time seemed to slow down—to wait. He felt God was testing him, waiting to see if Jamie Ross took him at his word. Waiting to see what Jamie would do with all that had been placed on his heart—entrusted to him, these past years. Did he truly believe that Jesus died on the cross so that anyone who confessed their sins and believed in him would be saved and enjoy eternal life with Christ—even Josiah Makoni? Then Jamie reflected back on a passage in Romans 3:23-26, *For all have sinned and fall short of the glory of God, being justified freely by His grace through the redemption that is in Christ Jesus, whom God set apart as a propitiation by his blood, through faith, to demonstrate his righteousness, because in his forbearance God has passed over the sins that were previously committed, to demonstrate at the present time his righteousness, that he might be just and the justifier of the one who has faith in Jesus.* Yes, Lord, I believe. Josiah's sins are no worse than my own sins in your sight. He can be forgiven, just as you have forgiven me. There is no sin too dark to be covered by the blood of your son.

Holding Josiah Makoni tightly, Jamie began to pray. Tears washed down his face as he prayed, all the time holding tightly to Josiah. After several minutes, Jamie pulled back and looked at Josiah. He felt a compassion he knew was not his own.

"Josiah, yes I am Chinyerere, but now I have a story to tell you. It is the story about a man called Jesus, who was the son of God. Jesus was sent to live on this earth, to teach us about God's love, his power, his grace, and his forgiveness. You see, Jesus did not want to die, but God's purpose was to send his son to die on the cross for us so that we, all of us who are sinners, can be saved. There is no man who has not sinned. When Jesus died he said, 'Forgive them for they do not know what they are doing.' And then, just before he died, his last words were, 'It is finished.'"

Josiah listened and stopped sobbing. He raised his head as Jamie continued.

Jamie could see in the dim light that the beard was gone and that Josiah's face was bleeding.

"Three days after he had been hung on the cross to die, Jesus arose from the dead. Yes, they buried his body in a cave, behind a big rock, but after three days the people came and saw, that even though there were guards, Jesus' body was gone. He had folded his grave clothes, rolled back the stone, left the cave he was buried in, and was alive again. Jesus then appeared to his friends many times telling them about the Kingdom of God. Then God took him up into heaven.

Despair washed over Josiah. "I have killed so many people. I still see those children and the baby girl lying next to her mother. I wake up every night. Even when I am drunk, as soon as I wake up, I hear the cries of those women and children calling to your Jesus."

Jamie put his hand under Josiah's chin. "Josiah, look at me. God knows what you have done. He understands. He is willing to forgive you, just as he forgave a man called Saul who was given special powers to kill the Christians.

"Special powers?"

"Yes. He was an important man, with authority, who was very successful in killing many followers of Jesus. Jesus made Saul blind and when he heard Jesus calling him he cried out to him. Jesus then sent Saul to a man who told him all about who Jesus really is and why he suffered and died on a cross for all the people of the world, back then, now, and forever. Saul was a new person. He was completely forgiven. He changed his name to Paul and there are many books in the bible describing how Paul spread the message of Jesus' love, his forgiveness, and how to live a changed life. You see, God knew back then, two thousand years ago, that we would all be sinners and that the only way for us, his children, to be free from sin and have peace, was to send his son to be beaten, nailed to a cross, lifted up, and left to die so that our bad deeds could be forgiven."

"This Jesus can take my bad deeds away—my killings? He can bring me peace?" Josiah caught his breath, desperately searching Jamie's eyes.

"Yes, Josiah. Jesus bore on the cuts of his back, and in the nails of his hands and feet, all the sins we have committed. The sins *you* have committed Josiah—all of them. He paid the price for you and me."

Josiah clutched Jamie. "Where can I find him? Show me where he is."

"Josiah, he is right here. All we have to do to be free is confess our sins, all the bad things we have done, and ask God to forgive us. This is not something President Mugabe or I can do. Only God can forgive you and give you peace."

Josiah could still hear the voices of those he had killed. He covered his head with his hands and trembled. "How can it be? I have killed so many people. I did so many bad things. Bring justice by taking me outside and shooting me. That is what your God would want."

"Josiah, may I call you Josiah?"

Josiah nodded.

"No matter what we have done, no matter how many people you or I have killed, God does not see these things if we confess them before him and ask him for forgiveness. He tells us in the bible that he removes them as far as the east is from the west. We must say we believe. Believe in his son Jesus, who died on the cross to wipe away these sins. It sounds so easy, but it is true. It is called the grace of God."

Josiah shook his head slowly. "Can your Jesus forgive even me? If I do these things what else must I do?"

"Josiah, all you have to do is to pray to God. Do it aloud so there is no doubt in your mind. Tell God that what you did in the past was wrong and ask him to forgive you. Tell God you believe he sent his son Jesus to die on the cross for you and that you believe in Jesus. Tell him that you wish to live a new life, following the teachings of Jesus as they are written in the Bible. When you do that, your old life is gone; you are born into a new life. Yes, with the same body, but a life of goodness and mercy where you can walk with God forever, not only in this life, but even when you die. Your body may die, but your body is just a place to live in while you are on this earth. The promise is that now you will live forever, walking with the risen Christ."

Josiah was quiet. Minutes passed. A peace came over him as he thought about all that Jamie said. "I believe you. I want this Jesus. Will you help me to pray?"

"Josiah, there are just three things for you to pray. Tell God that all you did in the past was wrong and that you are sorry. Ask God to forgive you. Tell God that you believe his son, Jesus, was sent to die on the cross for you and that Jesus is your Savior."

Josiah was trembling again. "I will do that."

Bending over, he opened his heart to God. "God, I cannot see you. Hear me now. I have done many bad things. I have killed many people—even women and children. I thought what I was doing was right, but I have not slept for four years. Now I know for certain that it was your spirit that protected Chinyerere. Please forgive me. Let me sleep again at night and have peace. I understand now what I have heard—that Jesus died on the cross for me. I believe in Jesus and will spend the rest of my life telling others about this wonderful thing. Teach me what is right and what is wrong so that I can teach others. I am your servant."

Jamie reached over and grasped Josiah's arms. "Josiah, stand up."

As the men rose, tears poured down the faces of both of them. Jamie wrapped his arms around Josiah and held him for what seemed ten minutes or more. "You are my brother now, Josiah. Once we were enemies, but now we are brothers. We are both children of God. I want you to spend the rest of the night in the church praying. I will bring blankets for both of us and we can stay right here. I will also bring you some food and water."

Jamie went back to the manse. Emily was incredulous. Her fingers trembled with excitement as she hurriedly gathered food while Jamie filled her in on the details. He carefully picked up the meal she had packed, as well as blankets and a jug of water, and returned to the church. Jamie remained with Josiah through the night. They prayed together, occasionally enjoying intermittent moments of silence as they humbly waited on the Holy Spirit to guide them into their next prayer. Josiah seemed to pour his very being out to the Lord. Jamie was filled with awe.

Several hours before sunrise, Josiah drifted off, but Jamie was too excited to sleep. He felt the power of the Holy Spirit urge him to continue to pray. As he looked at the tranquility on Josiah's face, he knew his new friend was also doing just what he was supposed to at that moment—sleeping. And Josiah did, peaceably. It was the first time in four years.

* * *

Jamie woke and his heart was still pounding. Picking up the phone he called John Whiting to share the news ...

Sunday morning was a new day. The wet earth steamed in the bright morning sun as Jamie led Josiah to the house. The dawn seemed full of deliverance. New life abounded. It exuded everywhere, even in the plants that had been refreshed from the previous night's rain. Josiah lifted up thanks.

Jamie knew that something in his own heart had changed during the night. He opened the door and allowed Josiah to step in first. Emily greeted them with a warm smile and a hot breakfast. She found fresh clothes for Josiah and offered him the spare bedroom. He attended church with them that morning. After services, Josiah sat down with the family to share the midday meal. Before they began, Jamie reached across the table with a book.

"Josiah, here is a Bible for you. I am also giving you some copies of the New Testament so that you can give them to others who need to hear about Jesus."

Emily spread out a feast before them, having begun preparations before the services. Josiah had no trouble finding his appetite. Jamie and Emily occasionally looked at each other and smiled as they watched him put away more food than the two of them and the children combined. Soon they learned that Josiah was hungry for more than food. He could not get enough of God's word. For the next six weeks he stayed with them and Jamie spent time each day teaching Josiah about the meaning of his salvation. Jamie had never felt such assurance that he was in the center of God's will and that the last several years had prepared him for these moments. Then, as quickly as it had begun, it ended. Or so Jamie thought. Early one morning, many days from the night Jamie first found him in the church, Josiah approached him.

"I thank you, my brother. You have shown me the way. You have set my feet on the right path and I sleep at night. Now, I must leave you. I have work to do."

Josiah grasped both of Jamie's hands in his own, shook them, and held them for several moments as he shared words of gratitude. He turned to leave. Jamie watched him disappear down the street. Just like that, he was gone.

* * *

It was late March, just before Easter. Jamie was in the garden trimming the rose bushes to encourage a late bloom before the winter. He was thinking. *Yes, God prunes his children. That way they will produce many blooms in their season.* Looking up, he saw a group of men approaching the front gate. His eyes immediately rested on a familiar face.

Josiah! But who are the others?

Dropping the pruning shears he walked toward the gate.

"Josiah! Who are these men?" They shook hands in the traditional manner.

"Chinyerere. I am back. These are my brothers. They were with me at Elim, every one of them. It has taken me many months to find them and tell them the story of Jesus. They have all accepted Jesus and now we have come to you because we want you to be our father and guide us. You have great wisdom."

Jamie felt a lump in his throat. He reached out to hug his friend, but Josiah continued with urgency.

"There is much work for us to do. There are many others that need to hear about Jesus—in the Honde, in the Sabi Valley, at Nyanyadzi, in Makoni, Marange, and even in Ngorima. This is where my brothers come from. They, too, want to share the good news in their villages. We want all the people to hear about Jesus."

Jamie put his arm over Josiah's shoulder and led the group to the house. "Come inside. Let us talk. Bring your brothers with you. Introduce them to me."

Emily beamed as Josiah walked in with his friends. They entered the living room and found a spot on the floor, not wanting to soil the furniture. Emily insisted they each have a chair and brought some extras from the kitchen. She quickly began mixing a jug of fresh lemonade and listened curiously from the kitchen as Josiah began.

"First, this is Enoch. He was also a leader among the comrades. This is Mangwende. Here is Isaac and his brother Mandebvu. The others are Amos, Mufara, Joseph, Chikunzi, Jeremiah and Manyase."

Jamie shook hands with each of them. Rachelle and Deanne excitedly took turns carrying cups of lemonade until all eleven men had been served, and then the whole family sat down to hear the stories. It was late in the afternoon before each had told how Josiah had found him and shared with him the good news. Afterwards, Jamie built a fire outside and Barrie barbequed steaks and mutton chops to celebrate.

The men had all brought blankets with them and Josiah led them into the church to spend the night.

In the morning, Jamie called his good friend, Pastor Fanie DuPlessis of Evangelism Explosion. Fanie, living in Mutare, organized teams of evangelists to spread the gospel throughout Manicaland.

"I'll be there right away," said Fani. "I've got a hostel where the new evangelists can stay. There's also a six week training program starting next week. This works out just perfectly."

Jamie hung up the phone—yes twelve missionaries had died at Elim, but now eleven new missionaries were going out to spread the gospel. "Yes, God, your plan is greater than anything I could ever contemplate."

Correspondence, whether by e-mail or postal service, is monitored. Anyone caught making a derogatory comment about President Mugabe, or the state of the economy, is subject to being shot, beaten, or thrown into jail.

As of this writing, over three million people have fled Zimbabwe, including most of the professionals, teachers, and medical workers. They are all seeking a better life, and new opportunities elsewhere.

Robert Mugabe, an avowed Marxist, assumed power in 1980 and, unbelievably, invited ex-Prime Minister Ian Smith to work with him in the transition. Determined to consolidate his power base he sent his North Korean Fifth Brigade into Matabeleland, brutally massacring between twenty thousand and thirty thousand of the opposition, and disposing of their bodies in abandoned mine shafts. The exact number slaughtered is indeterminate. Western powers turned a blind eye to the genocide as they recognized their responsibility for helping Mugabe assume power.

For ten years Mugabe amazed critics by following the constitution and implementing progressive policies, including the voluntary purchase of white-owned farms. During the next 10 years Zimbabwe continued to thrive both economically and as a political powerhouse. During Mugabe's tenure, however, the population doubled from six point four million to over thirteen million and the cry for land rose from among the peasant farmers. Soon Mugabe's popularity began to wane. In national elections in 2002, it is reliably reported Mugabe had the election results rigged in order to remain President. He did exactly the same with the elections that took place in March last year, refusing to acknowledge that he was defeated by the opposition. Election results were delayed for over one month and the Election Commission announced that a run-off was necessary, claiming no single candidate received more than fifty percent of the votes. Refusing to give up power, Mugabe sent out war veterans and armed youth militia. These so called war veterans were issued police uniforms and instructed to root out all opposition. Hundreds of opposition members were killed, thousands injured, thousands of women brutally raped, and hundreds of thousands left homeless. A fragile truce agreement was worked out with opposition leader Morgan Tsvangirayi. Mugabe, however, refuses to give up responsibility for the armed forces, the police, the justice department and finance, so the coalition remains very fragile—all the power remaining with Mugabe.

Mugabe has changed from a pragmatist and admired leader to brutal dictator and oppressor. Over seven hundred thousand people living in the suburbs of the two major cities had their homes bulldozed, and were displaced with no alternative shelter. The program was labeled 'Marambatswina,' or 'Get rid of the dirt.' These were the people in the townships of the major cities who had so dramatically opposed his re-election in 2002.

Mugabe issued orders for ex-ZANLA guerillas to seize white owned farms under the leadership of one of his cohorts, taking for himself the name, 'Hitler' Hunzi.

Zimbabwe's period of prosperity finally broke, giving way to chaos and a broken economy. What was once the bread basket of Africa has become a nation of starving millions. The white farmers fled with nothing, many going to Zambia and Mozambique where they remain today, struggling to develop new farms.

Twenty eight years later, hindsight reveals mistakes on all fronts. Firstly, Britain's refusal to compromise its position on an immediate transfer of power to a black majority yielded its consequences. This led to a unilateral declaration of independence by proud Rhodesians in 1965. Secondly, the Carter Administration's refusal to ratify the Kissinger Accord, coupled with support for Robert Mugabe, caused further unraveling. Thirdly, the Rhodesian government's obdurate concern with prematurely handing over power to those they felt were not yet qualified to lead—watching as other African countries fell into corruption and nepotism as new African leaders assumed power.

A prevalent thought is that the terrorist war of 1968 – 1979 was a struggle by unified Zimbabweans to oust the white controlled government of Ian Smith. Nothing could be further from the truth. Black rule was inevitable. The question was when it would happen and who was going to control the government. The Shona people, led by Robert Mugabe and Josiah Tongererayi, were determined to seize power and never be dominated by the Matabele who had conquered them a century and half earlier. They sought and received support for their struggle from China and North Korea.

The Matabele people, led by Joshua Nkomo, were equally

determined not to be ruled by the Shona, whom they had conquered and still considered subservient, notwithstanding the fact that the Matabele were in the minority. They sought and received support from The Soviet Union and Libya. The Soviets saw Rhodesia/Zimbabwe as the pathway to South Africa, and ultimately wanted both the economic and military benefits associated with control of the mineral wealth of South Africa, and the Cape sea route.

Despite the disaster we see in Zimbabwe today, Christianity is thriving. It is people like the Josiah Makoni's who are making a difference.

"If my people, who are called by my name, will humble themselves and pray and seek my face and turn from their wicked ways, then I will hear from heaven and will forgive their sin and will heal their land." 2 Chronicles 7:14

The author with the late Ian Smith – August, 2006